P9-BTM-095

Driving with the Top *Down*

ALSO BY BETH HARBISON

Chose the Wrong Guy, Gave Him the Wrong Finger

When in Doubt, Add Butter

Always Something There to Remind Me

Thin, Rich, Pretty

Hope in a Jar

Shoe Addicts Anonymous

Secrets of a Shoe Addict

Driving with the Top *Down*

Beth
Harbison

ST. MARTIN'S PRESS NEW YORK

This is a work of fiction. All of the characters, organizations, and events portrayed in this novel are either products of the author's imagination or are used fictitiously.

 Printed in the United States of America. For information, address St. Martin's Press, 175 Fifth Avenue, New York, N.Y. 10010.

www.stmartins.com

The Library of Congress Cataloging-in-Publication Data is available upon request.

ISBN 978-1-250-04380-1 (hardcover)
ISBN 978-1-4668-4218-2 (e-book)

St. Martin's Press books may be purchased for educational, business, or promotional use. For information on bulk purchases, please contact Macmillan Corporate and Premium Sales Department at 1-800-221-7945, extension 5442, or write specialmarkets@macmillan.com.

First Edition: August 2014

10 9 8 7 6 5 4 3 2 1

To Paige Harbison, for helping immeasurably with this book and cheering me along.

To Jack Harbison, who has shown great grace and maturity in the face of hardship.

To my mother, Connie Atkins, for helping us all through everything, all the time—you are the most generous spirit I have ever known.

And finally, this book is dedicated to the memory of the wonderful Matthew Shear. You will be forever missed, but your laughter lives on.

ACKNOWLEDGMENTS

Charlie Ugaz, you'll never know what your help has meant to me. Also all the little kindnesses—John will appreciate the flowers. Love, Long Legs ☺.

Thanks to Mary Rast for coming back into my life with your calm, cool, collected self and hitting the road to NYC with me. We could have been in this book!

Much gratitude to Cinda O'Brien for your friendship and generosity and the occasional dose of sanity, when needed.

AFIL, I'll always be your ADIL.

Connie Jo Brown Gernhofer, you have been a lifesaver. One of these days we have *got* to go to this store I've heard about called T.J.Maxx. . . .

Chandler, what fun times we've had! Our wine fest in Gettysburg was the best!

Kim Nash Amori and Dana Carmel, even in the worst of times

we are still our old selves, aren't we? Thank God (and Colonel Kieffer) for you guys, the best of friends.

Marianne Williams, this will probably surprise you, but you and your zest for life inspire me hugely.

Jordan Lyon, thanks for bringing your bright light into our house and lives.

Brian Hazel, thank you always for being such a great and positive friend—you are the bomb-diggity!

Jennifer Enderlin, thank you for your patience and brilliant input.

Annelise Robey, I am blessed to have you as an agent and a friend.

Meg Ruley, do you know it's been twenty-four years since Tina Isaak suggested you look at my manuscript? Thank you for taking me on!

Jen Lancaster, you raise the bar—not just for writing but also in furniture rehab. God bless Annie Sloan! See you in rehab . . . which I picture as your workroom, with lots of wine and old furniture and paintbrushes.

Quinn Cummings, I will never be as funny as you, and that makes me sad. But then I read your books and FB notes and they are funny, so that makes me happy. Quite the dichotomy. ☺

Denise Whitaker, you're the coolest long-lost cousin ever, and a great counselor as well!

Thadious Brookheimer, we've certainly been through hell together. Thanks for being there for me.

And Devynn Grubby, you've been a rock. A very witty rock. Thank you for bringing something wonderful into a difficult year—and welcome to the world, Miss Sadie Rose!

Driving with the Top *Down*

PROLOGUE

ONCE UPON A TIME, THERE WERE THREE HAPPY GIRLS, ALL BORN into charmed, sunshiny, shampoo-commercial lives. If into each life a little rain must fall, for these three, it fell after midnight, and by morning—as in the song from *Camelot*—the fog had flown. Though their lives were different from one another's and they lived in different towns, each enjoyed the best their world had to offer.

Each one could have come from central casting.

THE PERFECT HOUSEWIFE and mother—pretty, blond, thirty-four-year-old Colleen—leans against the Carrara marble countertop in her pristine white kitchen, one hand on her still-twenty-eight-inch waist, the other holding the latest, thinnest iPhone to her ear.

"Yes, let's get together soon!" She idly runs a finger along the bubble-glass front of her new cabinets, the perfect way to show off her grandmother's Spode Stafford Flowers china, the full set!

"Maybe we can even do a little antiquing!" Laughter. A private joke. Their husbands always rib them good-naturedly about their antiquing trips. Their acquisitions were meant to stock Colleen's shop, Junk and Disorderly, but Colleen always kept much more of the stuff she purchased and fixed up than she ended up selling on the showroom floor. "All right, Stephanie, I'll see you on Thursday!"

She hangs up, and just as the phone beeps off, the oven announces with a *ding!* that her neighborhood-famous pot roast is ready.

"Piper!" she sings up the staircase.

A moment later, a bedroom door scuffs open overhead, and Colleen's daughter, Piper, flies from the room and down the steps, their golden retriever, Zuzu, trailing her ankles. "Is it time?"

"Yes, ma'am!"

Piper is sixteen now. Still a little lanky and not quite filled out. But seemingly before Colleen's eyes, her nose has begun to thin out, she has lost her squeezable chipmunk cheeks, and beneath them, cheekbones have begun to appear. She pads into the kitchen in the knee-high tube socks she splurged on at American Apparel last week. Colleen doesn't have the heart to tell her that tube socks didn't always cost twenty-five dollars—they *used* to be tossed in with gym clothes and considered a truly dorky fashion item.

Colleen takes the pot roast out, raises the temperature on the oven, and brings the KitchenAid mixing bowl over to her daughter. "Drop the cookies on the pan, not in your stomach. You can't stay home from school tomorrow because of a cookie-making illness."

Piper raises her eyebrows innocently. "I'm not going to!"

She gives Piper a knowing look. These battles, Colleen knows not to fight. They are life's lessons, not hers to hand out. Piper would either be fine, or learn the hard way. She glances at the clock. Six forty-five. Kevin should be home any minute now.

She gets the ice-cold beer mug from the freezer and then pops open a Dogfish Head 60 Minute IPA. She hasn't even finished pouring it—carefully down the inside of the mug, to avoid too much foam—when the front door opens and she hears the familiar sounds of her husband coming home.

He might as well be Hugh Beaumont. Ward Cleaver.

A moment later, he comes into sight and says, "There they are—how are my two favorite girls?"

"Sup, Big D?" says Piper, holding up her hands in two mock gang signs, really sign language for "I love you."

"Whattup, lil' P?" He gives an upward head nod at her. This is some inside joke of theirs, its origins a mystery to Colleen.

Colleen looks at her husband. All these years, and she is still as in love with him as ever. Her heart pounds.

A moment later, their son, Jay, comes in the back door. He is twelve. Still young enough to be called adorable, but old enough to hate it.

Jay puts down the basketball he has under his arm and comes into the kitchen, heat radiating off him from the last few hours he has spent playing basketball in the fading sun with his friends down the road.

"Is dinner ready?" he asks. "I'm starving, but I need to take a shower first."

"Yeah, you smell like gym socks," Piper agrees.

"I'll go take off this monkey suit and make sure he's back down within five minutes." Kevin heads up the stairs after his son. Colleen hears them talk upstairs in the hall, something about a football player being traded—could they believe it?

Colleen takes a fingerful of dough, Piper does the same, and they pop each into their mouths, relishing the deliciousness of raw cookie dough and a happy childhood.

She has the best family in the world.

IN A HOUSE an hour south, Tamara—Teenage Girl–Prom Queen Type—sits on a couch, her hand holding popcorn she hasn't yet been able to shove in her mouth in the usual fashion, because she and her best friend are laughing too hard to even breathe.

It doesn't even matter what exactly they are laughing about. This is how it is with Tamara and Lily. Always laughing. Always having a joke.

"Oh my God," says Lily. "That . . . was . . . hilarious." She catches her breath at last and glances at her phone, which illuminated for a moment like a firefly. She hits a button to read the screen. Her eyes go wide. "Oh my gosh."

"What?" asks Tam, finally eating the popcorn.

"Mike and Ben are on their way here."

Tam almost spits the popcorn out. "No. Way. What?" She needs to put on makeup! Change out of her cat pj's! Take her hair out of this lazy ponytail and make it more Victoria's Secret!

Lily's eyes go wider. "I think Ben's going to ask you to prom!"

It's Tam's turn to go wide-eyed. Her heart pounds like a jackhammer. "No way! We have to go get pretty. Immediately!"

They both fly from the couch with the kind of speed mustered only when two teenage girls find out their crushes are about to come over in the middle of the night—and they have about thirty seconds to get ready.

Tam's layered hair spits out of her ponytail spunkily, and she pulls the band out, her hair falling into haphazard waves of dark honey. It wasn't bad. In fact, it was pretty good. She looked like herself. Felt like herself. If Ben didn't like her for that, then he wasn't the kind of guy she'd like anyway. That's how her mother has raised her.

Lily tries a little harder, putting on a little mascara and blush.

"Don't look like you're trying too hard," Tam cautions.

"Easy for you to say—you always look perfect."

"That's not true." But Tam's cheeks warm with pride at the idea.

"Oh, please, name me one guy who doesn't want to take you to prom this year."

Tam rolls her eyes. "I'm not going to sit here and name six hundred reasons my self-esteem should suck."

Lily give her an *a-ha!* look. "Because you can't!"

"Shut up." But inside, Tam is on top of the world. Lily's exaggerating her draw to the opposite sex, but if she's one-tenth as attractive to Ben as Lily would have her believe, then she just might score the guy of her dreams.

Lily's phone goes off again, and they both squeal—and then cover their mouths not to be heard and wake Tamara's sleeping parents.

"They're here!" announces Lily. "They say to meet them next door at the soccer field."

Whenever the two of them "sneak out," this is where they go: a hill right next door at the elementary school, within screaming distance of not only her own protective parents, but about twelve other equally attentive and caring suburban moms and dads too. So it's hardly a decadent escape. Sometimes they roll down the hill like little kids, or they lie back on a blanket and stare at the sky. They always have fun. One time, it even started raining, and they just ran around, laughing and getting drenched, not caring at all.

They meet the boys on the hill. Ben is looking nervous by the distant yellow glare of the school's outdoor halogen lights. With a butterfly flutter in her stomach, Tam notes his quick breath and the slight tremble in his voice.

"So," Tam says to him, hands clasped behind her back, "what's up?"

"Nothin' much . . ." He runs a hand through his perfect brown hair, leaving it just messy enough. "Uh, so I kinda wanted to ask you somethin'. . . ."

Prom. Lily was right. He's going to ask her to the prom! She will have this memory, and the great memories to come, for the rest of her life. This is it—this is her life blooming into full color, like that scene in *The Wizard of Oz* when the house blows out of Kansas and into the Land of Oz.

But this time? No witches.

Just dresses and pictures and limos and dinner and dancing to a song they will always always always remember as their own.

Her mom will take her dress shopping. She will help her do her makeup, working that cool two-color eye thing she was so good at. She'll get Tam new shoes!

She tries not to grin, biting her lip, responding with a *go on* nod.

"I think you're the prettiest girl in school, and I think you're really smart and funny, and . . . I can't imagine anyone that I'd like to go to prom with more. Would you . . . Would you wanna go with me?"

Finally not able or needing to hold back the grin, she nods and says, "Yes!" She throws her arms around him and he responds with his own arms before they both pull away, and they have their first kiss. They stand in each other's arms under the starry sky, and Tam thinks to herself: Everything is perfect. Everything is perfect.

She is the happiest girl in the world.

MEANWHILE, DEEP IN Winnington, North Carolina, Wilhelmina Nolan Camalier (formerly "Bitty"—a nickname referring to her trim figure) is speaking on the dais at a DAR meeting, discussing her husband's great-great-great-great-etc.-grandmother Rose Hampton and her brave acts during the Revolutionary War. Wilhelmina has made a study of the woman's life and works, and thanks to her efforts, an elementary school has been named in Rose Hampton's honor in the fine little town of Winnington.

She finishes her speech and asks if there are any questions. Everyone is surprised when the question session goes on longer than the speech itself, leading to a lively chat with lots of laughter and fun sprinkled in.

That's what everyone says about Wilhelmina Camalier—that she is an engaging public speaker and positively gifted when it comes to interacting with people. In fact, she is in such demand on the DAR circuit, as well as at historical societies in North and South Carolina (and bordering states occasionally), that she says no more often than yes. She has to—she has a family to take care of.

Family comes first.

Always.

She steps down from the podium and makes her way over to

the table where her movie-star-handsome husband, Lew, waits for her.

"You are amazing," he whispers in her ear after kissing her cheek when she sits. He puts his hand on her shoulder and pulls her closer for a moment, heedless of the impropriety of sharing so intimate a gesture in public. "I can't wait to get you home and into bed. We're going to have a howler of a night, baby."

She feels her face flush and knows it looks good on her, because one of the many compliments her husband has given her over the years is how pretty she always is, whether she's trying or not.

Once, when they were watching *It's a Wonderful Life,* he even commented that she cried pretty.

"Lew!" she whispers now in mock scorn. "You know the kids are there, we've got to be careful."

"Pffft." He waves the notion away and continues his own stage whisper. "We've got a babysitter and we're in the nicest hotel in town. Let's just hire her to stay over with the kids while we get reacquainted."

She chuckles softly. She's heard this exact same proposition before. Frequently, in fact. "Didn't we get reacquainted at the Hilton in Raleigh a few weeks ago?"

"I can't remember." He kisses her cheek again, then moves his hand to give her thigh a subtle squeeze under the table. "Guess we'll have to do it again. And again."

She can't help but laugh. "Oh, Lew."

"Come on, baby." He takes out the phone and pushes speed dial, then hands it to her. "See if the sitter can stay over."

Giving him a mock frown, she takes the phone and puts it to her ear, getting up and stepping outside the room to talk in the hall. A small voice answers. Lew Junior. Lewie. "Hi, sweetheart!" she says, her heart filling with a warm, familiar pride.

"Hi, Mommy!" He's eight. She wonders how long he will continue to be so happy to hear her voice.

"Whatcha doin'?" she asks, lingering in the moment.

"Lara and I are playing Monopoly with Miss Wendy. We both keep winning!"

She speaks for another moment to Lewie, then to Lara, who is every bit as happy with the evening's events as Lewie is; then she asks to speak with Miss Wendy, who happily agrees to stay the night. The guest room of the large Camalier ancestral estate is very comfortable, so she says she'll welcome the chance to do her back the favor.

Bitty thanks her and goes back to the dinner, trying to arrange her features into an expression of mock disappointment.

Lew sees right through her. He knows her so well, she can never fool him, she can't even hide Christmas presents from him; she always asks the maid to do it so she doesn't know where they are either.

"We're on," he says. A statement not a question. He takes her hand in his. "Let's blow this popsicle stand. I have a wife to adore."

She is the luckiest woman in the world.

THREE STELLAR EXAMPLES of the female sex. Three perfect lives. The ones they'd always envisioned for themselves, manifested like magic from their childhood hopes and dreams.

Three certainly happily-ever-afters.

Unfortunately, these are not the lives any of them really ended up with.

CHAPTER ONE

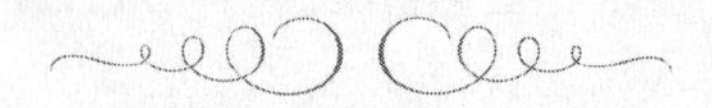

Colleen

COLLEEN BRADLEY HUNG UP THE PHONE—A TINY BEEP AT THE push of a fake on-screen button, as opposed to the satisfying slam of a good old plastic receiver—and rubbed her eyes in exasperation.

An hour and a half.

An hour and a half she had just spent on hold with that stupid hold music playing, and then the second she got a real person and not a robot, she was transferred, heard half a hopeful ring, and the call got dropped.

In front of her lay a pile of bills and papers. The satellite TV contract was up, and she needed to reup their service, after she first checked to see if there were any unadvertised specials. Last month, their phone bill was higher than it should have been, and she'd had to call and talk to them about it. The dryer was barely working, and she would have to schedule an appointment for someone to come look at it. And to top it all off, the basement carpet was all messed up from her son not letting the dog out before going to sleep, even though Colleen had warned him about that: If he didn't let him out, the dog would ruin the carpet. Lo and behold... Her life felt like a series of single steps forward and being shoved back three.

It wasn't that she didn't love and want her son—of course she did!—but maybe she'd spoiled him and created her own problem. ("Monsters are created," her mother used to say.) Maybe she'd made it too easy for him not to keep up his end of things, like letting the dog out, and now she was paying the price for the "laziness" of constantly telling him, "Forget it, I'll just do it myself," and then not following through in time.

Then again, Jay was the reason she had the life she did. She would never, ever forget that.

She took a deep breath and—determined to clear her in-box and knock at least that one thing off her to-do list—opened her e-mail.

Junk.

Junk.

Coupons for Pottery Barn. As if she could afford that, even with coupons.

Restoration Hardware?

They always lured her in with their beauty, but who could pay that much for a sofa?

An e-mail from her father. She'd read that later.

An e-mail from... Jay's vice principal?

She hoped it was a group e-mail, school spam, but as she feared, it was addressed to her alone, and about Jay specifically. His lack of motivation, bored attitude in class, failing grades even though he had the intelligence—they all knew that—to be doing much better and excelling in AP classes.

She sighed.

How many times had they had this conversation? A hundred? Two hundred? She felt her own frustrations with the school's increasing expectation of parental involvement in homework—she herself had always skated her way through junior high and high school doing her homework on her bed, usually while on the phone—but she was still willing to do what was necessary. Yet every time she asked Jay if he had any homework, he said it was done and she believed him.

Maybe it was just easier to believe him.

The truth was, she felt like his poor grades were her own fault. That is, Jay was responsible for his own laziness, but if she'd been hearing this story about someone else's kid, she'd be saying the mom had to be on top of things, no matter what. Kid failing? No more computer. No more Xbox. No more privileges until he got his grades up. It was obvious.

But what was he doing now? Playing games on the computer with his friends over Skype. She could hear him. She hated the nonstop gaming, but it was easier to pretend she didn't notice than to have the fight about it.

It was one more ball she was dropping. At this point, she'd dropped so many that in her mind, her life looked like a tennis court after group tennis lessons for ten first-graders.

She had to get her act together and start doing what needed to be done.

Now Vice Principal Richards wanted to meet with her and

Kevin (she already knew he'd be too busy at work to show) and *all* Jay's teachers before the end of term, which was two weeks away.

"Jay!" She yelled down from where she sat and just waited, too tired to get up and summon him for yet another Unpleasant Talk.

Finally, "Yeah?"

"Come here!"

After a longer-than-necessary wait, the tall, lanky fourteen-year-old came sauntering in. "What's up?"

"Got an e-mail from Vice Principal Richards." She gestured at the computer screen as if that would put the fear of God into him.

He quirked a smile. "How is he?"

"Not funny. You've got D's in two classes and an F in one."

"A's in the other three."

"You think that makes up for it?"

"It averages out to a mid-C."

"Jay." She put her head in her hands for a moment, then looked back at him soberly. "Now I have to go in and talk to every one of your teachers, your guidance counselor, *and* Mr. Richards."

"Just don't go."

"I can't just *not go*. That's the attitude—that right there—that's getting you in trouble. Do the work, Jay. Do. The. Work. It's almost summer vacation, you've got, like, three days to turn this stuff in. Being a student is your *only* job—can you just get it done?"

"Okay, okay. I'll try."

"No. No *trying*—just *do* it. Or you won't be going to Cooperstown with Dad." Empty threat; they both knew it. There was no way in the world she could cancel that trip now.

But they both pretended to believe it.

"I'm forwarding this e-mail to you, it's got your missed assignments on it. You can still pass without having to go to summer school. Go work on whatever isn't done now."

"Fine."

He went back downstairs and she waited tensely for a few minutes, then heard exactly what she expected: the sound of the computer starting up again.

So it wasn't that she was just being a persnickety old Felix Unger when she went into the kitchen and saw the mess; it was that she had completely had it with feeling like she was constantly taking one step forward only to be shoved back fourteen.

"Jay!" she yelled, eyeing the sink, the precarious pile of Fiestaware she'd gotten piece by piece off eBay and in antique and thrift stores, according to what she could afford at any given time. Some of the plates were chipped, one of the bowls had the mold-green remains of what was probably once Life cereal—and that was the one on top, so God only knew what the ones below looked like.

She didn't want to know.

"Jay!" she yelled again, then went to the top of the basement door and added, "Get up here. Again."

Her son responded with something muffled and indistinguishable from down and behind the rec room door.

"I can't hear you, come here!" Usually she had to go to them when she couldn't hear them, Jay or even Kevin. The onus was always on her to go hear, rather than on them to come be heard.

She waited about thirty beats and was half ready to go stomping down when she heard the door creak and saw Jay coming into the kitchen.

"What is it?" He blinked eyes reddened by what a more paranoid parent would have suspected was drug use, but which she knew were irritated because he'd just been sitting in front of the computer with the lights out.

"The dishes."

"I brought them up."

Seemed like such a small thing. She knew it seemed like a small thing. Maybe to another person it would have been. Maybe to her it should have been. But she was weary. Couldn't do his schoolwork, couldn't do the dishes, couldn't do laundry if someone offered to pay him, had no interest in playing organized sports or being in any other way organized. And all of it was a reflection, she feared, of her own laziness.

Or, not laziness—*exhaustion.*

"Okay, one, you have sworn to me for a week that you didn't have any dishes down there, so I'm not going to have a parade because you brought them back as science projects; and two, I told you not to eat downstairs at all. We're going to get bugs and maybe critters down there!"

Jay gave a laugh, and even she knew she sounded like a cartoon mom. "There's nothing down there."

"How would you know? You were okay ignoring this"—she gestured toward the sink—"atrocity for days!"

"Calm down."

Never good advice for someone who is angry, by the way. No pissed-off person ever calmed down because the object of their rage told them to. "I don't need to calm down—you need to listen and do what I say the first time. I shouldn't have to tell you things twenty times." Just talking about it again was starting to feel aerobic. "It's not fair for you to pile extra work on me like this."

"Fine. What do you want me to do?"

"I want you to do the dishes and stop ignoring the very few things I actually ask of you."

"Fine." He emphasized the *n*. "Jeez, you don't need to go off about every little thing. You could get the same point across by being calm instead of yelling, you know."

This was something he had said before, and something that bugged her every time. Not because it was true, exactly, but because it wasn't the typical fourteen-year-old line that the script called for. She wished it *were* true. She wished he really would listen when she spoke calmly, but he didn't.

"Apparently not." This was far from the first time she'd called him up to do something that actually would have been a lot easier for her to do herself. But she kept thinking that if she were consistent, he'd get so tired of always having to come back and do the thing he hadn't done, he'd just do it right to begin with.

So far, that strategy hadn't worked at all.

He turned on the sink and lamely rinsed absolutely nothing out of the bowl—the crud was going to need physical labor as well—before putting it into the dishwasher.

"Oh my God, Jay, do you see what's wrong with that picture?"

He actually looked at the walls, confused. "Huh?"

She pointed at the bowl, her words coming out with exasperated breath. "That. What do you think is going to happen to that in the dishwasher? Do you think there are tiny elves with trash bags in there who are going to go chisel that stuff off the bowl and carry it out to the trash so that bowl comes out sparkling clean?"

"That would be cool."

She sighed.

Of course it would be cool. But eventually the dishwasher elves would probably just end up sitting around, eating cookies, getting crumbs everywhere, and she'd be in charge of them too.

If she'd had another child—perhaps the daughter she'd hoped for after Jay until she'd finally faced the fact that she wasn't able to have more children—might she have had more support in the house? Could that longed-for child have made the difference that kept Colleen feeling like herself rather than a bland working machine that everyone took for granted?

"I want clean dishes to come out of the dishwasher," she said. "Not clean food."

"Okay, okay." He gingerly poked at the glued-on mess with a plastic straw he'd left in one of his drinking glasses (another of her pet peeves—it was like when her dad used to put his after-dinner cigarettes out on the plate, leaving it for the wimmin-folk to deal with). The straw bent feebly against the dried piece of Life cereal he was attempting to dislodge.

And suddenly it felt to her like this scene was never going to end. She just couldn't afford to stand here all night instructing him, moment by moment, on how to be a civilized human being.

"Pick a little, talk a little, pick a little, talk a little," Kevin would say. Unfairly.

Because what that amounted to was everyone perceiving her as a henpecker. Why was it so hard for them to comprehend her objection to their creating extra work for her? She'd work to clean the kitchen, just so she could get it out of the way and go on to do her own thing; then she'd come back and find this unsanitary mess. No one with a civilized bone in their body could have just left it there (one would think). So she then had to address it, one way or the other.

She watched for a few minutes as he limply rinsed the caked-on food, dislodging nothing, and stuck the dishes into the dishwasher, one after the other. Finally she couldn't stand it anymore—the impulse to just push him aside and say *Forget it, I'll do it myself!* was too great—so instead she turned and walked out of the room, onto the back porch, and into the cool June air.

Breathe.

Breathe.

It doesn't matter that much.

In a hundred years, none of this will matter.

Breathe.

What was going to become of her son if he couldn't clean dishes and pass high school? Was he just going to be one of those creepy loser guys with a ponytail pulled back into a thin snake down his back, bald on top, and willing to argue to the death about *Doctor Who* theories while rats crept through the kitchen, wiping bubonic plague germs all over torn bags of Doritos and opened cheese gone hard and dark on the sides and edges?

It's because of his mother, people would say. *She couldn't even teach him the basics.*

This used to be one of her favorite times of day. The pale blue twilight in the early summer. Almost warm, but with a lingering cool breeze. She had so many memories of this time of day.

She remembered being young and playing outside until dinner when the sky looked like this and her parents and their friends would sit out on their front lawns and drink—she suspected now *heavily* spiked—coffees. Sometimes she and her neighborhood friends would be allowed up past their bedtime on these nights because the parents were having so much fun.

Playing football on the beach when she was seventeen on a spur-of-the-moment trip to Ocean City. It had been cool enough then for jeans shorts, bare feet, and sweatshirts. And once the sun was completely gone, the sweatshirted arm of her hunky but ultimately unimportant boyfriend. That was the summer before college, and the weekend she'd had beer for the very first time.

Then the memory of standing in front of Kevin almost fifteen years ago, giving him the News: She was pregnant. After a shell-shocked moment, he'd told her it would be all right, but there was tension in his voice, and she knew the truth. They both did, and for just a split second, their eyes met and she knew everything she needed to know.

He didn't want this.

This was a *catastrophe* for him.

If she could go back, would she do it all the same way again?

CHAPTER TWO

Colleen

"COLLEEN?"

The voice came out of the darkness like a ghost.

Kevin. Appearing like magic just when she needed him most. It was almost annoying—did she ever do enough for *him*? Somehow she always missed her mark, was always just behind. Second place.

Always second place.

"Hey," she said with false cheer. "I didn't expect you until at least midnight. I'm glad you're here."

"I've been kickin' ass, getting all this work finished up before Jay and I go to Cooperstown next week. Tonight I finished up most of it, but decided to take the rest of it home with me."

"About Cooperstown—"

"Guys' trip," Kevin said, anticipating her question. This was a male-bonding thing, and she wasn't invited. She wasn't welcome. She was left out.

Colleen nodded. "You've mentioned that." She tried to keep the self-pity out of her voice. "What I was going to ask," she improvised, "was if you've checked the weather. Sometimes it's quite a bit colder up there, and I want to make sure I pack properly for Jay."

"You worry too much. He'll be fine. Let him pack for himself, he's a big guy now."

Physically, yes, but he was still her baby, and someone who saw his tall build wouldn't imagine how often she had to tell him things like, *You've worn that two days in a row, put it in the hamper. Good Lord, cut your nails—no wonder your shoes don't fit! Flush the toilet.*

No point in fighting over the packing; it was a fake question anyway. "Well, are you hungry? Maybe you can take a little break off from working right now and we can order a pizza and watch an episode of something with Jay." She really sounded desperate at this point.

He cocked his head in what she knew was him gearing up to nix the plan. "I wish I could, but I really have to get started. If you order a pizza, I'll have a couple pieces, though."

"Okay."

He came over to her and gave a quick kiss next to her lips, which she didn't have time to respond to. "I'm sorry. babe. After this trip, I'll have more time."

She knew she had no foot to stomp with, to tell him to just *damn it all* and take a half hour off to be with them. You couldn't do that while arguing with the sole breadwinner of the family.

"No, no, it's fine, I understand. It's okay, really."

"Did you call up the cable company?"

Her stomach prickled with remembered annoyance. "I tried,

but they disconnected me after I was on the phone forever. And I still have to call the dryer people and carpet cleaners tomorrow. Did you see the e-mail from Jay's vice prinicpal?"

"Yeah, he CC'd both of us. Have you talked to him yet?"

"Yes, I tried—" She was so sick of hearing the word come out of her mouth. "He just . . . He doesn't take me seriously."

She didn't know why that was. He took Kevin seriously, even though Kevin got to be the good guy. Wasn't one parent usually the cool one, the "good cop," while the other one had to be the enforcer? Why did Jay see Kevin as the enforcer *and* the good cop?

"I'll talk to him," said Kevin.

Again she nodded, knowing it would be a hundred times more effective than her conversation earlier. She shrank a little into herself, imagining that the question in his head was, *What do you do all day?*

"Look, there's something I need to talk to you about, so when you're done here . . ."

Her stomach and throat clenched. Those words. The slight variation on "we have to talk." She always feared it wasn't just some work thing he wanted to discuss, or a suggestion to, say, tear up the basement carpet and put in hardwood. She was always afraid of something else.

The thing she'd been half-expecting with full dread for years.

"I'll be in soon." She met his eyes, trying to read them, and nodded once more. He turned and she watched him head into the house, whistling tunelessly.

And she stood in the dark evening air, not particularly motivated in any direction. She remembered a time when she and her best high school friend used to sit outside on nights like this and look at the stars and plan their glorious futures while the moon crossed the sky. She didn't even realize at the time how precious those nights were or how sad it would be when they ended.

Somewhere along the way, they had ended, and a long time ago. Completely.

Now she stood in her suburban driveway, unsure which direction to take, whether to go to her workshop, which was almost painful to enter anymore, or to leave the comfortable shroud of night to go into the blaring lamplight of suburbia and, undoubtedly, a TV on too loud. Or worse, utter silence. A lifeless home.

She couldn't move.

Then it hit her. Not a bolt from the blue, but more like a weight that had been on her shoulders until finally her knees were buckling.

Something had to change. That was it. Something, somewhere in her life had to change.

She went to the garage side door, reached under a loose slate in front of it, and picked up the key. The garage hadn't housed a car for years. They decided not long after buying the house that it would be her workshop, where she'd work on the antiques she bought, repurposed, and sold at her Junk and Disorderly shop.

She flipped on the light switch and looked at her inventory. It was getting low. The best of farm auction season was over, and she'd barely gotten anything good this year. Most of what she had seen lately were things like chairs missing legs, shutters missing shutters, and trash cans from Target circa '98. Nothing like the dusty but grand headboards and slightly bent but still beautiful candelabras she found at the best time of year. At this rate, her stall at the sale would be all but bare and she'd lose her following as a result. Her clientele had been limited enough last year, and now she feared losing it all. Once upon a time, she had been kind of a rock star in the area. Her name was starting to mean something. But then last year she came up short on inspiration, time, and inventory, and did not do half as well as she'd wanted to or usually did.

Every year she fantasized about taking a road trip down the coast to go to auctions, and staying in quaint little bed-and-breakfasts, no chain hotels. She saw herself flying down the highway in her red convertible with a hitch attached, driving through dinky southern towns, pulling a Shasta trailer full of treasures behind her.

Unfortunately, she'd never had the nerve to up and leave on her own. She had grown timid, full of what-ifs.

What if the car breaks down on the road and there's no cell phone reception?

What if some weirdo watches me go into my motel room, then crashes through the window in the middle of the night?

What if I get sick and there's no one around to help?

It was ironic that a woman who spent her life fixing things—repairing antiques, repurposing "another man's trash," kissing booboos and wiping fevered brows—had such a hard time taking care of herself. Or at least feeling the confidence and independence of one who could and did take care of so much.

So a trip like that, while it might be a pure blast for another person, made her more nervous than she cared to admit.

Now, though . . . Now she had an additional mission. Yes, she needed inventory—she always needed inventory—and she needed the change of scenery to mix things up a bit. But what she really needed, she'd needed for fifteen years, and it was time to finally go after it.

She needed peace of mind.

She needed to confront the biggest mistake of her life and somehow come to terms with it.

She went to the refrigerator, where she had always kept extra lunch box fillers for Jay when he was younger. Now he just walked to the 7-Eleven with his friends at lunchtime. Now the garage fridge housed only bottled water, a box of wine that had been there so long, it was stuck like glue to the glass shelf, and the beers they almost never drank except for when there was company, which there rarely was. She considered the wine, but even at its best, it was too crappy to cook with, so instead she took a beer out and carried it to the tool bench to knock the top off with the heel of her palm. A trick from college days.

She issued a somewhat satisfying curse at the pain now shooting through her hand. She looked at the bottle. At least the top had come off clean—she still had that.

She sat down in a refinished French rocking chair, lavender with shiny gilding across the top—another thing she'd refurbished instead of working on herself—and let the beer—which she might once upon a time have referred to as "skunked," but which she thought of now as just "my savior in this moment"—trickle down her throat.

She sighed. What if she went her whole life without facing this? Fixing it, whatever that meant.

God, one sip of beer, and she was all drunk-philosophical-girl.

The old Colleen would have hated her.

Her imagination returned to the perks of the trip—the positives she'd enjoy: open road, new people, new places, and best of all, new old things and the fun she'd have fixing them up.

Like the portal window on her shelf right now. That was a find from an auction on the Eastern Shore a few years ago. So far she hadn't done anything with it, because she couldn't decide on what to do. The window had been salvaged from an ancient Victorian house near Rehoboth Beach, and its panes of water glass were original. She couldn't bear to ruin them and whatever past the piece might hold.

Had a lonely wife looked out that window, waiting for a husband to return from sea? Had he ever returned?

Or had it just been a dust-covered portal between a stuffy attic and the sky for decades before someone decided to upgrade the house and throw the window out in favor of something more modern?

Maybe it had hung over the sink, looking out over a garden through the many sunrises and sunsets of one family's life in the house.

That was what Colleen loved most about what she did—everything had a story.

Even if she had to make one up.

So, filled with romantic notions, at Christmas she'd hung the portal window on an otherwise empty wall in her own house, with a tea light candle behind the glass—then got so nervous about Jay or Kevin knocking into it that she took it back out to the workshop to think of something else to do with it.

She needed to begin living now, fully and honestly.

She took another sip of the beer, pulled her cell phone out of her pocket, along with the reading glasses she couldn't leave home without anymore, and sat down to start looking up auctions by state. There were more than she'd expected.

One hour and four empty beer bottles later, she had a list of auctions, a list of B and Bs, and a solid determination to hit the road.

"YOU'RE GOING TO do what?"

Kevin was generally supportive of Colleen, no matter what. Even when it came to what sitcoms in the '70s would have called "harebrained schemes"—like the time she spent an unusually large amount of money on old Erector Sets and various tools, with the idea of making retro robot sculptures. Most of the items she'd purchased were still in their shipping boxes, torn open and then cast aside. Usually he would sigh deeply with a resigned smile and encourage her to do whatever it was until the next whatever it was came along. This reluctance from him now was an entirely new thing.

Did he somehow sense her real mission? Was his resistance a sign she shouldn't go through with it?

"Kevin." She was calm. She was always calm. "What is your objection to me taking the week you're gone anyway to drive south and collect amazing things that I will make ten times more amazing?"

He gave a small laugh. "What if the proprietress at one of those quaint little B and Bs has an ax hidden under her crinolines?"

She had to laugh at the mental picture. It was exactly the sort of scenario she would have come up with herself. She liked that he teased her so familiarly. "Then I'm pretty sure I would, you know, *leave*. But don't worry, I didn't book the Bates Motel at all."

"Hm."

"Plus I saw this cool book once that has a list of places to stop along the way on I-95. All of them legit, and I can write off my travel expenses on our taxes."

"I want you to do what you want to do—I just want to make

sure you don't end up stranded somewhere, wishing I'd stopped you."

This was the right decision, and she knew it. "Kev . . . I'm so sick of not contributing. I'm so tired of trying to do this housewife thing and failing at it."

"You're not—"

"I am. I'm not great with the 'handling' of things. Finances and things like that. I know I asked to take over because I didn't want you to have to do everything, but . . . I felt so much better when I was bringing in actual *money* and had something to do with my days. My life can't be just failing at being an adult, failing at being a mom, and looking longingly at Pinterest all day, wishing I had anything to work on."

"Colleen"—he tilted his head a little at her—"none of that is true. You are a wonderful mom, and you're not *failing* at being an adult."

"I'm just not made for that—" She gestured at her phone, at the irritation of being stuck on hold earlier. "I'm just not made for that kind of thing. I'm creative. I have an art degree. And I'm not using it, and I think it's driving me crazy." She couldn't bring up what was weighing more heavily on her mind lately—that she hadn't been his first choice—she couldn't even say *why* the issue had become so compelling and awful. Maybe because Jay had left childhood and was careening so rapidly toward becoming a man. Those halcyon days of being Mommy, of being indispensable, were undeniably passing.

What did she have to offer Kevin, apart from parenting his child? What did she *really* have to offer that he couldn't get elsewhere, perhaps even with other bonuses (financial, sexual, and so on) thrown in?

Kevin sighed deeply. "Look. You know ordinarily I would absolutely be in support of this, my hesitation going no further than a few practical concerns. But there's one more thing."

The thing he'd wanted to talk to her about.

Nervousness hit her again. "Kevin, what is it?"

He gave her a pained look that could have suggested she'd unknowingly been exposed to some disease and that for the next few weeks, she was legally required to go into quarantine. Or maybe that she'd committed some horrid crime while in an Ambien sleep haze, and now they were awaiting her lawyer and the police.

But no. What he said was worse than either of those things. It began and ended with one word.

"Tamara."

"Oh God . . ." Tamara was Kevin's niece. Well, technically, Tamara was her niece too, but at age sixteen, the girl had already been in and out of the legal system so much that the cops in Frederick all knew her about as well as Colleen herself did: Tamara's name. Her record. Her birthday. Her address. (And even Colleen wasn't 100 percent on her birthday.)

She had known Tamara for only three years, actually, since the girl's mother died and Chris, Kevin's brother, gained custody of a kid he'd never even admitted having.

So what, she was afraid to ask, had happened to Tamara now?

"Chris was called out West for work," Kevin said. "He's desperate. There's no way he can leave her at home alone, obviously. You don't have to watch her if you really don't want to. Of course, I told him I would ask you."

"But . . . what does he usually do with her? When she's not in juvie, I mean. He goes out of town all the time for work."

"The woman he usually hires declined."

"Great. Even she can't deal with her."

"That's about the size of it."

Colleen sighed. She already knew she was going to be stuck with this if she didn't think of something—someone—fast. "He doesn't have anyone else?"

"He never would have asked us if he did."

She let out a deep breath. "Tamara hates me."

"She does not."

"Oh yes. Yes, she does. Ever since the Instagram Incident." Why the girl had posted pictures of herself smoking weed right there for everyone to see—and then made public plans to meet her friends behind McDonald's to do it again the next Friday night—was a mystery to Colleen still, but when she'd mentioned it to Kevin and he'd mentioned it to Chris, somehow Colleen's anonymity as the source was lost in the shuffle and Tamara had never forgiven her.

Even though it was possible that Colleen had averted an even worse disaster for her. A pretty girl messed up on drugs in some deserted field behind a fast-food restaurant off the highway was begging for all kinds of trouble.

"Look, I know Tamara is a huge responsibility," Kevin was saying. "You don't have to do this. I can cancel the trip maybe or—"

"No, no, no. I want you to go. Jay would be so disappointed. You're going."

He shrugged. "Maybe she can go with us."

She blinked at him. "I'm sorry? Maybe you can introduce our mercifully clean thirteen-year-old to a total delinquent near his age and have them hang out for a week on your 'guys' trip?" That galled her; it really did. Thanks a lot, Kevin. Way to make me feel unwanted *again*. "No thanks. I'll do it."

His face showed he was not surprised. "Honestly, I think maybe there's a small chance it could be good for you both."

"How do you reckon that one?"

Kevin shrugged. "She doesn't have a mom. She's messed up, but she's a smart kid. And for you, I don't know, I think it just might be a good thing for you."

He locked eyes with her and tightened his lips before looking away. He didn't have to explain. Colleen knew.

"It's not even the delinquent thing—I'm just afraid she still hates me and she'll just be one more thing I screw up."

"Stop thinking you're screwing up! Seriously, Colleen. Just look at her as a—" He searched for words. "—like a grimy, dull tiara or something. And you're going to polish her up and fix her just like your other stuff."

Colleen gave a soft laugh. "That was cute. A tiara."

He laughed too, and squeezed her shoulder. "I'll help him figure something else out if you really don't want to do it. But I don't want you to say no out of fear. You're a great mom. You're a great role model. And she needs both those things. You know I've spent some time around her when I'm with Chris, and I'm tellin' ya, she's not the worst thing in the world. She's smart."

"Sure, you said that. I mean how bad can she be?"

They looked at each other, and then looked elsewhere. They both had an idea of how bad Tamara could be: two tattoos, a pack a day, (at least) one delinquent boyfriend who'd been arrested for assault no fewer than three times, and a couple of stays in a juvenile detention center. That's how bad she could be. Or no—that's how bad she could get caught being.

Colleen knew nothing about dealing with a girl like Tamara. Yes, she'd been a teenage girl once too. But she had been a completely run-of-the-mill teenage girl. An embarrassing story or two, a pretty cute high school boyfriend who always drove the speed limit, and a couple of regrettable nights and punishing mornings from stolen beers and bottles of peach schnapps. She'd always had a date to the dance, but no queen titles; played girls' lacrosse, but never well enough to take it very seriously.

As far as her own delinquency went, she had none. She'd gotten detention three times in high school: once for tardiness, once for spaghetti straps that showed her bra straps beneath them (the height of sexiness at age fourteen, or so she and her peers were somehow led to believe), and one time for skipping school on Senior Skip Day. Which she'd been nervous about doing from the beginning of the year, but her friends had talked her into it. She was the last to agree and the first to get caught.

Story of her school career, actually.

She was no high school badass.

And now she would be going on a road trip with one.

CHAPTER THREE

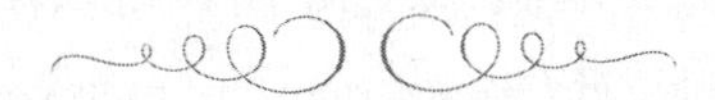

Tamara

TAMARA BRADLEY TOOK HER INDEX FINGER OFF THE TINY HOLE ON the side of the bowl and breathed in deeply. The smoke hit the back of her throat like a thousand knives, just as it always did. She held it in until it started to rebel, burning and tickling her lungs at the same time, and she exhaled.

Long and slow. Trying not to cough at the end rattle of breath.

The feelings that came next always hit her in the same strange and confusing succession: Dizziness. Relief. Hope for oblivion and, inevitably, a vague sense of disappointment that she was still present.

Then, always unexpected, a guilty tightening in her stomach.

After that, she just had to wait the next couple of minutes until she started to fade into the hazy cloud that started to soak up her thoughts like a single paper towel in a pool.

"Let me hit that." Her boyfriend, Vince, took the bowl from

her hand and then mimicked her, drawing the smoke in, holding out, and exhaling ungracefully, uttering, "Fuck, man . . ."

She stared at the TV surrounded by different game consoles and controllers. The number of nights she had spent down here in this ugly, wood-paneled, mildewed basement and watched as Vince and his friends played *Call of Duty* was too high to count. She and the other girlfriends would sit there and watch, like groupies. Every once in a while, the boys invited them to play a round, which was always embarrassing and presented like some novelty trick. Like, *Hey, look, the dog is in a hat! Like a person!* But instead it was, *Hey, look, a girl is holding an Xbox controller! She has no idea what she's doing!* The game wasn't really even any fun anyway, so why bother to figure it out?

Tamara usually declined at this point. Who cared anymore? Who was she trying to impress? She was just sick of all of it, and she got the sense that everyone else talked about her behind her back like she was just no fun. The pissy girlfriend who couldn't even play a fucking round and would rather sit there with her eyebrows up, flipping through her phone.

"I can't believe you're going to be gone for two weeks," said Vince, draping a limp arm around her shoulders. They were alone for once, something she always longed for yet always disappointed her when it happened.

"I know." She was dreading it. All that time on the road with the bitch who'd spied on her Instagram and basically ruined her ninth-grade year. It was like punishment.

"It's gonna suck, dude." Vince yawned. "I guess I'll have to start looking at porn again and everything."

Ew, she thought. Guys have needs, whatever. . . . No need to share with the rest of us. She'd seen *Don Jon.* She knew what guys were obsessed with and why.

She resisted the shiver of revulsion his words sent through her spine, for fear that he'd somehow be flattered by her reaction.

"Guess so . . . ," she said, still staring at the TV. She didn't even know what this show was. Some cartoon that was trying to be crass like *Family Guy* but wasn't funny at all.

"Babe." He burped loud. "Will you do me a favor?"

"Prolly not."

He laughed, mistaking her rudeness for a joke, as always. "I'm gonna miss you so fucking much. And—" He raced an extended palm up her crossed leg. "I don't want to have to think about anyone but you."

She resisted a sneer as well, and finally looked at him. He had a nice nose, good eyes, and sharp cheekbones. He was kind of hot. Almost hot. She still vaguely remembered when his slightly narrow frame had reminded her more of '80s rock gods and less of her Betty Spaghetty toy from childhood. His eyes had once seemed like chestnut brown, but now struck her distinctly as poop brown. She started to laugh without meaning to.

Guess the weed was kicking in. It rarely made her giggly anymore—but then, not much did.

"So I was thinking," Vince went on as if Tamara hadn't lost track of what he was saying, "that maybe I could . . . you know, maybe I could film you."

An unexpected image flew to mind. Her, in a Hawaiian dress, the skirt a blue and white map of the islands. It had been a gift from grandparents who were long dead since, and she'd waved at the camera for her mom, who was recording a video to e-mail to them as a thank-you.

Her mom was long dead now too. Or long enough to no longer be anything like the smiling pretty blond Barbie who'd always smelled like baby powder when Tamara was young. That was the mom she liked to remember. Not the desperate, shaking, bloated, and bitter alcoholic she'd become before she died. That was someone else. Someone unrecognizable.

Someone now dead.

Tamara played with that word, "dead," like it didn't hurt. Like it wasn't the most harsh word ever. She used it like an experiment to see if it still made her wince inwardly. It always did. But she couldn't stop doing it to herself. Sometimes Tamara pictured her mother underground. What did she look like now? Was she just a skeleton? How quickly did that happen? Were her clothes torn like a prop in the Haunted Mansion at Disney World?

What did her mom smell like now?

Stop it, she thought, chastising herself in her own version of her father's voice.

Tamara hated the thoughts, but couldn't resist them. She visited them now and then like someone opening the oven to see if a cake was almost done. As if she'd check someday to find the thoughts no longer cooking in her mind.

"So," Vince was saying in what she recognized as his persuasive voice. "Like, now?"

She shook her head in confusion. "Wait . . . what?"

"Maybe I could film you, like, giving me head." He held up his iPhone. The most recent generation of it, despite his insistence that his parents hated him and gave him nothing. In fact, he lived on the nicest street in Catonsville. One of the ones with big, tall, old trees, redbrick fronts, and actual mailboxes at the ends of actual driveways. The houses there looked like real homes. The kind people lived in on old Disney shows Tamara barely recalled watching.

Vince's place was just around the corner from the crappy row houses where he and Tamara hung out at night when they snuck off. He lived a couple of miles down from Tamara, who lived without a real mailbox, in a newish apartment building, void of any personality or homeyness.

Back when she really thought Vince was a tragic boy, unloved by his parents and unexposed to luxury, he had seemed like a fixable problem. A drowned boy she could breathe life into. A project she could complete with a feeling of satisfaction. In fact, she even thought they'd had things in common that might make theirs one of the stories everyone said couldn't happen. Young love that worked out for real.

She didn't have those kinds of dreams anymore.

Once she realized he was a spoiled little bitch boy with up-to-the-minute electronics littering his bedroom and basement, she became strangely less interested.

Her disaffection changed nothing, though. She had no intention of breaking up with him. He was better than nothing. She'd had too much nothing in her life not to know that. He was like a drug she knew would eventually kill her, or at least damage her, but since the worst hadn't happened yet, she didn't really see the sense in stopping herself now.

Much like, you know, the actual drugs she occasionally did.

But she wasn't going to buy her way into his good graces like this. Not by being filmed doing . . . anything. "Um . . . no. I don't want to do that."

"Aw, come on, why not? Don't be lame." He leaned back on the couch again, as if she were the most exhausting person he knew.

"Because, I just . . . don't want to."

"Are you saying you don't trust me?"

She was instantly defensive. "Of course not—"

"Then what does it matter? It's just for me, and I see you do it all the time." He looked at Tamara.

She raised her eyebrows and searched for an objection to this undeniably true statement. She wanted to say, *Yeah, and how lucky are you that you do?* But since she never said that kind of thing out loud, she just frowned instead.

He took his arm back. "Okay, whatever."

"Don't be pissed."

He shrugged but wouldn't look at her. "I'm not."

She hated this feeling: Guilt because she didn't want to do something she should never *have* to do. Guilt for letting him down, when he should be the one feeling guilty for being disrespectful enough to ask. "You obviously are," she said, when she knew what she should have been saying was, *Who the fuck do you think you are?*

"Tamara. I said I'm not."

She started to grit her teeth, then stopped and asked him to hand her the bowl and lighter back.

Three more episodes of *(Not) Family Guy* later, Tamara had begged him to do something besides sit in the basement. The idea of sitting there all night was enough to make her want to down half a bottle of NyQuil. But instead, they got out of the house for once. He'd texted a few people, saw what was happening, and then said they could go to a party.

In the Lexus—another luxury he bitched about constantly—he told her to put on whatever radio station she wanted. On his XM Radio. She put on Channel 7, the '70s station. The music wasn't Vince's kind of thing, but it was always cool of him when he didn't care what she put on. They pulled off of Edmonson Avenue and stopped at a gas station next to the liquor store.

He got out and told her to lock the doors. Maybe he wasn't so bad. He wanted her to lock the doors and be protected.

A voice somewhere in the back of her head told her that the fact that he didn't want her kidnapped—or maybe even his car stolen—did not exactly make him a loving and considerate boyfriend.

But when he returned from the liquor store with her favorite vodka—Three Olives Tartz, it tasted like SweeTarts—in addition to the Sailor Jerry, 94 proof, she thought maybe that did.

Yeah, between his fake ID and vague recollection of her favorite alcohol, he was practically a white knight.

After driving a bit more, they pulled up to a house she recognized as Jenna King's. Jenna was an annoyingly bubbly, perky, had-her-shit-together cheerleader type. Only she wasn't a cheerleader, she was a drama student, and had somehow turned that from lame to cool. Instead of seeming like a *Glee* character, she'd transformed herself into Megan Fox in the eyes of her peers. A cool, sexy actress. Not an overdramatic, limelight-craving drama kid.

Despite being the one to say they had to get out of the house, Tamara now felt annoyed, and wished she were—well, she didn't really know where. Not the basement. Not her dad's house—Lord, not there.

Just . . . somewhere else. Unfortunately, this was it.

There was nowhere else they could go without being watched or getting yelled at.

When they walked in, there wasn't much of a reaction. Everyone was caught up in whatever they were caught up in. Beer pong. Cards. Shots. More effing video games. It seemed like a disappointing display, but then, Tamara couldn't think of something more she had really been expecting.

She followed Vince to the people who had told them to come by, and everyone pretty much took the positions they would have taken back in Vince's basement. That put Tamara behind the lip of her vodka bottle, not bothering with a glass or a chaser.

After a while, she remembered she had a joint in her purse. It was rolled up and hidden with her cigarettes in a cute, vintage-looking cigarette case she'd gotten from a store in D.C. Her head was swimming already, but she didn't care. She wanted more Nothing. Holding the railing with a tight grip, she made her way upstairs and went out on the back porch to smoke it. She didn't feel like sharing her joint with Vince and his friends. It'd get back to her all soggy and gross.

She sat down on a creaky wicker chair. The squeak sounded almost like an animal. It was so loud. Had everyone heard that? Were they going to come up now and accuse her of holding out or being antisocial? She got the second one a lot. She felt a strange nervous tremor run through her, like a kid quaking at the sound of angry footsteps on the stairs.

She tried the lighter a couple of times with a shaking hand before it finally lit and she pulled the burn into the joint. She was alone out back, and took a couple of drags of the harsh smoke before hearing a voice behind her. "Um, do you think you could maybe not smoke that right next to a fucking window?"

Jenna.

"Right. Sorry."

Jenna gave a tight smile but didn't walk far enough away from the window before adding, "Fucking pothead. I don't remember inviting a bunch of burnouts to my party."

Tamara gnawed on the inside of her lip, a nervous habit, and pulled out her phone to distract herself.

"Shit," she muttered, seeing DAD, MISSED CALL (7). She slid over the alert to call him back.

"Hello, Tamara?"

She took a steadying breath and tried to sound normal. "Yeah, hey, sorry, I didn't have service."

"Where the hell are you?" He had on his mean Scary Dad voice.

"I'm at my friend—" She stepped away from the window and lowered her voice. "—my friend Jenna's house."

"Jenna?"

"Yeah, Dad, I told you about this." She hadn't, of course, but it's not like he listened to her anyway. On the rare occasions that they spoke. "She's the girl who does plays at school." He'd like that. Plays. "She dresses like a nun and sings about hills and the sound of music."

This Jenna sounded downright wholesome. Carrie Underwood, about to bravely take the stage in *The Sound of Music*. Or maybe even like the nun Maria herself.

"Oh. I don't think you told me about this."

She bit her lower lip hard enough to hurt so she wouldn't laugh. "Yeah, so her mom invited me to stay over tonight. They're making lasagna and playing board games. Is that fine?" She could hear him trying to decide if she was telling the truth, so she added, "I'll come home if you want, it's just, you know. Seems like it could be kind of fun. Whatever."

The saddest part of that lie was that it *did* sound like it could be fun. Not with Jenna, of course, but in general. Did anyone really do that stuff? She hadn't. Maybe it was just TV stuff and everyone knew it was bullshit and she'd just given herself away.

Apparently not. "I guess . . . I guess that's okay. But you have to come back by noon tomorrow morning."

"Why?"

"I'm taking you to Kevin and Colleen's, and we have to clean up the place and you have to pack before we go."

"Kevin and Colleen's." The hopeful, imaginative part of herself thought maybe Colleen would cancel and he'd have no choice but to leave her alone. If he did, she didn't even think she'd party that much. Just stay at home and blast music and not get yelled at for once in her life. "Dad, seriously, can't you just let me stay home?"

Some people walked outside, and Tamara drifted farther away from the house. She didn't want to be overheard sounding all teenager-y on the phone.

"No, I cannot let you stay home, Tamara. The place wouldn't be standing when I got back. What exactly do you take me for?"

"Nothing, I'm not . . . I wouldn't do anything wrong. I'm sixteen, I don't need to be babysat."

He laughed. Actually laughed. "I think there's a judge or two who would disagree with you on that."

She shook her head and said, "Fine. Whatever. I'll be there by noon."

Tamara walked inside, took her usual seat next to Vince, and downed another swig from her vodka. It lodged hot and hard in her throat, and for a moment she thought she might hork it right back up, but she held steady and waited for it to fade.

Vince didn't notice. No one did. She wondered if they'd even noticed that she was outside earlier, since so one reacted to her return.

She was glad when the weed and the liquor started to take control of her mind for her. Pairing them with the Red Bull she had before coming to Jenna's, she almost cobbled together something that resembled a good mood. As everyone got drunker, a few got higher, and the music got louder, she was out of it enough to really let go a little.

In the living room, the lights had dimmed, and someone was being a really good DJ. The songs playing were ones she liked, and she was dancing along with everyone else. She even had a fun moment or two with a group of girls, shouting along with the song.

It was following one of those moments that left her smiling and happy, that she turned to see Vince dancing with another girl. She was small—possibly too small to even envy—with a shock of red hair. Like, Hayley Williams from Paramore, atomic fireball red, not natural red. He had one hand on her back and one on her ribs as he said something in her ear.

Probably something about how much he hated the songs that were playing right now. She was probably agreeing and saying she wished they could go change it to some band she liked. Then he'd probably say, "Dude, you like them? No girl I know likes them!" And then she would probably be the kind of girl who didn't mind being called "dude" by a dude, and so would just nod and say, "Right on," or something equally annoying.

Fuck that redhead, Tamara thought.

She knew she could have gone over and pulled him away, but she didn't do that. If he was going to fuck up on her, he was going to fuck up on her. She couldn't stop him from cheating on her. Instead, she slithered out of the crowd to hide in a bedroom. She wasn't even sure why. It wasn't to cry, or to check her makeup. She just wanted to get out of it all of a sudden.

Pulling away from the mass of bodies, she headed down a hallway, losing her footing now and then and skidding her shoulder along the wall; then she pushed open a door. She shut it quickly behind her, not wanting to be followed by Vince or to become the token Arguing Couple at the party. She didn't anticipate, however, the voice that came from within that room.

"Uh."

She jumped at the sound, and then saw a boy sitting on the bed, holding a beer. He reached across the bed and paused the laptop that was playing some show or movie.

"I'm sorry," she said, her heart pounding as if he'd jumped out from behind a tree in a Halloween mask, "I thought the room was empty."

He gave a small laugh. "Why are you trying to find an empty room all by yourself at a party?"

She shrugged, returning the laugh. "Uh . . . I guess I just wanted to be alone for a second."

"You're at a party. You might be at the wrong place if you're having to hide."

She tried to focus in the dim light. He looked kind of familiar, but she could have imagined anything at this point. "You're alone."

"I live here."

"Oh."

"I'm Jenna's brother. Conor."

That was it. "Hi, I'm Tamara."

"I actually know who you are," he said.

"I . . . actually know who you are too. . . ."

They exchanged a look, and then he said, "I don't know why we all act like we don't see each other and hear about each other all the time. We go to the same school. And that's really not that big a world."

Tamara felt an internal cringe when he said "hear about each other." Yeah. A lot of people had heard about her. She didn't have the best reputation, and she knew it.

"I guess none of us wants to seem stalker-ish?"

"Probably." He ran a hand through his dark brown hair, the same color as Jenna's, but without the—in Tamara's opinion—hideous blond chunks. "So, I know you because you're Tamara the Jailbird. You know me because . . ."

She shrugged, feeling sheepish at his casual way of addressing the elephant that followed her into every room. It wasn't something she would ever have imagined herself ending up in the rumor mill for. "Just . . . seen you around." *Hate your sister, know her circle so I know who to avoid.*

"That's it, huh? Damn. I gotta work on my rep."

"Better than being called a jailbird, probably."

"Right."

Feeling the oncoming silence, and not wanting to be told to leave the room, she asked, "What are you watching?"

"*Breaking Bad.*" He shrugged. "Unlike the rest of the world, I never watched it. I'm super late."

She felt a sudden surge of enthusiasm. "Oh my God, I *loved* that show. Is this your first time watching?"

He splayed his arms. "Yup. I'm a virgin."

"What season are you on?" With more enthusiasm than she had felt in hours—or maybe longer—she walked over and sat on the bed next to him to see the screen. It didn't even strike her as a weird thing for her to do until she felt the heat from his body pulsing toward her through her thin Bon Jovi T-shirt (at fifty cents, a major score from the Goodwill by her house).

If he thought anything of her proximity, he didn't show it. "Four. It's probably the greatest show I've ever seen."

"Dude, just wait." She regretted the accidental use of Vince's word. "Dude" hadn't used to tumble naturally from her tongue at all. She used to sound like a mom trying to fit in with the kids when she said it. She'd hated feeling like such an outsider back then, but now it kinda bugged her that she sounded like any ol' no-real-vocab teenager. "Um. Yeah, it just gets better and better. I love it."

She looked back at him. He was obviously completely sober, save for maybe a beer or two. All at once, she wished that she could have the kind of conversation she had been imagining between Vince and the Redhead.

One that went: "I hate these parties." "Ugh, me too." "I'm not even drunk, or anything." And then they could leave and go to IHOP or something.

She knew it was stupid to imagine all this with Conor, someone who saw her as a jailbird at best and a dumb little kid at worst. He was a senior, and she and most everyone else at the party were sophomores. Two years, but it was a big difference. Particularly when in addition to those two years, there was the consumption of a half bottle of vodka and a joint between them.

And also the fact that he had a bunch of internship hours under his belt, when all she had was court-ordered community service.

"You don't usually wear glasses, do you?" she asked, gesturing at his thick-rimmed black glasses.

"Wha—? Oh, no, usually wear contacts. But when I'm just sitting around, I wear my glasses." He made a face and pushed the frames up into his hair. Was he embarrassed to be looking dorky around her?

No. That was in her head.

"Cool," she said.

"Not really." He laughed.

"I guess not." She smiled, and the expression felt unfamiliar on her face. She had the strange realization that this was the first time she'd smiled all night. The thought made her self-conscious, and all at once she felt like she was imitating the Joker or something. She pressed her lips together. Stopped the smile. "I'll uh . . . I'll let you get back to the show."

He nodded. "Yeah, you enjoy your party out there."

"Hey, at least it's good music. Not always the case."

He narrowed his eyes at her, and then said, "You're welcome for that."

"You put it on?"

"Yeah, it's my iPod. I figured if I had to listen to music through the wall all night, I wanted it to be mine."

"Makes sense . . . Um. Hey, so none of my friends even like *Breaking Bad*. So I never got to talk about it when I watched it. Do you want maybe to . . . ? Like, I could give you my number and you could text me after you get through a few episodes. I mean, if you feel like it. It's the kind of show you wanna talk about after things happen, I feel like."

No, she thought, that was super weird. She was just the weird little stoner girl who had somehow ended up at the party, and then in his room. Why was she being so weird? He probably had plenty of friends to talk about it with, ones who had watched it already. Probably a girlfriend. Probably a really cool girlfriend who had told him to watch it, and he was taking her advice. Some girl who was too classy and girlish to use the word "dude."

"Sure. Here, give me your number."

He pulled out his phone, and she gave him her number, certain he was merely being polite and that she had just totally embarrassed herself. God, she just couldn't help but look like an idiot. Her boyfriend was out there flirting with some stoplight, and here she was, giving her number out to the guy who clearly didn't want any part of anything out there. Which surely included her.

And it's not like she had even been invited. It suddenly seemed insane that she was hanging out at Jenna King's house, trying to fit in like it was her right to be happy there.

She said bye and hurried out of Conor's bedroom. Once she was back in the living room, Vince ran into her.

"Where you been? I've been looking for you."

God, she didn't even want to talk to him. Didn't want to hear his voice. Just wanted this night over. "Can we go back to your house?"

"Right now?"

"I really . . ." She scrambled to think of a way to leave. She used her frequent fallback. "I wanna hook up. I'm bored of this and I wanna go back and do that." A little piece of her died.

"What we were talking about earlier?" He looked intrigued, and she knew she had gotten him.

"Blow job." No matter how desperate she was to leave, she wasn't going to agree to become a viral video. Jailbird Gives Great Beak.

"Yeah. Whatever. Fine. Let's go." Some small, stupid part of her hoped he'd hear the hesitation in her voice and that some sort of decency would prevail.

No such luck. They were in his car and on the road in a flash.

Once home, and having snuck in the back door, they went to the couch, where he kissed her for maybe fifteen seconds before she felt the familiar push on the top of her shoulders. Not wanting to be yelled at or embarrassed more, she went with it.

She obeyed.

At first she didn't notice, being drunk and high and embarrassed, that he was holding his phone above her. By then it was too late to stop him.

"Hey—?" she started, giving the camera full view of her face before she realized what was going on.

"Babe. It's okay. It's just for me. I'm not going to show anyone. Now, finish."

So she did.

It wasn't like she had that much to lose.

Not two minutes after she finished him off, her phone lit up. A text from an unknown number.

Hey jailbird. It's Conor, just givin you my number.

It was like being trapped in hell and getting a postcard from someone in a happier world, living a happier life, with no clue what scene his innocent text had just been a chaser to.

She wanted to be part of that world so badly, she could almost taste it.

Almost.

CHAPTER FOUR

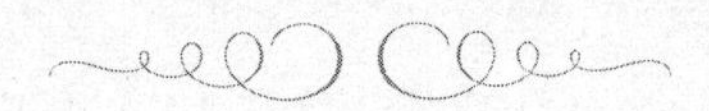

Colleen

IT HAD BEEN COLLEEN'S VISION THAT SHE WOULD RISE WITH THE sun the morning she was leaving, then stop at McDonald's—her favorite breakfast, truth be told—and hit the open road, blasting "Drive South" by John Hiatt. She had a whole playlist set up on her phone, actually. "On the Road Again," "Drive South," "King of the Road," "500 Miles"—technically a train song, but miles trumped method—and more. Forty-two drive songs in all. She'd felt completely inspired, dragging them onto her *Road Trip* playlist.

But instead of the sparkling clear June morning she'd envisioned, it was a drizzly cold leftover from what felt like October. The sky looked like a pile of wet towels at the gym, gray on gray on wet gray, swirling around the dank, still air.

A bad omen?

She shuddered.

Honestly, she was filled with trepidation about the whole thing, and every third thought was that maybe she should cancel the trip altogether and just stay home and babysit Tamara. At least that way, she could have some alone time and just check on Tamara now and then to make sure she wasn't lying on the bathroom floor like Nancy Spungen, with a needle in her arm.

"Trailer's all hooked up," Kevin announced, coming up behind her and looking brighter-eyed and bushier-tailed than she thought he should, given that he was about to lose his wife for almost two weeks.

He was probably just glad he wasn't going to be stuck with Tamara.

That wasn't fair. She was talking about a child, after all. A troubled one, to be sure, but Tamara had been through a lot in her young life, so it was ugly of Colleen to begrudge her this time together. Particularly since Tamara was probably looking forward to it even less than Colleen was. What a drag this was going to be for her!

"Are you sure the car can pull it?" Colleen asked Kevin. "It's not exactly a workhorse." In fact, it was exactly her toy—not her midlife crisis car, as Kevin called it. A red Toyota Solara convertible that she'd actually gotten because she always wanted one; since she was frugal enough to buy used, she hadn't had a choice of colors. She pointed out that he'd better hope she lived to be older than sixty-eight, but that hadn't stopped his taunts throughout the entire first year she drove it.

Then his Ford F-250 died and he'd had to borrow the Toyota, and all of a sudden he appreciated one more of the finer things in life.

"Piece of cake," he said. "You're perfectly safe. Just don't stop suddenly."

"What if a deer runs out in front of me?"

"Hit it."

"Kevin!"

He laughed. "Deer season isn't until the fall. Keep your eyes open and you'll be fine. You're more likely to have a clown dash out in front of you."

She had to laugh. "That I'd hit."

"That may be the only time I've ever seen a clown make you laugh."

"True."

"So." He stretched. "What time were they supposed to be here?"

"Nine." Colleen looked at her watch and tried to avoid making a snarky, impatient comment. Nine thirty. She'd hoped to have hit the road by now, grabbed McDonald's breakfast before they stopped serving (nothing worse than craving an Egg McMuffin and being offered chicken nuggets), then kept going until someone needed to pee desperately.

"I know," Kevin said, even though she hadn't commented.

"You don't suppose he changed his mind and forgot to tell us, do you?"

As if in answer, Chris's big blue boat of a Chevy turned onto the street and barreled down toward the house and into the driveway.

"Sorry I'm late," he said when he got out of the car. "We had a little trouble getting going this morning." He flashed a look at the passenger seat and said, "Come on, Tamara."

It wasn't that he snapped at her, precisely; there was just a subtle edge to his tone that caught Colleen's attention. The girl had already been collecting herself to get out of the car, but as Colleen herself had explained to Kevin time and again, any trip longer than ten minutes usually involved the removal of things from a purse that had to be hastily put back upon arrival at whatever the destination.

The less fun the destination, the more crap there was to put away.

It was like a law of nature.

Chris looked at his daughter for a minute, then sighed and turned his attention to Colleen. "I really appreciate your doing this. I didn't know what I was going to do. It wasn't like I could take her to Vegas with me."

"Sorry—Vegas?" "Out West" had sounded a lot more businesslike than *Vegas.* Suddenly his trip didn't sound so urgent.

He nodded. "Conference. The hotels there are cheaper than in other major cities, and there are plenty of flights. But can you imagine me trusting Tamara in the room while I wasn't there?"

The girl's posture shrank almost imperceptibly.

"I don't know," Colleen said, even though she might have said the exact same words to Kevin about leaving Tamara in a B and B room while she went to an auction without her. Something about Chris's dismissal of his own daughter got under Colleen's skin, though. Quickly and a little illogically. "I'm sure she'd be fine, if a bit bored sitting around in a hotel room."

"She hasn't been reliably fine in three years," Chris said, seemingly heedless of the fact that Tamara was getting out of the car then and could hear him.

Colleen noticed the girl's eyes dart toward her father, then away.

"Tamara, you remember your aunt Colleen," Chris said, stiff. Awkward. Like he was unsure of the name.

"Not really."

Colleen barely remembered her either, and definitely wouldn't have recognized the tall, thin girl standing before her with pale clear skin, no makeup, and dull black hair processed to frizzy, damaged ends.

"Be polite," Chris cautioned.

For a moment, Colleen thought he was talking to her, but then Tamara said, "Thanks for having me join you, Aunt Colleen."

God, this was uncomfortable. "You're welcome. Of course."

They all stood there in awkward silence for a moment, and Colleen wondered if it was twenty minutes to ten, based on the old Irish lore that awkward silences happened twenty minutes before or after the hour. For every time she'd been right in pointing it out to Kevin, there were at least five others when it had been nowhere near the mark, so she resisted saying anything this time, though she and Kevin locked eyes for just an instant.

"Well, we'd better get going," Colleen said. "I'm starving and I want to hit McDonald's before they start serving lunch. Are you hungry, Tamara?"

She shrugged. "I'm fine."

"This is to cover her expenses," Chris said, handing Colleen an envelope.

"Chris, that's not necessary."

"Of course it is. Take it."

No wonder Colleen had thought he was ordering her to be polite. He took on the same commanding tone with her that he did with Tamara. She took the envelope without comment and gave him a stern look he clearly didn't notice or care to notice.

He went to the backseat and took out a faded green backpack. "Tamara, where's your suitcase?"

"That's it." She gestured at what he was holding. "I don't even *have* a suitcase."

He looked annoyed. Maybe self-conscious of this small indicator of his parenting prowess. "This is all you packed?"

"Well . . . yeah. I mean . . . yeah?" She looked at him questioningly. "We're only going for a week, right?"

"Week and a half-ish," Colleen told her. "But don't worry, if we need anything else, we can certainly pick it up on the road."

Tamara turned her gaze to her father. "See?"

His expression darkened instantly. "Listen—!"

"Let's go!" Colleen said a little too forcefully. "Time's a-wastin'." Good Lord, she was turning into Ma Kettle. But whatever this girl had done—and she knew it had been stressful for Chris—her father was clearly way past the point where he could take anything in stride. It looked like he was one or ten all the time with Tamara, and Colleen didn't want to sit here and watch him go to ten.

Tamara looked uncertainly at her father, then went to him and gave him a cursory hug. He patted her shoulder with an open hand. Then Tamara came to the car and opened the passenger door to get in. She moved the front seat forward and tossed her backpack in, then started to climb in the back herself.

Colleen stopped her. "For Pete's sake, Tamara, I'm not your chauffeur—get in the front!"

"Oh." The girl hesitated, then got into the front seat.

Kevin pulled Colleen into a hug and said, "Bye-bye, baby." Then whispered in her ear. "This is a good thing you're doing."

She wrapped her arms around his lower back and gave him an answering squeeze before climbing in behind the wheel.

The car started with no problem—that was when Colleen

realized she'd been semi-hoping for a reprieve right up to the last second—and she put it in gear and backed out of the drive.

As soon as they started toward the main road, she felt a rush of anxiety and glanced at Tamara, who looked away the moment their eyes met.

"I'm starving." She'd already said so once, and repeated it even though it was pretty meaningless. If she were this lost for words the entire trip, it was going to be a very long couple of weeks.

Tamara nodded. "Yeah. You said."

"You look like you could use a little nourishment yourself." Wait, was that bad? Everyone said it was just as bad to tell a skinny person she needed a cheeseburger as it was to tell a fat person she needed to put the cheeseburger down. Had she just insulted the girl thirty seconds into their trip?

"I guess."

This was off to a bangin' start. Colleen was as nervous with a sixteen-year-old girl as she would have been with a sixteen-year-old boy when she *was* a sixteen-year-old girl. All tied up in knots about saying the right thing, not saying the wrong thing, not offending, not judging. It was all incredibly uncomfortable.

For both of them, no doubt.

She pulled up to the drive-through window and ordered her usual, plus a large coffee—even though she'd probably have to stop and pee a hundred times after drinking it—then looked to Tamara and asked, "Anything?"

"An Egg McMuffin," Tamara said, then quickly added, "And hash browns. The double one on the dollar menu."

No sooner had Colleen yelled the order into the microphone

than Tamara added, "And a biscuit. And a Wild Berry Smoothie." Then, as if that were going too far, she tagged on, "Small is fine."

Colleen placed the order, secretly glad the girl was going to eat, because Tamara really did look like she needed it. Not that Colleen thought Chris didn't feed his daughter; he probably just didn't take her tastes into account much. He was used to being on his own, and honestly, no matter who else came into his sphere, he probably wasn't likely to be very accommodating. That was how Chris was. That was how Chris had always been.

By the time they hit the road, it was a lot later than Colleen had hoped to leave, but at least it was with full stomachs.

Unfortunately, it was also with empty minds. At least conversation-wise. They drove for long, long stretches of silence, tied up in a long ribbon of D.C. traffic. Miles and miles passed, all looking the same—big buildings behind Jersey walls and construction. Brake lights. Horns. Extended middle fingers. This stretch of road felt like it went on forever, where if it had been a straight country road through farmland, it might have passed like a favorite song.

Instead the drive dragged like an amateur opera, made louder by the silence in the passenger seat.

There was no way to tell what Tamara was thinking, if she noticed or was uncomfortable with the awkwardness, but Colleen's mind was racing, trying to think of something—anything—to say. Initially she was aiming for witty and entertaining, but now she would settle for anything that was simply communicated out loud.

Meanwhile, Colleen's entire playlist was murmuring quietly over the speakers in the oppressive, muggy car, and the windshield wipers whipped out of sync to the music. She kept catching herself humming along, then stopped, embarrassed. She really wanted to belt out with it, but she was very aware of the presence next to her, and she could feel Tamara looking sideways at her now and then.

"So, do you have a boyfriend?" Colleen asked at last, even though it was exactly the sort of lame typical-adult question she'd wanted to avoid.

"I—" Tamara paused, then sighed and looked out the window, her posture tense. "No, not really."

That hesitation raised a lot of questions, but none that Colleen felt like she could ask right now without seeming really intrusive.

Instead she nodded. "I had a lot of on-and-off things at your age." Whatever that meant. How on earth could that be helpful? She was just trying to fill the gaps in conversation, and the effort was obvious to both of them. "What do you like to do in your free time?"

Tamara glanced at her and shrugged. "Listen to music. I don't know. Watch TV. The usual."

"Yeah? What do you like to watch?"

Tamara shrugged again. "I don't know. Whatever's on."

Right. Good start. "And what music do you like?" She was losing the kid, she could tell. How could she not? Her questions were so judge-y, Tamara's nonanswers even worse.

"Old stuff, mostly."

"Really?" That answer surprised her. Did this seemingly sullen, drug-addled teenager secretly harbor a love for Sinatra? Perry Como? Nat King Cole? "Like who?"

"The Clash—"

Oh.

"Sex Pistols, Arctic Monkeys, I don't know . . . all sorts of stuff. The Beatles. Bon Jovi."

"Bon Jovi?"

"Yup."

"Seriously?"

"Why not?"

"They're not that old, and not new enough to be in your current spehere. They're just like *in between*."

Tamara gave a laugh. "They've been around, like, thirty years!"

"No, they haven't." That seemed impossible.

"Yeah. They have. Probably longer." Tamara started fidgeting with the screen of her phone. "In fact, they're probably even before your time."

"No, they were hot when I was coming of age." Suddenly she was feeling really old. She didn't even use expressions like "coming of age"! Soon she'd be complaining that her crinolines were too stiff and her corset was too tight.

"Debut album, *Bon Jovi*, was released January twenty-first, 1984," Tamara read from her phone.

"Wow, really?"

Tamara held her phone up, as if Colleen could read the minuscule print. "It's a fact."

1984. A million years ago to Tamara. An era before she was a possibility. But Colleen's life had been in full swing. And it didn't even feel that long ago. And on the other hand, it also felt like lifetimes ago. How was it possible to feel so completely both ways at once?

"Okay, then, that's not before my time, exactly, but it's definitely really early in my time."

Tamara laughed. "Anyway, he was pretty hot. Bon Jovi."

"Still is."

Tamara gave a small shrug.

"Oh, I remember that feeling," Colleen said.

"What?"

"I remember being around older women and thinking their idea of hot was just depressing. Older women like older men, but when you're young you can't see it."

"Wait a minute, you're saying you wouldn't do Bon Jovi, version 1984?"

Of course she would. In a heartbeat. "We shouldn't be having this conversation."

That lit it on fire for Tamara. "Who would you do, if you had to: Bon Jovi from back then or"—she crinkled her nose, thinking—"the dude who supposedly stomped on baby chickens on stage."

"Alice Cooper?"

"Yeah, him."

"He didn't really do that. Urban legend."

"Good. Him or Bon Jovi?"

Colleen bit her lower lip, then said, "Not an appropriate game for us to play."

"So Alice Cooper, then?"

"No way."

"Bon Jovi! I *knew* it!"

"Easy guess. And his name is Jon."

"Jon Jovi?"

Colleen laughed. At least they had something to talk about. "No, Jon Bon Jovi."

Tamara sighed. "Points off for the stupid name."

Colleen could have explained that his real name was John Bongiovi, and that it was kind of a hot, romantic, sexy Italian thing, but that would have been revealing way too much about her old pop star knowledge in general and her Jon Bon Jovi knowledge in particular, so she let it go.

Then, just as quickly as it had come on, the moment was gone. More stiff silence.

Colleen tapped the volume-up button on the steering wheel with her thumb until the music was loud enough for them to listen to without being ultraconscious of the lack of conversation. They passed quite a few miles that way, and Colleen wondered how on earth she was going to get through the next couple of weeks like this. Every minute passed like an hour. And it was probably even worse for Tamara because all she could do was sit there and mess with her phone; she didn't even have the distraction of driving the car.

After they'd been on the road for about four hours, they stopped at Colleen's first marked stop, a salvage yard just south of Richmond, Virginia. The Yelp description had mentioned all kinds of intricate carved wooden pieces from buildings that had been glorious at the turn of the last century but which had been renovated recently. So Colleen wound around the back roads off I-95 to find it, turning around repeatedly on the road it was supposed to be on until finally she realized she'd passed it repeatedly. Far from the huge, glorious treasure trove described in the book, it was a small space with linoleum floors that had once been a foreign legion hall. It smelled like glue and mildew and something else Colleen couldn't quite put her finger on, but which made her want to run away. Light filtered dimly through old plate-glass windows, illuminating more dust in the air than merchandise for sale.

It had a lot of doorknobs.

Not interesting doorknobs, by the way, just the sort of handles you'd see in a 1970s elementary school or other public building on a budget.

"Is this the kind of thing you're on this trip to look for?" Tamara asked, clearly trying to be tactful.

"No. This isn't the kind of thing anyone is looking for. Except maybe someone looking for a quick fix in a cheap rental property." Who else would buy any of this crap? How did this place even stay in business? Was it just a tax loss for someone?

Tamara looked relieved. "I thought this was a little strange."

"Disappointing." It was.

"I'll say."

Colleen looked around and sighed. There was nothing of any interest whatsoever here. Nothing she'd even take for free.

"Do you need help?" a voice asked from only a few yards away.

Startled, Colleen jerked her head in the direction of the query and saw a gray woman—gray hair, gray complexion, even a gray tattered sweater—standing in the dingy light. It was like stepping into a dreary black-and-white movie and feeling your own color drain. Dorothy coming back from Oz.

"No," Colleen said quickly. She always felt a sense of guilt at not being interested in someone's merchandise, but she'd learned not to waste too much time pretending. "No, thank you." She ushered Tamara out.

The rain had stopped and they were able to roll the windows down and enjoy the warm night air. This added new elements to the drive—more fun and, mercifully, more noise.

"So what is it you are looking for?" Tamara asked.

"Oh, I don't know. Anything interesting. Unique. Cheap. Things I can paint and polish and fix up and sell in the shop."

"Like what?"

"Uh, well, last year I found an old bicycle and took the chain, spokes, and pedals off to make a candelabra."

"That sounds . . . weird." Tamara looked skeptical. "I can't picture that."

"It was cooler than it sounds. I also found some old colored glass bottles and drilled holes in them so I could put lights in and make them pretty little night-lights."

"Hm."

"Again, cooler than it sounds."

"And people buy that kind of thing?"

"They sure do."

"Who?"

"Mostly women with money who can buy pretty much anything they want, so they want something unique that no one else can buy." She wanted to add, *But don't get any ideas about turning a plate upside down and calling it a cake stand, because it's not as stupid and easy as it sounds,* but a comment like that would have been insulting to both of them.

"So you don't really have a thrift shop exactly."

No doubt that was how Chris had described it. "No," she said. "It's a cross between a boutique and an antique store, and people consign their own things there as well."

"That's cool. I wish I could make stuff and sell it."

"You could. It just takes some imagination. And work. And luck." Colleen smiled. "You're on the right trip, I guess."

"Better than some I've had," Tamara said cryptically, and Colleen didn't want to ask for an explanation, for fear of getting one she didn't like. "So this is kind of like that show on Channel 26?"

Channel 26 was PBS, and Colleen knew exactly what she meant. "I'd *love* to find an *Antiques Roadshow*–worthy find. I'm always looking for that needle in a haystack, but people have gotten a lot more savvy than they used to be. No one ever finds an unseen copy of the Declaration of Independence behind an acrylic painting of kittens."

"Like the copy where John Hancock spelled his name wrong in haste?" Tamara asked, quirking a smile. "You know, like when you're in a hurry and you scribble over your name and it looks wrong?"

Colleen laughed out loud. She had no idea Tamara could be clever. Kevin could, so maybe it was hereditary. A gene that had skipped Chris. "That would be awesome. Imagine what it would be worth."

"A Revolutionary War blooper."

"Exactly. Keep your eye out for that."

"You got it."

They fell back into silence, but Colleen was heartened that Tamara was a slightly livelier wire than she'd expected.

The drive past the worst of D.C.'s suburbia finally opened up to a dull highway lined with green. Nothing remarkable, but better than buildings. Once they got past Richmond, much of the traffic dropped off, and what remained seemed to be primarily big-rig trucks and family-packed minivans with Rubbermaid boxes bungeed onto racks on the back. Disney-bound, no doubt.

Colleen drove about half an hour past Richmond, then took an exit to a Sheetz gas station. ("Don't stop for a gas station until you can actually see it from the road," Kevin had always told her. This one was right off the highway.) She opened the door and turned to Tamara. "You want anything from inside?"

"I wouldn't mind some Doritos."

"You got it."

"Cool Ranch flavored!"

Colleen gave her the thumbs-up, went in, found some Cool Ranch Doritos, a tall bottle of Evian, and then hit the wine section to get a little something for later if she wanted it. On the shelf next to the fridge was a display of what looked like Reddi-wip but was in fact spiked whipped cream. Hazelnut, vanilla, and caramel. She'd never seen anything like it, so she added one of each to her purchases, making a mental note to keep it away from Tamara, who seemed perilously likely to help herself to it, whether she knew it was alcoholic or not.

They started back on the highway. But for the sound of the wheels on the road and the wind whipping over them, the miles passed in silence.

About half an hour from the North Carolina border, a truck bore down on them and slipped beside them into the right lane.

Colleen put her foot on the brake to let him pass, but he slowed down with her. When she sped up, he sped up too.

A nervous tremor crossed her chest.

"Do you know him?" Tamara asked.

"I certainly hope not."

"He's gesturing at us. Do you think something's wrong with the car and he's trying to warn us?"

Colleen glanced in the rearview mirror. Everything looked as it had the whole time. There was no odd pull on the wheel; the drive felt normal. Except, of course, for the apprehension she suddenly felt, remembering old urban legends about truck drivers seeing murderers lurking in backseats and trunks and so on and trying to warn drivers, who just blew them off and treated them like pests.

She wondered if she should pull over and check everything out, but he was pretty good at keeping pace with her, and there were no exits within view. There was no way she was going to pull over right now.

They were about ten miles from the Henley exit, though, which happened to be where Colleen had gone to college. That would be a good place to pull off and just check everything out for safety. Besides, the Henley Diner was incredible, and after McDonald's for breakfast and nothing but junk food since, she thought they could both probably go for an incredible meal.

"The car's fine," Colleen said with more confidence than she felt. "Who knows what he's doing?"

"Okay." The doubt in Tamara's voice was clear.

The trucker kept pace with them, tracking their speed relentlessly. The road maneuvers went from seeming like they might be a coincidence to being clearly on purpose to feeling downright scary.

They were almost at Henley when Tamara said, "Oh my God! No *way*! Creeper!"

Colleen's nerves were so frayed by then that the words startled her. "What?"

"He's . . . ew."

"He's what?" Colleen glanced but couldn't tell what Tamara might be talking about. The trucker was gesturing still, rather broadly, but she couldn't tell what it meant. Was he brandishing a gun or something? "What's he saying?"

"Ugh. I don't know, but I think it's something like 'Oh, baby,' and he's— Ugh, it's just too gross to say."

"Huh?" Colleen looked again and saw that the driver had somehow raised his pelvis up and appeared to be— There was no way. "Is he doing what he looks like he's doing?"

Tamara met her eyes for a moment. "Does he look like he's beating off?"

Colleen returned her eyes to the road. "Yes, he does."

"Then I think yes, he is."

"Oh, God." Well, this was going to look great on her Résumé of Superior Guardianship when Chris saw it. Day One of her Excellent Adventure with Tamara, and so far they'd had fast food and convenience store snacks, seen a bunch of unremarkable doorknobs, and caught a middle-aged man masturbating. Add some roadkill and a motel room that smelled of bug bombs, and they'd have a banner Day One under their belts.

"Ew!" Tamara cried, and looked away. "So *nastyyy*."

No kidding. This was the crescendo of their first day together? This? Some pervy trucker whacking off and, in so doing, subtly undermining Colleen even further. She was the impossibly boring straitlaced aunt taking a teenaged girl on a long drive south with old music and awkward spits of conversation—and now this? Asshole.

At that moment, the sign for Henley appeared, just like Brigadoon in the mist. "Okay, hold on, Tam, we're going to lose him." She gunned the motor and shot ahead of the truck, then swerved into the exit lane, thinking he wouldn't have time to do the same.

Unfortunately, he seemed to have experience with this game of cat and mouse and moved into the lane behind her, quickly closing the gap between them.

"This is so creepy," Tamara said, looking fretful. It was amazing how fear transformed that hardened mask of an expression Tamara had been wearing all day and made her look like the vulnerable child she actually was.

"There's no way he can take an eighteen-wheeler on these back roads," Colleen assured her—but was there?—and took a sudden left onto the main road into town.

He followed.

"Get your phone out and call 911," Colleen said then, wondering why it had taken her so long to think of that. The idea alone made her feel a flood of relief.

Tamara looked at her screen. "No reception."

Sudden panic surged through her with the force it can have only after a moment of false relief. "Shit! I mean *shoot.*"

"I think he's about to."

Colleen looked at Tamara, startled for a moment, replaying the comment and trying to figure out if the guy had taken out a gun or something, but when she met the girl's eyes, she saw a tentative laugh in them.

And then they both burst out laughing. The kind of hard, breathless laugh that felt like it was never going to stop. It had been a long time since Colleen last went on a laughing jag like that.

"I cannot believe you said that," she said.

Tamara turned down the corners of her mouth and shrugged. "I can't believe you got it."

"Ouch. Come on, how old do you think I am?"

Tamara's laughter quieted. "Actually, I *don't* know. How old are you? Like . . . forty?"

Ugh. "Thirty-six."

"Oh." Tamara didn't look surprised at the news, so it was hard to take the "forty" guess that personally. "I'm not very good at guessing people's ages."

"I'll say." Colleen smiled to let her know it was okay.

There was an old winding road into the mountain on the right, and Colleen couldn't remember where it led, if anywhere, but she was positive she could take it at the last second and he'd overshoot it—everything was a pun suddenly—then even if he turned back, there was no way he could safely drive it.

She took the turn and the trailer fishtailed behind her. She'd forgotten all about it. Fortunately, it righted itself and she gunned the motor onto the small road, watching the truck pass the turn in her rearview mirror. It was no time to get complacent, though she had to keep driving until she could get to a safe turnaround spot. That way, at least she'd be pointing in the right direction to get reliably into town, where she could drive straight to the sheriff's office.

They drove for about ten minutes until the quiet around them took over and it felt like they were well and truly safe. Colleen slowed the car and did an eighteen-point turn to reverse her direction and face the highway again.

This time she drove slowly, wary of the trucker's return, even while the possibility seemed excessively unlikely.

"Once when I was little, a guy pulled up to the intersection in my neighborhood and said, 'Did you ever see one of these?' to all of us kids playing," Tamara said. "I didn't go over, but Amy Williams and her sister did—and he was . . . exposing himself. They went home and told their mom and she called the police and my mom totally freaked out."

"Did you freak out?"

Tamara considered that for a moment. "No, I wondered what it looked like." She looked at Colleen. "I mean, I'm not sorry now that I didn't see—it was just that at the time, that was all anyone could talk about and I couldn't even picture what it might look like."

"Unfortunately, I can." Colleen shuddered at the idea of a grown man doing that to children.

"Me too. Now. It's really messed up to do that to kids."

"People are sick."

"More people than you think, probably," Tamara agreed, then closed her eyes and leaned her head back against the seat. "Weirdos are everywhere. It's more weird not to be weird."

"You may be right."

"Pretty sure I am."

Colleen turned left on Birch Street and was surprised to see that not only was the diner not there but it also looked like it never had been there. There was a gas station and a crummy wooden house, and the rest was overgrown brush. "I could have sworn this was where it was."

"Did you say the Henley Diner?"

"Yes."

"Right there." Tamara pointed not at the diner but at a billboard so small, with lettering in script, that it was hard to read at all. But the building in the picture was unmistakable. "Turn around and then go right. It's a half a mile away."

"Thank goodness one of us can see." She carefully maneuvered the car around and followed Tamara's directions until, sure enough, the familiar old diner came into view. Blue-gray wood slats outside, a chimney shaped like R2-D2 pumping out delicious scents, and a small assortment of old pickup trucks and a few scattered practical college student cars in the parking lot.

This was the place.

It was hard to believe they had left her house in Frederick only that morning. Of course, her hunger and the fact that she'd had only crap food were probably contributing to her disorientation.

But something told her everything was about to take a turn for the better. A good meal, a great dessert, a few more miles across the border into North Carolina, then they would stop for the night and get up bright and early to start again in the morning.

Hopefully, then things would fall in line with her carefully mapped-out plans.

CHAPTER FIVE

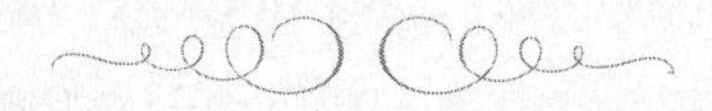

Bitty

Dear Stranger,

Everyone should have somebody to write a suicide note to. People kill themselves and leave suicide notes behind every day. Always addressing their children, parents, friends, anyone. I don't have anyone to write mine to. So I'll write it here, and whoever reads it . . . well, I guess you're my closest friend.

I'm currently writing from a booth at my college diner. That's why I'm using this cheap spiral notebook paper. It was all they had at the drugstore. Do they still call them "drugstores"? I always wonder if that's somehow politically incorrect or something. Anyway, if I'd thought more carefully ahead, I'd have gotten better paper. And something to put it in, I guess. I'm not sure where to leave this.

I'm not very good at drama, I guess.

Though, boy, I sure had a lot thrown at me this week. I mean, the truth, now that I look back on it, is that I've been putting up with a low-level hum of bullshit—yes, I said bullshit—for a long time, but I ignored it, pushed it away, whatever. I was the dutiful wife, right?

So dutiful that I apparently had zero idea who my husband was or what he was capable of.

I guess that's the first thing you should know about me: I'm a blind idiot who doesn't even know her husband of thirteen years, and I'm not very good at planning suicide.

We're not off to a good start, are we, New Friend?

Oh well. I'm a letdown for everyone, always have been. A fraud, even when I didn't know it. There's no reason I should be any better to you than I am to anyone else.

So, getting back to the point, I'm here in the Henley Diner, in a sticky vinyl booth that's probably been torn for twenty years, and is imbued with the smells of every greasy thing that was ever fried up here.

A year ago, if you'd told me I'd be here, ordering fried green tomatoes and pecan pie, it would have felt like a slap. Not me. Not Wilhelmina Nolan Camalier. (I never had a middle name, because my parents were so set on me keeping their last name that they forced the issue by planning for it to at least be my middle name when I married.) (By the way, not having a middle name is kind of a drag when you're in school and all your friends think there's something weird about you because your parents were too stingy to give you more than one name.)

Anyway, I'm not exactly sure why I came here, of all places, two hours east of my house when my plan was to go south. For some weird reason, I wanted to see it one last time. I guess it feels like the last time I was sure I was happy was here.

No. I'm kidding myself. You probably saw right through me, huh? Close as we are? This isn't a place of great joy for me, it's just the last place I ate really well. When I ordered my fried chicken with mashed potatoes and broccoli, and consumed all but the greens in about six minutes flat. That was the last time I had fried chicken, incidentally. In fact, it was the only time, and I loved it the way they warn people not to try heroin because they'll love it. But that was a bad day too, though not so bad as this day, and I came here for comfort food and I got it. The place has hardly changed.

I haven't either. Oh, I know I look different, even though you would probably be kind and tell me I look just the same. I've told that lie to people too. Maybe there's a certain symmetry to my coming back here. Full circle. At least closing one circle.

My friend Colleen and I sat in a booth—that one right over there, I can see it now. I sat with my boyfriend, Blake, and she sat with Kevin. We were on a happy little double date. I probably asked for my Diet Coke to be refilled six times along with everyone else, not feeling like I was actually drinking the equivalent of six sodas—half a case of sodas. Later that night, everything had changed, and I didn't ever want to come back here.

I guess I could go into what happened that night, but why bother? I'd come off crazy, like I'm still upset about some dumb breakup that happened all those years ago. Which I'm not.

That's not why I want to kill myself.

I don't even want to go into the details of how I ended up at this spot, in this booth, having my last meal. It doesn't even matter. My life is just like anyone else's sob story. I was raised by a withholding mother, and an overprotective father who didn't know how to talk to or interact with a young—or older—daughter. I did well in high school, never got in trouble, then went to college, just like you're supposed to, then I graduated and married my boyfriend, thinking I knew the life I was in for, and was excited about it.

Happily ever after.

But that didn't happen. I don't believe in that anymore. I remember when I did, as clearly as I remember believing in Santa Claus. And I miss believing in happily ever after just like I miss believing in Santa Claus. A lot of magic went out of life with the realization of how ugly and stark and unfair things can really be.

You've probably danced with that a little yourself, whoever you are. Seems like everyone has done their time with disappointment. I know some people have had it worse than me, much worse, but some have had it better. It's not really about what everyone else is doing in life, or how they handle things, it's about what you can handle and what you can't.

I couldn't handle the change in my life.

So everything fell apart, and now here I am, frustrated and alone, with no one to call. No one to cry to. No one to even write a suicide note to. I think that's the most pathetic thing of all.

I have a gun in my car. There's no way to say that without sounding dramatic. But I do. It's a cute Smith & Wesson. Very girlie. I'm trying to decide where to do it. Maybe on the side of the bridge? Maybe in some pretty church. I don't know yet. After I leave here, once my favorite diner now my Last Supper (pardon me the grandiose moment), I guess I'll drive around until somewhere seems right.

CHAPTER SIX

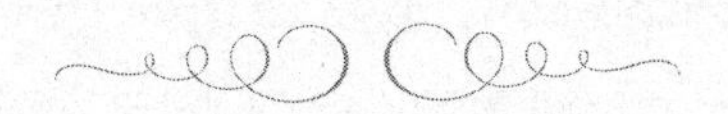

Tamara

"I USED TO COME TO THIS PLACE ALL THE TIME WHEN I WAS IN COLlege. It was cheap, greasy, and good." Colleen collected her wallet and things, and opened the car door.

Tamara got out too, taking the little jump that was necessary to get from seat to ground.

"You went to school around here?"

"Yep. Small college right outside of town. So, basically, this is the college town right here." She took a deep breath and looked around. The light from big ugly parking lot lights illuminated her face and she looked . . . alive. "I can't believe how *the same* it looks."

Tamara also looked around. There was basically nothing around. It didn't look like how she'd always thought of college towns. She had been to Towson University once, when Vince was sure they could get into a bar there, and that had felt like a college town. The big long street was crowded with college students going from bar to bar. People played cornhole outside one bar, everyone was dancing inside another really loud bar, and at one place there had even been some semi-legit band playing.

The bar they had been assured they could get into, Lil' Dicky's, was a cramped hallway of a place. It was kind of awful, but still, it felt like what you expected out of a college area, full of energy. This was more like a place you'd hear that the walk-in fridge in the back was haunted. By old potato ghosts. Before they were chopped up and turned into French fries.

She laughed a little to herself as they went into the diner, and thought briefly about sharing her mental image of an evil Mr. Potato Head floating like Casper in the back kitchen, but she decided against it, figuring that was too weird, and would probably be a fast way to have Colleen call up her dad and say she was on drugs—or maybe just actual-crazy.

She didn't need anyone else making him think that.

They were taken to a table next to a bunch of girls, all shrill and squealing at each other. Tamara wondered if Colleen was the type of adult that would tell them to calm down, or if she would just get really annoyed until they left or passive-aggressively change tables. If she had been sitting there with her dad, he would have muttered that they were a bunch of PILs, which stood for "Pigs in Lipstick." It was a nasty term he used for the kind of girls who were generally average looking, but put on "a hot-girl costume." Too much makeup caked on, fake hair color, usually wearing a dress or outfit two sizes too small and not made properly for their shape. The kind of accoutrements they thought made them hot, but really only made them cartoonish.

Every time he remarked on this, it stung a little. It just didn't feel right for a man to talk about girls like that. Any girls, but especially not ones who were so much younger than he was. Plus it sucked because since he was always saying that kind of thing, now she noticed it whether she wanted to or not.

Now Tamara was thinking way too much about these girls she'd never know. Just a weird girl at the table next to them thinking about them.

Colleen, on the other hand, didn't seem aware of them. She didn't acknowledge the chatty volume at all and just opened her menu and said, "I could eat everything on this menu. One time, one of my girlfriends and I ordered six different things just to share them all." She shook her head at the fond memory. Days so long past, they didn't even seem real anymore.

"We paid for it using the money we had just gotten back for selling our textbooks. That was a good night. But let me tell you, even with a young metabolism, combining pancakes with chicken tenders with a cheeseburger and cinnamon French toast and God knows what else—that'll give anyone a horrible stomachache."

"I bet," replied Tamara. She recognized that she sounded uninterested in the story, when actually she was just thinking how good all those things sounded.

And how she wished she had a friend she could pig out like that with. What a lame and pitiful thought: *I wish I had a best friend.*

Tamara didn't really have anything resembling a best friend. She used to, back home at her mom's, but they had lost touch. At home, all she had were "the girlfriends." The other groupie girls who watched the boys play video games and went off to make out or do more whenever the guys said to.

She shivered, thinking of Vince and the fact that he had recorded that video. God. How could she have been so careless, letting him do that? Not that she "let" him; she was just too lazy to stop him. No, not lazy. Tired. Painfully, sickly polite. Something. At any rate, she knew she didn't trust him, despite his promises it would go no further. Knowing him, it could very well be on Reddit or 4chan or something else by now. Her private moment with him, being upvoted and downvoted by creepy unattached losers sitting at home, feeling high and mighty with their job as judge, no idea that it was a big deal to her.

Hopefully she was wrong. Maybe this time he was telling the truth when he said he wouldn't tell anyone. She just feared that by "anyone" he had meant "anyone who would tell Tamara they saw it."

She bit on the inside of her cheek, and decided that cinnamon French toast was a lot easier to think about than Vince exposing her.

"I'm getting that French toast," she announced.

"You are? Hm. I was thinking about it too. But we can't both get the same thing, then we'll miss out on swapping bites." Colleen smiled. "What else sounded good to you?"

Swapping bites. Not something Tamara was used to. Neither was getting to help pick out more than one thing. Both sounded okay at this moment.

Her answer was quick, as every time she went to a restaurant that served breakfast food—not very often—she had trouble picking between something sugary that would make her fall asleep in half an hour and something with protein to keep her going. "Uh . . . the mini meat loaves with mashed potatoes. Is it weird to get something so dinnery and so breakfasty, though?"

Colleen thought for a second. "No. I think it's quite civilized, actually." She flagged down their waitress. "I'm going to get the mini meat loaves." She gestured at Tamara to order.

"Oh. Um. Cinnamon French toast." Tamara noticed Colleen let her order her first choice and took the second one herself. It was a small gesture that didn't really mean anything, probably, but still Tam thought it was cool.

The waitress made a scribble that couldn't have been letters on her pad. The movement was too big, too scroll-y. Was she drawing pictures? A picture of a hot dog instead of the words "hot dog"? . . . Tamara almost laughed at the idea of a pile of Pictionary-style doodles of the food wadded up in the trash can at the end of the night. "Got it," said the waitress, whose name on her tag was so faded, it looked blank. (Why put it there?) "Should be out in about ten minutes." She took the menus, tucked them under her arm, and left. Then she was gone, and it was back to just being the two of them.

Silence.

Blech. These awkward silences kept happening. When Tamara was a kid, she had filled every silence. Been talkative and enthusiastic about everything. She remembered her mother being responsive when she was young, and she remembered her dullness and single-word answers—sometimes not pertaining to anything at all—before she died, but Tamara didn't remember when she had changed from one personality to the other. It was like she was remembering two different people.

When Tamara moved in with her dad, her talking had stopped altogether. Not only was he quiet, and not the type to sit around chatting, but he was always telling her to be quiet or calm down too. One time, when she had been delighted to be taken to lunch on her birthday—her only plans for the day—he stared at the screen the whole time, watching football. She had chatted on about things going on in her own life, not needing a response and knowing she wasn't really going to get one. When he broke his silence, he snapped at her, saying, "Are you ever going to stop talking? You haven't taken a breath since we walked in here." When he didn't do something like that, he would tell her to leave him alone for a few minutes. The "few minutes" never ended, and she could never wait long enough for him. Real soon she'd learned not to come back at all.

All this left Tamara with an irritatingly restless feeling whenever there were silences, but with a reluctance to fill them as well.

Maybe even a determination not to.

She got that her father had never planned on actually having to *live* with her. She understood that her existence had not been welcome news . . . just eighteen years of payment for his freedom. That's if things worked out "ideally"—but her mother had died and he ended up taking care of a daughter he'd never wanted, and no matter how many strained or guilty smiles he gave after saying something short-tempered to her, it was always 100 percent clear that Chris Bradley was not a "single father" so much as a "single man with a finite obligation."

They both knew the deal, even though they never talked about it.

But this road trip seemed like a scenario where she probably should do a little more talking. Colleen owed her nothing. Truth was, Colleen didn't owe her dad anything either. Tamara really ought to do her best to make this trip as smooth as possible from her end.

Problem was, she sucked at making conversation.

So she said, "I can't believe we got jacked off at tonight."

Colleen snorted and seemed to have to stop herself from spewing coffee from her nose. Tamara laughed, especially when Colleen glanced at the table next to them. Given the facial expressions turned back toward her, at least some of the girls had heard her say it.

"Shh!" Colleen tried to keep a straight face, but a spike of laughter came out before she collected herself and said, "But . . . yeah. How disgusting. What could the aim be there?"

Tamara laughed.

Colleen's face showed puzzlement, then realization. "No pun intended. But honestly, did he think we were going to pull off to the shoulder and rip our clothes off for him?"

Tamara shrugged and spun her straw around her Sprite. "It's not even like he was hot. Like if Ryan Gosling were doing it, that'd be one thing."

"Ryan Gosling would never do that," Colleen mused. "But if he did, it would have been a lot more distracting, which, really, would have been a lot more dangerous. Though I would have thought less of ol' Ryan for doing it."

Tam considered. "So really, we should have thanked the driver for being so butt-ugly, since it wasn't distracting to you."

"I think you're right."

"We owe our lives to that man."

"You might even say he's a hero."

They both sneered then, and gave a cringe before laughing.

"And now, here we are at my college diner!" said Colleen. "So, in all seriousness, I kind of am thankful to him." She made a face. "Not that I like to admit that."

Tamara was too, but she didn't say anything more about him. "I don't remember the last time I went out to eat."

"Really? I wouldn't think of Chris—your dad as being much of a homemade meals kind of guy."

"He's not. When he's home, we order food or he brings home subs or whatever. When he isn't, I'm either at someone's house or I make easy mac or something."

"Nothing fresh?"

"You mean like an apple or carrot sticks?"

"Or real cheese from a block, raw meat that you cook how you like, and, yeah, an apple now and then?"

Tamara shook her head. "Not really."

Colleen looked at her like she'd never heard anything sadder. If that bothered her aunt, she definitely couldn't handle the rest of the tragic details in Tamara's life.

"I mean it's fine," said Tamara, trying not to sound pathetic. "I like mac and cheese."

"Well, of course, who doesn't? But still. Everyone needs a nice home-cooked meal every once in a while. One that doesn't come out of a blue box and have a two-step cooking process. And maybe something green that is supposed to be green."

Tamara shrugged and gave the sort of empty sentence she often did. "Yeah. But, I mean, it's . . . whatever."

Their food arrived, and it was better than she had expected, and as good as Colleen had promised. The mini meat loaves were succulent softballs of tender meat that, when cut into, spilled melted cheddar onto the plate and into the gravy and mashed potato mix. Swirl a forkful of meat loaf on the plate, and you ended up with something that could probably cure all the ills of the world.

The French toast was no less remarkable; this was not the thin, anemic slices of Wonder Bread dipped in egg that her mother had made her as a child, but thick slices of tender light bread, crisped golden on the outside and dusted with powdered sugar with real maple syrup on the side. The place also had a thick slice of smoky-sweet tavern ham and a buttery mix of tiny diced potatoes and onion, which clever Colleen had requested grated cheese and sour cream for.

Food like this could eradicate war.

"This really is awesome," said Tamara, adding extra butter to the already-buttery toasts.

"Told you. I never lie about food. That should be punishable by law. If I see a sign that promises the world's best cup of coffee, and it isn't? I'm ready to call the authorities."

"It is pretty bad to be disappointed like that." She shoveled in another bite. "Vince—my um . . . boyfriend thing . . . he's always saying that things are the best or are way better than anything, and then they never are."

"Really?"

"Yeah. Like the other day he said we had to drive to Northeast because they have 'the best pizza ever,' but it was gross."

"Best pizza ever is Grotto Pizza in Delaware."

"Ohmigod!" Tamara's face brightened. "I love Grotto!"

"You've been there?"

"Yes! I used to go there when I was younger." She reeled herself in. Enthusiasm didn't suit her. "It's really good."

Colleen put down her fork and gaped at something behind Tamara.

"What?"

"I think . . . I think that's—" She shook her head. "There's no way." She returned her attention to Tamara. "Sorry."

Tamara glanced behind her but didn't see anything remarkable.

Just a scrawny kid, coloring or something, in a booth by herself. She didn't see a celebrity or anything. "You think that's what?"

Colleen squinted and frowned. "I think that's my friend from college." Again, she shook her head. "Is this some weird time warp?"

Tamara turned in her chair and looked more carefully, but didn't see anyone. "Was she with the kid in the booth?"

"What?" Colleen focused on Tamara, then behind her. "Oh. No. That is her in the booth."

"Wha—?" Tamara looked again and saw, yes, the person was older than she'd initially thought. The woman stood up and tucked a spiral notebook under her arm just as the waitress had done with the menus, and exited the place with a group of students. A big, dark, buff guy stopped and held the door for her and then followed her out. "The one who just left with that group of college dudes?"

"I am sure she wasn't with them. But what on earth would she be doing here?"

"I mean you went to school here, and you two were friends when you did. Makes sense, doesn't it?"

"I think she moved a few hours away. Like the rest of us." Colleen shrugged a single shoulder. "Almost no one lives here. So." She shook her head some more, like this was impossible and she just couldn't make sense of it. "What are the odds?"

Apparently, the odds were good: Two minutes later, after a few wordless chews, Colleen said, "Oh my God, it's her."

Tamara looked, and the woman was coming back through the door, headed to the booth she'd been sitting in previously. She looked older than Colleen. Gaunt. It was hard to imagine them in school together.

"Are you sure?"

"Weirdly, yes . . ." She frowned, looking like she was trying to figure out a math problem in her head. "Pretty sure."

"What's her name?"

"Bitty. Well, it's actually—"

"Hey, Bitty!" Tamara called her name and then went back to eating, like she hadn't said anything.

"Tamara!" Colleen said through gritted teeth.

With her back to the woman, Tamara asked, "Did she look?"

"Didn't even flinch."

"Then maybe it's not her."

"It's her." Colleen focused her gaze behind Tamara. "What on earth is she doing?"

Tamara was dying to turn and look, but that would have been so obvious. "What *is* she doing?"

"I think . . . I think she's crying. She's sitting back in the booth and she just put her head in her hands and—" Colleen sucked air in through her teeth. "I should do something, but I don't want to embarrass her or . . . I don't know, what an awkward time to have a little reunion."

Tamara could tell Colleen was talking more to herself than to her, so she just made a noise of assent.

"But if something's wrong . . ." Colleen's voice trailed off.

"Just go talk to her!"

"It's not that easy."

"Why not?"

"Because—"

Tamara heard the sound of someone blowing their nose, probably on a rough, cheap diner napkin, and watched Colleen's gaze snap over to her.

That's the kind of response a mom had. Or was supposed to have. That nurturing thing. Ready to help. Willing to help.

Wanting to help.

"I have to do it." Colleen took a breath and stood up. "Stay here, I'll be just a minute."

Tamara gave a shrug to indicate *Take your time.* She didn't see how this could take a minute.

And it didn't. Three Sprite refills and a bunch of phone apps later, Colleen came back to the booth with the woman. Thin, creaky-looking, pale-faced, and dark-circled, she looked like something out of a zombie movie. How could she have been Colleen's friend in college? It looked like there was about a twenty-year age difference.

"Tamara, I'd like for you to meet someone."

Tamara didn't know Colleen well, but she could already tell that her aunt's voice was not her own. She was uncomfortable.

"This is my old friend—"

"Wilhelmina Camalier," the woman said, reaching a claw out to Tamara.

Seriously, did Tam look to her like a hand-shaking hoity-toity lady?

Still, she took the icy appendage into her French toast–greased palm and gave a squeeze, the way she saw her dad do when he ran into someone he didn't know well. "Nice to meet you," she mumbled.

The woman, who seemed to Tamara to be an icy cold bitch already, said, "I wasn't really prepared."

Well, excuse me, lady. Sorry we didn't give you warning.

Colleen gestured at her clothes. They were just normal clothes, but to Colleen, they seemed proof of something. "We weren't planning on running into anyone either. We were just sidetracked by everything. Road trip, you know. Never know what's going to catch your eye or take you off course." She made a dopey, gung-ho gesture.

"To . . . here?" Wilhelmina Camalier asked.

"To . . . No, this isn't where we're road-tripping to, but when you see the sign for this exit, it's impossible not to remember."

"Yes." The lady didn't look like she wanted to remember whatever it was that came into her head when she heard the word "remember."

The two of them still hovered, standing there, clearly neither sure what the next physical move was going to be.

"We're going on a little tour of the South to stop at a bunch of farm auctions to pick up some antiques," Colleen said. This was unusually awkward. "I refinish them and sell them."

Wilhelmina clearly had nothing to say, but nodded as supportively as she could seemingly muster.

"But, of course, that's not the issue right now," Colleen went on. "You said you called the police?"

Tamara was immediately on alert with a plunging stomach and hot cheeks. Habit. Police?

"Well, I—" The woman looked down and to the left before taking in a deep breath. Lying. Tam's mom had always said that. Down and to the left was lying. Up and to the left was remembering. She didn't know what the other two were. "Yes, I did. They took a report."

"That was fast," Colleen said.

"There was a policeman in the parking lot." The woman looked at Colleen. "You remember how they always hung out here."

"I do."

Another lengthy, tense silence.

"Why don't we sit down?" Colleen asked, sliding into the booth.

At first the woman said nothing. Didn't move. Didn't leave. Didn't say "fuck off," as she looked like she wanted to. Just stood there.

Colleen patted the seat next to her. "Come on, sit down. We can call for a cab or car rental company or something."

She settled into the booth next to Colleen, each of them looking uncomfortable at the proximity. The seat next to Tamara was occupied by Colleen's purse and Tamara's hoodie. Thank God.

The waitress returned, and Wilhelmina Camalier said with a head shake and palm that she wasn't going to order anything.

Colleen looked annoyed by that for some reason.

What the hell had happened between these two that they were so freaking awkward? Tamara wondered.

"So what happened that you needed to call the cops?" Tam asked. "Or, whatever, flag one down in the parking lot?"

"Her car was stolen," Colleen answered.

The other woman's eyes filled with tears and she looked down. All she had was her purse and that notebook Tamara had noticed earlier. "And my money. Almost all my money was in there."

"You keep your money in your car?" Tamara asked.

"Not usually. I just went to the bank and had it in an envelope and stopped in here for a quick bite."

That woman didn't look like she ever stopped in anywhere for a bite. Looking at her, Tamara believed Wilhelmina might actually mean One Single Bite of Food.

"I can't believe no one heard anything if someone broke into your car," Colleen said, evidently not feeling the same bullshit vibe Tamara was from this story.

"I guess they didn't really break in," the woman said. "I left the keys in it. You know, only because I was coming in here for just a moment, and who ever stole a car or anything else around here?"

"But, honey, you can't expect to leave anything unlocked these days without risking losing it. Come on."

"It's not like that where I come from."

"You come from here."

The woman straightened her brittle-looking spine and argued, "No, I don't, I come from Winnington, North Carolina, where people are civilized and don't just help themselves to others' property, whether it seems easy or not."

At that, Colleen all but put her hands up in surrender. "Okay, okay, got it. But that still leaves you with a problem."

Tamara could see the irritation cross Colleen's face. Wilhelmina could argue all she wanted, but evidence supported the fact that Colleen was obviously right. If the question was *Should you leave your keys in the car?* then the answer was *Obviously the hell not.*

"I know it does." Wilhelmina looked less defensive and more upset again. God, was she always pitiful like this? She'd practically begged to get ripped off; it was unbelievable that she was so stunned by it.

"Will Lew come and get you?" Colleen asked.

The woman scoffed and then straightened up. "No. Lew's . . . out of town. So I was . . . taking my own little vacation. Headed for a spa or something to take a few days to myself."

Wow, Tamara thought with a raised eyebrow, she was a terrible liar. Not that the truth could possibly be that interesting, because the lies sure weren't. But society ladies like this would probably say anything just to protect their reputation, whatever it was. If she had a stain on her skirt, she'd probably claim it was the work of a fancy new designer.

Tamara had no patience for liars.

Fortunately Colleen didn't seemed fooled. Points for her. "You were just driving off aimlessly for a vacation with no destination?"

The woman's face colored. "Yes," she insisted. "If he can go off and do . . . his own thing, then why on earth shouldn't I? If he wants to hang with the boys, let him." She looked down.

Maybe her husband was having an affair with a younger woman. That happened. It was certainly the kind of thing a person would lie about.

"So you just took off by yourself? No girlfriends or anything to keep you company?"

"Oh, no. Not this time. I really just wanted some time alone to get my head together." She gave a dry laugh. "Guess I didn't do a very good job, though, given that I was so absentminded, I got myself robbed."

Colleen's face softened. "Well, all isn't lost. Just a few hours. You can still salvage your trip, especially since you're flexible about it."

"Yes." Firm nod. "I'm going to finish what I started. I just need to find another way."

"Hm. Maybe we can give you a ride to the next big town or airport or something, so you can rent a car," Colleen suggested. "I doubt there's a place here, and if there is, it's probably not open right now. Which way were you headed? You must have some idea where you wanted to go, right?"

"South," the woman answered, though it sounded like she was talking more to herself than to Colleen or, obviously, Tamara. "To . . . Florida. Though I was open to anything interesting along the way." Again, it sounded like a bullshit answer without serious planning behind it, but if she was pissed off at her husband and his blond floozy mistress and showing him two could play at his game, then maybe it didn't matter to her where she went, as long as he was left wondering. That was kind of understandable, actually.

"No kidding! We're going to Florida!" It was obvious that the words flew out of Colleen's mouth before she'd really had a chance to stop and think. By then it was obviously too late, and the words just kept coming: "Why don't you just hitch a ride with us? The police have your number, right? Come along, and if you see a stop you prefer to Florida, just rent a car."

The woman balked immediately, much to Tamara's relief. "No, no. Thank you," she added, though it seemed like an afterthought, "but I don't want to impose."

"It wouldn't be an imposition—we were good friends once." Colleen's voice had changed, but it seemed to be working back toward supportive. Sincere, anyway. She was obviously a chronic savior. "Some strange coincidence brought us both here tonight at the same time. I don't know how long it's been since you were here, but it's been years for me—"

"Me too."

"—so maybe it's fate."

"Or hunger," Tamara tried. She didn't want to ride in that little car with this woman for God knows how long. Awkward conversation with Colleen was bad enough; she couldn't even imagine adding this particular brand of discomfort to the mix.

"Hunger." The woman met Tam's eyes, and for just a second they were probably on the same page. "Like you said, when you see the exit for Henley, it's impossible not to remember and I just needed a piece of this pie to fortify me for the road."

"So let's get you back on it," Colleen said. "We're going to stop in a couple of hours for the night anyway. If you prefer, we can stop in a bigger town so you can find a Hertz or something."

The woman looked hesitant, but more than that, she looked ragged. Worn down. Beat up, without the bruises. She didn't have any fight in her. She didn't look like she ever had, actually. She looked how Tamara imagined herself to look after most conversations with her dad. So it wasn't a huge surprise when she gave a limp shrug and said, "Thank you."

Tamara's heart sank, and she took a moment to think worse of herself for having such an uncharitable reaction to someone who was obviously as fucked over as she was. At least in some way.

"Good," Colleen said, and it was obviously her Mom Voice. "Then it's settled. We'll pay up here, hit the road, and aim for—what, do you think? Rocky Mount? Farther, if we feel like it. But at least Rocky Mount. I'd hoped to stay only in little bed-and-breakfasts, but our day got hijacked, and at this point I'd welcome a bed in a Hampton Inn."

"What happened to your day?"

Tamara was more than willing to answer that one. "We were driving, and this truck driver pulled up next to us and—"

"He was driving very aggressively," Colleen interrupted, throwing a pointed look at Tam. "It felt threatening, so I took the first exit that felt safe, which was Henley."

"Ah, so you are the coincidence here. I came for the pie, but you were just escaping."

"I might have stopped for the pie too, though."

The woman smiled, and for the first time, Tamara could see how she could be pretty. Or maybe once was. If she'd ever had any sort of meat on her frame instead of just looking like skin stretched over a plastic skeleton. She was what people meant when they said that skinny didn't equal hot.

"The pie was always worth it."

"We should get some for the road."

Tamara's mouth watered at the idea. They weren't leaving the good food behind now; they were taking it with them. Truth was, this beat the hell out of easy mac or canned spaghetti or anything else she ate on a regular basis.

"Coconut cream to go?" Colleen asked, looking to both of them.

Both agreed, though Tam did it louder and with more urgency.

Colleen called the order out—it was that kind of place—and the waitress said she'd box it up.

Another one of those pregnant pauses stretched between them.

"So," Tamara said, unable to quell that old instinct to fill it. "I'm sorry, but I'm not really sure what you want me to call you . . . Mrs. Camalier? Or—?"

"Bitty," the woman interrupted. It was the strongest her voice had been the entire time they'd been talking. "My name is Bitty Nolan."

Wasn't she Wilhelmina Camalier a minute ago? Whatever. "Cool. Bitty. I'm Tamara. Or Tam." She took the nickname she had somehow gotten from Colleen and used it. Lame as it was, it felt good to have one, and she wanted to use it.

Wilhelmina-slash-Bitty wasn't the only one who maybe didn't want to be herself tonight. Tam liked the idea of taking a break from being a screwed-up teenager and, instead, maybe just being a normal girl.

With a nickname.

Why not? It wasn't like she was ever really going to see this woman again. She probably wasn't even going to see Colleen again after this trip was over. That's how it was in Tamara Bradley's life—people didn't stay. They didn't even come in on purpose, but if they found themselves there, they left as soon as possible.

So why not be whoever she wanted to be in the meantime?

CHAPTER SEVEN

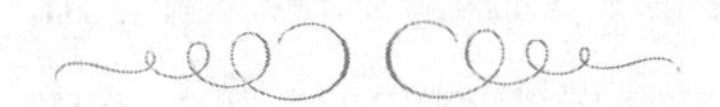

Colleen and Bitty, the past

"I JUST DON'T SEE US FITTING IN THAT CAR. ALL OF US? NO WAY."

"Oh, Bit," said Colleen, looping an arm through hers and resting a head on her shoulder. "Don't be such a worrywart—we'll be fine. We'll fit."

Bitty shook her head. "It's not safe. We should get another driver."

"There is no other driver! Tom's the only one willing to stay sober, so just relax."

"I could drive."

"Hell no—I don't know one of us who needs a drink more than you do."

Bitty sighed, and Colleen rolled her eyes good-naturedly.

"What seems to be the problem here, ladies?"

Blake Leon, always in busted-up jeans and a backward hat, stepped between the two girls and put an arm around each of them.

Colleen reached for his wrist, which dangled over her left shoulder, and said, "Bitty here is worried we won't fit in the car. So she wants to get another designated driver and car."

Blake stepped away, pulling his arms from around them, and placed a hand on each of Bitty's shoulders. "I didn't want to have to tell you this . . . but I happen to be a *Tetris* master."

Colleen snorted with laughter and sat on the thigh-high cement wall they stood in front of.

"And I don't mean to brag," Blake went on, "but my clown-car work has been featured in magazines. I'm pretty popular for it."

"Oh yeah, magazines like what?" Bitty cocked a head, playing along as Colleen continued laughing.

"Uh, jeez, where do I start?" He scanned the sky for names. "There's *Clowns Weekly,* obviously. And *Car Crammers*—that one described me as 'dashingly handsome,' but that's pretty subjective. And, you know, a few others. Guinness wanted me for its world records, but I"—he paused and let out a long breath—"well, I didn't want the press."

Bitty's jaw clenched with repressed laughter. "Well, then I guess I have no choice but to trust you."

Blake sighed, his face frozen in a resigned expression. "I didn't want to have to work on the weekend, but I'll do it for you, Miss Bitty."

He went back to the group of guys waiting for Tom a couple feet away.

Colleen stood and went to Bitty with a look that said, *So, is he not as hot as I said?*

"He's pretty cute," Bitty confirmed, clearly reading Colleen's expression.

"Pretty— Oh, Bitty, you're a fool. He's adorable as hell, and he's a good guy. I don't understand your constant trepidation."

"I just don't date that much."

"Um, yes, I know this. I'm your friend, remember? I see you sitting around Not Dating all the time." Colleen shook her head. "I can't wait till someone pulls you out of your shell. And I feel like Blake just might have the right amount of disarming charm to do it."

Tom pulled up in his crappy Corolla, no doubt as tiny as Bitty had feared it would be, and the loading in began. First the guys filled up the backseat; then Colleen crawled over the laps onto one of the guys. Bitty followed as you might if you were about to slowly lower yourself into an ice-cold pool. First a toe, then the foot, then finally waist deep, until finally she was all in, but still trying to keep her face and hair dry.

Colleen was laughing about something with one of the guys already, and Tom had some loud punk rock band turned up.

Bitty sat on Blake's lap, him readjusting her when her rear end trenched into his thigh. "You're all bones, girl."

She stared out the window, avoiding Colleen's *Oh my God, date him—you guys are too cute!* gaze, but Colleen noticed a small smile playing at Bitty's lips.

Blake thought she was hot; he'd already unabashedly admitted so to Colleen. He was a straight shooter. She knew it was going to be hard to get Bitty to loosen up—she was always slow to feel comfortable. Of course, when the two of them gabbed, Bitty would be uninhibited and not nervous at all. But get her in front of a group of people, and she retreated, like a hermit crab scrambling back into her shell.

They finally got to their destination—down the highway, into the woods, where you would never expect to find a bar, and inside

Woodchuck Couldchuck. A band was playing, and now that they were newly twenty-one, Colleen could finally force Bitty to go out and do some things.

They spilled from the car, Bitty straightening her white miniskirt and black blouse, and Colleen pulling her Daisy Dukes down a little and straightening her belt.

"It'll be fun," Colleen promised, shoving her a little with a shoulder as they made their way inside.

Once there, all of them getting a hand stamp that said they'd shown the ID proving they were twenty-one, Colleen walked straight up to the bar and ordered two Sea Breezes and two shots of whiskey.

It was the age of not minding if she drank two completely separate kinds of liquor, and of not paying for it in the morning.

She handed the shot and pretty pink drink to Bitty. That was one fun and unexpected thing about Bitty—she came off like something of a priss, but the girl could throw back a shot of rail whiskey without batting a lacquered eyelash.

They took the shots, and Colleen grinned at the look of surprise on Blake's face when he watched Bitty. His eyes shifted to Colleen and she gave a small shrug, one that said, *Yep, my pal is awesome. Told ya so.*

The band started in, and not long after, Bitty had already loosened up. She was getting chatty, and had those rosy cheeks that always proved she'd had a few drinks.

Colleen couldn't hear what Bitty was saying to Blake, but judging from the way she stood with one hand stirring her drink by the straw, her hair swept to one side, and wearing a challenging smile, she would place good money that her friend was flirting. And judging by the raised eyebrows and intrigued grin Blake was returning, he was enjoying it.

"I'm such a good little matchmaker," Colleen said to her semi-beau, just to call someone else's attention to the cute scene before them. She didn't know why she was always so determined to set people up. She'd been burned doing it more often than not, inevitably breaking up with her boyfriend while her friend continued on with his friend, putting her in an icky position of heartache and jealousy.

But she was a romantic soul and maybe something of a control freak, and so she liked to be the one responsible for helping two poor lonely souls find each other and true love.

This, however... This might have been her biggest challenge yet. Bitty wasn't an easy sell, and she definitely wasn't a pushover. She was shy and picky and hesitant and skeptical all wrapped into one pretty package.

But by the time they loaded back into Tom's car, hours later, Bitty wasn't hesitating. She had climbed into the car and sunk down into Blake, allowing him to put his arms around her.

Bitty felt his warm, hard chest on her back. She wasn't going to go all the way with him. Not tonight. Not next week. Not anytime in the foreseeable future. Bitty had been holding on to her virginity like a child held on to a security blanket. Everyone who knew her knew that. Even then, it had seemed kind of quaint, old-fashioned, and more annoying than anything else.

But this was a start, at least. She was open to Blake. Open to the idea of him. She was touching him and not tightening her mouth into a hard judgmental line and walking away from this.

So there was hope.

Maybe Bitty would fall in love and get her happily-ever-after after all.

CHAPTER EIGHT

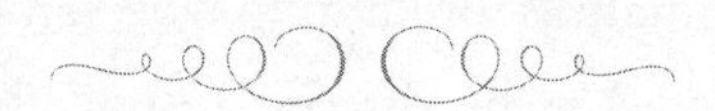

Colleen

THE ICED TEA FROM THE DINER KICKED IN PRETTY QUICKLY, AND they went right on past Rocky Mount, then detoured off 95 south into Raleigh, North Carolina. Thanks to some nimble-fingered Yelp work on Tamara's part, reading descriptions and clicking in numbers, they had reservations at a place called the Velvet Cloak Inn. Colleen had insisted they give it a try because the place sounded much more appealing than any ordinary La Quinta or Motel 6 on the highway.

Tamara sat in one of the high-backed *Alice in Wonderland*–type chairs in the lobby as Colleen checked in and got the key.

Next to her, Bitty was trying to get her own room.

"I'm sorry, ma'am, without some form of identification and a credit card guarantee, I'm not able to give you a room," the poor hapless clerk was telling Bitty. He looked like the kind of kid whose face was always kind of red, but it was absolutely blooming now in response to Bitty.

"Do I need to talk to your manager?" Bitty asked. "Because I don't believe you are allowed to be prejudiced against a person simply because they opt not to be licensed drivers and have the good sense not to get caught up in the mire of credit cards."

"But if something were to happen to the room—"

Bitty stepped back and splayed her arms. "What do I look like I'm going to do to a hotel room? Do I look like some raunchy rock star who's going to trash the place?"

"Well, you could get porn all night and not pay-per-view it," Colleen said with a smile.

Bitty shot her a look. "Not helpful."

The young clerk's face grew even redder. "We're not able to turn the pay-per-view options off."

"I'm not going to be watching pay-per-view!" She gave Colleen a *See what you started?* look that Colleen actually recognized from the old days.

"Bitty, why don't you just stay in our room with us? I've got two queen beds and a daybed—there's plenty of room."

"Thank you," Bitty answered in a controlled tone. "But there is no legal reason why I can't get a room. I have enough cash to pay for it."

The clerk excused himself to go speak with his manager, and Colleen imagined he would be swabbing his forehead plenty as well, since he didn't look like he was very comfortable with conflict. Little place like this, it wasn't surprising. They probably got plenty of guests, but they were probably all just weary travelers looking to rest for a few hours before hitting the road again. Or drunk kids looking to stay within a cheap cab ride of downtown.

They were the weary travelers. And only five and a half hours from home.

A beefy man came out of the back, wiping what appeared to be chicken wing grease from the corners of his mouth. The clerk was behind him, looking like a child in comparison.

"Ma'am? I understand there's a problem?"

"There is," Bitty said, "but I don't understand it. I need a room for the night. Not even for the night, for a few hours. And I'm being told that because I don't drive or rack up debt, I'm ineligible."

This was getting ridiculous. Colleen knew this look, this tone. Bitty was standing on a principle now, not arguing for anything that actually mattered.

"No license or state ID, no credit card for incidentals, no room," the man said, and honestly, there was clearly no arguing with him. Even if Bitty had a point—and she kind of did—it was really obvious that this guy wasn't in the mood for it and he wasn't likely to care what the legal technicalities were; he just wanted to get back to whatever greasy stuff he was eating in the back.

"Bitty, I'm serious, come to our room with us. We're all tired, and this is going to go on forever if you fight it—and you're still not going to win."

Bitty glanced self-consciously at the clerk and manager. She didn't like to lose either.

But Colleen didn't care. "You're never going to be back here again, just give it up for now. We'll figure out the lost cards tomorrow. Come on."

Bitty sighed. "Fine. I don't want to keep you up all night, and I know you won't go to bed as long as I'm standing here."

"That's right."

"But I'm not pleased. I'll definitely be writing a letter to the owner of this place. Which I will never visit again."

Colleen almost laughed at the look of relief on the clerk's face. The manager, on the other hand, looked like he just could not care less.

The room was less interesting than the description Tamara had read to her, and certainly less elaborate than the lobby would have suggested. The two queen beds clearly dipped in the middle, under thin linens and bedspreads that looked like the cheap "bed in a bag" sets sold at discount stores. There was a vanity with two yellowed sinks at the end of the room, embellished by a mirror that was going black in spots, and the toilet and shower—more accurately a "shoilet"—were closed off by a flimsy particleboard door. There were small chipped tiles on the floor and an ill-fitting plastic bathtub cover that must have been what they meant by "recently renovated."

Clearly all the motel's funds had gone into creating an illusion in the public areas, because the room may as well have been in any dinky roadside chain lodging in the world. But it was clean, and had two queen-size beds and a daybed, as promised.

They'd started to get ready for bed, shoes off, bras slipped out from under shirts, teeth brushed, when Bitty pulled Colleen aside. "Do you think I could borrow your car for just a few minutes? I need to run to the store to get a few things. I noticed there was a CVS when we pulled off the exit."

"Oh." Colleen hesitated, and then felt stupid for hesitating. What could the harm be? "Yeah, of course. Are you comfortable driving with the trailer hooked on? I could take you, if you want."

"Oh, no, it's fine," Bitty said quickly. "Can't be nearly as bad as driving a horse trailer with two spooked mares in the back."

"No, I guess not." There wasn't much in the trailer yet, so there wouldn't be any shifting loads. Why not? What was she worried about? She took the keys out of her bag and tossed them to Bitty, who caught them with surprising agility.

"Thanks. I'll be back soon." Then, seemingly an afterthought, "Do you need anything?"

Colleen had brought every single thing she could think of for every possible eventuality. She was prepared for an unexpected menstrual period or a tsunami. "No, I'm good. Tamara?"

"Nope."

"All right, then. Thanks for everything." With that, Bitty left the room.

Thanks for everything?

Almost a full minute passed before either Colleen or Tamara spoke.

Finally Tamara broke the silence. "So she's super weird."

Colleen thought she should defend Bitty, respond with something adult and appropriate, but she didn't know what to say. Bitty may as well be a stranger now. She didn't know her anymore. She'd just given her her car and her trailer, ignoring the pit-of-the-stomach feeling that told her not to. She looked at Tamara, whom she was charged with taking care of, and gave a slow nod. "She wasn't always." And she sincerely, sincerely hoped there was nothing to worry about now.

"Did something, like . . . happen to her?"

Colleen shrugged. "Hard to say. I mean, she didn't live through a massacre or anything. That I know of." And no, she was pretty certain Bitty hadn't literally lived through a massacre, but what had she endured? What was her life now that she had become such a narrow little spooked thing? Or had she always been that, except during some drunken, carefree college days when Colleen just happened to have known her?

"You said she was your college best friend, though, right?" Tamara looked as if she were really trying to puzzle this out. "How come you guys aren't friends anymore?"

"Kind of hard to explain." It really was, Colleen thought to herself. What happens to friendships that you thought at the time were going to last forever, but which fell away, all but unnoticed? "We just lost touch somewhere along the way. Moved in different directions."

"Did you know her husband, or did he come later?"

"I met him a few times. He was a grad student doing some intern stuff when we were in our last semester."

"What's he like?"

Colleen tried to imagine how Tamara would envision Bitty's husband. A tall, handsome Disney Gaston, or a meek Walter Mitty? "He was nice enough. Polite, anyway. Very wealthy, his family basically owned his hometown. Pretty smart. Not incredibly hot, but nice-looking, in a soap opera–actor sort of way. I think anyone would have said he was good husband material. A catch. And she came from a good family too, so they were a good pair. *Suited,* as they say."

"Then . . . why's she running away?"

"Running away?"

"Yeah. I mean . . . right? Her story's all over the place, she's a rich lady with no credit cards, she got her car stolen but she's not freaking out about it. . . . I mean . . . She's obviously a total runaway right now."

As soon as Tamara had said it, Colleen wondered why that

possibility hadn't occurred to her. She had taken Bitty's excuse at face value.

To think of her—or any woman their age—"running away" just seemed crazy.

She couldn't buy it. "I don't know that she's running away. It just sounded like Lew made plans without her, so she wanted to do the same back at him. Keep him on his toes. I could understand that. The poor thing just must not have a lot of good friends she could confide in, or who could take off at a moment's notice with her."

"Think there's a reason for that?"

"She lets very few people in. She's got a guard up. She always has."

Tamara raised an eyebrow. "Yeah, I know that feeling."

"Then you understand we shouldn't push her on it." Colleen watched her, unsure if she should ask more or let it go. Tamara clicked on her phone, and it became clear the moment was gone.

The two of them got ready for bed, and then clicked on the TV. A rerun of *Saturday Night Live* was on.

Colleen looked at her own phone. Bitty had been gone almost an hour. To the pharmacy down the block. That seemed like a long time.

Tamara, evidently noticing it had been a while too, said, "Do you think you should call her or something? Seems weird it's taking so long, right?"

"I'm sure everything's fine."

"Hopefully she didn't steal your car and camper thing."

"Tamara! Don't be ridiculous."

"Just kidding."

Of course, Colleen was starting to have the same kind of thoughts. Which was dumb, because even though she didn't know the inner workings of Bitty's mind today, once upon a time, she had known her well, and she couldn't imagine that her friend's moral fiber had changed so much. "I'm sure everything's fine. I just hope she didn't get lost."

Colleen did know it was not like Bitty to get lost. She was a competent handler of things. If she was taking this long, it was on purpose.

"If she did, she could ask directions."

"That's right."

A little more time passed. Probably not much. But as soon as Colleen realized Bitty had been gone for too long, every minute seemed like an eternity, adding to the oddness and making her feel stranded. She had always hated going anywhere and being without her car in case she needed to leave, and now she was in some nothing town, miles from home, with no way out except to believe in someone she hadn't known for more than a decade.

When Colleen looked at the clock for perhaps the thousandth time, she felt Tamara's gaze turn to her, hitting her cheek like a laser.

"Why don't you just call her?" Tamara asked. "If you're embarrassed for her to know you don't trust her, then just pretend you need tampons or something and ask her to pick them up."

"I can't."

"Why not?" Tamara pushed. "I'm sure she'd get why you're like, 'Hey, where's my car?' "

"I don't have her number."

CHAPTER NINE

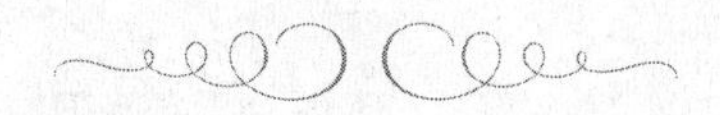

Bitty

Dear Stranger,

So far, suicide isn't working out very well. I had my plan in place, stopped for some good old comfort food at Henley's as a goodbye—because, who cares? I figured I wouldn't have time to get fat from it. If anything, it would just back up the illusion that my death was a tragic mistake—you're the only one who knows better now—because the autopsy would reveal I was full of fried chicken, sweet potato fries, real vanilla Coke, and coconut cream pie.

"She didn't do this on purpose," they'd say. "Look at this, she was clearly happy. No one kills themselves after Henley's coconut cream pie!"

But the best-laid plans . . . you know. Obviously I couldn't go through with my plan, because, of all things, my car got stolen. Apparently, an old XJS isn't that hard to hot-wire. People used to trust each other more and security systems weren't built in till fairly recently. This is what I've learned from Googling it on my phone. But I have to point out, I did lock it. But I guess this Podunk town doesn't see a lot of Jaguars driving through, so it was conspicuous. If anyone can hot-wire anything, it's a bored country boy.

So that was that. Car gone, and with it, the five thousand dollars I'd stored before in my safe at home. I have about $240 in my wallet now, which, to be honest, would have been enough anyway, since I wasn't planning on being around that long, but it's nice to know you have the resources to go out in style.

Instead I ended up trapped in my college diner with no hope until—miracle or catastrophe?—Colleen Wilcox showed up. Colleen Bradley, now. Blast from the past. I could tell she didn't recognize me at first, and when she made the offer to take me to Florida, she wasn't really sure it was a good idea. Especially since I'm not all that fast on my feet as a liar, so she had to doubt my story about Lew being off with the boys.

Even though that part is obviously true.

Anyway.

I wasn't sure it was such a great idea either, but I can't afford to sift through the quality of ideas right now. I was thinking Florida might be a good place to go down and rent a boat, drive out into the ocean, and just . . . disappear. Leave 'em wondering forever. That wasn't the original plan, obviously, you know that already. I'm not into uncertainty and I'm sure not into pain, so I think the gun idea was the best. (They say women don't shoot themselves, because they're too vain, but at least there are no variables.)

Now I need to rethink. I said I was going to Florida because I wanted to think of someplace far enough away that they wouldn't volunteer to just drop me off, but when they said they were going to Florida, well, it seemed like a good omen. I was watching *Nancy Grace* sometime ago when this woman had disappeared and they said she could be reduced to nothing but bone out in the Florida elements in just a matter of days. Under a week. I find that to be a plus. I don't know you, so I don't know if you're squeamish about that kind of thing, but at least you'll know now that I'm not. I like the whole "ashes to ashes, dust to dust" thing much more than, you know, traditional burial.

The only thing I'm not so sure of is how I can spend the days necessary with Colleen and her niece, acting like everything's normal, socializing, taking part in life, when I have already mentally checked out. This is a toughie.

Right now, I'm sitting in this old rattletrap of a convertible of hers, complete with an embarrassing old trailer attached, with the heat blasting, and I wouldn't be surprised if the carbon monoxide got me. That's not my plan, but, hey, if it happens, it happens and it means the car wasn't safe for those two so, actually, my last act will be altruistic. Unfortunately, I feel fine. Everything around me is completely and utterly normal. I'm in the parking lot of CVS, watching a sprinkler spit at some little tomato plants in a house just a few yards away right now.

I feel kind of bad because I asked Colleen if I could borrow her car to go to the drugstore, and now I've been gone—I don't know—an hour or so. Maybe more. She's probably wondering where I am, and if I'm the same Bitty she knew. Thinking she can't trust me. She's right, I guess. And the answer is no, I'm not the same Bitty she knew. I'm not the Bitty anyone knew, not even myself.

I guess I'm no one now.

Of course, you already know that. You're holding the proof in your hand, this suicide letter written to Dear Stranger. How pathetic is that? If I heard this story on the news, I'd think it was one of the saddest things I'd ever heard. Maybe a letter like this floated up on some shore in a bottle or something, and some kid dropped his beach ball and opened it up hoping it was a treasure map and found, instead, that it was a middle-aged woman's angsty ramblings. Maybe even attached to a name. "Authorities suspect the letter might have been written by Wilhelmina Camalier, the woman missing since June of last year, but the water damage is too great to definitively identify her writing. . . ."

Or what she's saying.

I guess I won't send this off to sea in a bottle, now that I think about it.

Anyway, before the car debacle, I pigged out at Henley's, and, let me tell you, that felt good! Best I've felt in ages, honestly. Let them know I died happy, will you? Okay, not happy, obviously, but I went on my own terms. Had peace of mind. Then I started writing to you and felt a real sense of purpose. Is that crazy? Well, of course, you'd have to say anything I said right now was crazy, wouldn't you? I mean, facts being what they are. Or will be. But being there, alone, in that place where I'd spent so many good times before my marriage . . . it reminded me, somewhat, of who I am. Was. I can't ever be her again, I'm too far down the rabbit hole to climb back up and have a normal life, but for a few random moments here and there, I could feel myself twisting deep inside, like a toddler beginning to wake from a nap.

So when Colleen walked in—jeez! I just didn't know what to make of it. At first she seemed like an echo or a memory, but memories don't age. Not that she looks old or anything; she actually looks great. She has the face of a woman who hasn't seen too many sleepless nights. No Botox, no fillers, a few lines, but the unmistakable mask of a woman who has seen mostly contentment, if not much excitement.

Or maybe it's just the bloom of the Well Fed. She's as curvy as ever, with one of those old-fashioned hourglass bodies that would be criminal to call fat, and doesn't seem to care what she eats as long as it tastes good. Same old Colleen.

The girl was always there to pull me out from my slump, so leave it to her to magically arrive the night I decided to kill myself.

Apparently, she's going to antique auctions down the coast, picking up old furniture for a business she has. Made sense. Whenever I pictured Colleen, which I didn't do often—it kind of hurt too much to think about "the old days"—I always imagined her covered in paint. In her baggy, torn-up jeans covered in sawdust and acrylic paints, the tips of her fingers stained from the alizarin crimson she painted with—the color that always looked bloodlike.

So it made sense to me that she would still be doing something like that. Still working late into the night, hair in a ponytail, accidentally getting a pretty swipe of paint across her eyebrow.

I wonder if she still paints. She "fixes things up" for some sort of antique store she has, she says, but that doesn't necessarily mean she's doing oils or sculpting anymore. That's the kind of thing that, all too often, depends on the support of a spouse. I wonder what her marriage is like. I was invited to the wedding. I probably should have gone, but I didn't.

I was too caught up in my life. My life was supposed to have been new. Not just a new chapter in my life, but a new book entirely. *Bitty's Life, Volume 2: Wilhelmina.* Back to my ridiculous given name, which most people cannot even take in when they look at it.

Wilhelmina Camalier.

But alas, my marriage, just like my death, didn't go as I expected.

Oh my God, an old man just knocked on the car window. Hang on, I'll be back.

I'm back.

And that was unpleasant.

First off, it wasn't an old man, it was a wizened old woman who looked like a man. In fact, to be perfectly accurate, she looked exactly like the Mayor of Munchkinland—and that's who she seemed to think she was, because she was trying to pull her stupid RV into the parking lot and said my camper was in the way. She had, like, twenty feet on either side of her, which she should have known because her ridiculous pink flamingo string lights lit the entire parking lot like the UFO landing gear in *Close Encounters of the Third Kind,* but, nooo, she needed me to move.

I would have argued, I swear I would have gone all Towanda

on her, like Kathy Bates in *Fried Green Tomatoes,* but I don't really know how good Colleen's insurance is, or if it's different coverage that doesn't allow someone else to use your vehicle, or whatever.

So I got out of the car, to point out how much room she had, and how little room I had to maneuver, and, honestly, the woman was like three foot nothing. I towered over her.

But despite that, she started yelling at me! I mean profanities, flailing arms, the whole nine yards. I tried to speak quietly, because in normal situations, people respond faster and listen better if you are quieter, but in this case, she just bulldozed me. So I raised my voice—just to be heard, you understand—and then she raised hers (when you wouldn't have thought that was possible), and all of a sudden, people filling their gas tanks at the station thirty yards away were looking over, and people were coming out of the food mart into the gas lanes to see what the commotion was.

When I told her to please stop yelling, she screamed, "Don't threaten me!" as if I'd pulled a gun on her.

(Which I could have, if it weren't for my car being stolen! More bad luck! I mean, what would I have had to lose? And what a satisfying moment that would have been!)

Anyway, as you might imagine, the scene everyone thought they were witnessing was five-foot-seven-inch me towering over this tiny person, threatening her, frightening her. I don't know, maybe some even called Child Protective Services. It was humiliating!

So, just to end the nightmare, the little bitch got her way and I moved the car and trailer, only to hear this horrible screeching sound. So I got out and looked, and the bumper had gotten caught on the broken base of what must have been a parking lot light once and it was pulling off. So I lifted it up and over the damn cement base and pulled the trailer around, then pushed—well, sort of shoved—the bumper back into place.

It seems to be okay now.

Nevertheless, I'm going to run into the pharmacy and get some Krazy Glue in addition to sleeping pills.

I'm back again. So I glued the bumper in place, and if those old commercials with a guy hanging midair from his hard hat, held in place only by Krazy Glue, are any indication, the bumper should stay in place now.

I have less confidence in the sleeping pills. I'm sorry, the No-Somnias, which I think is a pretty poor pun on "insomnia" and kind of sounds like it too, indicates "no sleep" but it was two bucks cheaper than the Tylenol PM, and I have to watch my dollars in case this doesn't work. No telling how long that $222 (now) is going to have to last me.

It's tempting to take them all now, but the car is getting low on gas, and I can't leave Colleen with a corpse and an empty tank. Talk about tacky.

And I can't do that to the kid either. Did I mention Colleen had this kid with her—this sullen girl—who is apparently her niece, her husband's brother's child, so no relation to apple-cheeked blond Colleen. She has dull, charcoal hair—dyed, of course—and skin so pale, it's almost green. This time of year! When I was her age, I would have been out trying to get a Bain de Soliel tan but instead she's on this road trip with a woman twice her age. She must be bored out of her skull.

Too bad I'll never know more of her story.

Still, tempting as it is, I can't do myself in in this car, right where they have to get back in and drive another thousand miles and back. The kid would freak out. I remember being her age. Weird thought: I'm alive now and maybe strike her as weird but not frightening. Not creepy. But the minute my life leaves me, I'm something else entirely.

Better that I don't do it in a space they have to keep regardless.

So, what am I on now? Plan C? Got to keep thinking.

Meanwhile, I guess I should put at least a few bucks' worth of gas in the tank, considering the fact that I must have used up quite a bit sitting here writing with the engine running.

I may be planning "the ultimate selfish act," but I don't want to be inconsiderate.

CHAPTER TEN

Colleen

FARM AUCTIONS WERE COLLEEN'S FAVORITES. YOU NEVER KNEW what you were going to get. Where traditional antique auctioneers brought up one fussy item at a time and there was absolute clarity on what you were getting—though you could still get a great deal—farm auctioneers always seemed grizzled and a little bored, and inevitably, about three hours in, they'd start selling multiple boxes of unidentified, uninspected items. Sometimes they'd even sell an entire tableful just to end the thing and, presumably, get on home to pop a beer and watch some tractor pulling.

For Colleen, these auctions were just like Christmas mornings of old, when she'd excitedly run downstairs to dump her stocking onto the floor in front of the fireplace, eager to see what Santa had left, even though it was 80 percent gumdrops and a good half of the foot was taken up just by the orange no one ever ate but that her parents always included anyway.

That's exactly how farm auction lots were.

Once, for just two dollars, Colleen had gotten a lot that included, among other things, an orange outdoor extension cord, a plastic hard hat that she wasn't sure was real or a toy, a small wooden box of rusted chains, a bingo ticket cage like a hamster wheel for mixing up the tickets, a fourteen-pound bowling ball in a bag, and a heavily tarnished Tiffany sterling silver trumpet vase, which someone threw in there because they were too lazy to walk an extra five feet to the recycle bin.

All she'd wanted was the bowling ball bag. She thought she could make it into a cool purse. That it had a ball in it surprised her. She made that into a candle holder, wondering if anyone would seriously want it even though she thought it was awesome, and it had been the first thing to sell the morning she put it out. The Tiffany vase was the last thing to go that day, but it went for twelve hundred dollars. That was the sort of profit that kept Kevin encouraging her to keep on doing what she was doing, but it was the bowling ball candleholder that actually kept her interested in what she was doing.

So everyone won.

Except today, when Bitty and Tamara both looked so miserable that instead of enjoying the down-home atmosphere, strong coffee, and over-fried cinnamon doughnuts, Colleen was self-conscious that she wasn't showing them a good enough time.

Which wasn't fair, because she wasn't here to show them a good time; she was here to collect inventory for her business and somehow—through very little fault of her own—she'd ended up with these two sullen strays.

"See anything of interest?" Colleen asked Tamara after she'd wandered alongside a table of items, peering into the boxes like she was looking into exhumed coffins.

"There was an old Easter basket filled with pink plastic grass and three dead wolf spiders."

Colleen was not rising to the bait. "Do you plan to bid on it?"

"Do you think the spiders come with it?"

"I think you could negotiate a deal with the auctioneer." She glanced toward a very tall man with a very large gut barely covered by a PIGS R US BBQ T-shirt, who was wearing a Peterbilt hat over what Colleen just knew was a sparsely covered scalp.

Normally she loved this kind of sight.

Tamara looked in his direction and literally turned up her nose, though she probably didn't realize she did it. "No, thanks."

"I did see a box of old albums over there," Colleen said. "Did you notice them?"

"You mean like photo albums?"

"No, records. Vinyl. I thought kids were all back into that these days."

"Oh, yeah. My—Vince's brother, this guy I know, he's into that. But you have to have special equipment to listen to it." She shrugged. "Why bother when you can just put on Spotify?"

"I agree," Colleen said, thinking of the many times she'd moved in her younger days, hauling crate after crate of LPs from one place to the next and setting up her stereo with the nickel and two pennies taped to the needle so it played over the skips on her Duran Duran albums.

"Where's that girl?" Tamara asked.

"Girl?"

"Woman, whatever."

"Bitty?"

"Yeah. She was talking to some guy about guns."

Colleen gave a laugh. "Bitty hates guns."

"She didn't seem to."

"I'm sure she was just being polite."

A sudden light came into Tamara's eyes. "What if she wants to kill her husband?"

"What?"

Tam shrugged. "What if that's what all this is about? She's mad because he went away with the guys one time too many and now—*boom!*—she finds herself in some obscure town—"

"Raleigh, North Carolina, isn't obscure."

"—and she thinks she can buy some old gun at this place no one would ever associate with her, and bump off her husband with an untraceable gun."

"Are you finished?"

"The question is, is he finished?" She raised both her eyebrows in a gesture that said, *Right? Seems possible. . . .*

Colleen had to stifle a smile. At least the kid was imaginative. "I think Lew is safe from Bitty, at least for the time being. The untraceable gun isn't bad, but the dissatisfied wife with a grudge is always the first suspect in a case like that. She'd be caught in an instant."

"Not if she had an alibi."

"Okay, I'll bite. Who's the alibi?"

"We are!"

"You've lost me."

"When we bring her back home, she asks us to wait outside while she goes in to make sure, I don't know, that the door's unlocked or whatever, and then she shoots him, comes running out, screaming that her husband has been murdered and, 'Quick, call the cops!' and all that jazz, and she throws the gun into the trailer and the cops never suspect her because she's been with us the whole time, which we can testify to, and then you and I drive away with the evidence."

Colleen looked at her earnest, excited face for a moment, and saw that there really was kind of a creative soul behind all the blasé disaffected teenage cynicism she sometimes projected. "There are a few flaws in your logic."

"Like what?"

"Like what does she think we're going to do when we find the gun when we're unloading?"

"She assumes you're going to protect her." Tamara raised an eyebrow. "Wouldn't you?"

"No way."

"No? Your best friend?"

"My friend from college," Colleen wasn't sure why she felt so compelled to correct, "and, no, I'm not holding on to a murder weapon that could, presumably, then be pinned on me for someone who has already proven herself to be capable of murder."

Tamara shook her head. "Some friend." But there was a smile in her voice.

"I'm not doing it for family members either," she added. "So don't go counting on me ever being an alibi for you."

Something crossed Tamara's expression.

"Not that I expect you to cross the law," Colleen hastened to add. She suspected Tamara had probably been accused of a lot of things in her young life, whether she'd done them or not. Not murder, of course. Tamara went to juvie for getting caught driving drunk with three ounces of weed in the car—not her car, maybe not her weed, who knew? Chris had shown zero patience with any of this, so there was no way for a fourth party to know the truth. She suspected Tamara was acutely aware of that herself, that her father would always leap to the worst conclusion. It was time the girl had someone she could count on, someone who would accept her for who she was instead of constantly being disappointed in her for who she wasn't.

It was such a shame her father didn't see that. Or care. Maybe he truly just didn't care. Had Tamara's mother? Colleen took a moment to imagine what it would be like if she died and Jay was left with no one who strongly advocated for him. The thought was too much to bear. She couldn't stand it, so she pushed it away.

Bitty joined them, then, wordlessly.

"Did you get a gun?" Tamara asked right off the bat.

Bitty looked alarmed.

"She's kidding," Colleen said quickly, shooting a look at the girl. "She was just commenting on how little there is of interest to buy here."

"Someone just got a saddle for seven dollars," Tamara added.

"What?" Colleen could have used a saddle! Her profit on that would have been huge! "You guys occupy yourselves. If you want to bid on anything, you have to go register—otherwise, I don't know, have coffee, eat doughnuts, complain about me, whatever, but I'm going to bid."

Two hours later, after fiercely fighting the guilt instinct that had her thinking about cutting out early in order to quell the bored beasts, Colleen did have a saddle (twelve bucks, though, and it was

English, not as nice as the ornate Western one that Tamara had pointed out earlier), as well as a large collection of molding scores (easily over a thousand bucks' worth for twenty-two), a box of antique tools in excellent condition with some plumbing pieces they'd added in for free, and a huge plastic Tupperware box—just like one her grandmother had used to keep cookie cutters in—full of miscellaneous kitchen items and candles.

And, perhaps most important, she'd established that they were playing by her rules. This was her trip, her business, and she wasn't going to let two sourpuss interlopers ruin it.

All that said, though, she was secretly glad for the company. Although there had been many tense moments, from the initial stony silences and awkward attempts at conversation with Tamara to the anxiety of waiting for Bitty's hour-and-a-half trip to the CVS half a mile away—explained away by some far-fetched tall tale (ha) of a fight with a midget and a faulty gas pump—the truth was that the road got dark and lonely at night. It was one thing to picture herself singing along with the radio on a sunny, warm day, cruising through the Carolinas and stopping here and there for barbecue or shrimp and grits, but drop the temperature a few degrees, add some cool night rain, and put the top up, and the movie changed from a chick flick to a potential horror movie in the blink of an eye.

But at least she wasn't alone when she stopped at an all-night truck stop for gas in some tiny unnamed town at 11 P.M. on the way out of North Carolina, as she did tonight. At least someone would notice if she didn't return from the grimy, sticky-floored bathroom with the vending machine in the stall offering colored and textured condoms as well as matchbook-sized "books" offering SEXUAL POSITIONS FROM AROUND THE WORLD and KAMA SUTRA WAYS OF LOVE.

Actually, for seventy-five cents, she'd been unable to resist buying the sexual positions from around the world one, which was how she knew they were the size of matchbooks. (She intended to give the book to Kevin as a gag gift, and its miniature size made the prospect all the funnier to her as she slipped it into her purse.)

So she'd grabbed some ginger ales plus two white wines in small containers that looked like juice boxes, so she and Bitty could make their old college concoction when they stopped for the night. She also grabbed a caffeine-free Coke for Tamara and an assortment of chocolate and candy, including Jolly Ranchers, a sticky candy she hated but that Jay had always had a strange fondness for, ever since some dentally irresponsible elementary teacher had given them out as an incentive for good work, so she figured Tamara might like the same.

And, in fact, she was right. That was the first thing Tamara went for.

"Your cousin likes those too," Colleen commented, pulling the car onto the lone highway and clicking on her brights.

"Why didn't he come?" Tamara asked, mouth full of sugar.

"He went to the Baseball Hall of Fame with his dad. Guy stuff. There was no way I could compete with that."

"How old is he?" Bitty asked quietly.

"Thirteen. But you should see him—I swear he's already over six feet tall. Practically a man." She went on, talking more and more about his growth spurt at thirteen, his skills at baseball, his good manners, sense of humor, unfortunate love of video games, sloppiness, and everything else that came to mind, because once she started thinking about him, she missed everything about him, and home, and Kevin. Suddenly she felt like she was in another world, one where she didn't quite belong.

She'd never believed much in astrology, but she was a Cancer, the sign associated with homebodies who got homesick easily, which described Colleen to a T.

"Sorry," she said when she realized she'd long since lost her audience. "I don't mean to be a bore. God, imagine how bad I'll be when I have grandchildren. I'll have one of those ridiculous 'brag books' that folds out like an accordion, and I'll be showing total strangers my babies." She gave a laugh, but she was the only one.

"I think it's nice," Tamara said, a response that surprised Colleen.

Bitty, in the backseat, said nothing. Colleen actually wondered if she'd bored her to sleep. But after a few minutes, she heard a sniffle from the back. Then another. Then Bitty made some joke about being allergic to South Carolina, and Colleen instructed Tamara to get a pack of tissues out of the glove box and hand them back to Bitty.

She offered Benadryl as well, since she always kept some in her purse in case anyone had an allergic reaction to anything (she'd been terrified of allergic reactions ever since hearing horror stories about bees and anaphylactic shock as a kid), but Bitty declined, and pretty soon her sniffles stopped and they turned up the radio and headed for the Bunker Inn in Florence, South Carolina.

CHAPTER ELEVEN

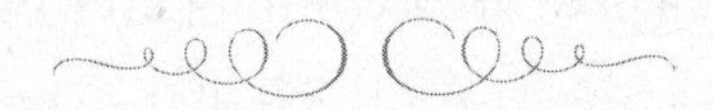

Tamara

THE NEXT B AND B WAS KIND OF A SHITHOLE, IN TAMARA'S ESTIMATION: It was like someone's house. No lock on the door, no private bathroom, just a small room in a hall of four, one of which was clearly the master suite and coincidentally where the "innkeepers" slept. The little soaps and shampoos in the hall bathroom (with childproofing on the cabinetry) didn't match each other and looked like they'd been lifted from another hotel visit somewhere along the way . . . maybe sometime back. The conditioner was missing about a third of the little bottle, and the shampoo was crusted around the screw top. But who was Tamara to complain? She rarely stayed in hotels at all, and couldn't remember ever going on something she could have called a "vacation"—most of her overnight stays had been in transit from one place to another, often in an emergency. So it wasn't like she really cared enough to notice if it was a nice place or not, but she noticed Bitty's nose had been turned up ever since they got there.

The funny thing was, she was clearly trying not to show it. Like, her determination to seem like she was just rolling with it became that much more conspicuous when they showed up at what Colleen's notes had described as "a charming Colonial bed-and-breakfast with a tearoom and traditional English breakfast," but which even Tamara could see looked like a regular suburban house with a table with teacups set up in the laundry room and the washer and dryer covered over with a quilt with a small rose print on it.

Very English. Ha.

The trip here hadn't been all that rewarding either, so Colleen and Bitty—whom Tamara was thinking of as Bitchy—probably would have been happier at some glamorous spalike place where someone relieved them of their bags upon entry, and they had gotten lost between the last auction and there, running out of exit signs loaded with fast-food restaurants and gas stations, with bright hotel logos shining up from the trees off the side of the road. And here they ended up, Colleen announcing that "at least we're somewhere," and saying that if they were going to run out of gas, she'd rather do it with charged phones by daylight.

Tamara had asked if they could just use a car charger, but apparently, the cigarette lighter thing didn't work in the old car.

They weren't in the room longer than five minutes when the gravity of how gross the place was really hit home. Tamara walked into the bathroom and was nearly murdered by a *Jurassic Park*–worthy flying bug. She screamed bloody murder.

"What, what's wrong?" said Colleen, jumping into Mom mode as Tamara fell backwards and covered her head with her arms.

"Pterodactyl," she said with a muffled voice into her knees.

She looked up and saw the huge bug fly toward Colleen, who also squealed and ran away from it.

Bitty, however, watched it as a cat might watch a mouse—in a cartoon—and then jumped onto one of the ugly blue chairs to try to catch it.

Yeah, no—catch it. Not kill it. Not hurl a phone book at it or anything. But to catch the nasty thing.

With her bare. Freaking. Hands.

And she did, on her third try. She looked over her shoulder at the other two, her hands cupped around the thing—she could hear its nasty crunchy wings flapping against her bony fingers. "Could one of you wimps please get the door?"

Tamara was still frozen on the yellow tile floor, something that was probably far more dangerous thanks to germs than the huge bug, so Colleen rose from the bed and opened the door.

Bitty did the boy trick of acting like she was going to throw it in Colleen's face, and then gave a big laugh when she shrieked.

She set it free, the way a Disney princess might let go of a bluebird.

"Holy crap," Tamara said once the heavy door shut, leaving the three of them, thankfully no longer four, inside. "I can't believe you just . . . caught that thing."

Bitty walked over and washed her hands as daintily as if the scene had not happened at all. She laughed. "Why not?"

Tamara didn't know how to say it, and instead glanced to Colleen, who was standing with her hands on her hips, looking warily about the room. "She can't believe it because you come off like a total prissy pants."

Tamara stared at Bitty, suddenly fascinated.

Who was this older woman who didn't eat and who considered a satin sleep mask to be a middle-of-the-night essential (yeah, that was the kind of crap she had come back from CVS with), who didn't consider a stolen car to be a huge deal, but who could catch enormous crunchy bugs and not mind?

"Everyone's got little quirks like that. I guess that's mine."

Colleen took some ones out of her wallet and handed them to Tamara. "You want to go find us some vending machine stuff?"

"Sure. Anything specific?"

They both shrugged, and then Colleen said, "No, whatever looks good. If there's a healthy thing or two in there, grab some, but I doubt there will be."

She was right. There were Doritos and candy bars, but nothing you could exactly call "healthy."

Tamara looked at the soda machine and got an idea. She picked out three separate sodas, all ones she would drink, one of which was diet, which she suspected Bitty would want. But really who knew anymore; clearly, the woman was weird.

She walked back through the door and announced, "I have an idea." They waited for her to go on. "Have you guys ever played Never Have I Ever?"

Colleen and Bitty exchanged a look. Tamara couldn't tell if it was because they were more familiar with it than she could realize, or if they had never played it and were feeling old and out of touch.

"Well, you hold up your hands and say something you've never done, and anyone who has done it puts down a finger. It's fun. It's—well, it's usually a drinking game, but I brought sodas."

A few minutes later, they had laid down a sheet on the floor from the closet and set up a little junk food picnic, and had poured sodas—Bitty indeed opted for the Coke Zero—into the small, plastic-wrapped foam cups by the sink.

Tamara put on a Spotify radio station that would play stuff that maybe Bitty and Colleen wouldn't know, but which probably wouldn't bother them. Ed Sheeran, Of Monsters and Men, etc.

"So, for example," Tamara said, popping a Flamin' Hot Cheeto into her mouth. "I could say, 'Never have I ever caught a big gross bug with my bare hands.' "

Getting the game, Bitty smiled and put a finger down. "Okay, so now it's my turn?"

"Yes."

"Hm. Okay. Never have I ever . . . Hm. This is hard."

"You can use your turn defensively. Like if you know something Colleen might have done."

"That puts you at quite the advantage," Colleen said with narrowed eyes.

Tamara laughed, trying not to sound too eager. Like a kid who hears an adult swear but doesn't want to react too much.

"Never have I ever thrown up in my own hair," said Bitty, pointing the question at Colleen.

Colleen put a tongue in her cheek and put a finger down.

So did Tamara.

"Okay," Bitty went on. "Never have I ever . . . been to Disneyland. Or World."

None of them put their fingers down. How sad was that?

"My turn," said Tamara. "Never have I ever had a nickname."

Nope, that was sadder.

Bitty put down a finger.

"What's your actual name again?" asked Tamara.

"Wilhelmina."

"Wilhelmina?" Tamara asked, not comfortable enough to laugh, but wishing she could. It was so . . . so *serious.* So *stern.* So old-lady-ish. So . . . well . . . actually, maybe it fit her perfectly, come to think of it.

"Yes?"

"How did you get Bitty from that?"

Colleen supplied the answer. "Because in college—and still, she was itty-bitty. Just like she is now."

Tamara frowned slightly. "Huh. Do you know what 'bitty' means now? Like to people my age, I guess?"

Bitty looked woeful, and Colleen looked prepared to do damage control.

"It's not bad! It's not bad. It's just kind of a way to refer to hot girls. Like. 'I hooked up with this totally hot bitty last night.' " She found herself using the voice she used when she imitated Vince.

"See, now, that's not bad at all," said Colleen, looking relieved. Heaven knew what she'd been afraid Tamara was going to say.

"I've heard worse." Bitty sighed and shook her head. For a moment she looked like she was going to say something else about it, but instead she said, "My turn. Never have I ever smoked pot."

Tamara eyed Colleen, who was eyeing her. "Honesty is the best policy, Colleen," she said, intentionally leaving off the "Aunt."

Seeming reluctant, Colleen lowered a finger, but then said, "Okay, yes I did, but I hated it, did I not?" She pointed at Bitty for backup.

"You did. You thought you were having a heart attack."

Colleen laughed. "Yes, I ended up crawling into bed with Bitty and crying about— What was it?"

"The extinction of the dinosaurs."

Tamara cracked up. Then, reluctantly, Colleen did too. Even Bitty started to laugh.

"And maybe you don't have to wonder why I never tried it, then," said Bitty.

No one seemed to notice Tamara had put down a finger, but she was also pretty sure they knew and just weren't saying anything.

"Okay, fine," said Colleen, a challenge in her eye. "Never have I ever been caught climbing up into the rafters of a closed-down coffee shop to dump a gallon of milk on anyone."

Tamara tried to make sense of the image, and then looked to Bitty, whose already tight cheekbones sharpened as she recognized the memory and put a finger down.

"You did that?" Tamara asked.

"Yup!" Colleen tipped backwards in laughter.

Bitty finally laughed too, and then said, "It was once."

"I don't think that's the kind of thing that needs to happen more than once, Bit."

Tamara smiled along, not feeling like she knew enough details to laugh. "Why did you do it? Who did you do it to?"

"So . . . okay, I had this boyfriend Blake. And we got into a . . . well, kind of a prank war. We were . . . gosh, I guess juniors in college?"

"Yep. End of our first junior-year semester. I remember because it was December and freezing."

"Well, he deserved it." It was the loosest sentence Bitty had spoken, Tamara noticed. "Anyway. He started it, for one thing. By sneaking into my apartment and taking all my spoons and forks."

Tamara laughed. "That's so random."

"When I say that, I mean he also took anything that could be used as a spoon or fork. He did that because I was, you know, pretending to be upset with him over something tiny, and that was his way of getting me to go get food with him."

"Aw, that's cute, though!"

Bitty looked wistful for a moment. "Yes, it was." She smiled, but it looked like it was more to herself than to the conversation. "But then I hid his car key in a loaf of—" She started laughing again. "—a loaf of sopping wet bread."

"That was his fault too," Colleen chimed in. "He shouldn't have said to us that he thinks soggy bread is the grossest thing in the world. He just shouldn't have!"

Tam laughed, but didn't want to say anything. She wanted them to keep going.

"So then his last prank before the milk was that he put a lock on my closet. Like, came in and used tools to install a lock."

Colleen trilled with a laugh. "Oh my God, I forgot about that! You came to—" She dissolved into laughter Bitty was now sharing. "This girl arrives to Astronomy in Blake's jeans and a tank top."

"Because he was a genius and knew I always slept in my underwear and a tank top. So he left me my least favorite of his pants, and that was it."

Tamara laughed at the image. "I can't picture that at all."

"No, she was a skirt and dresses girl. Everyone noticed."

They caught their breath, and Bitty concluded, "Yes, so, he got doused in milk!"

"All of yours have to do with food, I feel like," Tamara noted.

"Well, when you never eat it—" She rolled her eyes and took a sip from a plastic cup.

After another couple of stories, Bitty became the first one out, surprisingly, and Tamara said she was going to go make a call. But really it was because Bitty and Colleen were, like, rebonding or something, and she thought she should probably give them a few minutes without the kid in the room.

Tamara ambled down the motel steps and sat down on a parking block. She opened her cigarette case and took one out. She already knew she'd probably smoke two back-to-back.

She let her legs splay out, staring at the ground. A spider crawled by, and as sometimes happened, a nursery rhyme popped into her head:

Little Miss Screwup sat on a curb
Smoking her jacks and pot
Along came a spider, who wouldn't even sit beside her,
and crawled to a different fucking parking spot.

She gave a small laugh at how lame her thoughts sometimes were. When she was a kid, she had often made up her own nursery rhymes, or changed the ones everyone knew. Over time, her frame of reference had changed, but the habit stuck.

Sometimes the rhymes were really fucked up. The play on Jack and Jill on the day of her mom's funeral was almost unrepeatable, it was so dark. And that one had been pretty messed up to begin with.

She checked her phone as she inhaled, already about 75 percent through the cigarette.

No texts.

This wasn't wholly unusual or anything. She didn't have any friends she talked to outside of the basement or school or whatever. It was mostly a walkie-talkie for her father to call nine hundred times and make her come home from wherever she was.

But, lamely, she had kinda hoped to hear from Conor. Jenna's brother. The guy she had talked to for two-point-five seconds, who had called her a jailbird and obviously wouldn't think of her again. It was dumb to think otherwise, and she knew it. She had known that much when she gave him her number to begin with.

Maybe, though . . . Maybe she should just text him anyway?

No, that was stupid. Or was it?

See, these were the times a girl needed a best friend to talk to, she thought to herself. A friend that would say, *Oh just go for it, what do you have to lose? Just do it! Click send!* And a friend who, if he didn't answer, would be there to rationalize with you when he took too long, or who would say, *You know what, he's not even that cute anyway,* if he never did.

"Ow, shit," she muttered as the cigarette between her fingers got down to the filter, and to her skin. She stomped it out and lit another, summoning the guts to send a text.

Hey Conor! It's Tamara Bradley. We talked at the part—

No. Way too enthusiastic.

It's Tamara. Did you finish season four yet?

No. Weird.

Whats up Conor? It's Tamara. Just wanted to see if you've finished—

That sounded like the transcript to a voice mail.

Hey, it's Tamara! (the jailbird) Have you seen the epic season 4 finale yet?

That was pretty good, she decided. She tagged on another question mark, to show her enthusiasm for the show, and then let her thumb hesitate over the send button. With a grit of her teeth and a very deep breath, she pressed send.

Immediate regret. She was super weird. She was being crazy. A clingy weird little freakshow who— *Ding, ding!*

A text.

Conor: *This show. Is fucking crazy.*

She dragged on the cigarette and let it sit between her lips as she answered.

Right?? That whole episode I was like dying. Did you start 5 yet? Her foot was tapping quickly as she saw that he was typing.

His answer was immediate again. *No, I don't have it. I'm thinking about buying it but I'm flat broke haha. Do you have it?*

Her heart skipped. *Yeah I do actually. I mayyyy or may not have watched every episode more than once. Or twice. Haha.* Sent. Oh no. Stupid stupid stupid. The "haha" was too much. Too self-conscious. Now he thought she was a total spaz and he was going to want to scrape her off quickly.

Apparently not. *Hah awesome. Wellll any chance you wanna be a doll and lemme borrow it?*

Yay! *Of course, yeah. i have it at my dads, but i'm actually on a road trip right now.*

This seemed to impress him. *No way? For real? With who? Where you goin?*

I'm with my aunt, she's buying stuff for her store. she does something with furniture and like little yard sale things. She wondered, fleetingly, if it had been too uncool to mention her aunt. Like she was a little baby who had to be babysat. Which, actually, was pretty much what was going on.

Fortunately, Conor didn't make fun of her for that. *Thats awesome. When you gonna be back?*

Liiike a week and a half. I've been on the road for fowr days now.

Shit. *four* i'm not illiterate. Haha*

Dammit with the "haha" again. No one laughed that much! *No one!*

Four days huh? Soo you haven't tried the new pho place that opened THREE days ago right next to school?

Was he leading up to asking her out? *Omg i forgot that was happening. What's it called? Pho Sho or something, right?*

She could almost hear his voice in his answer. *Haha yeah. I haven't had it yet either. What do you say in exchange for letting me watch your season 5, i'll hold off on getting it (which is a huge sacrifice btw) and we can pho together when you get back?*

Tamara's inner monologue was suddenly a steady stream of *ohmygodohmygodohmygod*. She hesitated, her fingers over the letters, trying to think of just the right response, but her text dinged again with another message from him before she could.

Unless that's weird. in which case you can go pho yourself.

Relief. Okay this time, it was okay to laugh. *Hahah no no that sounds awesome. Yeah i'll let you know when I'm back in town.*

Schweet. Hey do me a favor. Text me pictures of the five most awesome things you see while you're gone.

She immediately thought of the truck driver, but he'd said "awesome" not "horrible," so even if she'd thought to take a picture—ew!—she wouldn't have sent it to him. Still, he presented an interesting challenge. What would she send pictures of? She couldn't wait to hit the road with new eyes. *Will do. You text me the five most boring things that happen while you're at home.*

Ha! Perfect.

Her stomach was in knots, and she had the dorkiest grin on her face. She didn't even realize she hadn't had any more of her cigarette. She stomped it out and headed back inside, feeling like maybe, just maybe when she went home, things might be different. Maybe she could try to be a normal girl. One who didn't live underground with no natural light or clean air, and instead just electric, fuzzy TV light and pot-filled oxygen.

Maybe she could fix herself before it was actually too late.

CHAPTER TWELVE

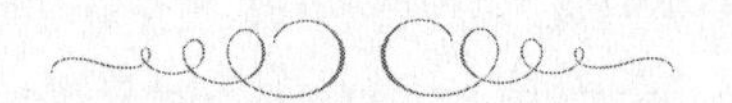

Colleen

"SO HOW'S IT GOING, THEN, ARE YOU FINDING A GOOD AMOUNT OF workable things?" Kevin asked.

"Sure, yeah," said Colleen, her phone between her ear and shoulder as she mixed the two packets of stevia into Bitty's Black Eye, which had been her request from Starbucks when Colleen said she was going there. She wasn't even sure what was in the Black Eye, only that it smelled like an ashtray and looked like regular coffee. For herself, she had gotten a Peppermint White Chocolate Mocha. A friend's daughter had worked at Starbucks, and informed her that the Venti, whole-fat White Mocha latte she was prone to ordering had almost a thousand calories—if not more—once she added the peppermint. Colleen's response had not been, *You're not supposed to tell us these things, you bitchy barista,* but she had really wanted to say it. She'd picked out a Chocolate Chip Crème Frappuccino for

Tamara. She had wanted caffeine, and Colleen said yes, but ultimately went with no caffeine. For God's sake, Colleen didn't have her first cup of coffee till she was twenty-five, so she didn't need to be slugging stimulants down a kid's throat. But Tamara could use the calories.

"That doesn't sound like a very enthusiastic answer. Are you not finding as much as you hoped?"

"No, I am." In truth, she'd been distracted and found less than she probably would on an average day of garage sales in Frederick. Which was not nearly so much as she had hoped. The justification for leaving the shop for this long was to find unique items for low prices that she could repurpose and sell at a large profit, thereby writing off her travel costs and any losses incurred while the shop kept limited hours under Lydia's eye.

So far, there was no real justification for the trip as far as Kevin would be concerned, but it wasn't over yet. She still had her main goal ahead of her. Florida. Palm trees and blue skies, the happiest destination for so many people, but Colleen sort of felt like she was headed for a firing squad.

She just prayed Kevin would never find out what she was doing.

"Good, then, I'm glad it doesn't feel like a waste." He took a breath, and she knew he was concluding the trip was a failure and he was also concluding why. "How's the juvenile delinquent?"

"Actually, she's been surprisingly easy," Colleen said, careful not to sound too enthusiastic, lest she should become the regular go-to replacement mom, but at the same time, wanting to share the good news. "I really thought she'd be more of a handful, but it hasn't been too bad."

This was actually an understatement. Tamara so far had been

well behaved and even fun at times. A little mopey every once in a while, but ever since their game of Never Have I Ever, she seemed to have perked up a little. Colleen was finding she enjoyed her company, and was even grateful for the buffer Tamara provided in the awkward relationship with Bitty.

"Well, good. I'm sorry again I can't be there with you."

No, no. He would hate it. And she would be tense the whole time, knowing he was hating it. She was really glad he wasn't here. "Oh it's fine. How's Jay been? Are you guys having fun?"

"It's been a blast, actually," he said, then with fractionally less enthusiasm added, "We both keep saying we wish you were here."

Colleen was 99 percent sure this wasn't true. But it was the kind of thing that didn't have to be true to be nice.

"Aw. I'd say I do too, but I'd probably get bored with all the boys talking sports the whole time." She gave a laugh. "I'm such a girl."

"I think you'd be surprised by how many women are here. You know Sam Riley? The kid that busted his ankle in soccer last season?"

She tried not to let on that she'd immediately tensed. "Yeah, he was in Jay's fourth-grade class, I think." She remembered his single mom *quite* clearly. His very hot, flirtatious single mom. "Did Kelly go?" Her forced casualness sounded comical to her own ear, but she didn't let on.

"Yup, she's a huge sports buff, apparently. Never know it looking at her, right?"

No, never. Not the five-foot-eight waif with Gisele Bündchen legs and Kate Hudson hair. Or maybe that's just how Colleen was remembering her. She was definitely pretty, though, and definitely didn't look like she'd be into sports. Even though it was inaccurate, she would rather picture some hardened woman who looked like she could take a punch as being the "sports type."

"No," she said, trying again to sound light and like this news didn't change how she felt about the trip. "Yeah, she definitely doesn't strike me as that. So what are you guys doing tonight?"

"I think the kids are going to hang out in the rooms, and the rest of us are going to watch the game at the hotel bar. They've got Old Bay wings and Dogfish Head on tap here."

"Sixty Minute?"

"Yup."

"Your favorite, that's very cool."

So they'd all be getting drunk together. With Kelly. Probably a bunch of guys, and her as the only woman. They'd joke and tease her, and they'd all probably flirt with her and she'd play it up like she didn't notice this crowd of husbands was ogling her.

Not that Kevin was that guy.

Ugh, that would probably make it even worse. He'd probably be the only one not after her, so by virtue of that, she'd probably like him the best.

Colleen squeezed the bridge of her nose. She had to get out of her head. Stop thinking so much. She let her imagination run wild with this sort of thing. It probably didn't help that she couldn't remember the last time she and Kevin had just *hung out.* That was one of the problems with marriage.

When you were dating, there was always that certain level of pretending to like the things your boyfriend did. Colleen could easily recall sitting at a bar and hanging out with him and drinking beer. Ordering the same beer as he did, even though she didn't like it, just in an effort to seem easy-breezy. Watching football—God, those games lasted an age—which she understood but didn't care about, and reacting when everyone else did while trying not to come off like the poseur she was.

Then you got married or got comfortable, and you didn't have to fake it on that stuff anymore. So your interests split off, and suddenly you weren't spending that time together. Then some hot thang like Kelly came along and filled in that "fun girlfriend" role. And worse, she genuinely liked whatever it was.

Colleen shook the thoughts from her head. "Well, that sounds like fun, babe! I'm really glad you guys are having a good time."

She wasn't sure now what she envied more. That Kevin and Jay had this thing to bond over in a father–son way, or if she wished she were the one bonding with Kevin again.

"It's fun. Okay, sweetie, I gotta run—we've got a private tour of the Hall of Fame museum here."

"Okay, I'll text you later."

"Okay. Love you." It was a perfunctory statement. Made every time they hung up the phone. Did he mean it?

"Love you too."

THE AUCTION IN Glidmore, South Carolina, was—thankfully—better than Colleen had anticipated. Conscious of the possibility of coming back with virtually nothing if she didn't focus and use her imagination and bargain-hunting skills, she decided again that it wasn't her problem if Tamara and Bitty were bored; she was going to do what she'd come to do.

The first thing she bought was a box of old rusted horseshoes for a dollar. She felt Tamara's questioning eyes on her and added "judgment" to the mental list of things she was going to ignore. With a little paint, a little glitter, some glue, feathers, rhinestones, whatever she could think of, blinged-out horseshoes sold really well in the shop. She couldn't even say she didn't understand it, because a couple of them had turned out so well that she'd hung them up and not sold them. They were pretty. Unique. A rusted horseshoe over a door, well, that was commonplace. Everyone had seen that before. But a pale pastel horseshoe, that familiar shape, embellished with rhinestones, pretty paint, and—on one occasion you'd have to see to believe—feathers, it took the traditional and made it girlie, and people went nuts for that.

Who didn't want luck?

And who wouldn't prefer it pretty?

Actually, that was the kind of thing maybe Tamara could do—the painting and decorating. Colleen caught herself at the thought. She only had Tamara for another week—she wasn't going to be around to do art projects or shop things, she'd be going back home.

Still, Colleen could tell her about it so maybe she'd take the initiative to come up with her own projects and do something productive instead of smoking those damn cigarettes she always reeked of.

Colleen hadn't said anything, she didn't want to be the nasty old aunt wagging a finger and telling Tamara she was "bad"—but, jeez, the cigarette habit was not only nasty and led to wrinkles and yellow teeth, but how on earth could she *afford* it? Cigarettes cost a fortune these days!

But after the auction, the opportunity came up.

"What are you going to do with all those horseshoes?" Tamara asked. Skepticism clear in her voice.

"Paint them. Make them glittery. BeDazzled. Basically turn them into art. Are you up to that?"

"What, making horseshoes into art?"

"Yup."

"Me?"

"Why not?"

"Because I'm not in this business, I don't know how to do that. Like, *at all.*"

"Did you ever paint pottery as a kid?" Colleen thought this was a given—didn't every kid go to a pottery shop to make some ghastly *MOM* platter that their mother had to display from embarrassment right on through to extreme melancholy?

"No? . . ." Tamara looked blank.

"What about school art projects that you brought home?"

"What, like those turkeys made out of our hand outlines?"

Colleen hesitated. It was a pretty rudimentary definition of art, but it would do. "Sure."

"Once."

"Okay." Irritation suddenly took over. "If you can get inspired and make those horseshoes into beautiful decorations, you're hired. If you can't, forget it, have another cigarette."

Tamara looked wounded for one fleeting moment. "I don't smoke that much."

Colleen had no patience for it. "*Any* is too much. But I can't stop you." She shrugged. "Do what you want."

Uncertainty flitted through Tamara's expression. "So, these horseshoes. You just want them decorated?"

The triumph was so small that Colleen could barely claim it as hers, even to herself. "I want them beautiful. And I can do that, but it takes time. If you can do it, I'll pay you. But not to just do a slipshod job, to do a really good job. Let me know if you're interested."

"Okay," Tamara agreed. "I'll think about it."

And they left it at that, even though privately Colleen thought it was a really good offer for pay and to nurture her creativity.

A few more lots came up, including an old box of Christmas music books, which Colleen got for three bucks. A little bit of glue and some German glass glitter, and those pages could become beautiful decorations that would go like mad during the holiday season.

She was also psyched to notice there was a music box in the bottom of the crate. The label on the bottom said it would play a variety of songs from *The Sound of Music,* but when she cranked the key, it buzzed and rattled and played a few discordant notes of "My Favorite Things." It was disappointing, but not a huge loss, since she'd gotten what she intended to get with the sheet music. The music box would just have been a nice bonus.

But that, she had discovered a long time ago, was how life was: Sometimes a little glow in the road ahead gave you hope for a moment but turned out to be a mirage. And sometimes that mirage was pretty enough to keep you going just a little bit longer.

THE NEXT DAY, they hit another auction, and this one was the shizzle. Truly. After she registered and started to look at the merchandise up for auction, Colleen couldn't believe her luck.

She was particularly gratified to look around at the unsophisticated-looking rubes who were there to bid against her. There was no telling—there was *never* any telling—but she had that feeling deep in her bones that today might be a very profitable day.

They brought up a salvaged window eave, everything but the glass, that was said to be from a historic Charleston hotel that had been torn down a decade or so previously.

"Oh my God, imagine that with a mirror where the window was," Colleen said to Bitty.

"The bidding is starting at four hundred dollars," Bitty countered. "How much would you have to sell it for to make it worth it?"

"Well, *any* profit is profit—"

"Hauling it home, refurbishing it?"

"I could make a decent profit if I sold it for six-fifty," Colleen said, assessing the piece, which was easily five feet tall and almost that wide. "But I'd price it at eleven hundred initially, and odds are pretty good that I'd get it."

Bitty turned the corners of her mouth down and nodded. "Impressive for a single piece."

"That's my aim."

Bitty smiled. "You always were an entrepreneur. I was only a shopper. Let's hope this works."

Colleen felt a little irritation with the implied negativity. This was what she'd been doing for ten years now. More if you counted the time she had a stall at the local tag sale. She'd built her customer clientele, built her reputation, built everything to become a self-made, self-employed woman. She couldn't afford to just "hope" things went well—even though that's exactly what this whole trip had become, thanks to a bad couple of years—and she sure didn't like others treating her business as if it were some hopeful whim.

But what could she say? If she whipped Bitty down with all that, she'd just be the jerk who'd attacked an old friend. She'd never prove anything, because the proof was, as they say, in the pudding, and Bitty was probably never going to see the pudding. She was just along for the ride for a short time.

"I do," Colleen said, in simple answer. "I do hope it works."

And it did. The bidding on the window frame was unenthusiastic and she got it for two hundred dollars. She also got a dusty 1940s dresser mirror, a double bedframe that was more than one hundred years old, and a miscellaneous handful of tchotchkes she'd inspect later.

"I know the saying about one man's trash," Bitty said, picking up a dingy brass powder compact, "but sometimes one man's trash is another man's trash, you know?"

"I know my business, Bitty," Colleen warned.

"And I don't, admittedly. So educate me." Bitty held up the compact. "How would you sell this to me?"

"Well—" Colleen took it from her gently and held it up. "—do you see the insignia on it?"

"I see that there's some lump of *something* there."

"Look more closely. Do you see what it is?"

Bitty examined it dubiously. "Some sort of . . . I don't know. An anchor or something?"

"It's the eagle, globe, and anchor for the U.S. Marine Corps. But the compact, as you can see"—she held it up again—"is shaped like a heart. So this World War Two item was used by"—she opened it up to show the half-used powder and puff still in place—"some girl probably waiting for her boyfriend or husband to come back from the front lines."

Bitty furrowed her brow. "Okay?"

"The fact that it's been used, obviously more than a few times, says that it meant something to someone, wouldn't you say?" Colleen held it up a third time. "I mean, how often do you dig this deep into any of your makeup? We just buy new stuff all the time, right?"

"That's true."

"But this was special to someone. And then it went unused. At some point she used it for the last time and didn't use it again. Why?"

"I don't know." Bitty looked anxious. "We can't know."

"Right," Colleen agreed. "We'll never know. Except that there is this irreplaceable trinket, which I will polish to new on the outside and leave exactly intact on the inside, because so many people prefer the original content. And somewhere out there is a woman, maybe a current marine girlfriend or wife or maybe a marine herself, for whom this will spark the imagination and inspiration, and she'll want it and pick up on the history of some other woman from long ago."

Bitty had the dreamy look of one getting a massage.

Colleen couldn't tell her that so many of these romantic stories came to her because she'd never really had a romance of her own. She'd never admitted, even to Bitty, that she'd been Kevin's second choice. That the unexpected shift in circumstances that had led to their marriage might be the only thing still holding them together in Kevin's heart. She didn't know. She was so afraid to ask. So she carried on like the dutiful wife, did her best, and every time she felt she failed, it was magnified ten times by the underlying idea that she was never really supposed to be there in the first place.

But she wasn't going to admit that to anyone.

So instead she laughed. "See what every day is like for me? I opened the shop because I kept buying everything I saw that I could make up a story for. It was out of hand. Kevin finally suggested it might be better for me to make a profit than to crunch through all of our savings."

"He was always financially clever, that Kevin."

"Isn't he, though?"

"So do you make a good profit at the shop?"

Colleen tipped her hand side to side. "It's okay. Some years are better than others. I haven't been very inspired this past year, so it's been a loss. That's what I'm hoping to rectify now. I need to find great stuff on this trip, or I'm afraid I might have to—" She gave an exaggerated shudder. "—get a real job."

"Well, now that I know what you're looking for, I can help. For instance, I saw an old, beat-up clarinet over there." She gestured toward some lots that were coming up next.

"Beat up?"

"Yeah, I mean, I'm sure it's not *playable,* but, you know—" She shrugged. "—you could do something else with it."

Colleen considered, then raised an eyebrow at Bitty. "Like what?" She glanced at the auctioneer as a new box of stuff was brought up.

"I don't know, maybe . . . maybe wire it and make it into a mantel lamp or something?" Bitty suddenly looked uncertain. "Is that stupid?"

"No! That is so cool! I *love* that idea! Which lot is it in?"

"I'll go look." Bitty ran off, sneaking up to the upcoming lots with a look of secret delight on her face.

Colleen could have waited for them to bring it up and describe it, of course, but with Bitty *finally* being positive about something, she wanted to keep the mood going.

It wasn't that she wanted to convert Tamara and Bitty into replicas of her, going gaga over antiques and painting and all that; it's just that there was something for everyone in this world, and if getting them busy and out of their heads was going to help, then she was going to try to do it.

"That one," Bitty said, pointing to a red milk crate that was probably three lots down from the current one. There was one of those old push toys for toddlers that made a popping sound when pushed. That was probably worth something too, but Colleen wasn't in the thrift store business. Usually she just took what she wanted from a lot and left the rest where anyone could help themselves. Plenty of people like her were here, eager to scarf up a deal.

Colleen waited as the auctioneer went through the other things for a few minutes, and she could feel Bitty's growing excitement. It was funny, really. Finally, the lot came up, and after several minutes of fierce bidding with a man who probably wanted the outdoor electrical extension cord, she won the lot for five dollars.

Bitty was delighted. "Score!" She put her hand up for a high five.

Colleen hit it, then asked, "Where's Tamara?"

"Last I saw, she was going outside. I think she was probably having a cigarette." Bitty shook her head ruefully.

"I hate that."

"Me too."

"Glad I didn't do it past seventeen."

"Me too."

Colleen went outside, and after a few minutes that stretched into a few panicked minutes—Had Tamara been abducted? Had she gotten so bored, she decided to hitchhike out of here? Was she passed out somewhere on some sort of drugs Colleen didn't realize she was taking?—she saw Tamara in the shade of a tree, stubbing out a cigarette that was long since extinguished and looking as if she'd been crying.

"Tam?"

The girl looked up, startled. "Oh! Sorry! I was just . . . On a call. Or trying to make a call. No answer." Quietly she added, "As usual."

"Everything okay?"

"Just trying to check in with my dad. It seemed—" She shrugged. "—like something I should do."

"He knows you're safe with me. If he's in a business meeting, maybe he can't be interrupted."

"Yeah. I guess." Tamara flicked the cigarette butt away.

Colleen looked at the cigarette butt, then back at Tamara. "So I must say this in my duty as your aunt—you know that gives you wrinkles, brown teeth, and unwanted facial hair, don't you?"

"Unwanted facial hair?"

Colleen crossed her heart. "True story."

"Okay, well, it's out now."

"I wish you knew how important it is to stop now before it's a lifelong habit."

"No offense, Aunt Colleen," she hadn't said "Aunt" in a couple of days, so this was the equivalent of a parent calling a child by first, middle, and last name, "but I've got enough *shit* going on that

I don't need more of it. I'm sorry, but—" She closed her eyes tight and shook her head. "I'm sorry."

Colleen knew when not to poke a bear, and this was definitely not a time to poke the bear. She didn't like the smoking *or* the disrespect, but it was really clear this outburst was about something very different, and Tamara had no one to talk to. Maybe if Colleen could ride it out, Tamara would realize she could talk to her.

"Okay, miss." She reached her hand down, and Tamara took the help standing up. "We've all got shit going on, not least of which is we have a bunch of *shit* to pack in the trailer, so come help."

"Yes, ma'am. You don't need to use that language."

"Apparently, I do. It's the only way to be heard by some people."

Tamara's mood shifted, like a kite in the wind. "I had a bad day, okay? It was nothing personal."

"Want to talk about it?"

"No. Thank you."

"That's fine. But keep the storm squalls to yourself, then, got it?"

Tamara rolled her eyes but smiled reluctantly. "I'll try."

Colleen remembered trying herself. It wasn't always easy. "Good. Try."

And she left it at that.

CHAPTER THIRTEEN

Colleen and Bitty, the past

"DO NOT PUSH ME INTO THIS WATER, BLAKE LEON, OR I SWEAR I'll—" Bitty squealed, the sound followed by a loud splash. She came up from the water, smiling but play-angry. "What did I tell you?"

She pulled Blake into the lake by his ankles. Bitty knew he didn't have to budge. The guy was a six-foot-two brick wall, made of lean but strong muscle. But still, he let her pull him in.

A few yards away, Colleen was with Kevin. He was sitting, legs extended, leaning back on his palms, and she lay in his lap, her hair a long, twisting sheet of blond and brown. As she looked up at him and he laughed at something she said, Colleen thought, *Yes. I finally found him.*

They met in a way she could already imagine retelling for years to come: Colleen had been walking between classes on a winter afternoon when the light was getting low early, and a guy had approached her, his hoodie pulled down low, and tried to take her purse. She'd screamed, of course, and started to fight him off, when the cute boy from her Statistics class—Kevin Bradley—appeared from nowhere and pounded the guy until Colleen begged him to let him go.

She never told Kevin that she thought the perpetrator had been Guy Wilkins, from her Badminton class, who had arms like dental floss and who couldn't have harmed a small, slow fly. He just had a weed habit he was trying to support, and somehow he'd decided Colleen was a good mark.

It was a mistake he probably wouldn't make again. With anyone. So it was a good thing Kevin had been there, really.

And it was a good thing Kevin was there, because he had protected her—and whether the guy was a wimp or a hulk, Kevin would have done the same, and that had made Colleen giddy with adoration. He was willing to get his butt pounded to save hers.

It was just as people always promised it would be.

It'll be when you least expect it.

When you know, you just *know.*

I feel like I've known him my whole life. . . .

Then, when she ran into him and his buddies at Henley's a week later, the destiny seemed complete. Admittedly, he and his friends had been a little toasted, but she told herself that his wild enthusiasm for her that night was because that's how he really felt, unfiltered by some idea of propriety.

It might have been the first time she had ever been sure of anything in her life. She knew from the second they'd started talking that he was the man she would marry. Of course she couldn't *know* know. But she was pretty sure she knew.

Here they were. Bitty and Blake were perfect, Colleen had known that too, from the start. And now she had Kevin, with whom things had been perfect and blissful for two months. No, it wasn't that long a time, but it had been so perfect. She was always laughing. She was always having fun. They were both game for anything, so the world really felt like their oyster.

There was talk of a recent ex-girlfriend, but she was an *ex* for a reason, right? Nothing to worry about there.

And Bitty . . . Oh, putting Bitty and Blake together might be her greatest accomplishment to date.

"They're so cute, aren't they?" Colleen said, stretching her head back and watching Bitty and Blake flirting in the water. You'd think they were newly matched or something. Not that they'd been together for over a year and a half already.

"So cute," said Kevin, joking. Of course, he was a guy; he didn't think they were cute.

"Really, though," said Colleen, sitting up. "If they don't get married, I'll lose all faith in love."

Kevin said nothing, his joking smile fading a little.

"Kev? What was that?"

"What? Nothing."

She tilted her head at him. "Kevin."

"Nothing. I don't know anything."

She raised an eyebrow. "You've already given away that you do, just by saying that. Spit it out."

Colleen could see that he really, really regretted letting on that he knew something. Especially since honesty was their one and only real rule.

"Kevin, I won't say anything—you know I'm good at keeping secrets."

He seemed to consider that, and then brace himself. "Blake is leaving."

Colleen's heart wrenched. "Leaving? . . . Where is he going, what do you mean?"

He sat up and dusted the dirt off his hands. "His mom is sick. She lives in Georgia. She can't make any money or anything, and she's all on her own. He's going out there to help her out. Clean the house, make some money, help her with the bills and all."

"Oh, no . . ."

"He's telling Bitty really soon. I think he's kind of freaking out about what she'll say."

"What she'll say? I mean, she's not going to, like, go banshee on him. But she's going to be really upset."

"Yeah. Sucks."

"Is he . . . so is he dropping out?"

"He has to."

"With only a semester and a half left? That is— No, he can't do that. He can't!"

"Life gets in the way sometimes, I guess."

Colleen's eyes shifted from Kevin's guilty face to Blake and Bitty.

She had never seen Bitty the way she was now. Once upon a time, her friend had worried constantly. She was hesitant. Quick to feel insulted. Shy to a fault. Always looking perfect, and trying to act perfect. But since getting together with Blake—he had asked her to be his girlfriend while they drank Coke, not Diet Coke, in the back of his pickup truck. Not anywhere special, Bitty had said. They didn't look out at a pretty skyline or gaze up at the stars. It was just a parking lot, with other cars, people walking by. "But," Bitty had told Colleen, "it may as well have been the top of the

Eiffel Tower, clinking champagne glasses. Only somehow, it was ten times more romantic."

Colleen felt sick to her stomach for Bitty. Bitty was in love. Bitty was happy. Bitty was free. She had Blake, and she knew it. Once she'd had him, her worry had fell away. What did it matter if someone insulted her anymore? She had Blake. If some guy at the bar wouldn't name her the hottest girl there, how could Bitty possibly care? She had Blake.

But now, Bitty was going to lose Blake and be left naked, with her guard down. Colleen already feared the wall that Bitty was sure to rebuild around herself. She wondered if she'd even let Colleen see beyond it anymore.

BLAKE DIDN'T TELL her until the next Friday. They all ate at the diner, and afterwards, Kevin and Colleen left, and Bitty told Colleen later what had happened, in a few strangled words. She and Blake sat outside the diner in his car, and he'd told her. Told her he had to leave for a year or so. He couldn't say for sure when he'd be back.

He couldn't say for sure *if* he'd be back.

He was sorry.

And that was the end.

CHAPTER FOURTEEN

Bitty

Dear Stranger,

When it comes to suicide, you'd think it was sort of a beggars-can't-be-choosers sort of thing, wouldn't you? Like, once you've decided to do it and you're on your way to the pharmacy to pick up a prescription for sedatives and you slip in the street and fall in front of an oncoming truck, that's just fortuitous, right? Means it was meant to be or something.

That's what I would have thought, anyway. Until today.

We went to another auction, and I darn near enjoyed myself. But this is a tough position I've put myself in, it's like every choice I've made has been stupid. Losing the car, losing my money, then hitting the road without a solid plan. It was bad enough becoming a barnacle on Colleen and Tamara's trip at first, feeling like an outsider, knowing they were both unsure what to do with me or what to say. I can only imagine what they said in private. Snarky comments from Tamara about having a stranger intrude on their time to get to know each other? Apologies from Colleen for allowing the weirdo on board?

All of the above?

So obviously, I have been aware of needing to take care of this—the sooner, the better. But there was just no obvious way for me to do that with no money and no credit cards.

But the last thing in the world I can do is go crawling back to Lew and kill a little time before Plan B. Or am I on Plan C now?

The auction was in a large, cold building that was like a mixture of half barn and half elementary school gym. Big, flat, formless building with no climate control but ugly scuffed linoleum floors. One wall had large wooden shelves in front of it, holding, among other things, a wheel of fortune they probably used for game nights. Another wall had large, heavy curtains pulled back like a young girl's ponytails, and a low platform that must have been a stage, though honestly it was only about five inches off the ground.

I wondered how often they held activities here, what kind of people came. We were in South Carolina and the accents were thick. Would a northerner like me be at a disadvantage playing bingo here? Was the caller saying *A* or *I*? How embarrassing to stand up and yell, "Bingo!" (1) at all, and, (2) if you were wrong.

This is the kind of thing I think about. The many ways to be publicly humiliated. I don't know why, but I've always been like this, always afraid of something embarrassing happening. It usually does too.

You're probably thinking self-fulfilling prophecy, and you're probably right about that.

While Colleen was busily looking over the inventory with a notepad, writing down all the things she wanted to bid on and what her maximum bid would be (she writes it down so she doesn't get competitive in the moment and overspend just to beat some fat-gutted farmer in a contest over who wins a rusty scalding tub), and Tamara was outside under a shady tree, obsessively checking her phone in private, I went and got a hot dog and Coke.

I'd forgotten how good hot dogs are. Not that this is relevant, but, seriously, if you're reading this, go and get yourself a hot dog. Don't live a life of lack—enjoy the simple things. A hot dog with ketchup and mustard and relish. I could do with the raw onions too, but this rinky-dink place didn't have them. It was just plain generic store-brand hot dogs in buns so cheap, they wrapped around the dog as thin as paper, and little packets of condiments. I put on three of each. I could not have ordered something more delicious from Morton's.

When I was young, my friend Pam Slade had this thing called a "hot dogger," and it was this probably dangerous device that had electric probes set up so you could spear six hot dogs on each end and push a button, and in sixty seconds you'd have an electrocuted meat product smelling vaguely of burning rubber, dripping with buttery grease, and ready for the party. I wanted one so badly, I can still remember the ache. My mother, of course, said no way. She didn't want to encourage me in any way to eat more junk. Eating, she said, was "unlovely" and it was the responsibility of a proper young lady to be lovely. For her family and, someday, for her husband. Implication: Eating will screw you out of a fine prospect and a happily-ever-after.

I'm here to tell you that's bunk. On every single level. Eat what you want, drink what you want, enjoy every bite, every sip, every breath you take doing what you want to do. Don't listen to the naysayers. They will always be there to promise doom and gloom. Ignore them.

Do it. You'll thank me.

After the hot dog (well, hot dogs—I had to get another one), I went back into the barn-a-teria and was looking for a clock to see how much longer before this infernal thing started and therefore ended, when I saw a corner full of ladders and other equipment. The reason I saw it was the best part: There was a little girl with black hair and a bright pink T-shirt standing there alone, crying and looking up at a gray and white cat up in the rafters in the "stage" area.

I'm such a sucker.

Assessing the situation in one quick moment, I rushed to her to quell her crying.

Everyone else was all wrapped up in the potential acquisition of moldy leather tack, rusty band saws with frayed electrical cords from the '50s and, if I'm not mistaken, a set of Volumes 1 through 20 of Nancy Drew Mysteries with the old blue covers with a black silhouette of Nancy being sleuth-y with a magnifying glass.

I asked the girl what was wrong, and she pointed to a cat high up in the rafters. She was worried he was going to fall. I don't know much about cats, I've never lived in a home that allowed pets, but you didn't have to be Jack Hanna to know if the cat *did* fall, it wasn't going to be pretty. I asked her if it was her cat and she said no, and my first, uncharitable, thought was that she was a little too hysterical over this cat that wasn't even hers.

I asked her how old she was, and she said seven. Was that too old to be sobbing away like this? I know less about kids than I do about cats. One of my earliest memories was of the end of first grade, which I think was when I was seven, and my mother had my bangs cut too short, in the manner of every hideous ad from the '50s and '60s. I looked like a joke. She pretended it had been a conscious fashion choice, and that I was being impertinent to question it, but I noticed that every time she took me to get my hair cut after that, she was always very quick to caution them about my "dramatic cowlick" in the front.

I had cautioned stylists the same way for my entire adult life.

Anyway, the secret thing about me (my secret superpower, if you will) was that I grew up as kind of a tomboy. My mother worked damn hard to "girl" it out of me, but I was not afraid to climb one of the many farm ladders that were right there and get the damn cat down so I could do something slightly worthwhile before meeting my Maker and having to give a report. If the pearly gates were anything like school, I could really play up the compassion for the crying child aspect, then give short acknowledgment to the saving of one of God's creatures.

I was pretty sure God would be more impressed by the compassion. He could have saved the cat Himself if He was so damn worried about it.

I pulled a ladder out slightly to a solid angle, making sure to keep it off the linoleum and on the platform stage, which was covered with some sort of indoor/outdoor carpet. Then I made sure the rakes and other tools were out of the way of the ladder, so if it slipped, it wouldn't send everything clattering to the floor.

I guess the fever of bidding frenzy that makes people illogical once the auctioneer begins his spiel was contagious, and all I could think about was the feeling of accomplishment I'd have—however small—when I'd saved that stupid cat.

So I began to climb the ladder, rung by careful rung. A couple of them shifted and rolled under my soles as I went, and the last thing in the world I wanted was to bang my way down four and a half feet to a noisy landing in a box of Christmas costumes for some live nativity scene or something. Rising slowly from the box with Balthazar's velvet hat on my head at a rakish angle, dusty frankincense wedged up my nose, and clutching a now-headless baby Jesus.

As I got higher, I started to feel more confident. I was getting pretty high up, and the ladder was pretty sturdy after all. They just don't make things like they used to, do they?

For some reason, the rungs at the top of the ladder were more stable than the lower ones, I guess because whoever owned it previously was a wimp and used it for only minor, low-lying jobs. I got to the top pretty quickly, luckily I was never afraid of heights, and took another look at the auction-goers.

Would you believe not one person was looking in my direction? I mean, that was fortunate for me because of how it went. I didn't need an audience watching the whole damn thing. Or filming, even, so I could be the next YouTube fool. But you get my point—there's a person climbing thirty feet up over the scene, and no one noticed.

Not even when I had to stop for a sneezing fit from the dusty curtains! Wouldn't you think it would register for someone that those sneezes were coming from an odd place?

Apparently, not the case in Tinytown, South Carolina. So I

made it to the top, took a deep breath, said a prayer (I didn't tell you I still had some Presbyterian left in me, did I?), and started to reach toward the cat, calling *kitty kitty kitty* the way everyone does, though I have no idea if it helps.

I looked down. The tools weren't so far out of the way as I'd thought when I moved them. This was exactly the sort of thing parents feared when their kids got around tools, and for good reason.

I looked back at the cat, who was watching me impassively. I made little kissing sounds that left him completely unimpressed.

Well, now what was I supposed to do? I couldn't just climb back down and tell that little girl that I called the cat twice, by a name that surely wasn't his, and he didn't come, so I gave up.

I had to do something worthwhile, and this small task had presented itself. I couldn't fail at this. I reached for him, and the ladder shifted slightly. Reflexively, my hand shot back to the rung and I cussed at him.

I swear the cat yawned.

Finally, in desperation, I stepped down a rung to get at a better position, and reached for the cat. There couldn't have been more than an inch between my fingertips and its fur, but it might as well have been a mile.

What was I going to do? I mean, there was just nothing I could do except climb all the way back down, move the ladder a couple of inches, then climb all the way back up. That seemed so unnecessary, since I was already up here and so close. So I stood there like a dumb, unseen moron, unable to make this patently, clearly, horribly dangerous situation actually, you know, worth it.

Thank God there were no security cameras in a place like this. I could just imagine the viral video making the rounds on the news. The sort of thing where the newscasters aren't supposed to laugh because it's really a very somber story at the heart of it, but inevitably someone, probably the weather or sports guy, would say some little smart-aleck joke and everyone would chuckle.

One more step down and I tried again. They didn't know it, all those unwatching witnesses, but they'd given me a chance at a mulligan. I stood on my tiptoes and reached for the cat, making contact. For one brief moment I had him, but then he meowed loudly and leapt to another rafter. Startled, I overcompensated and the ladder started to tip. Backwards. And it kept tipping.

And here's where you'd think I might have just seen this as serendipity. I'd wanted to kill myself and even though this wasn't how I had planned to go, it was an opportunity that had presented itself handily. It would have happened fast, and from that height it would have been over instantly. Best of all, it wasn't even my fault, really—I mean, yes, I was the dummy who'd climbed up there to get the cat, but it was because a little girl was crying, so in essence, I would die a hero. Sort of.

But no, instinct kicked in, I screamed, and without even thinking, I reached for the curtain as the ladder blew past and slammed to the floor.

That got their attention.

Everyone looked at the ladder. From my perspective, I could see that human beings have roughly the same reactions and timing, because their heads all seemed to move at the same time, turning first to the source of the clattering, then to the oddball trapped in the top of the curtains, sneezing her head off.

There wasn't even time to think of what to do.

The instinct to live, to save yourself, at a time when all your muscles are engaged in doing exactly that in a manner not unlike rigor mortis, is stronger than any scheme Lucy and Ethel or I could ever come up with, however "heroic" it might be on the surface.

So for one endless moment, I remained there, frozen in the most embarrassing position I'd ever been in.

But before anyone could, or did, move, the curtains started to tear. Slowly. Evenly. One might even say sarcastically. The sound was like a record being scratched, and when I instinctively reached up to grab the rod, my sleeve got caught in the hook. It was one of those surf brand T-shirts—Roxy, I think—with the thumb hole at the wrist. Purely decorative, as it was made out of fabric so thin that it didn't matter whether it had sleeves or not—the shirt wasn't providing any protection from the cold.

I'd actually had that thought that morning when I'd put it on, since the hooks on my bra weren't meeting comfortably all of a sudden (a fact I'd attributed to the doughnuts I had at the last auction—it's really amazing how fast weight piles on me, my mother was right!) and I left it off.

So down I went, like a new member of Cirque du Soleil on the first day of training, taking the curtain with me and leaving my shirt behind.

How long did it take? Three seconds? Maybe four? An hour? A week? A year?

I have no idea. To me, it felt like forever. Kind of like when you're sitting there waiting for people to finish singing "Happy Birthday" to you in a restaurant with a frozen smile on your face.

When at last I hit the ground, one of those rakes I'd tried so carefully to move out of the way had been knocked when the ladder fell, so my right foot landed directly on it, puncturing right through my shoe and knocking the rake up to hit me in the head.

I was a Stooge. Or Jerry Lewis.

I was ridiculous.

Really, it was my fault for having such uncharitable thoughts about how dumb and blind these people were, thinking to myself that they wouldn't notice John Wilkes Booth walking into a theater with a machine gun.

They were noticing me now.

I barely remember getting up and dusting myself off. At the time, I didn't feel any pain, but I'm a little achy now, so that was probably just the adrenaline. I went over to a shocked Colleen (thank God Tamara was still outside) and told her I would be waiting in the car.

Naturally, she didn't leave me there for long; she came out as soon as she paid up, but in the meantime I did get a chance to think. And, seriously, when I started to fall, why did I stop myself? Is the human impulse to survive so physically strong that it doesn't care what the mind thinks? Where was the brain that had been planning suicide for the past few months? Suddenly hiding behind the muscle, urging it to hold on. Crazy.

I'd thought my road was so clear. How could I fail at this one final thing? There is no way to fail at suicide as long as it works. Failing at suicide is failing at failure.

At this point, I'm beginning to feel I'm so bad at living that I might never be able to end it. Wouldn't that be ironic?

CHAPTER FIFTEEN

Colleen

"WHAT IS THAT SMELL?" TAMARA ASKED AS THEY ROLLED ALONG the endless miles of I-95 through Georgia. The road was a long black Sharpie line in front of them, flanked by guardrails and, for the past five miles, Jersey walls with low, swampy water extending far to the left and right. Smokestacks billowed in the distance to the east.

Jersey walls made Colleen nervous, so she was glad to have something to say—anything—to try and distract herself. "Paper factories," she said, gesturing toward the smokestacks. "They smell like sulfur."

"It's disgusting."

"Yeah, well, that's the smell of Georgia for you."

"I hate it."

Colleen wanted to snap at her, and say that she could deal with it or keep bitching, but either way, it was going to still stink. She kept her mouth shut. She knew she was only irritable because she had been able to get ahold of Kevin for just a minute here and there over the past few days.

"Bad time to have the top down," Tamara went on, her tone dripping with nasty attitude.

Shut up, Colleen thought. Tamara had been really good, really agreeable, for most of the trip, so maybe it was an uncharitable thought, but still, *Shut up shut up shut up.*

"We should stop at Paula Deen's restaurant in Savannah," Bitty said. "What's it called? The Lady and Sons?"

Colleen glanced sideways at her. How fast could a person put on weight? Bitty had been eating nonstop, and she looked great. She actually looked like a *normal* person now. Colleen had never seen her resembling anything other than a twig. They'd even stopped at a Target so Bitty could get some new clothes. She'd only gotten yoga pants and a couple of sleeveless exercise shirts, though. Colleen wondered if she was running out of money or determined to lose the weight again.

Seeing Bitty gnawing on peanut brittle they'd bought at the last gas station, it seemed like it was more likely the former. The map of this trip was starting to look like a Candy Land game board.

Not that she'd gained *that* much weight, of course, but a little really showed on Bitty. Obviously, she needed it—her body was soaking it up. Once, Colleen had gained five pounds from Thanksgiving and the following day of leftovers—mashed potato pancakes fried in butter!—which had stayed on her until she finally stopped thinking she was "bloated" and went on an actual diet to lose them. So how much could Bitty gain in a week? After Colleen's weight gain, she'd looked it up and seen that, actually, it was frighteningly easy to consume the 3,500 calories required to gain a pound. There was a regular-sized milk shake at the local ice cream store that had more than 2,000 calories alone.

She used to love those things.

Not anymore, though.

"Isn't there something wrong with Paula Deen? She did something messed up, right?" Tamara asked.

"There is nothing in the world wrong with Paula Deen," Bitty said. "Except that she doesn't use as much real butter and cream anymore on her TV show."

"You watch her TV show?" Colleen asked, surprised.

Bitty took a sip of her Pepsi. Real Pepsi. Not diet. That was 250 calories right there, and she'd had a bunch of them.

Colleen used to love real Pepsi too, till she'd looked it up.

"I used to," Bitty said. "I did it instead of eating. I know it sounds weird, but it was kind of a substitute."

"That would *kill* me. Watching someone make pound cake while I was on a diet? I don't know how you did it."

"I did it because I *had* to. I did everything because I had to." Bitty paused and looked off to the west. Her brown hair was taking on tinges of auburn in the sunlight, and freckles were starting to dot her nose because they'd had the top down. Colleen had offered her sunscreen, but Bitty waved it away as if Colleen were offering her a dead squirrel in a clown suit.

"I don't need that."

"You *need* it! Good Lord, I don't know when the last time you were out in the sun was, but I'm pretty sure I was there. With your complexion, you're going to burn like crazy."

"I'm fine."

"Tamara?" Colleen handed the bottle back and felt Tamara take it. "Smart girl." Then in the rearview mirror, she saw Tamara look at it, shrug, and set it on the seat next to her.

Colleen groaned. "You're both going to be sorry."

There was a sign for a rest stop a mile ahead, and she decided to pull over and reapply the sunscreen herself, fix her ponytail, which was getting blown out by the wind, and, of course, pee. Because the moment she hit the road, it felt like she had to pee every few minutes.

Also, she didn't mind getting a moment of alone time. Even if it was just in a bathroom stall.

"Again?" Tamara asked.

"Thank goodness," Bitty said, draining the last of her Pepsi and burping. It was a ladylike burp, but still a complete and utter shock coming from Wilhelmina Camalier.

Colleen looked at her in disbelief. "Are you kidding?"

"I'm tired of always being perfect and proper."

"I'll say."

"That was rude, though. Sorry."

She pulled the car into a parking space and put on the brake. Bitty and she opened their doors, and she turned to the back. "Tam?"

"No, I'm good." She returned her attention to her phone. Her brow was furrowed.

"It'll be a while before we stop again." God, she sounded like such a nag, even to her own ears. This was what kids did to you. Somehow they ended up looking like the calm cool ones while the adults who were just trying to get them to do the right thing ended up seeming shrill. "Okay," Colleen said in a singsongy voice, mentally adding *desperate need to pee* to the list that had begun with *peeling sunburn.*

"You go on," Bitty said, digging through her change purse. "I'm going to run over to the vending machines too. I'm just dying for a Nutter Butter. Anyone want anything?"

"Nope," Tamara said.

"No, thanks," Colleen said, thinking that Paula Deen's restaurant had actually sounded good and Nutter Butters were a pretty far cry from that.

She went to the restroom, and as she came out, Bitty was going in. "Oh, good. Will you hold these?" She thrust two packs of cookies and another Pepsi into Colleen's hands before looking at the otherwise-abandoned restroom. "God, these places are spooky. It would be the perfect place to murder someone, wouldn't it? If I'm not out in three minutes, send in the national guard."

She gave a laugh that was followed by a weird look, and then went inside.

Colleen gave a laugh of her own, but she could hear the genuine edge in Bitty's voice. "I'll wait on the bench so I can hear you scream, how's that?"

"Thanks." Bitty looked grateful.

Colleen went over to the bench a few yards away and set the cold Pepsi and cookies down next to her. There was a North Carolina newspaper folded up on the brick wall to her right.

All these people on this road, she thought, everyone passing the same things, stopping at the same rest areas. How many people had been through here this year alone? This month? How many people did she actually know who had stopped here in her lifetime? Anyone famous? Had Ava Gardner ever taken the trek down from her eponymous museum in North Carolina to, what, Boca Raton or someplace fancy in Florida? Had she stopped here herself? When had she died, anyway? The '80s? After she'd been on *Knots Landing.* Colleen used to watch that show with her mom. This rest stop had definitely been here in the '80s. It was entirely possible Ava Gardner had peed here.

Wow. She was getting punchy.

She glanced back at the paper, now half expecting to see an article on Ava Gardner, but what caught her eye instead was a small picture in the top right over the caption WINNINGTON WOMAN MISSING.

Was that—? Could it be?

No way.

Was that *Bitty*?

She picked up the newspaper, vaguely aware that she had no idea who had left it there or what was all over their potentially grungy hands, here outside the toilets. But she had to see.

The paper was dated yesterday.

WINNINGTON WOMAN MISSING

The mysterious disappearance of former Winnington socialite Wilhelmina Camalier deepened today when her car was found on a remote road near Henley. Her purse and keys were in the Jaguar, and there did not appear to have been a struggle.

It is uncertain exactly when Mrs. Camalier went missing; no sources recall seeing her for several days before her car was found. Having separated nearly a year ago from her husband, Lew Camalier, she had been operating under extreme distress ever since the split, according to many sources.

Police haven't entirely ruled out foul play, but Winnington deputy Marc Penskey thinks the case is cut-and-dried. "This is a woman in great duress. In layman's terms, you might say she's come unglued and is wildly unpredictable."

Apparently, Mrs. Camalier left all her personal belongings in her home, including her license and most credit cards, so it is thought that she cannot get very far. Mr. Camalier says no money is missing from their bank account.

"I just want Wilhelmina to come back," Lewis "Lew" Camalier says. "To get the help she—

"Reading the comics?"

Bitty's voice started Colleen so much, she gasped. When she looked up at Bitty, she could tell the color had drained from her cheeks.

What on earth was she going to do? Why hadn't Bitty told her all this was going on? What was the significance of that huge omission, and what on earth should Colleen do with it? She couldn't ask Kevin for advice, because she already knew he'd tell her to drop Bitty off at the next ER.

"Colleen?" Bitty prompted, frowning.

"Oh. Sorry," she said, apologizing for the thoughts Bitty didn't even know she'd just had. "I'm getting that nervous, spacy feeling I always get when I've had too much caffeine."

Bitty nodded. "I remember." She held out a cookie. "It always helps to get something into your stomach."

"No thanks," she said. She didn't even have the appetite for a cookie. "I've got to watch it."

"That's all you guys ever say," Bitty noted, picking up her Pepsi and the other cookies. "You're making me feel like a total pig."

"Welcome to my world," Colleen said automatically. "About time the tables were turned."

As soon as she'd said the words, she hoped there was no room for misinterpretation or insult. Nothing to potentially *set Bitty off.*

"What does that mean?" Bitty asked.

"I have no idea. Honestly. I'm punchy."

"You're acting weird. You know that, right?"

"I'm fine," Colleen said, then made a show of sighing. "I just talked to Kevin, and he and Jay are having such a good time without me, it kind of made me feel sad. Like they don't need me."

"Oh, Colleen, that's terrible. God, men can be such jerks sometimes. We'd probably all be better off without them."

Colleen looked at her sharply, but she went on.

"But then life would be pretty boring. Still, I wish Kevin hadn't made you feel that way."

"He didn't mean to." How far was she going to have to take this lie? "I could just tell they were having a really good time."

"So are we!" Bitty put an arm around her shoulders and gave a squeeze. "Right?"

"Right." Colleen rolled up the newspaper and stuffed it awkwardly into her bag. "Let's go. Time to hit the road again."

IT WAS CRAZY. Once upon a time, Colleen had known Bitty well, and now she was suddenly a missing person and had totally neglected to mention it. If Bitty was found with her, did that mean she would be considered somehow an *accessory* to . . . something?

No. This was crazy. Bitty was fine. She'd just left a jerky husband. A jerky husband who wielded a lot of social power and probably had that article planted to save face for himself. The stupid thing was written by a man. He probably came this close to mentioning PMS. And it was badly written, to boot. Just a little bit of gossip in an otherwise-bored newspaper. Reporters this far out of the major cities didn't have anything worthwhile to say about Jennifer Lawrence or Halle Berry, so they just had to make drama in their own midst.

Surely that was all it was. And even if it wasn't, there was no mention of Bitty having done anything illegal or being in any way dangerous—she'd just, basically, taken off. Big deal.

Who didn't want to do that now and then?

Colleen accelerated down I-95 as the sun went down. Her playlist had reached its old-time music section at just the right moment, and Frank Sinatra was singing "Witchcraft" as the sun sank into the horizon under a scribble of lipstick pink sky.

Colleen glanced in the rearview mirror and saw Tamara mouthing the words. "You *know* this song?"

"I'm not an idiot."

"No . . . you're just sixteen. Not a lot of sixteen-year-olds are familiar with Sinatra's oeuvre."

"I don't know what that means."

"I'm just surprised you know it, that's all."

"Okay, well, mostly I liked *American Horror Story,* and I heard this on it and Shazamed it, so don't go freaking out that I'm in some sort of Satanic cult or something just because it's about witches."

Colleen laughed. "I wasn't going there."

"My dad would." In the rearview mirror, Colleen saw Tamara roll her eyes, then turn her head to the scenery, jaw clenched. "He's such an asshole sometimes."

"Men, I'm telling you," Bitty chirped.

"Stop," Colleen said. "Not all men are bad. What"—she tested the waters carefully—"what made you so mad at Lew?"

"Who said I'm mad at Lew?"

"Basically everything you say about him or men sounds like you're mad at Lew."

"Who's Lew?" Tamara asked from the back.

"Bitty's husband."

"Soon-to-be ex."

Colleen turned to her. She was opening up. Good sign. "Really?"

Bitty nodded. Clearly she didn't feel like elaborating.

That uncomfortable feeling churned in Colleen's stomach again. "What happened?"

"Look, I know you didn't like him. You don't need to remind me of that."

"I wasn't—"

"Just drop it. It has been rough. He's an asshole. I shouldn't have married him. I don't need it piled on that you told me so."

Colleen didn't want to argue with Bitty. Even though it was absolutely insane to act like she had been gearing up for an almost two-decades-delayed *I told you so.*

Even though . . . she had totally told her so.

"Tam." Colleen glanced in the mirror. "I think we're getting close to the B and B for tonight—can you check the map?"

"What's the name? And"—she looked around—"where are we?"

"Almost in Savannah."

"Okay."

Tamara clicked around on her phone, and Bitty bit her lip, her elbow resting on the top of her car door. Colleen could tell from knowing her that she was seething. The kind of brokenhearted, angry Bitty that Colleen had seen only once before.

"I could just . . . I could just kill him."

"Better him than you, huh?" Colleen joked.

Bitty didn't laugh. "One of us, anyway."

CHAPTER SIXTEEN

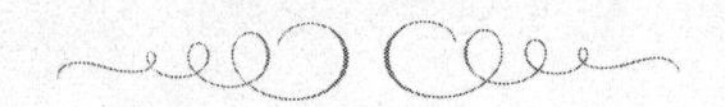

Bitty

Dear Stranger,

Colleen is acting weird with me.

I feel her looking at me sidewise while we're driving, like she's suddenly assessing me. I wonder if she's getting some sort of cabin fever or something, where she can't stand having so many people around her.

I kind of am.

I mean, I'm grateful to her for including me, this has been a very interesting week so far, but there are three of us in this little car for hours every single day, and with all of us being women, I guess it's natural for us to start to prickle around each other.

Plus, I don't know about the other two, but I'm starting to

feel distinctly premenstrual. They say women sync to each other's cycles. I wonder how long it takes for that to happen. Probably more than a few days, even if some of those days *do* feel endless.

I also wonder, though I hate to say this, if she's watching me judgmentally for eating so much. Not that I'm eating more than an average person, I think, but I probably look totally piggish to her. Particularly since I have never really indulged in food much in my life.

I started because I didn't think I was going to live long enough for it to hit my hips anyway, but the funny thing is, I think it's starting to make me feel a little better. Can food really be an antidepressant? I know there are a lot of books that make that claim, but could it be true?

Probably not. At least not peanut brittle. I guess it's more likely that getting away from the tiny biosphere of Winnington alone—for the first time in decades—has lifted some of that black cloak of Camalier-ness from me.

I felt like I couldn't make it without Lew when I was there. Without an identity as a wife. And everyone there backed me up on that, make no mistake. There was no question that I was valuable only when basking in the reflected glow of the Camalier name.

Candy Fitzgerald-Sonner—the new wife of an old bore, who clearly has her eye on taking over virtually all my social roles—might learn the same lesson. Or she might grace society with her unfunny bons mots until she's an old woman, like Lew's mother, and dies a glorified death and sinks into the legend of this place that feels so big when you're in it but looks so small and even unreal when viewed from a seedy truck-stop diner in Nowhere, Georgia.

Winnington exists only unto itself. Almost no one in the outside world is aware of it at all.

Socrates' cave allegory.

It was easy to suck me into that, of course, because that's how it was for me growing up. My mother was the grande dame of Barlowe society and taught me everything I needed to know about getting a certain kind of man and keeping him, by starving and serving and bowing and scraping.

She'd never admit that, though. She'd say she simply taught me to "behave like a lady."

Sometimes—okay, frequently—I wonder what would have happened if Blake hadn't left. I know that's silly, wondering "what if" about a boyfriend from what was practically childhood, but I really loved him. Even looking back now, with everything I know about life—which, arguably, isn't much—everything I've endured, all the pain and the losses and the humiliations and, yes, the glories, I still wonder what would have happened if he hadn't left.

I think we would have stayed together. After a year and seven months together, we weren't losing interest. We rarely disagreed, never "fought," and I always felt valued by him. Loved. Accepted for who I was.

Would you believe that when I got together with Lew, I stopped singing in the car with the radio? Small thing, I know, but I used to love that, rocking along with Mariah Carey or whoever, I listened to everything and loved to get in the car and belt it out with them. Blake used to just laugh and shake his head indulgently. It charmed him, I think.

But Lew always asked me to turn down the radio, not to sing, because he had a headache. He had more headaches than the proverbial disinterested wife! And with that simple dis, he practically took away my voice.

When I cooked for Lew—not too often, since he didn't like my cooking—I'd turn off the radio the minute he came in. Then I'd work in silence. Or several yards away from where he sat, watching the hushed weirdness of golf on TV. Or *Golden Girls* reruns. *That* was discordant, but did I ever say, "Hey, what's with you and *The Golden Girls*? Am I just too young? Is that why we never make love?" No. I didn't want to hurt his feelings or insult him.

In fact, I *never* mentioned the complete lack of sex in any way other than what I thought was a seductive come-on. I'd say stuff like "I want you so bad," because I did—I craved touch and affection, but I never asked why he wasn't interested, why he couldn't get it up for me, why so often, even in our dating time, he wasn't able to *keep* it up. I just treated him like he was a king.

I had no idea he was a queen.

Foolish me.

Sad thing is, to me he *was* a king, for far too long. As long as I could keep Blake out of my head, I was able to see Lew as the be-all and end-all. I was *proud* of him when we went out to events. I was *proud* to be Mrs. Lew Camalier.

I wasted too many years doing that.

The New Age people are always talking about taking care of

yourself, loving yourself first, and so on. I used to think that was nonsense. Silly. I thought I was taking care of myself by taking care of my husband. I thought pleasing him gave me more pleasure than anything else could.

But you know what I've found out?

Despite the occasional tense moment/hour, I have felt more . . . *freedom,* riding in this convertible through the South, the wind blowing, the sun shining, surrounded by people I'll never know or see again, in cars I'll never remember, than I have ever felt in my life.

And freedom feels good.

I wonder what I'd be like if I'd never gotten married.

Probably lonely. I think I know myself well enough to know I need a companion. I need to feel *needed.* Of course, *wanted* would be awesome as well, but beggars can't be choosers. I was just never one who wanted to strike out on my own and subscribe to *Working Woman* magazine. I wanted to be . . . Well, I wanted to be exactly what I became.

Be careful what you wish for.

Once upon a time, I loved another man. Looking back, I guess I should characterize a twenty-year-old as more of a "boy" but at the time, I thought he was my forever. Good guy, solid, salt of the earth. Not moneyed or cultured, my mother never would have approved. But I didn't care about that. I'm not heading toward some *Romeo and Juliet* b.s., I loved him and wanted to be with him forever.

He left me.

He had to, it was a family thing, not worth boring you with it now, but the thing is, of all the possible Other Life scenarios

I think of, that's the one that I have the most questions about. What could have been? We've passed hundreds of palm readers and neon psychic signs outside of ramshackle huts on this drive, and every time I see one, I think I'd like to go in and ask about my fate.

At this point, though, not only am I afraid to hear what my past could have been, but I'm *really* afraid to hear about my future.

CHAPTER SEVENTEEN

Colleen and Bitty, the past

BITTY SAT ON THE RICKETY BACK BUMPER OF COLLEEN'S CAR, hyperventilating into a paper bag.

Colleen was silent, one hand on Bitty's shoulder, the other anxiously grabbing her own thigh. She had known this was coming, and she didn't tell Bitty. Didn't prepare her for it. But she hadn't known what to say. What was she *supposed* to say? It was between Bitty and Blake; it was really none of Colleen's business. Plus, she had known for only a few days.

Bitty took in a deep shuddering breath. It was the first time she stopped wheezing since Blake had driven away. She had screamed at him to go. Yelled at him and thrown her soda at him.

That's when Colleen arrived.

He clearly hadn't wanted to leave. He said he had wanted to explain more, but she hadn't wanted to hear it. Privately, Colleen wondered if he was going to ask Bitty to go with him, or if he might have given her some promise to return, maybe even proposed. People had separations all the time because of extenuating circumstances—that didn't mean they had to be apart forever.

But there was no telling Bitty that. She was in full hysteria mode. It seemed like she was physically unable to calm down.

She sat up and shook her head at Colleen. "How is this ha-happening?"

"I know, sweetie—"

"No, seriously." She swatted Colleen's hand away and stood to pace in the dirt in front of them. Her emotions were made worse by the shots they'd had before the night went sour. "How is it possible that the *first* time I ever feel anything real for someone, it's just being"—she gestured wildly—"taken away? How is it fair?"

"It's not."

"It's not. Exactly. I have never felt like that. At all. I love—" Her voice was swallowed by tense tears in her throat.

"I know," Colleen said, because there was nothing else to say.

"All my life," Bitty said, "I've thought of duty before happiness. I never dreamed I could actually fall in love and be so"—she shuddered—"so *blissfully* happy. But I was, you know?"

"I know."

"We got along just *so well.* We agreed on everything. Everything except whether there should be strawberry milk." She gave a feeble laugh. "He only hated it because it was pink and he wouldn't have wanted anyone to think he was a sissy."

"I don't think anyone would ever take Blake for a sissy."

"Right?" Bitty looked at her with eyes so red and bleary, it burned just to look at them. "That was another thing I loved about him.

He's so protective of me, and I always feel—I always *felt*—so safe with him. I never realized how much I prized masculinity until I was in his arms." She started crying again, shuddering sobs that racked her thin body. "And now I'll never be in those arms again. It's all just over."

"Did he *say* that?"

Bitty splayed her arms. "Do you see him? He's burning down 95 as we speak, headed to Bumfuck, Georgia, to some dinky town where he'll undoubtedly get back with his high school girlfriend and they'll get married and live next door to his parents so they can babysit when he and she want to go out for bowling night dates, and he'll forget all about me."

Colleen gave her a squeeze. "You're really buying yourself pain here unnecessarily. You're making up stories that make this hurt even more than it has to."

"It couldn't hurt more."

"Bitty, he could be back."

"Here?" She shook her head. "He's not coming back here. He's leaving school in his senior year. By the time he got back, if he ever even tried, everyone he knows would be gone. He'll be older than everyone. It would be like Rip Van Winkle going back to elementary school."

"So you're making this impossible for him in your mind, even while that's the most hurtful thing you can do to yourself," Colleen pointed out. "Can you see that? I'm surprised you haven't decided he's going to have a car accident on the way down." The minute she said it, she regretted it. All she needed was to add that worry for Bitty.

But apparently, that wasn't on Bitty's list. Again she shook her head. "Oh, no. Nothing's going to happen to him. He's going to go to Georgia, and I'm never going to hear from him again, and I will wonder for the rest of my life what ever happened to him. He will always be the one."

"Come on." Colleen took her by the shoulders. "This is so melodramatic. He didn't go back in time, he just went back to his hometown. They have phones there. He can call you."

"No." She sniffed. "I told him not to."

"Why?"

"Because I know how these things go. If he left with some intention to come back for me someday and I sat around waiting for that, it would just prolong the agony. It still wouldn't work out. These things never do. So I'd get my hopes all built up, live the life of a nun or a sea widow while waiting for my man to come back, and then he wouldn't and I would be lost."

Colleen didn't point out that Bitty seemed pretty lost right now as it was. She couldn't understand why her friend wouldn't rather cling to some sort of hope, especially since chances were really good that Blake would be back sooner than anyone expected. Not that Colleen hoped for that, because it would mean his mother didn't make it, but realistically, that's how cancer went sometimes—it took over quickly and mercifully.

There would be no reason for Blake to stay down there, then. Especially if he still had Bitty to come back for. Colleen couldn't understand why she wasn't clinging to that driftwood of hope.

"I think he'll be back."

"But what if he doesn't?" Bitty demanded. "What if I wait and wait and he never comes back? Because, I have to say, the way he's leaving, the way he told me *on his way out of town,* it sure doesn't seem like my feelings are any sort of priority for him here." She dissolved into heaving sobs again. "I didn't s-see this c-coming. N-not at all!"

Colleen watched helplessly, rubbing her hand on Bitty's upper back and making soothing noises to no effect.

Finally, Bitty recovered herself. "I love that guy more than anything. And the fact that he can just leave—"

"But you know why he has to," Colleen said firmly. She'd had enough—she couldn't just watch Bitty have a nervous breakdown without acknowledging the other facts of the situation, the other people involved. "It's his mom, Bitty, he can't turn his back on her when she's dying. What would you think of him if he did? I know it sucks, but you must understand how—"

"Wait, wait, wait." Bitty held up a finger at Colleen and tilted her head. "How did you know that?"

Colleen's face drained of all warmth. She hadn't heard them fighting; she'd arrived at the tail end, when Blake was leaving. And Bitty hadn't told her all of this yet—she'd been crying too hard to calmly detail the whole conversation for Colleen.

Colleen knew because Kevin had told her. And Kevin knew because Blake had told him. And that meant everyone knew before Bitty did.

And that math problem was formulating and resolving in Bitty's mind right now.

Bitty's eyes narrowed as she realized that this night and what had happened was clearly not news to Colleen.

"You *knew!*"

"I didn't—"

"Don't *even* try to lie."

Colleen took a breath, frantically trying to find a way to justify the unjustifiable. "Okay, Kevin told me just the other day, and I didn't know what to say! I didn't hear it directly from Blake. What if Kevin had misunderstood or something? It would have been wrong of me to say something when I didn't know the facts."

Bitty took a step back. "No, no—I'll tell you what you say, you say, 'Hey, my supposed friend, your boyfriend's about to leave you, so start preparing yourself for that.' "

"How was I supposed to say that? I wasn't supposed to know at all! And I *didn't*! I didn't know *anything* for sure."

"No, but you *did*. And so you should have told me."

"Blake would have been so mad at Kevin, he specifically—"

"I don't give a damn about Kevin getting grief about telling his girlfriend. This is about *more* that that."

Bitty never swore.

"This isn't about us."

"My life falling apart and my best friend knowing it and not warning me *isn't* about that?"

"This is just a bump in the road, not your whole life falling apart! Think about it!"

"Easy for you to say!"

"It's *not* easy for me to say. I *hate* seeing you this upset, but you're making this all about you and your feelings when there are really big things going on that no one has control over."

"You did."

"How?"

"You could have warned me. Given me a heads-up so I could think about this, digest it. Maybe force the issue with Blake so we could have talked about it when his car engine wasn't running, waiting for him to just get in and leave me forever."

"I'm sure he waited because he couldn't bear to tell you."

"Or he was afraid. You were all afraid."

"It wasn't my place *or* Kevin's."

"And if I knew Kevin was doing some other girl, would it *not be my place* to warn you?"

Colleen's nerves tightened, and she was tempted to ask what Bitty meant—but she knew there was nothing there, that Bitty was only making a point. "It would be for *Kevin* to tell me," she said firmly. "If you told me something like that, there's always the risk that it was a misunderstanding and you would have gotten me all upset over nothing. And that's exactly how I felt in this case, Bitty. I didn't know the real facts. I didn't know he was leaving today. I didn't know anything for certain—it was up to Blake to tell you everything."

"All I know is that he's gone, and you knew he was going and watched me skip around on air, all la-di-da, having no idea. I realize you and Kevin have been together only a couple of months and you don't know what it's like to be so tight with someone, but Blake was my whole world and now he's gone. Hundreds and hundreds of miles away. *Gone.*"

"Bitty, stop, please—it's really serious that he has to go home for this, and I just didn't know how I was supposed to give you this news. No matter what, it wasn't mine to tell."

"You know how I feel about him."

"Yes! Which is exactly why it would have been so hard to break news to you that isn't even my news to break! And which is based on something else *also* serious that I know zero about. Don't lose sight of that, Bit—this is a really serious family crisis."

Bitty shook her head. "You should have told me. I will never, *ever* forgive you for this."

"Bitty—"

She held up a hand to say stop, but said nothing.

Colleen halted and melted a little. Bitty looked away and walked to one of the waiting cabs that always sat outside of Henley's diner.

CHAPTER EIGHTEEN

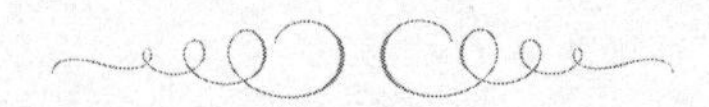

Tamara

THE PROBLEM WITH GETTING A TEXT FROM A CUTE BOY WAS THE number of minutes, hours, and—nauseatingly—days that went by where you heard nothing. She had even taken a picture of a statue she saw in one of the restroom stops they'd made in some anonymous town (characterized by a complete lack of character in the gray Jersey walls, skid-marked pavement, and weedy brush) that no one would ever think about, of a dog smoking a cigarette. She'd put her fake Ray-Bans on him and thought that it was a hilarious picture. But the picture had gone unanswered. Why had he asked to play that little game if he didn't even seem to care?

It had been days since their last interaction, which was making her feel irritable and moody. She hated being a fool over a boy, but there you go. All she had now was Vince texting her. Even he wasn't texting her that much. Just answered her. Their conversation the night before had gone as follows:

Hey V, how's stuff?

good, im at this big ass house rite now. the pool is fuckin awesome

Wish I was there, that sounds like fun

No answer, so she went on. . . .

My trip is kinda boring.

prolly shudnt of gone then

It bothered her beyond belief that he could act like it was her choice. He knew she was dragged kicking and screaming on the trip.

it's not like I had a choice!

whatever. when u back again?

Really? He didn't even remember?

Soon, like next week sometime.

No answer again. No enthusiasm at the prospect of her return. Just silence. Desperate for some kind of flirtation, she continued. . . .

You wont need that video anymore, you'll have the real thing ;)

Even texting that made her feel gross. She stared at her phone, waiting for the three little dots, the telltale sign that he was answering her. But no. Just the time stamp that said he had read it, but that he wasn't answering.

And he didn't answer. Not all night or anything.

Tamara wasn't even aware of Bitty and Colleen. They were all at a BBQ place, and all she could do was check her phone every two seconds. She wasn't even eating.

She was *that* girl.

Like, what could Vince even be doing? She *knew* his phone was always on him. She *knew* that. She knew he had seen it. She hadn't done *anything* to make him mad. What the hell was his problem?

She got on Facebook and typed in his name. Maybe that would explain something.

"Tam?"

She looked up. "What?"

Bitty gestured a little shyly at her plate. "I asked if you were going to eat your fries."

Colleen piped in. "Or your sandwich—you haven't even taken a bite!"

"I'm not really all that hungry. You can have the fries, Bitty."

"We aren't leaving until you eat half of that," Colleen said matter-of-factly.

"But—"

"Uh-uh. You heard me."

Tam groaned and took a big bite. She was hungry, she realized, but eating just didn't feel like something she could really handle right now.

She started as she saw a picture posted of Vince. Posted by Lauren Fellows. Lauren Fellows? Who was that?

She clicked on her profile picture. Oh no. No, he did *not*.

The redhead from the party. The one who Tamara figured probably *hated* the music and who was just so freaking cool with her crazy Paramore hair and her quirky interests, and use of the words "dude" and "chick."

That stupid red-haired bitch.

She went back to the picture. It was him, surrounded by thick smoke, on a balcony of some kind. Just looked like one of the crappy apartment complexes that littered Towson University, his favorite place to go get messed up. Tamara scanned the picture for any signs that might give her more of an idea of what he had been up to. Her eyes stopped when they landed on a foot with pink toenails. On his thigh. Barely making it into the frame.

Her head spun a little, and she pushed the sandwich away from her, suddenly feeling simultaneously weak and bursting with rage.

She got up from the table, saying something that hopefully sounded like, "I'll be back in a minute."

It was hot out, and that only made her flushing red cheeks feel more like they were burning. She crouched against the wall at the side of the building, phone still tight in her hand. She was tempted to throw it. Oh, how good would it feel to just hurl that stupid little rectangle down the alley, into the puddle that had formed in the middle from God knows what. But she didn't. Only because she knew the shit-fit her dad would throw if he found out she broke it. Make up an excuse or not, he would be livid and scream at her until she crawled even further into herself. If that were even possible.

So instead, she just leaned against the wall, piecing it all together.

He hadn't answered her. The second she'd left town, he hung out with that girl. That meant either he had got her number that night, while she had been right there, or he'd asked about her. How embarrassing for her to be the stupid fool of a girlfriend off on a road trip, while other people knew that Vince was asking around about some hot little thing from some stupid party?

What had it all been for? All the countless, endless nights and days she had hung around him, basically acting as a lapdog. She had sat and watched him play his stupid games for hours without complaint. When she wanted to go to the movies or something, she would pay, because she'd rather get him to go than not be able to go at all. She had admitted to having a boyfriend, never trying to move on or meet someone new, because she had promised to be with him.

But why? For how long? Until they got married? Until he knocked her up? Until someone else saved her?

Shamefully, she tried not to admit to herself that the last part was the right one. She wanted to be saved. She wanted someone to come along and tell her she deserved better. Someone who she could hang out with like normal people do, who would do cute little dumb surprises—even if it was as small as grabbing a bag of her favorite candy when he filled up his crappy old car. She wanted the Prince Charming on a white horse to come in, maybe even have a little showdown with Vince. How would it be to be desired and wanted so badly that someone would fight for you? She both could and couldn't imagine it. She could be out on some cute date with this imaginary guy, getting ice cream and walking around Old Ellicott City, with its stone walls and cobbled streets, and that one store that she had never been in, filled with glittery girlie things.

They'd go to the movies and on the way run into Vince, skateboarding with his stupid friends, and New Boyfriend would stop and give Vince a piece of his mind. Something that included sentiments like, "I don't know who you think you are," and "This is the greatest girl I've ever met, and you were lucky you got even a moment of her time."

But that guy didn't exist. She had never met anyone who even seemed to consider doing something like that. No. And why would they? Meeting Conor was a case in point. To them, she was just some burned-out—or at least burning-out—pothead loser with a record. She'd gotten caught with weed, big surprise, got probation because it wasn't that much, and then made the mistake of being the "mostly sober" driver home from a party. Without a license. Right in her neighborhood. It was dumb, yeah, but it was hard to get in too much trouble going twenty miles per hour on empty streets. She hadn't even been pulled over. Her mistake was in not noticing the bored cop sitting on the street corner, whose eye was caught by a car unloading a bunch of teenagers.

And now she was a jailbird.

At least she didn't have crazy piercings or wild hair. Wild, stupid, red hair. She did have the two tattoos, though. One was her favorite quote, YOU ONLY LIVE ONCE, BUT IF YOU DO IT RIGHT, ONCE IS ENOUGH. From Mae West. Supposedly. She had gotten it because it seemed to support and justify her desires to party and not give a damn about anything or anyone. But it was still true. Perhaps maybe her definition of "doing it right" was the part of herself she wanted to change.

Or the part of herself that she was desperately begging someone to help her change. Whatever.

And now, her crappy, unloving boyfriend—that, let's be honest, she didn't even *like*—had cheated on her. She knew it. Even if he hadn't hooked up with Lauren Fellows, which she just knew he had, he did lie to her. And he had ignored her. And that was cheating enough.

So if she was expecting some Romeo to come along, did she really expect him to act like that? She couldn't even hang on to *Vince*.

And the part that killed her the most—the part that had flown to her mind like a bullet to the head—was the fact that he had that video. He had that fucking video of her demonstrating her blow job technique and her stupidity all in one fell swoop.

She let her head fall into her crossed elbows, and gritted her teeth hard as the tears started to come. With Tamara's fury always came tears. An exasperating trait she wished she could be rid of. The number of times her dad had screamed at her or been harsh, and she had burst into weak tears was too many to count. And if you want to argue with a level head, gasping for breath in between sobs was not the way.

"Tamara? Tamara . . ." Colleen had rounded the corner and was walking quickly and officially toward her.

Tamara took a deep breath and tried to wipe away the tears with her shoulders as if it weren't obvious from her crouched position what was going on.

"It's nothing, not a big deal, I'm sorry—"

"Why are you saying sorry? And I'm sorry, but I'm calling b.s. on the fact that nothing is wrong. Tell me." She crouched down in front of her.

"No, I don't want to talk about it."

"You can tell me anything that's going on."

"I don't want to! Okay? Jesus Christ." Tamara stood, getting a surge in her chest at spending some of the anger that was building in her.

"Hey!" Colleen said, standing too.

"Just stop! I don't want to talk about it, and it doesn't have anything to do with you, so can we just fucking drop it and go?"

"Watch your language, Tamara."

Tamara laughed. "Right. Yeah, no, I'm gonna go ahead and say fuck that. Don't tell me what to do. You're not my mom, and you don't know what's going on, so just— Ugh!"

She stomped off toward the car. She knew she shouldn't be yelling and acting like this. But it was all she knew how to do. Close into herself and keep a repellent force field around that blasted people back when they tried to edge in.

They rode in silence for the most part. Bitty and Colleen tossed a few words back and forth, but Bitty seemed to have as much on her mind as Tamara did, and Colleen just seemed kind of over it all.

Whatever. Tamara didn't really blame her for that. She also didn't have it in her to do anything about it.

She couldn't decide what to do. Text Vince, ripping him a new one; write to redhead and rip *her* a new one; or—she was still kind of considering it—throw the phone out the window. Instead, she was finding that she was just sitting angrily in the backseat, torn between crying and screaming.

The worst part was that she couldn't freak out. If she made him mad, he might do something with that video.

Her phone buzzed. Her heart leapt, and she wasn't sure why. What exactly was she hoping to hear, and from who?

CONOR, TEXT MESSAGE (1)

She took a deep breath before opening it. Finally, something. Something to take her mind off Vince and all the humiliation.

Hey . . . sorry I haven't answered your picture. It was pretty funny, ha. But I just didn't really know what to say.

Oh. Well I mean I only sent it cuz you told me to take a picture of five different cool things, so . . . idk that's what I was doing I guess.

She watched him type via the little ellipsis that showed up during messaging. Then he stopped typing, and her heart sank, before he started up again. Then finally the text appeared.

It's just, I don't know, I saw this thing . . . you did? And I'm not sure if like you know about it or what, so I haven't known what to say, and it's not like I know you like that.

Her stomach fell with a gush into her shoes.

What are you talking about . . .

Her fingers were trembling. Her eyes were blurring. Her heart was pounding. No. No no no no . . .

Then he sent a link. There was no telling what the link was from the jumble of letters he sent. No real words, just a shortened URL.

She glanced up at the front, and then plugged her headphones into her phone before clicking the link.

With a shudder, a video popped up. With a little tag that read MY DIRTY XGF on the bottom right, her video started to play.

Her eyelashes, slightly furrowing brow, the freckle on her right cheekbone, and her . . . doing what she did to Vince. Doing what she already couldn't have imagined doing again. It played in front of her eyes like a slow-moving car crash.

The view of the top of her head, then some of her face, then her realizing the video was on. Her weak, "Hey—?" as her eyes widened with fear and her lashes sank with sadness and embarrassment as he said, "Babe. It's okay. It's just for me. I'm not going to show anyone. Now, finish."

And the look in her eyes as her gaze dropped from the camera and Vince's face down to nothing, and then as they shut and she did as she was told.

She watched the video, feeling sick, from start to end.

When it finally stopped, she saw 71 COMMENTS. . . .

That would be too much. She closed the window and looked through tears at the text from Conor.

She started to say a million things, but then gave up and shut the phone off. She covered her eyes and cried, making 100 percent sure that no one would hear her.

THEY GOT INTO their hotel room, got settled, and then Colleen suggested they all go to dinner.

"There's this Cajun-sounding place called Harry's downstairs and around the corner—it looks good."

"I'm actually not all that hungry," said Tamara.

"You aren't skipping another meal."

"No, just . . . Do you think you could bring me back something? I'll be hungry later, and I kind of want to be alone."

It was like feeling sick and knowing you had to wait to throw up until you got to the bathroom. She was filled with unspent tears and probably a good scream, but she had to wait to be alone to spend it all.

And, to be honest, puking was not completely out of the question.

Colleen made a face. "I don't know—"

"Look, no offense, but I could do with being alone for a little bit. It's been pretty close quarters."

Tam knew Colleen couldn't argue that. She seemed to be torn before finally saying, "All right, but don't go anywhere, please. And keep your phone charged and on you."

Tamara raised her eyebrows in agreement. She was suddenly melancholy for the carefree moments with Colleen, where she wasn't being a snotty teenager. Or, whatever, carefree moments in general. Any moment before she had porn on the Internet that even people like Conor had seen. If it had been sent to him, that meant everyone had seen it. It's not even like she had friends, really, but anyone who knew her had seen her at her most vulnerable.

The door shut, leaving Tamara alone with her everything. She didn't even get a breath in before her chest started to convulse with sobs. She cried her heart out for a good minute, and then the tears started to subside. She was almost disappointed. She felt like there was more in her that she wanted to get out but she couldn't.

She sniffed and walked over to the mirror to right herself. God, she looked ill. Better, honestly, than when she had left. But she had once been quite pretty. Now her skin was verging on yellow without a hint of pink in her cheeks, and the bags under her eyes were gray and blue and sunken. She was probably looking at herself in extremes and seeing things worse than they were—but maybe not. Maybe she was just seeing herself accurately. Complete with damaged, overprocessed hair, it was safe to say she was the worst physical version of herself that she had ever been. She was an "after" picture in a "What Drugs and Drinking Could Do to You!" article.

The silence in the room was suddenly too much. She turned away from her reflection, yanked open the door, and left.

She pounded down the cement steps of the motel—it was nicer than it had sounded, but still had that wraparound porch-type look—and walked out into the streets of whatever downtown she was in.

She kind of liked not knowing. That way she didn't have to say, *I remember that time in ________ when I was the saddest I ever was.* At least this way she could say, *I don't know where I was, but I know I hated myself.*

Tam be easy
Tam sucks dick
Tam gets filmed
Now just click

God, she was melodramatic.

She walked around for twenty minutes before realizing she

had forgotten her cigarettes. She stopped at the next group of approachable-looking people who were smoking. Luckily, since it was a nice warm night and it seemed like a pretty walkable southern downtown, there were a lot of people doing that.

She had another crazy imaginary flash in her mind. Of being in a place like this with friends. Just, like, two girls or something, sitting outside of . . . say, that burger place over there. Drinking sodas and chatting. Maybe a couple of shopping bags at their flip-flopped feet. Maybe going to a movie later on. Or maybe having a sleepover. Something. Not aimless basement-sitting.

She fluffed her hair a little and walked up to a relatively cute dark-haired guy. He was leaning over, his elbows on his knees, laughing at something another guy said.

"Um, excuse me . . . could I bum a jack?"

The guy looked up, and then sat up. "I didn't hear the magic word." He cupped his ear at her, smiling. He was teasing her.

She smiled back. "Please? . . ."

"That's better." He rested his cigarette between his lips and pulled out a cigarette from his pack. They were Camels. She never smoked those.

She held out her hand. "Thanks."

"Now, hold on, Grabby," he said, the cigarette still in his mouth. "Now, I'm thinking for this, I deserve to know your name, and for you to have a seat with my friends and me here. Jake, move."

Jake—one of the friends who had been watching the exchange with amusement—scooted his chair over. The main guy, who had called Tam "Grabby" reached behind him for a green plastic chair and set it next to him. He patted the seat.

Tamara looked up. It seemed to be a bar. This was confirmed when she saw everyone was drinking. Of course.

She took the seat, and then the cigarette.

"I'm Rich."

"Well, then, I'm interested." She immediately regretted the joke. It was probably over his head, and now he thought she meant something she didn't mean.

He raised his eyebrows and inhaled. He leaned back and surveyed her with a seemingly expanding opinion on her. "Funny girl, huh?"

Rich smiled at her, and it was such a boyish and endearing smile that she grinned back. He lit her cigarette and looked back to the other guys. They had all started talking to each other again. Clearly, if the girl was to be claimed, she already had been.

"So, your name is—?"

"Tamara. Tam."

"Which one?"

"Tam . . ."

"All right—cool, Tam. You visiting or do you live around here?"

"Just passing through."

"Where're you going?"

"Florida somewhere. I don't even really know. I'm with my aunt and her friend."

"Aunt and her 'friend' or, like, aunt and her friend?"

"What—? Oh God no, they're not, like, undercover lesbians." The very thought made her laugh again. "No, just her actual, like . . . *friend* friend. My aunt refinishes furniture and is going to farm auctions and stuff."

"Cool cool. And you got dragged along."

"Yep . . ."

"So, then, uh . . . you're probably pretty bored, huh?"

"Yeah. Had a kinda shitty night. Whatever."

"I can tell. You already burned through that cigarette."

She looked down. It was almost to the filter. "Oh . . . yeah. I guess it kinda shows, huh?"

He lit up another one and handed it to her. "Do you like to party?"

"Um . . . yeah, sure." Was she agreeing to go somewhere with these guys?

"Well, if you wanna tag along on something actually *fun,* we are going to a house party, like, right around the corner from here."

She knew she looked nervous and hesitant. "Um . . ."

"It's walking distance. You don't have to get in our big white van, little girl."

That boyish smile again. It made her trust him.

"Okay, sure, I guess . . . I guess why not, then?"

She knew why not: Because she didn't know these guys. Because her phone had, like, only 25 percent left of its battery, and because she had said she'd stay in the room.

"First, let's do a couple shots. Hey, Tom." He got the attention of a waiter in jeans and a T-shirt bearing the bar's name.

"What do y'all need?"

"Lemme get four shots of Fireball."

She counted. There were five of them, including his friends and her. Oh, she thought, maybe he wasn't including her. She felt suddenly embarrassed for temporarily thinking he would. Also, she supposed that meant that he *was* twenty-one. And maybe he knew she wasn't.

But when the shots came, he took all four in his hands and handed her two.

"Two?"

"Yeah, boo, you gotta catch up."

She smiled, somehow taking all this as a compliment, and took one of the shots. Then the second.

Then he handed her his second one: "Like I said, you gotta catch up."

She took it. Like a champ. Her head started to spin after only a few minutes. On the walk there, it occurred to her that she really should have eaten that sandwich earlier.

CHAPTER NINETEEN

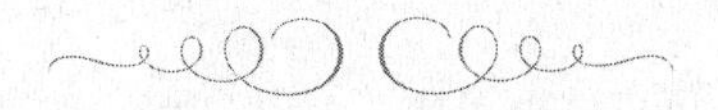

Colleen

THE SECOND THE DOOR SHUT BEHIND THEM AND THEY TOOK OFF down the steps and onto the road, Colleen realized that this was the first time she and Bitty had been alone together since college. The thought of time passing so much and so quickly sent shivers down her spine.

Next to Harry's, Colleen spotted a martini and wine bar.

"Would you want to maybe grab a drink before dinner?"

"Absolutely," Bitty answered before Colleen had even finished asking. It had been a long day, and they both needed to relax.

They sat at the bar, and each ordered a perfectly respectable glass of white wine. Chardonnay for Colleen and a sauvignon blanc—preferably one from New Zealand, if they have it, she asked nicely—for Bitty.

"Probably best to fit the alcohol in while we're out of sight of the truant, huh?" Colleen said with a slightly nervous tinkle of laughter. "Don't want to set a bad example."

Bitty bit her lip and then put her hand up to flag down the bartender. Colleen watched, wondering if Bitty was going to change wines. It was eight dollars a glass, an extravagance to Colleen, so she'd drink it regardless of whether it was perfect or not.

"Two double SoCo and Lime please," Bitty said to him.

Colleen's eyebrows shot up, along with the corners of her lips. "Ha! Really?"

Bitty took in a deep breath. "You only live once, right? So far, anyway."

"Whoo. Our old go-to shot. Doubles, even."

The bartender, who clearly didn't get a lot of shot requests in this sleepy tourist town, took the Southern Comfort off the shelf, put two rocks glasses in front of them. Each was filled with a very decent amount of brown liquid and garnished with a lime. Colleen's tongue prickled with the remembered sting she was already anticipating.

"Bottoms up," said Bitty, holding hers up to cheers with Colleen.

And the next thing that happened, Colleen wouldn't have seen coming in a million years. Old habit kicked in, and they did their old tradition without saying a word.

Put lime in the left hand.

Cheers glasses.

Tap bottom twice on bar.

Hook arms.

Take the shot.

Suck the lime.

They both locked eyes, brows furrowed from the burn, and started to laugh like kids.

"I guess that confirms that we did too many shots in our youth," said Bitty, now dabbing her lips daintily with a bar napkin.

"You say 'in our youth' like we're *that* old."

"We're not in our youth anymore—that much is for sure. We're damn close to middle age, if we're not already there. You want to tell me you look at Tamara and say that *that* age doesn't feel like a million years ago?"

Colleen watched Bitty as she spoke, her cheeks starting to get a tinge of pink from the alcohol. Now that she was alone with her and looking directly at Bitty, she felt like she could really see her. When they'd first spoken again at Henley's, she thought Bitty looked old. Not *old* old, but aged. But now as she saw her up close, she realized she didn't really look that way. The most noticeable signs of her age were by her eyes, and they didn't even look bad. They weren't actually wrinkles so much as faint lines. It was the way she set her face that made her look older.

Once upon a time, Bitty had had alert, almond-shaped eyes, cheekbones that didn't stick out like a skeleton's, but rather tightened in constant amusement. She might have been an occasional prude and hard to get out of her shell every once in a while, but Bitty was bright and sweet, and undeniably pretty.

Now her face was generally set in a bit of a frown, her cheekbones were skeletal, her nose a little too thin, and her eyes looked worried and sad-dog. That was what had given her the look of more years passing. Not real aging.

That said, the fact that she'd been actually eating and drinking this past week instead of dieting psychotically, *had* plumped her out ever so slightly. When they first met up, there had been a skeletal quality to Bitty's face that was now noticeably softened.

"I agree that seventeen years ago was seventeen years go," said Colleen, shaking herself from staring at Bitty. "But we've probably got a good second half of our lives left in us yet. Hopefully longer."

Bitty seemed to give a quick laugh—it was hard to tell—before taking a generous sip of her wine.

"Bitty, what is going on with you?" The SoCo had already given her the voice that had gotten her in trouble more than once.

"What do you mean?"

"You know what I mean. Something is up. I can tell." When Bitty took a long few seconds of silence, she added, "Is there more to the situation with Lew than you said?"

Bitty shot her a look. "If you're lucky, right?"

"What?"

"I know you never liked Lew, so you must be dying to say 'I told you so.' "

"I'm not— This has nothing to do with any feelings I might have had about Lew a thousand years ago—"

"So you admit it was a lifetime ago."

"Oh, Bitty, knock it off. It's really clear that you are stressed beyond your limit, yet when you talked about it the other night, you sounded so calm, so reasoned, like your husband going off with another woman was just *one of those things.*"

"Yeah, well."

Silence. "*Well* what, Bit?"

Her arms were crossed, and her face was expressionless. The way she tended to look when she was both embarrassed and terrified to discuss something.

"I'm curious. What exactly was it that you didn't like about Lew back then?"

"What does that matter? It was college—I also thought chasing Rumple Minze with Corona was a good idea. I didn't know shit from apple butter."

The southern saying slipped from her lips before she could stop it.

"Just tell me what you remember. What was it?"

"I told you then. . . . I thought he was a dick, frankly. He was possessive and controlling, and once you were with him, you spent ninety percent of the time apologizing for your actions or rationalizing his anger at you. You hate controversy and confrontation, and here you were faced with a guy who antagonized the living hell out of you, and rather than confront him or cause an issue, you always just put up with his crap because it—to you—seemed easier than arguing your point."

"I needed that, though. I needed discipline, I liked a little of being told what to do. I used to do that with everyone, just let them walk all over me. He wouldn't let me do that—he helped me grow a little."

"Oh, sure, okay, but one of the things he hated so much was when you went out and had fun with me. I was the enemy to him, and eventually you just got so sucked up in him that you dropped me."

"I needed to grow up, Colleen, I couldn't go out taking shots and—"

"You were on the President's List, never missed a class, and went out only sometimes with us! You had every right to do that—you were twenty-one and in college!"

"Yes, I was, and was about to graduate and become an adult. I needed what he gave me. I can't regret that now, or my entire life will have been a waste."

Colleen took a swig of her chardonnay. "That's not true. If anything, it proves how much better off you are without him. Do you want to feel like your life with him was 'worth it,' or is it better to feel like your life without him is going to be *a million times better*? You hung around and put up with his crap, I don't even know how much you blocked out on a daily basis, but he said unforgivable things to you. He just wanted to whip you into shape to become his perfect little Stepford wife, and you were more than willing to comply, for whatever reason."

Bitty narrowed her eyes and bit the inside of her cheek. "Duty. Always duty."

Colleen fought an internal battle of whether or not to say what she wanted to say next. "Fuck duty! How could that even have appealed to you after what you'd been through? You had already been in love. *Truly* in love."

"What, with Blake?"

"Yes, with Blake!"

"That was young, stupid love." She clenched her jaw, a muscle ticcing. "It was meaningless."

"I'm calling absolute bullshit on that."

"How? That's exactly what it was."

"No, it wasn't. Let me paint you a little picture here: When you were with Blake, you smiled and laughed all the time. You didn't let any of your responsibilities fall by the wayside, but you didn't stress over every little thing. When you got together with Lew, you were quick to anger, tired, and constantly living on the defense and walking on eggshells. I don't know how you can think that a person making you happy ninety-five percent of the time versus five percent of the time can possibly be called meaningless. If I could have chosen a person for you to be around, it would have been him every time!"

"Yes, well, Blake didn't exactly leave either of us with that option, did he? And how can we act like Blake cared more or was better for me?"

Colleen bit back the next comment. That Blake had loved her, and that Lew had looked at her like a convenience, and that it had been painfully obvious even back then. Good timing. Pretty little wife. Somewhere inside, Bitty knew it—she'd always known it—but for some reason, she wasn't allowing herself to see it even now.

Colleen took a deep breath and said, "I remember perfectly what you told me about each time they said they loved you."

Bitty didn't look at her, but tilted her head toward Colleen in attention. "I don't remember."

"You said—"

"Two more," said Bitty as the bartender passed.

Colleen caught the look of surprise on the bartender's face. He came back with two more.

"Okay, go on," said Bitty, taking a sip from the glass without the college performance this time.

"What you told me about Blake, was that you had been sitting on the back of his pickup truck, eating tacos from that gas station."

A small smile tugged at Bitty's mouth, and Colleen saw again how still-young and bright she could look. "Those tacos were so flipping good. It was so weird."

"Yeah, I remember everyone talked about them, and I didn't

believe you until you said they were good. And then I tried them. And they really weren't that great."

"You're crazy! They were incredible."

"Well, anyway . . . you told me you had just been laughing over something, and then he put an arm around you and pulled you in. You were sipping on your drink, and he said—"

"He said, 'I love you so fuckin' much, you know that?' " Bitty rolled her eyes, her cheeks lifted with a smile she didn't want to convey.

"Yep." Colleen let her live in the moment a little, before going on. "And when Lew said it to you, it was at the end of a long night of fighting, where you had tried to break up with him. And he had sat next to you on your couch and said—"

"Lew said, 'I'm not sure if you want me to say this or not, but I'm in love with you.' "

Colleen nodded again. "Look, I'm not saying your choice was always between the two of them. But at the time, I was angry on your behalf. I felt like you were scared of losing someone that mattered so much to you again, so you went with the next person you could. He was rich, did the right things, like taking you to dinner and buying you presents, and he told you he cared. He took the right steps, and you knew you'd end up where you wanted to be. I can't blame you for your choice, but that was why I was so mad. That's why I screamed at you and said how much I hated him for you. That's why I was a bitch to him."

Also he had been a jealous freak, who was angry all the time, and got pissy like an unlikable-girlfriend character on a sitcom.

"Yeah. I get that. I always . . . I mean I always got it. But it's what I did. I wanted it to work out with him, and you weren't happy being a part of that particular picture, so . . ."

They both knew "so" what. So they had stopped being friends. Not been part of each other's lives anymore.

"I'm sorry if you think I feel righteous or something about this. I don't. I wanted to be wrong about him. I want you happy, I always did. But you compromised your real happiness for what you thought you *should* want, and the reason I'm bringing *any* of this up is because I'm afraid of you still doing that."

"Yes, well, turns out you were right. You told me so."

"I don't want that. But the thing is . . ."

"What?"

"I'm worried about the power he still has over you. The power to grant you mercy or not. You know?"

"He has no power over me." Clearly, Bitty still didn't want to bring up the news article or anything it had said. Colleen wanted to push her, but didn't want to push too far and end their good moment. Or, if not *good* moment, at least real moment. The first real moment they had had in years. One Colleen wished they could have had seventeen years ago, saving themselves the nearly two decades without a best friend.

Colleen's phone rang on the bar, and they both glanced to see that it was Kevin.

She had a moment of guilt that her husband was calling just as Bitty was admitting how much things had sucked for her.

"I'll be right back."

Bitty waved a hand to say *no rush,* and picked up her wineglass by the stem.

"Hi," Colleen said, her voice ever so slightly strained as she stepped out onto the sidewalk alongside the route AIA. "How's it going? Everything's okay?"

Kevin gave a short laugh. "You need medication, worrywart. Everything's fine. Just calling to let you know Jay and I are heading back day after tomorrow because we want to stay an extra day."

"Having a great time, huh?" she asked, feeling both pleased that her family was having fun and miffed that they were having fun without her. And a little exhausted from how tense the last few days had been on her trip. Had a *family* vacation ever been extended? She couldn't remember that ever happening.

"Really great," Kevin said. "And I have actually been able to get some work done while he's hanging out with the other kids in the evening, so no time has been wasted."

"Good, I'm glad. What are your plans for tonight?"

"The kids are all going to do the whole hang-out thing, and the rest of the parents and I are going to be hanging downstairs at the bar. Some band is playing that's supposed to be pretty good."

Great. Sounded like he was spending a lot of quality vacation time with all the other dads—and mom—drinking Dogfish Head 60 Minute from the tap while she drove around a moody teenager and a moody non-teenager.

"That sounds like fun. Hey, have you heard anything from Chris?"

"Nope. Why, is something wrong?"

"No," she said, knowing Tamara's bad attitude didn't merit complaint, since it was what they had all expected anyway, "but isn't he curious how things are going for his daughter?"

Kevin snorted. "You know Chris—out of sight, out of mind. He probably doesn't even remember he *has* a daughter. We'll have to reintroduce them."

She pictured Tam's face. Tam laughing. She'd been so tentative at first, but she was opening up now. And that was just in a few days! How did her father not feel that a hundred times more? "That's horrible."

"That's Chris."

Okay, yes, she knew Tamara had been difficult for Chris. The idea of being a bachelor and suddenly taking in the daughter you'd had very little contact with, beyond sending a monthly check in her direction, was also a difficult one to imagine—Tamara's mother had effectively separated the two since the girl was born, and Chris was never moved to do anything about it. In its own weird way, that made them pretty compatible. But when she died and he'd found out he had to take Tam in, there was really no choice, except the one to man up and be a good father or to accept your responsibility in a minimal way and try to change your lifestyle as little as possible. Chris had chosen the latter.

Great guy.

"Gotta go," Kevin was saying. "Just wanted to let you know about the change of plans. Will you call the kennel so they keep Zuzu an extra day?"

Why can't you? she wanted to ask, but she knew why not. She'd long since created a dynamic where she handled everything and all but pushed his hand away from any task he tried to initiate and said, *I'll do it.*

So he expected her to do it because she did *everything.*

She fixed things. Antiques, relationships, name it.

"Sure," she said, as usual. In the background, she heard a spike of a woman's laughter, and the manly chorus of laughter that followed. At least it had sounded like a woman. Was she just overreacting and imagining things now?

"Thanks, babe. Have fun!"

It was only after she hung up that she realized he hadn't really asked much about how it was going for her. But he wasn't a phone guy, never had been, so she couldn't allow herself to take that personally.

Could she?

She went back inside and sat on her barstool.

"So how's the perfect husband?" Bitty asked with the tiniest edge to her voice. She had a smile on her face like it was a joke, but Colleen knew her well enough to know the dig wasn't 100 percent in jest.

"I never said he was the perfect husband."

"Okay . . ."

They were both quiet for a minute, until Colleen dropped the bar napkin she had been twisting in her fingers without noticing, and said, "Look, I'm sorry things are rough or whatever they are with Lew. Believe me, I deal with my own struggles too. Things didn't just work out blissfully for me either."

"Okay," said Bitty, shaking her head with a laugh.

"What?"

"I mean, isn't that a little silly? Like a supermodel insisting to a handicapped person that life sucks for them sometimes too? Yeah, it's probably true, but I'm pretty sure I win. Or lose. However you want to look at it."

Colleen felt the indignation rise in her throat. Just like Bitty, she wasn't ready to lay everything all out on the table, but it pissed her off that Bitty felt like her situation could beat anything Colleen was going through.

Which was what, exactly? This stupid problem she hasn't been able to get past in her seventeen years of being with Kevin? That question that had always nagged at her?

"I'm not going to get all into it or fight about whose life sucks more, but I will say that we all have the monsters we battle in life."

Bitty looked at her dubiously. "Are *you* fighting a monster?"

"I'm about to." A shiver of nerves rocked through her core as she thought the thoughts she had avoided even admitting to herself this whole time. The reason she was here. The reason she had decided that now was the time. The reason she had hopped in her car and ended up in Florida, and the reason she thusly ended up spending the last two weeks with her messed-up niece and former best friend.

The reason she hadn't said aloud yet. And yet now time was winding down. She was about to fight her battle. About to come face-to-face with the thing that had held her down for the last seventeen years.

Sometimes, when you're close with someone, or even if you used to be, they can read your thoughts.

Bitty's almond eyes were wide as she looked at Colleen, who was staring at the debris from her shredded napkin. "I have a question."

Colleen braced herself. "Hit me with it."

"What did you mean earlier, about Lew having the power to grant me mercy?"

"Oh." Here it was. Everything on the table. "I saw the article."

Bitty looked genuinely confused. "What article?"

"The one in the newspaper about your disappearance. By some coincidence, the paper was at the rest stop and I just happened to see your picture." Bitty looked blank. This was so awkward. "I'm sorry, I probably should have said something, but I didn't know what it was all about, so I thought I should just feel you out."

"I don't know what you're talking about. What newspaper? What article?"

"Are you serious?"

Bitty sighed and tilted her head. "Does this seem like a good time to joke?"

"Then you don't know that you're regarded as missing in Winnington?"

Bitty gave half a shrug. "Missing in the sense that I didn't report to my soon-to-be ex where I was going, but how is that newsworthy?"

"Oh boy."

"What?"

"Honey"—Colleen signaled the bartender—"you're gonna need another drink."

CHAPTER TWENTY

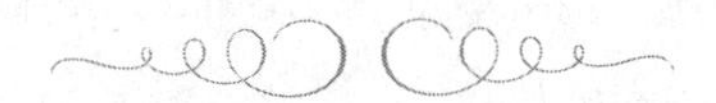

Tamara

THE HOUSE SHE WENT TO WITH—WHAT WAS HIS NAME? RICH?— and his friends was pretty cool. It was a duplex that was kind of trashy and worn down, but in that beachy way that doesn't make it all that gross. It was surrounded by big lush tropical plants, and inside was like the inside of a stoner-surfer guy's slightly altered brain. Outside, surfboards that were obviously often put to actual use were kept near a rack of kayaks. Inside, the walls were plastered with pictures of hot girls, beach scenes, and surfing. On every surface was beer, a bong, other paraphernalia, or Sex Wax. Slung over the couch were Volcom sweatshirts. She would go on to find Hurley bathing suits slung over the shower curtain rods, and not one but two *Endless Summer* posters hung in the bedrooms.

She floated around a little at the party before finding a comfortable piece of couch to sit on. It was one thing to be at a party and know only the small group you came in with, but an entirely other thing to be at a party in a city—where was she again?—you've never been to, where the only people you know are the people you actually *don't* even know.

Looking around the party, she realized how similar it was to the ones back home. It was almost exactly the same, but seemed like a theme party. An "Everyone Dress Up Like Floridians" party or something. But the people were all the same. The girls were still squealy and annoying. The guys were half-douchey, half-hot. And she felt alone in a crowded room. Not really that much different.

Except these people didn't know she had a blow job video online.

With an awful icy clutch of her heart, she realized that they could very well find that out. Anyone there could stumble across it. Maybe even recognize and remember her. *Hey, isn't this that chick who came to our party once?*

That could happen at any point. She could buy bubble gum at a gas station, and the age-spotted old man could recognize her from it.

She resisted the urge to cry.

"Hey—hey, what was your name?"

Glancing up, she realized Rich was talking to her. "Tamara?"

Why had she phrased it like a question? Was she unsure who she was? *Wow . . . way to overthink things,* she thought to herself.

"Tamara, right, do you wanna do a dab?"

"A what?"

He laughed, and so did other people. Why?

"Do you smoke? Weed?"

"Yes . . ."

"And you've never heard—? All right, look, if you smoke, it's the same shit. It's out of a bong and everything. You'll be fine."

More people were looking at her than would have she wanted. "Is it pot?"

"It's hash, yeah."

"Um . . . okay."

She followed him out to a patio and glanced at her phone. It had been about an hour. But she'd just smoke and go back. She'd be fine.

Everyone seemed to know each other pretty well here, she noticed. That made her feel even more out of place. Especially when she thought about how it's not like she felt more *in* place back home.

Whatever.

She watched as Rich's friend used a butane lighter to do something to whatever was in the spot where weed usually went on the bong.

She was really going into this with a lot of knowledge, clearly.

Rich hit it before she did, then handed it over to her.

"Just like normal?" she asked.

He coughed and nodded at her, handing her the lighter.

At first it felt like normal. Made her cough. Pulled her away from reality just enough without being scary. But then it was too different. She was in a side room with Rich and his friend. It didn't feel sinister. They were watching something. Some YouTube clips on the TV and laughing. She was sitting up on a bed. There was a puppy on the bed in front of her.

She scratched the puppy's ears. "Who's this?" she said, her voice sounding startlingly normal. It was disturbing that she could sound like everything was fine, when she felt so not normal.

Rich and his friend exchanged a look. "That's Roxy."

"Oh . . . why's that funny?"

"Because you just asked that." Rich laughed but gave her a good-natured smile.

"Shit," she muttered, looking at the puppy. Maybe Roxy did sound familiar. Or was that because she had just heard that a second ago? She shook her head, trying to right herself.

She looked at her phone. It was 10:33. She felt like it was 3 A.M. But hadn't it been only nine fifteen last time she looked at the time? It had been, because she was supposed to go home. Or, not home, but back to Colleen and Bitty.

Bitty Bitty Bitty. Colleen. Clean.

Their names sounded like they were from a different life. One she didn't live in anymore. But in reality, it hadn't been long since she was last with them.

And in reality, she really would rather be with them. She wanted to be with Colleen, to have that Mom-ish presence around her that she'd never really had. She wished she were in a hotel room with them, watching something dumb on TV, eating vending machine snacks, and not feeling this sour nausea in the pit of her stomach.

She wanted Colleen to come pick her up, like she was just a kid in school, going home to the safety of family.

Which was stupid, because Colleen was only the babysitter. And here Tam was being the dumb kid who accidentally called the babysitter "Mom."

She stood up. No, no, standing was not happening.

"You leavin'?" asked Rich.

Why, did he want her to leave? Was she unwanted *everywhere*? *Stop overthinking!*

"Uh . . . no, I need just a min—just a minute."

She crawled back onto the bed, and lay almost facedown. She heard them laugh at her, but couldn't do anything to stop it. She was desperate for revival. Would a minute or two give her strength again?

Her heart was jumping out of her chest, but also felt like it was slowing down. She lay there, wishing she hadn't done this. Wishing it was tomorrow, when this would be over.

More time passed. She didn't know how much. She heard their conversation but immediately didn't retain it. Couldn't respond.

No, her heart definitely felt like it was slowing down. Like to a scary level. It felt like work to keep breathing. Could that happen? It was supposed to be involuntary to just keep breathing, whether she chose to or not, right?

But it felt so much like work. If she stopped breathing, she was sure she would just die. Her heart would just slow down. All she had to do was let go. She felt sure of that. This was what dying felt like. This. She was separate from her life. Close to death, something that terrified her. She had no idea what was ahead of her if she chose to let go. This, though, this was what it felt like to know you were about to die.

She took in a deep breath and felt better briefly until everything slowed down again. If she could just let go and be dead, if her involuntary reflexes were somehow rendered useless by whatever she had smoked, did she want to hang on? Or did she want to let go?

What was the point? *What* was the point of going on? She had nothing. No one. All she had was a school full of people who had by now certainly seen her video.

Suddenly she became aware that Rich and his friend were just messing around. The laser they'd had earlier—when was that? She hadn't remembered it until now—they were using it to have the puppy crawl over her. She could hear them pointing it at her butt and in that region. She couldn't stop them. She was too lethargic. Too brink-of-death. Too high.

She just had to put up with it. Like she did with everything.

Finally they lost interest and left the room. Tamara looked at her phone—10:42. What? It had only been nine minutes?

Impossible.

She curled her arms up under her and tried to fall asleep.

IT WAS SOMETIME later that she felt someone crawl into bed with her. At first she panicked and started to squirm. What was about to happen to her? Did she have it in her to fight someone off right now?

But whoever it was just pulled her in and seemed to go to sleep. She wanted to cry. She felt used and worthless. But she could do nothing.

So she went to sleep.

SOMETIME LATER—MINUTES? hours?—she awoke still feeling loopy but far more normal than she had been. She must have slept in one position for hours, because her right arm was tingling and her jeans were binding into her right hip. Fortunately, no one was in or around the bed with her. Not that she expected evidence of some unremembered event—she remembered the night, if in a somewhat surreal, detached way—but she didn't know if anyone had come or gone while she slept.

As she looked around, she decided that the memories of that hour and her flip-flops could be the property of this house now. All she wanted was to get the hell out.

She had expected sleeping bodies and dark rooms to tiptoe

through, but it turned out the party was still going. Her phone was dead, so she had no way of knowing what time it was. Maybe it had only been another nine minutes.

No one seemed to notice or care much that she was leaving. Rich, the only person she might have said a word to—and she wasn't sure which word—was nowhere to be found.

It had grown a little chillier outside, and the rocks were cold under her feet. She tightened her arms over her thin T-shirt. She walked for a few minutes. She had remembered passing the post office. And then that weird little store with the monkey statue. But how had she missed the enormous glowing building next to her? She stepped over to it. It was a school.

"No way," she said, looking into the courtyard beyond the wrought-iron gates.

She walked up the pathway, past a huge fountain with frogs spitting water, and walked up into the building. Enormous doors were propped open, welcoming her in.

Her bare feet flapped quietly on the marble floor, and she let go of her trembling arms. It was a big, huge, beautiful hall with steps that led up and to the left and to the right, just like in old houses in movies. She walked toward the stairs and stopped to read some of the flyers hanging by big dark wooden doors that were shut tight.

FRIDAY IS MEXICAN NIGHT IN THE DINING HALL! TACOS, FAJITAS, VIRGIN MARGARITAS Y MAS!

SUMMER CLASS STRESS GOT YOU DOWN? COOL OFF AT SATURDAY'S POOL PARTY! REFRESHMENTS PROVIDED.

GET THE JUMPSTART NOW! PICK OUT NEXT SEMESTER'S CLASSES IN YOUR CATALOG TODAY!

This world felt so foreign to her. A world where people only a couple years older than her could choose to go to a pool party, or go get Mexican food from the dining hall on a whim if they were hungry.

She kept walking and ended up on the second floor, which looked over the downstairs. No one was there, except for one girl reading a textbook and gnawing on a highlighter, and her presumed boyfriend who sat across from her, holding a novel with one hand and her ankle in his lap with the other.

"Hey, do you have your ID?" came a voice from behind her.

"Oh . . ." She was immediately defensive. What had she done? She was trespassing, probably.

"It's just, I'm locked out. I swear I go here." The girl laughed. She had a spunky blond ponytail, and a T-shirt that read FLAGLER COLLEGE VOLLEYBALL. "I think I left my wallet in my room, and my phone is dead." She held up a pink Droid phone and rolled her eyes to show that she knew how dopey she looked.

"No, I, um . . . I don't . . . I don't go here."

"Oh. *Oh.* Okay, well, sorry to bother you. Are you . . . Are you visiting a friend or something?"

"No, I was walking around and I just came inside. I'm probably not supposed to be in here."

"Whatever, it's the summer, who cares?" The girl sat down, pulling her yoga pant legs up to her chest. "Are you in high school?"

"Yeah, I'm a junior."

"Are you thinking about applying here?"

"Maybe . . ." Tamara looked around.

"It's pretty cool. It's small, but you know, that way you kind of make a lot of friends and everyone knows each other and stuff. I transferred from a bigger school. You ever have that feeling when you're surrounded by a ton of people that really you're just alone?"

"I know what you mean, yeah."

"Sorry, I'm all deep about everything right now." She laughed again. "I'm taking philosophy, which is *kinda* useless, but still fun. And my teacher?" She rolled her eyes back. "Drop-dead gorj."

Tamara laughed. "Probably makes philosophy feel a little more fun, then."

"Totes. That's fucked up, right? Oh well. Anyway, I'm going to go ask that hipster couple over there if they can scan me in. Otherwise, I'm mildly screwed. It was nice meeting you . . . ?"

"Tamara."

"Tamara. I'm Taylor. Good luck getting in—maybe I'll see ya around!"

"Thanks."

The girl bounced off, and Tamara saw that the back of her shirt said, GIRLS, UNDEFEATED, BOYS, 8–7.

The girl was let in by highlighter hipster girl, and waved goodbye to Tamara, who then left to walk back to the hotel. Once back on the outside of the wrought-iron gates, she cast one more look behind her before heading back.

For some reason, the visit had made her sadder than ever. That girl—Taylor—had believed Tamara went there, for at least a few seconds. But she was so far from that.

She was lost for fifteen minutes before finally spotting the street the hotel was on. She wiped away tears she hadn't known she had cried, and straightened up. She had to go back to Colleen and Bitty and just pray they weren't too mad.

CHAPTER TWENTY-ONE

Colleen

THE FIRST ORDER OF BUSINESS FOR BITTY AFTER LEARNING OF THE newspaper article was to call Lew. She and Colleen had discussed the possibilities—calling the police, calling the newspaper—and had finally decided that calling Lew directly was the best course of action. He'd started it; he could stop it.

"Tell them I'm not some unhinged scorned wife," Bitty hissed into the phone. "Tell them I'm not a dangerous, bereaved, abandoned wife on the run, or I swear I will tell them the truth. I swear it. You have left me with nothing left to lose. You don't know where I am, and neither do those Keystone Cops in Winnington, so I could slip in when you least expect it, and get you—do you understand?" She made the sound a gangster in a bad movie might make to indicate slitting a throat.

Colleen had to try not to laugh.

Obviously Lew was arguing back, but then Colleen saw a light come into Bitty's eye.

"I didn't want to have to do this," she said, then bit her lip for a moment, a gesture Colleen recognized as what she did when she wasn't sure where she was going. "Listen to me, Lew. Are you listening? Good. You know how you're always impatient for me because I don't know how to work this damn iPhone?" She waited while he obviously agreed she was an idiot. "Well, you're right. I can't. I didn't want to tell you this, but when I got home that day, I thought there was an intruder, so I turned the thing on so I could call the police if I needed to. But earlier I'd taken a picure of the prettiest little blue jay. Right outside our kitchen window. Well, I guess it's *your* kitchen window now. And— What? Okay, I'm getting to the point! When I turned on the phone, I accidentally hit the movie button. I recorded the whole scene I walked in on. You're not on-screen the whole time, but there is no doubt about what was going on. Gosh, I'd hate to smudge our name by showing that around, but it might go some distance to explaining this . . . *misunderstanding* . . . about me." She waited. "Lew?"

Colleen had to hand it to her. If this worked, it was brilliant.

"Ah," Bitty said, a smile crossing her face. "I had a feeling you'd understand. Make sure you correct this immediately. I mean *immediately*. I'll look for a retraction in tomorrow's paper online. Right? Good. Bye, now, Lew. Your lawyer will hear from mine."

"Feel good?" Colleen asked when she hung up.

"Pretty damn good."

They walked over to Harry's restaurant, ate some good old spicy Cajun food, got an order of fried chicken fingers for Tamara, and went back up to the hotel room.

Where Tamara wasn't.

"Good Lord, where *is* she?" Colleen asked, throwing down her purse, only to immediately pick it back up and retrieve her phone.

As Colleen dialed, Bitty looked in the bathroom and then out in the halls, and came back in shaking her head.

Colleen's phone rang, rang, then voice mail.

Rang, rang, then voice mail.

Rang—voice mail.

Voice mail.

Either it died or she had turned it off.

"This makes no sense."

"You know phones sometimes lose all reception in a tiny pocket of space. Maybe she's in a store or went to the pizza joint. Give it a minute."

"You're right," Colleen said, trying to believe it. "I'm sure everything's fine." But she wasn't. She wasn't sure at all, and what had she done? She'd gone out and done shots and had wine instead of staying on top of her responsibility to keep an eye on this kid.

She called Tamara's number again. And again.

And looked at the clock.

"This is not okay," she said. "Something is wrong. What am I going to do?"

Bitty shook her head. "I don't know. I've never had a kid. I don't know what to do in this situation."

One more call; then she left a voice mail: "Tam, it's Colleen. It's almost eleven. I don't know what's going on or why you're not answering, if you're upset or something is up, but come back to the hotel. Call or text me the *second* you get this. Please, I'm worried." She hung up. "I don't want to yell at her or she'll never come back."

Bitty frowned. "Do you think she's gotten into something worse than just smoking cigarettes?"

"What, drugs? *Here?*"

Bitty nodded. "Here or something she had with her? I don't know. She was acting strange today, didn't you notice?"

Colleen hadn't. How could she not? She'd thought she was doing such a great job picking up the slack Chris had dropped. "What do you mean she was acting strange? In what way?"

"Really quiet. Kept checking her phone. Biting her lip. Eyes darting everywhere around us, like she was looking for a spook."

"Well, since I was driving, my eyes were on the road, Columbo, but if you noticed all these signs of something being amiss, why didn't you say something?"

Bitty looked surprised.

"I'm sorry," Colleen said quickly. "One of my biggest faults: I'm quick to worry, and when I'm worried, I'm snappish. Something doesn't feel right. What time did we leave for the martini bar, did you notice?"

"No."

"Me neither." She groaned. "God. You know, I'd actually been toying with the idea of asking Kevin if we should take her in, you know, try and give her some feeling of family. Turns out I couldn't even keep track of her for a week!"

AN HOUR LATER, Tam still wasn't back and Colleen was certain all her worry was completely justified.

And she was completely convinced that she'd blown a huge opportunity, the opportunity to have that daughter figure around that she'd always imagined would be there someday, somehow. Tam had started to fill that role. Even with all her quirks and the worries that buzzed in Colleen's brain, she'd started to feel like something necessary was missing with Tam not there.

She and Bitty were walking around St. Augustine, looking for her in the long row of shops along the narrow alley that was St. George Street. Tourists crowded the place, and some of the stores seemed to extend back forever.

"Do you remember what she was wearing?" Colleen said, recalling how Kevin always said she'd make the world's worst police witness.

"Cutoffs," Bitty said, now that she'd revealed herself to be Captain Observant. "Orange flip-flops and a retro Clash T-shirt, *London Calling*. Unfortunately, it was black and dark gray, so it's not really going to stand out."

Colleen took out her phone and dialed Tamara again. Her call log showed that she'd now called her thirteen times in a row. She was losing hope that the girl would answer.

They stopped everywhere. Nothing in the shell shop. Nothing in the kitchen shop. Nothing in the three vintage shops. Nothing in Hot Stuff Mon, the shop devoted to hot sauces and cooking stuff but with the catchy name that might have attracted a teenage eye.

At one point, they came upon a cheap old hotel with a pirate theme that looked exactly like a teenage hangout, but when she opened the door hoping to find a reception desk, there was just a narrow staircase painted with the words TO A PIRATE'S LIFE FOR ME.

Nothing.

"Do you think we should call the police?" Bitty asked.

"I keep thinking that myself, but they would probably view it as a huge overreaction. After all, she hasn't been gone *that* long, at least in their eyes. It would be hard to convince them it's an emergency just because we're worried about a kid we've spent only a few days with and don't really know the habits of." Though she knew enough about Tam's habits, at least her previous ones. It was kind of hard to reconcile the fun sweet girl she'd begun to see as a comrade on this trip with the drugged-out wild child she knew Tamara to be. Maybe a few days of good was her limit, and she'd gone out trying to score something.

Or maybe she brought something with her, and had waited as long as she could, trying to resist it, but took it today, hence her odd behavior, and had wandered off in St. Augustine and gotten lost. Or had just been waiting to get far enough from home to run away and never be found. Maybe she had even walked right into the water and drowned. The thought sent tremors through her. If something terrible were going to happen, would she have had some sort of feeling in advance or could she totally be ambushed by it? Was it truly possible something was terribly wrong right now?

They walked through every street and alley in the main part of town, even though with every step their efforts seemed more and more hopeless. The place was so crowded and loud that Tamara could actually have been inside any one of the places they'd checked, and they might have just missed her anyway.

Anger was now mingling with Colleen's nervousness. This was incredibly irresponsible of Tamara. Selfish. She couldn't have called when she knew time was getting on? Even texted?

"I'm sure she's fine," said Bitty.

"No, you're not. Of course you're not sure. You can't be."

"Well, I know, but what am I supposed to say in this situation?"

"I don't know, maybe nothing?"

Colleen's fear was getting the better of her. As they walked along finding nothing, and she dug through every gaggle of teenagers with her eyes, she became more and more afraid. What if Tamara's phone really had died? And she hadn't been sure where their hotel was? That could happen easily. Maybe she went for a walk and got lost.

Maybe someone around her had seen her and offered her help.

"I'm not just angry," Colleen admitted to Bitty, "I'm really *afraid* something has happened to her."

"Don't you know her to be kind of wild, though? It's been two and a half hours or so, right? For a rebellious teenager, that's nothing. She probably met some people and is inconsiderate enough not to let you know, but is ultimately fine."

"You were the one who suggested maybe she had brought drugs along on the trip with her!"

"Yes, but that's not . . . Well, it's as likely as anything else, but I'm sure she didn't bring along something she's never done before, if she did bring it. Or maybe she didn't do that at all, she doesn't know anyone here, and who wants to do drugs by herself?"

"People who are addicted to drugs do, Bitty."

"Well . . ."

She seemed to have no real response. They walked in silence some more. The shops were emptying out, and the bars were certainly letting in only people with IDs at this hour. Although, who knew, the kid probably had a fake.

They walked to the fort, Castillo de San Marcos, where Colleen remembered Kevin telling her ahead of time that there were visible bullet holes still left in the stonework. It was dark there, and an ideal place for an angsting teenager to crouch against a wall, feeling sorry for herself. But no. Still no Tamara.

The last real shot at a good place to find her was on the Flagler College campus in town. They walked in the grand entrance, into the women's room off the main hall, up to the rotunda, where kids sat doing homework and eating vending machine food, and then down onto the grounds. Through gazebos, the lawn where some mini-adults sat having "dates." Into the library and the student center. But no Tamara.

"She's dumb," said Bitty. "If she wanted to get away for a bit and have a good time, this is where she *should* have come."

Colleen managed a laugh, before stopping and sitting down on one of the low stone walls. "Should I call the police?"

"They won't do anything about a teenager who's been missing in a college town for, what, maybe two hours?"

Colleen knew that was true. If the police were called every time a bored student moved from one party to another without telling anyone, they'd never get any of their important work done. Never mind that this *felt* important; it also wasn't outside Tamara's established behavioral patterns. This was *exactly* the kind of thing that had gotten her into trouble to begin with: reckless behavior with no regard for the consequences. Admittedly, maybe she hadn't had anyone watching for her and worrying in the past, but she knew Collen and Bitty would be.

Didn't she?

Finally, Bitty said what Colleen was thinking. "Do you think we should go back to the hotel? That's the one place she knows *we'd* be if she came back looking for *us*."

Colleen nodded. It was the only thing they could do right now.

"I lost my friend's dog once," said Colleen. "And I was up all night trying to find him. All night, just driving up and down and up and down the roads, looking for this fat ugly bulldog, and I knew that I couldn't give up. Because if you give up, then you lose all chance of finding him."

"This is different. She's a sixteen-year-old girl. And she's smart. She might be, you know, a little foolish, but she's not stupid. She'll come back. She'll find a way."

"I'm not afraid she's run away forever so much." Though now that she'd said that, she *was* afraid of it. "I'm afraid something happened to her. I'm afraid that she's led a life of messing up, and that tonight is the one night she didn't set out to do that, and she ends up hurt. Like Alice Haylon in school."

Alice Haylon had been a smart girl who went a little crazy at parties. She drank almost every night of the week, was loud and showy and definitely rather reckless. The kind of girl who never turned down a dare. But ultimately, she was a great girl. So when she died in a car accident, it had broken everyone's hearts, but not necessarily shocked anyone. The shock had come when it was discovered that drugs and alcohol had had no play in her death. So the number of times Alice had gone to parties or driven back with someone who was a little buzzed—or hell, sometimes definitely shouldn't have been behind a wheel—she had survived. And one time when she was on her way to do whatever, she had died. It had hit everyone who knew her like a one-two punch. First she was dead. Then she was dead, but not for the reasons people had assumed.

"I know what you mean," said Bitty, a shadow crossing her face. "I know exactly what you mean."

"I feel like she's so close to being okay, you know? She's smart. She's kindhearted. She's just bored and has nobody. Nobody in the world she feels truly loves her or would be there for her, no matter what. Everyone deserves that. Everyone. I don't want to feel like there's any chance in the world I could lose her before I get a chance to try to help her."

THEY SAT AWAKE for hours, the TV on, but not getting any further than the screen. Colleen and Bitty were silent, not wanting to overthink things too much. They just sat there in tense silence, Colleen's worry colliding hard with aggravation that this might all be the inconsideration of a teenager, ruining her night on a trip she'd planned to take alone for her own reasons.

She was lost in that thought when there was a clumsy scratching and bumping at the door, and in stumbled Tamara, white faced, red under the eyes, with tear streaks. Bitty was sitting at the small table, and looked at Tamara with alarm.

"Where have you been?"

Colleen had set out to ask it harshly and angrily, but it came out desperate and relieved. She didn't feel like she knew Tamara well enough to run up and embrace her, and she also didn't know how angry she should be yet.

"I'm sorry."

Colleen stood, suddenly with all the energy in the world, and stared Tamara down.

"I just went for a walk, and . . . and I got lost."

"Why are you such a mess?" Bitty asked. "You look like you've been through a war."

Tamara looked past Colleen to the mirror, seemingly startled by the horror-movie survivor she saw staring back at her.

Tamara took a deep breath and said, "I met some guys and asked them for a cigarette. They invited me to a party, it was right there, walking distance, so I went. They offered me weed, and I haven't smoked since I left, and I just kind of accepted out of habit. But it was different. It fucked me up. Sorry for the language." She hung her head. "It was called a dab. I don't know anything about it. I thought I was going to die. And then my phone—well, my phone did die. And then I came here as soon as I could."

Colleen was in shock. At the fact that Tamara had been honest. At the fact that she was here, and okay. At all of it.

"Should we go to the hospital?" asked Bitty.

"No, I feel normal now," said Tamara. "I'm just so sorry I did that. I'm so so sorry—"

Colleen was inclined to reach for her and tell her it was okay, she was just glad she was alive. But again, she couldn't do that.

"Let's look it up," said Bitty. "Tamara, charge your phone. Colleen, can you look it up? See what it is?"

"Good thinking."

Twenty minutes later, after Colleen had texted a friend who was a nurse, Bitty had accessed her premium membership to a medical Web site, and Tamara had Googled it, they knew what dab was. She should be okay. It wasn't inherently dangerous. But it could make you feel like hell on earth.

And it had.

"I don't know what to say to you, Tamara. I was really worried about you. I don't know what I would have done if something had happened."

Tamara looked surprised.

And Colleen, in turn, *felt* surprised that Tam should feel surprised. Had no one ever worried about her before? Had no one ever told her they were glad she got home safely?

"I thought you guys would just go out to eat and . . ." Tamara's voice drifted off.

"And what? See if you showed up again? Get in the car and go on without you? There was *nothing* we could do but sit here until you returned. Unless, of course, you were gone twenty-four to forty-eight grueling, nerve-racking hours—at which point, I could call the police. The lack of consideration for our feelings, for *my* feelings, is incomprehensible, Tamara. I was scared out of my mind."

"I'm sorry," Tamara said. "Really."

Colleen wasn't through. "I really thought you weren't doing this kind of thing on the trip. As a mother, my rule is that you can't get in trouble if you tell the truth. I'm very glad you were honest. But I'm still so sad that you felt the need to go do this."

Tamara nodded sadly. "Me too."

"Did something happen, Tamara?" asked Bitty. She rarely spoke, but when she did, she seemed to ask the right questions.

"Yeah, it's nothing. Just dumb teenager stuff. I overreacted and freaked out."

They both waited for her to choose to go on.

She didn't. Unsurprisingly.

Colleen shot Bitty a quick look, then said, "Tam, come outside with me for a minute. I need some fresh air."

"I just came in."

"Come out." She put a hand on Tam's narrow shoulder and guided her outside.

It was beautiful outside. Now that she was able to relax, Colleen could see it. There was nothing quite like looking at a clear night sky behind palm fronds on a really warm night. It never seemed to get this warm at night in Maryland.

"What happened?" Colleen asked without preamble.

"Nothing." Tam wouldn't meet her eyes. "I just went for a walk. It's cool here, and I doubt I'll ever be back, so . . ."

Colleen struggled with an impluse to reassure her that, yes, of *course* she'd be back and that her life would have many happy events—big and small—in the future. But it wasn't up to her, and for all she knew, and all she suspected, Tam might *not* ever go anyplace nice again. Maybe she'd just rot under Chris's court-ordered care until she was eighteen and could be booted out (or married some stringy loser to get away) to face a life of struggle without the foundation that a nurturing family unit gives. People succeeded against the odds, certainly. All the time. But did Tamara have that drive? Colleen just didn't know yet.

And it was beginning to feel like she wasn't going to have time to find out.

"Is that code for you don't want to talk about it?"

"No," Tamara said, but so defensively, it sounded like *no-wahhh.*

Colleen looked her in the eye. "You don't have to talk to me. But don't ever lie to me. No one wins when someone's lying."

Tamara looked right back at her. "I don't want to talk about it."

Which left Colleen with the very ultimatum she'd just implied. "Okay, then. But you listen to me, Tamara Bradley: I'm not giving up on you. You can't just push me away with some attitude and a brick wall of protection. I'm your family forever, and even if I weren't, I'd care just as much just from having gotten to know you as I have.

So my offer stands right now, and it will stand in a month, and it will stand in ten years. If you ever want to talk, you are safe coming to me. Do you understand?"

"Yeah, thanks, that's cool," Tam said, looking away and sounding for all the world like a dull-witted, burned-out teenager.

But Colleen had caught the glint of tears in the girl's eyes as she turned her face toward the light. "It's late," she said. "If you're hungry, there's fried shrimp in the fridge. We both need rest. Tomorrow's going to be a big day."

CHAPTER TWENTY-TWO

Colleen

THIS WAS A STUPID PLAN. CHILDISH. LIKE SOMETHING FROM A UNIversally panned chick flick.

So why Colleen kept driving south of St. Augustine instead of just admitting the trip was going badly in every possible way, she didn't know.

She just had to do this.

She had to confront her.

Julia. The woman who would be Kevin's wife if Colleen hadn't stepped in and ruined it for them.

Maybe it was just because she'd been haunted by Julia for so long that Colleen reached a wall where she either had to have resolution or . . . what? Give up? No, she wasn't going to *give up* or stop living or leave her marriage or anything, but she was going to continue on the path of self-doubt she'd been on for fifteen years, and where would *that* lead? Obviously not to any sort of mecca. Just a quiet extinguishing someday.

It was midafternoon on Sunday. In a few hours, she and Bitty and Tamara would be heading back north, and all this would be behind her. She just had to get it over with.

The house was a typical expensive Florida Mediterranean model, on a generous lot. Colleen could hear the ocean beyond it—nice backyard. As she parked the car and walked up to the front door, she felt vulnerable; there was no turning back, no way to dodge out and go to the place next door and pretend to be looking for some-one else or something. Of course, no matter what she could come up with, it would be a dumb lie, so why was she even considering it?

The truth was dumb enough. But she'd committed to it, and now she had to follow through.

She took a deep breath and knocked on the door.

Turn back turn back turn back RUN! ran through her mind like a drumbeat. But she was frozen, rooted to the spot. The sun, nudg-ing toward the west at her back, burned hot, and she felt sweaty and rumpled. She probably smelled hot. She hated the smell of hot hu-man coming into cool air-conditioning.

The door opened, and there she was: Julia Markham. Kevin's first real girlfriend.

The *real* love of his life.

And she looked gorgeous, of course. Slim, tall, perfect in a pale blue shift dress that, unlike any shift dresses Colleen had ever tried on, emphasized every curve without looking self-consciously sexy at all. Which made it even sexier, of course. This was not an easy person to compare herself to.

There was no comparison.

"Julia?" Colleen said, even though she knew.

"Yes?" The woman frowned her arched eyebrows, not a hair on her head astray, and tilted her head slightly, clearly trying to place the mess before her.

Colleen felt her face grow hot. "I know this is really weird—and, believe me, I am wishing I were anywhere but here at this moment, but here I am and . . . I'm Colleen Bradley. Kevin's wife?"

Understanding came into Julia's chocolate eyes. "Oh, yes! Colleen! I've seen your picture." Understanding left and reality overtook it. "I don't understand, though—" She searched the landscape behind Colleen. "—is Kevin here?"

"No. I'm by myself. I was hoping to talk to you." This was crazy. How had this ever seemed like a reasonable idea?

"Of course." Julia's composure slipped for just one barely detectable moment. "Where are my manners? Come on in." She took a graceful step backwards, opening the door to Colleen, and the clean, sun-filled house bloomed behind her. It was almost as if angel music played.

Colleen's house would never look like this.

Never.

"This way." Julia led her past an all-white kitchen to an all-white sunroom. There was a pitcher of ice water with lemons in it already on the coffee table and a copy of *Architectural Digest* lying open, facedown, on the sofa. In Colleen's house, it would have been a Diet Coke and a dog-eared *People* magazine.

"What's on your mind, Colleen?" Julia asked. There was a slight crispness to her tone, which Colleen took to be caution. Who wouldn't be feeling cautious under these circumstances? Your college ex-boyfriend's wife shows up at your door, a thousand miles from where you know they live? She must have been wondering if Colleen was wearing a diaper and packing heat.

Colleen added *brave* to the list of Julia's attributes.

"Look," she said quickly, "like I said, I know this is really odd, and it was probably a harebrained scheme, but I wanted to apologize to you. I've wanted to, or at least needed to, for a really long time."

That appeared to take Julia aback. "Apologize to me? What on earth for?"

Sudden, unstoppable tears filled Colleen's eyes. "For"—words failed her for a moment; she had to choke them out—"for ruining your life. Yours and Kevin's. I—I think."

Julia's shock could not have been more clear. "What are you *talking* about?" She smoothly handed a box of tissues to Colleen from the end table next to her.

Colleen sniffed and dabbed at her eyes. "I didn't know Kevin had a girlfriend when I met him—"

"Technically, he didn't," Julia said carefully.

But he had. They both knew it. He and Julia had just had a fight. After two and a half years of dating, college sweethearts, Julia and Kevin had a fight and Kevin went out and got drunk with his buddies, which was where and when he met Colleen.

All she knew at the time was that he was gorgeous and older and funny and smart—and drunk—and that he was going after her pretty enthusiastically. Egged on by his friends, who were undoubtedly trying to get him to get over Julia by just "getting right back on the horse"—even if it was a different horse. That's how guys were.

And girls tended to be too blind to see it until it was too late.

"Okay," Colleen agreed, "that's true, technically you were 'on a break.'" Wasn't everyone sick to death of that old *Friends* reference now? Yet it was completely true. "And I didn't know about you at first—honestly, I didn't."

"Of course not," Julia said with an ease and distance as if she were talking about a general situation, one not her own. "What guy's going to tell a new girl that he just had it out with his old one? There was no reason for him to explain me to you, nor for him to explain you to me. We were over. I truly hope you haven't been carrying that all these years, Colleen. Truly. It was just a silly teenage romance."

Colleen took a breath. "That's gracious of you. But I know the truth. Kevin was in love with you. He was planning to get back with you, you were *both* planning a wedding, and before he could tell me—and I realized later he'd been planning to break it to me, maybe even that day—I had to tell him I was pregnant."

Colleen, the past

It wasn't possible. They'd used protection. It was 99 percent effective, and the other 1 percent was if you used it as a party hat. Or if it broke or had a pinhole in it, but that almost never happened in real life.

So how could the four sticks on her sink (she'd done two, then decided the package must be faulty and gone out to get another two) all say the same thing?

Positive.

Pregnant.

It was impossible to fathom. A month ago, she had been Not Pregnant, and her whole life was ahead of her—every choice open to her, or at least it seemed that way (there was no telling whether she'd ever *really* want to run for president) and now a huge percentage of those choices were gone. Boom. Like pipe dreams.

Naturally her "options" had occurred to her. She was strongly pro-choice, but she couldn't imagine choosing to end this in practice and wonder forever what could have been.

Likewise, she admired the hell out of people who were strong enough to give babies up for adoption, but she didn't think she could live a lifetime constantly calculating the age of any child or person she saw who might look vaguely like her or Kevin or a combination of them both. It was selfish, she knew, but giving her baby away would torture her.

So she decided she was going to keep the baby. She was going to raise him or her, no matter what. She was prepared to do it alone, if need be. And need might be, because she had no idea how her parents were going to react to this tidbit the minute after she completed her costly education.

And a year before the baby's father completed *his* degree in architecture.

How was she going to tell everyone?

How was she going to tell *anyone*?

Even Bitty had just left for her home in North Carolina, heartbroken over Blake leaving. Colleen couldn't burden her with this too. She'd feel like she had to *do* something, and when nothing could be done—because, really, nothing could be done—she'd think she failed Colleen. That's how Bitty was, always dutiful, always trying to be whatever she thought people needed her to be.

Colleen, frankly, couldn't face telling any of them.

But she had to.

And it had to begin with Kevin.

And first it had to begin with sleep.

When she woke up in the morning, she had that moment of disorientation when she remembered *something* was wrong, but she was too sleep-fogged to recall exactly what it was.

Then it came to her. Crashing down in all its reality, as unreal as it was. She even went into the bathroom and glanced into the trash can, in case it had all been a vivid dream—but no, the four pregnancy tests were still there, and the tampon wrappers she would have expected to be—her period came like clockwork every month—were not.

Later she would not remember the drive over to Kevin's, apart from the way her hands shook on the steering wheel. This was unreal. It felt like being in an improv class; she had to find a way to say the unsayable. She had to find a way to live with knowing she was about to change someone else's life—in addition to her own—forever. She had to tell him she was pregnant and that she'd made the decision to keep the baby, so forevermore, no matter what happened between the two of them, he was going to be a father. He would know, whether he acted on it or not, that he was a father. And she would know she'd done that to him.

She parked the car out in front of his apartment, took a deep breath, and went to the door. It took a long moment for her to knock, but when she did, he seemed to open it almost immediately.

"Hey," he said, clearly surprised.

"Hi. I'm sorry to come unannounced. But we"—she took a shuddering breath—"we need to talk."

Was that relief that crossed his expression? "I've been thinking the same thing," he said. "Come on in, have a seat. I know it's only noon, but do you want a beer?"

She gave a dry laugh. "No, thanks."

"Mind if I have one?"

"Please do." *Please have six.*

He popped open a can of Bud and sat down at the hexagonal table he and his roommate had gotten from Goodwill. "Have a seat," he said again.

"That's okay, I'm a little nervous."

He nodded. "I think maybe we're feeling the same way." Later those words would register for her, but her first reaction upon hearing them was that maybe her nerves were so blaring, he couldn't help but pick up on them.

"The thing is . . ." Words failed her. Just stopped.

He waited a moment, then prompted. "What?"

"I . . ." Her palms grew sweaty, instantly. She felt like she could puke, though it was nerves not the baby. This should be so straightforward. In a way, so easy. But it was like she was a character in a fairy tale who'd lost the ability to speak.

"Maybe I should start?"

She wanted to shake her head, to stop him from what she feared he was going to say, but she couldn't move. She just felt her eyes widen and burn with unshed tears.

"I think you're great," he started. "I mean that, you're one of the greatest girls I've ever met—"

"I'm pregnant!" she blurted, then felt herself stepping backwards. She didn't know why; she wasn't afraid of him. Was it some instinct to back out of the place and run? She didn't know, but she felt behind her with her hand until the wall impeded her, and she stopped and took a bracing breath to try and face him.

He'd gone pale. Seriously pale. All the blood must have left his entire head. "What?"

She nodded spastically.

"Are you sure?"

"Yes. I took more than one test."

"How?"

"I don't know. We used protection. Did you notice anything, ever, that went wrong with that?"

"Obviously not."

Well, obviously *so*, but she didn't say that.

"There was that one time we didn't have anything, so I pulled out," he said, frowning, thinking.

No, there wasn't. That had never happened. She never would have taken the chance on purpose.

It must have been another girl.

He must have realized that too, because he amended, "No, we didn't, what am I talking about? My head is spinning. We were careful every time—this isn't possible."

"I know. But it's true."

He drained his beer and went to the fridge. "Are you sure you don't want one?"

"Can't. Pregnant."

He came back with two anyway, opened them both, and drained one after the other. "So does that mean you've made your decision?"

"Yes, I'm keeping it. But you're not obligated in any way. I'm only here to tell you so you know, so you can participate as much or as little as you want to. This can be *my* deal alone if you want it to be, but I wouldn't feel right if I didn't give you the choice to be there as everything . . . progresses."

He looked down for a long time, and she watched the muscle tic in his jaw. He did that during sex too, when he was trying not to come. She'd thought it was sexy then. Now it just made her feel small and troublesome.

Finally he looked up. "I want to be there, of course."

She hadn't expected that. "What?"

He stood up and came to her. She could smell the beer on his breath as he approached. "I want to be there for you, for you both. I'm not leaving you alone with this, you know that."

"I don't expect anything from you."

"That's what I like about you," he said, and pulled her in for a hug. He kissed her forehead. "You're so kind that you're worried about what this means for me rather than what you're about to go through."

"Well, I'm worried about both," she said against his chest, and gave a half laugh.

He gave a half laugh too. Nothing was really funny, but what else could they do? "We'll make this work," he said.

"What did you want to talk to me about?" she asked. It had sounded serious. The words he had gotten out wouldn't register until later on, when she tried to piece together her memories of the conversation.

"Nothing. It doesn't matter." He kissed the top of her head again. "I don't even remember."

JULIA LOOKED AT her glass of water, then back at Colleen. "Would you like something stronger than this?"

"I'd love it, but just one. I'm driving."

"I'll just be a moment." Julia walked over to the kitchen, opened the freezer, and took out a bottle of Belvedere Vodka. She poured a couple of fingers into a juice glass—at least she wasn't such an immaculate hostess that she happened to have measuring tools and a shaker at the ready. But then, Julia had been a bartender in school. Just one more thing that made her cooler than Colleen. Another skill she had that Colleen didn't—she tried to make a mojito once when a mint plant got out of control in the backyard, and had ended up with a sugary, alcoholic salad in a glass.

Julia came back to the sofa and sat down, looking only a little bit less gathered than she had when she first opened the door. "I like you, Colleen. And I respect you. And I see no need to try and paint things a different color because I want you to believe everything I say now. Yes, it's true, Kevin and I got back together shortly before you learned you were pregnant. And yes, there was talk of getting married."

A lump formed in Colleen's throat. She was never going to get over this. Now that it was confirmed, it was really true. How *could* she ever get over this? How could she ever get over feeling second best? If she was even second—maybe he had better choices ahead of her. "I'm sorry for that. At the time, I didn't know all of that. And, honestly, even if I had, I don't know what I would have done. I was scared and lost and . . ." She shrugged, out of words.

"And following your destiny," Julia finished. "Living the life you were meant to live. Kevin and I weren't meant to be together. We were, as I said, just a teenage romance. At the time, yes, it felt devastating. I got a lot of angst mileage out of it." She gave a light laugh. "But it disappeared into my rearview mirror pretty quickly. This is your *life,* but it was only my . . . lesson. One of many, many experiences that led me here."

Colleen was awed by her grace and the kindness Julia was displaying under the probably creepy (to her) circumstances of having an ex-boyfriend's sweaty wife sitting in her living room unexpectedly. "I know he still talks to you." God, she hated to admit that. It was so rife with all the ugly, embarrassing implications of wondering who he was talking to and looking at phone bills and joining Spokeo to look up the number and thereby getting the address and employment information and— Ugh. It all seemed so seedy now.

"Sure, we talk now and then," Julia said. "Mostly about how proud he is of Jay and his baseball playing and, mostly, of you and your creativity and your shop. I love the name, by the way—Junk and Disorderly. I could never come up with something like that, but there's no way in the world I wouldn't stop in if I were driving past."

He'd told her that? "Thanks," Colleen said uncertainly.

"We don't talk that often, maybe two or three times in a year, but remember we were basically childhood friends. It can be very comforting to have those people in your life. But there has never been so much as a *whiff* of an implication that he wishes things had gone differently."

"I'm—I'm glad to hear that." She still didn't believe it entirely. "A little amazed to hear it, honestly."

"Good heavens, from the minute Jay was born! Well, I don't know about the *minute,* because *obviously* he didn't call me the *minute* Jay was born, but by the time I talked to him around Christmas that year, he couldn't shut up about how great Jay was and what an amazing natural *you* were as a mother. I almost felt like he was lording it over my head, pointing out that he felt like he'd dodged a bullet by getting you instead of me." She stood up. "Wait, I have something to show you." She disappeared into another room for a moment and came back with a card in hand. "I'm afraid this proves how pitifully behind I am on putting away the last of my holiday decorations, but I need a new card box." She held it out to Colleen. A generic Christmas card with a picture of Colleen and Jay, with a note in Kevin's familiar hand that said, *My beautiful family—I am the luckiest man on earth! Here's wishing you and Rick all the best in the new year!*

This was a shock to Colleen. She couldn't imagine it. Not after spending fifteen years imagining Julia, and not after what she was seeing now, looking around this glorious house for the past fifteen minutes. "But—"

"But what?"

Colleen was losing track of her convictions. "I took his choice away. And yours. He didn't *choose* me; he chose *you*. He was *stuck* with me."

Julia shook her head. "That's a sad way to look at it. And inaccurate, I might add. He picked you in the first place because he wanted you. Maybe Jay came along a little earlier than you two might have planned, but maybe he *had* to so that Kevin didn't make the worst mistake of his life and come back to me! It wouldn't have served me either, Colleen. We were that old story. The kids who got together really young and couldn't let go of each other. It wasn't until we were forced to that we both realized what a huge mistake it would have been to stick with each other out of habit and routine. At the time, yes, he was such an integral part of my life, I was so used to having him around, that it seemed impossible that there was a world that existed without him in it. But that's not because he was right for me—that was because I was used to him and we were such good friends that it was easy. I have a good life. A good career. Everything I could ever want." She leaned forward and looked Colleen in the eye. "But you have given him more than I *ever* could have. You have given him his whole life."

And as soon as the words were out of Julia's mouth, Colleen knew they were true. The card was proof she hadn't needed—or shouldn't have needed to see. It had been self-indulgent, in a way, wondering for all these years if there were an option. Almost looking for ways to make herself feel she didn't fit in.

For fifteen years, she'd been tense, always guarded and suspicious and insecure—that wasn't giving her best to herself, her husband, *or* her son. She'd held Julia up as a symbol of her failure when Julia was, as it turned out, just a small off-ramp on Kevin's—and now Colleen's—road.

"I was embarrassed as soon as I arrived," Colleen admitted. "I'm about a hundred times more embarrassed now."

"You shouldn't be," Julia said. "I've wanted to meet you for years. And now that I have, I feel like I have a new friend."

"You're more gracious than you need to be." Colleen smiled.

"My clients don't always say that when they get my bills." She smiled back. "But I will mention it to my husband when he gets back in town."

"You're married?" Spokeo hadn't mentioned that. God, that was even worse! She'd come here based on completely unreliable information. It was incredible that she'd even ended up at the right house.

"Ten years now. My husband and I have an architectural firm in Jacksonville, but he's in Chicago right now, consulting on a new building on the pier."

"Wow. I had no idea. Kids?"

Julia shook her head. "I'm not the maternal sort. Neither is Rick. We're too selfish—we like our alone time and our vacations."

"What are those?"

Julia laughed. "See?"

Colleen stood up. "I do. Thank you so much, Julia. I appreciate your time and your patience. Honestly, I feel like such a jerk, but also *profoundly* relieved. It's like a weight has been lifted off me, and I didn't even know how heavy it was."

"Then I'm really glad you came by."

They went to the door and hugged, though a bit stiffly. Colleen noticed Julia smelled faintly of cigarette smoke, in addition to a crisp, apple-y perfume.

Kevin hated smoking.

And, actually, the smell of apples. It reminded him of stinkbugs; he said so all the time.

Colleen thanked Julia once more and went back to her car, feeling like her mission—as ill-advised and foolish as it may have been—was accomplished.

She looked at the sky. Dark gray clouds were gathering. It was time for them to hit the road before the storm hit them.

CHAPTER TWENTY-THREE

Bitty

Dear Stranger,

I don't want to end up in the *Guinness Book of World Records* for the world's longest, most circular suicide note, so I guess I'm going to have to be the world's most boring diarist. I'm starting to get curious about how things turn out here, so I guess suicide's on the back burner, and I have to set about the more difficult task of trying to figure out how to live until, you know, I die.

I thought I'd tried already, once. But staying in Winnington after what had happened with Lew was just ill-advised. A stupid idea. No one would ever accept me in that role. I've now been gone long enough, and reported crazy on top of that, that Candy Fitzgerald-Sonner has taken over my reign—and good luck to her. She might not have the same problems with her husband that I had with mine, but hers played grab-ass with me, and probably countless others, at last year's Winnington Christmas parade, so I suspect she will be another one of the mighty fallen someday.

So now it's time to tell the truth. I'd been taking the high road here, but I'm over that now. I don't owe Lew any more respect or dignity than he offered me.

Here is what happened.

It was any old Thursday night, just a day in my life. And as was a normal part of my daily life, I was hungry. I am always hungry. I've been on a diet for as long as I can remember; my mother had probably limited my formula intake as an infant. (Heaven knows Jean Nolan would never have risked saggy breasts by nursing a baby—I sometimes wonder if my mother had even carried me or if, more likely, she'd purchased me on her way out of Bergdorf's one day as a fetching little accessory.)

Usually I was able to pick up my husband's favorite calamari dish from Luigi's without problems because the smell didn't appeal to me, but a waitress had just walked past with a sliced loaf of Italian bread and a garlicky-cheesy olive oil dip that smelled so good, I was almost willing to do an extra three hours on the treadmill the next day in order to eat it.

But I couldn't. I knew I couldn't really have it. It was all well and good to make exercise promises in anticipation of eating, but once I was finished, and in the food coma that would undoubtedly follow such a splurge, I wouldn't feel like getting up and moving.

My self-discipline was pretty good, but it wasn't that good. Easier not to eat the thing in the first place than to work it off later.

But, man, it had smelled good.

"Mrs. Camalier?" I heard them calling my name before I realized I was hearing it. "Wilhelmina Camalier?"

I snapped to attention. Me. Show's on again. "I'm sorry, I'm Mrs. Camalier." They knew it, I'd been in there many times before, but Lew had drilled into me to always point out "I'm Mrs. Camalier," ideally calling whomever I was addressing by their first name, if it was written on a name tag.

Big me, little you.

It has become second nature to me.

The hostess held up a bag. "Your order's ready."

I stood up and went over to retrieve it, handing the hostess thirty dollars in cash. "Keep the change."

"Thank you!"

I didn't even know how much the order cost. I'd overtipped, for sure, but I couldn't stand there and smell the bread and pasta any longer. The temptation was too great. I wasn't made of stone.

I continued to obsess about food on the drive home. All of the things I'd love to have if only they wouldn't ruin my figure and therefore my life. I had an image to uphold. I was a pillar of Winnington society, and almost everywhere I went, at least some eyes were on me. And most definitely judgmental.

Looking good was the only job I had.

Ever since I'd married Lew Camalier, great-great-grandson of Winnington's founder, Lew Wallace Camalier, part of the Winnington population had looked to us with admiration and part had looked on us with scrutiny, seemingly always hoping to find some reason to discredit us. Lew swore it was because the descendants of Wyatt Smith hoped to resurrect their already-disproven claim that their ancestor had founded Winnington and Lew Wallace Camalier merely took the credit.

Personally, I suspect people were more interested in exposing my husband for the jerk he is, more than looking to raise a new statue in the town's Founder's Square.

Of course, I couldn't tell Lew that. He would raise holy hell at the very suggestion that his lineage was less than what he—and his mother before him, and his grandmother before her, and so on—had proclaimed it to be.

Which was, in fact, why I was bringing home the Calamari Concession. Last night, I'd raised the subject of children again—as in, it's getting way past time, if we're ever going to do it, we have to hurry up—and he had gotten upset with me over the "pressure."

After fifteen years of marriage—in which we'd had sex so infrequently, I could probably count it on my fingers—if I could remember the occasions well enough to tally them, there was no possibility of "waiting to see what God wanted" or "leaving it up to fate." If we didn't make a concerted effort, it was never going to happen.

Truth was, he had me over a barrel. This decision, like every other, was his. He got to dictate my entire life because without him, I had no life. I was Lew Wallace Camalier's wife, and it was a pretty good title. I, Bitty Nolan, never did anything of note. I didn't even think I knew how to go back and be Bitty again. Imagine that—knowing who you once were but finding that person irretrievable. It was hell.

I punched the code in at the front door and stopped in the

dining room on my way to the kitchen to grab one of the nicer serving dishes to display the food on. It was a rippled crystal platter that I always thought looked like a rainbow fish.

"Lew?" I called, but there was no answer.

I busied myself arranging the dish, opened the wine to let it breathe (despite conflicting reports on whether or not that was useful—it was the way my mother had done it, so it was the way I did it). Finally I got some strawberries out of the fridge, cored them, and sprinkled a little crystal sugar on them to make them pretty as a delicate little side or dessert.

Shoot, I thought, I should have left some out to eat before I put the sugar on them. I had picked one up, considered it, then put it back. If I started, it would be hard to stop and I didn't need all that sugar or food guilt. I could just imagine Lew's reaction if I started piling on the pounds. He was a pretty thin whip of a man, and he didn't want his wife getting wider than him and making him look even smaller. I couldn't really blame him for that. I didn't want to feel like an Amazon next to him either. At five feet six inches, I was just two inches shorter than he claimed to be, yet I could look directly at his hairline, so, at least fashion-wise, my life was centered around low heels and narrow-tailored clothes.

It was fair. It was the deal I'd made. In exchange, I not only regularly appeared in the style section of the newspaper, but I was also on the cover of *Carolina Society Lifestyle* magazine once.

"Lew!" I had called again. A glance out the window showed his car was there. It was Sunday, so he'd have gone to church, but usually he stayed in after that. I thought for a minute: Was he traveling this week? Last week he'd gone to Tampa, but this week he was in, right?

A small dread crossed my chest. but I dismissed it quickly. Whenever things are even a little bit off, horrible scenarios spring to my mind immediately. A pool of blood spilling out from underneath a closed door; a body hanging, bug-eyed, from the rafters; a uniformed police officer at the door, hat in hand. It was a wonder I was sane at all, though sometimes I wasn't really sure I was.

"Lew?" I started up the stairs and heard movement overhead. Relief flushed over me like cool water. God, why do I always have to go to ten on the worry scale? It's ridiculous.

There was a bang in the bedroom.

I went up.

"Good Lord, Lew," I said, opening the door, "what on earth are you doing, cleaning out the closet with a battering—?" I stopped.

My hand clapped to my chest.

Lew was naked on the bed, on his knees. The first thing I noticed, as discordant as it was, was that the soles of his feet were perfectly clean. That's how fastidious he is—he never even takes off his shoes long enough to make the soles a different color from the tops. Well, rarely.

They were off now.

His back gleamed with sweat. His forehead too, when he turned his alarmed face to me, he had a sheen that suggested it had been a long afternoon. His chest heaved, though I couldn't yet say if it was exertion or shock.

Likely both.

"Wilhelmina!"

He always called me by my whole name. I could understand

why he wasn't on board with Bitty. That wasn't a cool name, and it didn't even come from a particularly good trait—it wasn't necessarily cool to diet so much, everyone called you Itty Bitty—but he'd never come up with anything else, anything affectionate, even some shortened variation of my real name.

It was always "Wilhelmina" in full.

Even, apparently, at the defining moment of our marriage. Or, rather, the end of our marriage.

"I—" I started. But what? I *what*? There was no reasonable follow-up. I had just purchased one of my husband's favorite treats as a surprise for him, I'd set it up downstairs, complete with wine, and come to find him so I could serve him.

I'd even worried about him when he didn't answer my calls.

But here he was, the man who wasn't attracted enough to me to kiss me on the mouth, much less create babies, pretty spectacularly en flagrante with someone else.

Blond?

Yes, of course. The cliché.

Younger?

Yup. Younger than both of us.

Before I even saw a face, I could tell it from his smooth thighs and . . . tight scrotum.

Because, oh yes, male?

You betcha.

Lew was in bed with a man. Naked. Sweating. Kneeling in front of the man's mouth. There was just no mistaking this situation for anything other than what it was.

And I'd never even seen it coming. No pun intended.

All this comprehension churned into me quickly, like an

avalanche. Every impression topped by a next impression and a next impression, giving me a slide show of different facts I could view forever and never feel even remotely okay about.

No one ever talks about how the person looking at the deer in the headlights has much the same expression as the deer. That's how I felt while I looked at that moment. Frozen in shock.

I tried to swallow but couldn't. My mouth was dry. My throat was tight. My eyes burned, but I couldn't look away.

Time passed in a blur. How much? I don't know. Minutes? Seconds? Fractions of seconds? I just felt my head spinning and went to turn away, leave—I guess try to erase the entire thing somehow.

"Wilhelmina, you need to not tell people about this." Lew started to get off the bed, and I noticed, with shock, that he was still hard.

How was that possible? This had to be as horrifying a moment for him as it was for me. This was a revelation he clearly didn't want made and I didn't want to know. That was usually the perfect recipe for wilting. Was this guy he was with such a huge turn-on that he couldn't help it? Was he hoping to move me on out of there so he could finish what they'd very clearly started?

Not that I was objective, but the guy really wasn't that hot. Early twenties, the kind of blond I usually attribute to Sun-In. He had a bit of a moon face and fettucine arms. He was not a guy you risked your entire reputation on.

Maybe Lew had taken the Viagra I'd been oh-so-subtly suggesting for the past couple of years.

Whatever it was, the sight of it made me wince and avert my

gaze. A reflex. "Should I leave while you finish?" I asked sharply. "Maybe wait downstairs with the goddamn dinner I brought you until you're ready to resume your role as my husband?"

"This isn't what it looks like," he said to me with surprising conviction.

That brought my gaze right back to him. To them both. His friend was looking at him with as much curiosity on his face as I felt in my own expression.

"It's not?" I asked.

"No."

"Okay . . ." I took a breath. The scene was so surreal and seemingly endless that, in a weird way, I was growing used to it. I could almost pull up a chair and chat. "Tell me about it."

"Jared—" He gestured at the young man whose shoulders lowered fractionally, like a dog's ears, upon hearing his name. "—is my massage therapist."

I gave a hard spike of laughter, involuntarily, and noticed that Jared—assuming that was the guy in my bed with my husband and not a totally different guy involved in a different story or possibly about to come out of the bathroom—also frowned and drew his head back.

"Is this Jared?" I asked, gesturing toward the guy, then met his eyes. "Are you Jared?"

"Yes?" His answer sounded like a question.

"Are you a massage therapist?"

Long hesitation. "Yes . . . ?"

"Tell me, what kind of massage therapy necessitates nudity and my husband's penis in your mouth?"

"Uh—"

"That's not what's happening here," Lew snapped, getting off the bed and pulling on some boxers he'd left on the floor.

As horrifying as the entire scene was, I couldn't look away. This was the end of my life as I knew it—there was no doubt—everything from this moment on was going downhill, probably to the bottom, so I had to take in every single detail until that moment.

"Jared, what's happening here?" I asked.

He looked at me like I'd just asked him the twenty-fifth number to the right of the decimal in pi. "We're— I'm— This is a massage."

"Prostate massage?"

"I don't know." He looked at Lew. "Maybe?" He mouthed the words *I don't know what to say* as if I couldn't see him. It was then that I noticed on his right hand, ring finger, a thick gold band, not unlike a wedding band, dotted with diamonds. The ring Odessa had told me she saw Lew buying. He'd given it to Jared! "Nice ring," I tossed off.

He looked at it awkwardly. "Uh. Thanks?"

Incredibly, Lew threw a robe on, then marched over to me and grabbed me hard by the arm to pull me from the room. "Stop it," he hissed.

"Me?"

"Yes, you."

"Stop what?"

"Stop hounding him."

I would have been less stunned if he'd just punched me in the face. "Stop hounding him? Are you kidding? Have you gone crazy? I just walked in on you with a man—well, boy really, is he even of age?" How was this happening? How could I get lost in the details now when the point was so painfully clear? My husband was having sex with a man in our bed and here I was, noticing his feet were clean, wondering if he was taking Viagra, and now asking how old his partner was.

Worse, Lew was ready to jump right in and play up the madness. Instead of apologizing or explaining or getting in a time machine and going back in time to erase what I'd just witnessed, he was being contentious about the whole thing, scolding me.

"He's twenty-four," he said. "Not that it's any of your business."

"Isn't it?"

"This has nothing to do with you."

"That"—I pointed in the general direction of his privates, which had mercifully gone down—"has nothing to do with me. This"—I gestured at the bedroom door—"has everything to do with me. This is my marriage, my husband, my reputation"—my voice caught—"my life."

I might as well have said nothing.

"Obviously, no one is going to find out about this." He said it as if that were a given. An order.

"Really?" Only then did the thought occur to me that this wasn't the first time. Of course it wasn't. For one thing, Lew looked quite experienced with it, and for another, at his age, it was unlikely he was only now figuring out his sexual preference. Particularly given how long it had been since he'd had sex with me. "How long has this been going on?"

"I told you there's nothing going on—"

"Call the Mad Hatter so we can get some clarity here, would you? That was definitely not nothing going on in there!"

"He's my massage therapist, and he has some . . . unique therapies that, yes, might look a little peculiar, but you had no right to grill him like that. He doesn't know anything."

"Apparently, that's totally in keeping with your taste." This kind of thing didn't happen suddenly. If there was a hapless idiot here—someone who didn't know anything—it was me. I'd tried for years to lure my husband's sexual interest back in, tried like hell to please him and have, at the very least, a normal marriage.

Every single time I saw an *Oprah* episode where they talked about "the average number of times a year the average couple had sex" I cringed. Per year? "Per lifetime" would have been a better measurement for me. Lew and I had had sex, or tried to. (Is it really sex if it resulted in both parties just giving up rather than climaxing?) In the beginning, our relationship had been one where we both "wanted to wait." We didn't want to "rush into things." We didn't want to "make the same mistakes."

Apparently, the reason our relationship had been so old-school and so respectful was because the entire time, he was dreading the day when he would have no excuse.

"You could have told me a long time ago our sexual problems weren't because of me," I said. My voice was strong and angry, but inside I was crumbling. It would be a stretch to say the shock was wearing off—it was hard to imagine the shock would ever wear off—but the truth was forcing its way in. "Could you not give me that single small mercy? If you'd allowed me the benefit of the truth, then maybe I could have made better, more educated decisions about my life."

"Like what? Are you saying you would have left?" He gave a hurtful dagger of a laugh that went right through my heart. "You had too much to lose."

"Yeah, a husband who had no feelings for me." God, how I'd tried. I'd tried everything, over and over, for years. I'd tried tonight. The proof was downstairs on the counter, going bad as quickly as my marriage.

Lew didn't appear to care at all. "You weren't any more in love than I was!"

Wow. That just wasn't true. Once upon a time, I'd thought I was very much in love with him. Well, maybe not "very much." It was nothing like Blake, but maybe one couldn't expect adult love to be like youthful passion. But certainly I *loved* Lew. I wouldn't have married him otherwise. Certainly I'd come to understand my role as his wife in the years that ensued, and eventually I'd had to give up the idea of a passionate romance, but I most definitely had entered this marriage, and fought for it, based on the belief that it could still be a good and strong marriage even if it wasn't what you might call hot.

"I loved you," I had said quietly, the words hard to force over the lump in my throat.

"You loved this life." He gestured around them. "And that hasn't changed." He dropped his arms at his sides. "In fact, this is liberating for us both."

I think my jaw literally dropped. He was actually working up to spinning this into a good thing? "Are you about to tell me this is going to strengthen our marriage?"

He considered me for a moment. "Yes."

"Oh my god." I started to turn away from him.

He took my arm and wrenched me back to face him, easily. "You listen to me. You are my wife."

"At this point, I don't even know if that's true. Is a marriage based on such a major lie real, or is there a legal loophole there?"

He shook his hand off me. "You are my wife," he said, low and firm. "And as such, you have a position in this town, a standing based on my reputation and the reputation of my father, and grandfather, and great-grandfathers past. You took on that duty and, by God, you're going to fulfill it."

"In exchange for what? What do I get out of protecting your secrets and pretending everything is just hunky-dory?"

"You get everything you already have. What you win"—it was hard to say later whether something in his face or tone actually went cold or if his words just made it seem so—"is not to lose."

I didn't leave right then and there. Crazy, right? You'd think I'd have happily turned on my heel and left, and never looked back. What a betrayal. What a fundamental lie. And letting me think, all these years, that it was because of *me* that we didn't have sex, rather than because I could never, ever be what he wanted, no matter what.

But the embarrassing truth is that I was so used to being Mrs. Camalier that I didn't have the confidence to just up and leave. Or, wiser still, point toward the door, like Death in *A Christmas Carol,* demanding *he* leave. I had rights. But in a marriage like that, it was hard to keep a grip on that fact.

So I found a place to rent, under the pretense of making it into a little art studio for myself, and slowly moved in. It didn't take people long to figure out what was going on, of course, and in a small, self-conscious town like this, it didn't take long for them to look at me like I was something the cat had brought in from the woods.

I gave it a game shot, though—really I did. I see now that the error was trying it there, but by that time, Winnington felt like the only home I really knew. But then one day, they wouldn't accept my check at the grocery store. No reason. I'd never bounced anything there. I think Lew just told them I had nothing, and they believed him. I could have given them a card, of course, or even cash, but that was the line right there—the uncrossable line between the illusion of dignity and the reality of humiliation.

And it was at that moment that the truth hit me full force.

There was no way for me to win. I'd already lost.

I'd lost before I even began to play.

CHAPTER TWENTY-FOUR

Tamara

THE WEATHER WAS HIDEOUS. THE RAIN WAS COMING DOWN SO hard that, from her place hunkered down in the backseat, Tamara couldn't see the road in front of them at all. She only hoped Colleen could, but she was scared. It wasn't unfamiliar to Tam, this heart-pounding lack of control, but somehow this felt more dangerous than anything she'd ever done.

She also wasn't used to caring so much whether she lived or died. God, how many reckless things had she done without a care for what happened to her? Or even what happened to her friends. That Tamara was starting to seem like a stranger.

Replaced, evidently, by this seat belt–clutching sissy girl.

Bitty must have shared the sentiment. "This is bad," she said. "We should probably pull over."

"I was thinking the same thing," Colleen agreed, "but for the past twenty minutes, I've been looking for an off-ramp of some sort and we haven't passed one. There must be one coming up soon."

"What about the side of the road?" Bitty pointed to some cars that had already done that and put their hazard lights on.

"I've heard too many horror stories. Look how some of these trucks are blowing by. We do *not* want to get rammed by one of those jerks. Oh, look—is that a service road?"

Tam sat up and squinted but couldn't see anything.

"It's a turnoff of *some* sort. As long as we can get the trailer far enough off the road too, we should be okay."

Colleen made the turn, and a large but low, neon sign greeted them with an announcement of XXX 24 HOURS LIVE GIRLS.

"As opposed to what, dead girls?" Tamara asked.

"Great, now I'm poisoning a child's mind."

"It's okay," Tam said with a humorless laugh. "I'm not as naïve as you might think."

"Oh, dear," Colleen breathed. She inched the car forward through sloppy mud puddles until it was well onto the service road, then put it in park and sighed. "Think it's going to let up soon?"

"I think we should build an ark," Bitty said.

Tam laughed. She'd never been one for Sunday school, but even she got that reference.

They sat in silence for a moment, then Bitty said, "You know, I swear I keep feeling water drops falling on me." She looked up and felt the roof. "Here." She held her hand to a spot right over her head. "There's a hole here."

"I think there's one back here too," Tam said, remembering how she'd kept wondering how she was spilling her Coke when it was secured in the cup holder. "Just a small one."

"This is the problem with convertibles in anything but great weather," Colleen said. "They are muggy and cramped and unreliable. Come on, crew, let's get in the trailer. At least there are snacks back there." She opened the door, pulled her seat forward, and helped Tam out. Bitty got out the other side and they both slammed their doors and ran for the door to the trailer.

When they climbed in, it was incredibly dark and dank.

"There," Colleen said in the darkness. "Isn't that better?" She gave a dry laugh, opened the curtains, letting in the flashing neon glow of the sign, then said, "I've got some candles here somewhere. They were in that carved box I got at the auction in Florence." She felt around. "Got 'em." And started to set them on the little Formica table. "Now all we need is matches." She frowned and looked around, then said, "Tam?"

"I—" Tam started uncertainly. "I think I have a lighter, hang on." She dug around in her purse until she found it and handed it over to Colleen. As if lighting the candles herself would prove she knew how to use a lighter and *that* would be the damning thing.

As the glow bloomed before them, the trailer took on a pretty, albeit cramped, ambiance. Colleen took out a bag of trail mix and plopped it on the table. "Best I can do."

"You have the Whipped," Tam suggested.

"The what?"

"The Whipped." She pointed. "That you got at that gas station on the way down."

"Oh, yeah." Colleen got up and brought the cans over to the table. She wrestled the plastic lid off one and squirted it into her mouth. "Not bad. Not bad at all." She handed it over Bitty. "Try it."

Bitty didn't even question why this would be a good idea but opened her mouth and took some in. "Mmm. What is this?"

"Whipped cream and fifteen percent alcohol."

"No *way!*" Bitty took another hit.

"Can I try it?" Tam asked. As if she hadn't had it a hundred times before.

Colleen looked shamed, as if she'd been caught being rude. "I'm sorry, honey, it's alcohol. Not that strong, but still. That would be irresponsible of me. But Bitty and I will put it away."

"Like hell." Bitty took another mouthful and said, "Let 'er 'ave some." She swallowed. "Jeez, it's not like *you* never drank when you were underage."

"True," Colleen conceded slowly, "but I'm supposed to be looking out for her best interests."

"And it's in her best interest to relax and have a little fun since we're stuck here in the shadow of Ron Jeremy land." Bitty handed Tam the bottle. "I'm making an executive decision. Go ahead."

Tam looked at Colleen, who nodded her assent but turned her head slightly away. "I didn't see."

"No, because you were busy opening the hazelnut one." Bitty gestured. "Get on it!"

Forty-five minutes later, Colleen had clearly lost track of her intention to keep track of Tam, and they'd gone all the way through the vanilla bottle, and the hazelnut one was starting to feel a bit light too. The rain continued to pelt down on the roof like pennies being hurled from heaven.

"Looks like we're here for the night," Bitty commented.

Colleen looked at her. "Because we're drunk or because the Revenge of Noah is spilling out of the sky?"

"Well . . . both. Probably mostly the drunk thing."

"Amen."

Normally Tamara had a pretty high tolerance, but this stuff was getting to her too. She didn't say anything, though. She didn't want the small, rational part that remained in Colleen to come out and close up shop.

"Is anyone tired?" Colleen asked.

"Not me," Bitty said.

Tam shook her head. "Me neither."

Colleen looked at her watch. "It's only nine P.M. This is going to be a really long night."

"We could play a game?"

"I don't see the opportunity for a lot of dares or anything," said Bitty.

"Yeah, that and you always puss out when you get dared to do anything you don't feel like doing." Colleen rolled her eyes.

"No! Well, *yes,* but I was always being dared to do things like knock on a door in the boys' dorm naked."

Tam laughed. "Did you do it?"

"No, she didn't," said Colleen.

"But Colleen did." Bitty fell back a little in laughter. "I couldn't believe she really did it."

"Yes, I did. I actually got a date out of that dare."

"Yeah, no shit. You knock on a guy's door naked, and he asked you out? Shocker!"

"Whatever!" Colleen tossed her hair. "Point is, what game would we play? I should have brought some kind of card game or something."

They all thought for a second, until Tamara spoke up. "We could play Never Have I Ever again."

"All right, I'm in. Who starts?" Colleen put a hand up.

"I'll go," said Tam. She racked her brain for a question that wasn't boring, but wasn't going to get her in trouble either. She wanted it to be good, though. She kind of liked hearing Colleen and Bitty's stories. "Never Have I Ever . . . made out with a stranger."

Colleen looked to Bitty, whose eyebrows had shot up, and who was avoiding eye contact. She put down her thumb and cleared her throat. "And moving on—"

"No, you have to tell her!"

"Tell me!"

"It wasn't even a dare. I just . . . well, I felt someone standing behind me once at the bars and just leaned back and kissed him, thinking it was my boyfriend Blake . . . but it wasn't. It was someone I didn't know from Adam . . . but at least he was hot."

"And a good kisser, you said."

"Yes, but not as good as Blake."

"Oh my god!" said Tam. "Was Blake pissed?"

"He thought it was hilarious! He watched the look on my face as I realized it wasn't him. Apparently, I looked as horrified as I felt."

"Your face was *bright* red. And that place was lit up by black lights, so it would have been impossible to tell if you had been a shade lighter than lobster Red."

Bitty shook her head and pinched the bridge of her nose. "Yes, classy times."

"Okay, Bitty, your turn."

"Ha. Okay." She tilted her head at Colleen. "Never have I ever gotten lost on Halloween, only to be found after two hours, dancing with a bunch of people dressed up like musical horns."

"Oh my god, I didn't *mean* to be lost!"

"Yes, you did! You stormed off all pissy," Bitty said, and then looked to Tamara. "Word of advice: Never go out for Halloween in Fell's Point in Baltimore and decide you're angry over nothing, amble off dressed as Madonna, and get yourself lost."

"The guy I was dating made some rude comment—"

"No, he didn't!" Bitty squawked. "You admitted you misheard him."

"Well, whatever. I *thought* he said something rude. So I stomped off. And. Yes. Got lost immediately. In a time before cell phones. And was not found until hours later. Maybe if my *friends* were a little nicer and found me sooner, I wouldn't have had to accept the free shots from the Justice League, and start dancing with those horns."

"She made a fool of herself. Lesson here, Tamara, is that drinking can make you unreasonable and get you lost. And give your best friend blackmail material, like a picture of you backing your butt up on a man in a trombone costume."

Tamara smiled. She had dreaded this trip and been so mad that her father made her come, but now she was sitting here with two of the coolest betches she'd ever meet. She wished she'd known this Colleen, and not the Instagram-reporting one, a long time ago. It would have been nice to have her to go to with some of her problems.

Maybe it still wasn't too late. . . .

"Okay, *my* turn." Colleen put up her hand, now with four fingers.

A couple rounds passed, and the rain got harder. Tamara laughed at their old stories, at first, really enjoying them. Then becoming stupidly, childishly jealous of the fact that they had each other, and that at the end of the day, she still didn't have someone to share all those best-friend experiences with.

Finally, running out of things, Tam shrugged and tossed out, "Never have I ever not found out the person I was dating until recently is really a cheating asshole."

Both of the women looked at her.

"Vince cheated on you?" asked Colleen. Tamara found it nice she had taken the time to remember his name, but also felt like it was a waste. He was a waste.

"Yep."

"I'm so sorry, honey."

Bitty put down a finger.

"Wait, what?" said Tam.

Bitty spritzed a little more Whipped into her mouth and nodded slowly. "My husband cheated on me."

Colleen said nothing.

"My turn, right?" asked Bitty. "Never have I ever been married to a straight man."

Tamara's eyes widened into half dollars, and Colleen went, "Whoa! What?"

Bitty nodded again. "Yep. Walked in on my husband with another man. We separated a year ago. Here I am today."

"So when we ran into you at Henley's—"

"I wasn't in a good place. I was kind of on my last leg, I guess." The look on her face confirmed it. "You know, I mean, I did what I'm supposed to do, you know? I tried to get back up on that horse and be *okay*. To just simply keep on living. I got a little apartment in town—well, a little outside of town. And I knew I'd lost my position as a leader there, but I still spent the next year doing my best to be part of coordination for events and gallery openings and all. It's amazing how even a Race for the Cure can become a political thing in the society of a small place like that."

"What happened then?" asked Tamara. "Were you sad or what?"

She took in a deep breath. "I was utterly alone. I had spent my entire adult life piecing together this life, and it was irrevocably shattered into dust. It wasn't just that he cheated once with a pretty waitress or something. This was fundamental and not going away, no matter how I handled it. So. Yes. I felt hopeless, and once I was on my own, it was so much worse. I'm sorry, I shouldn't be saying all of this, especially in front of you, Tam."

Contrary to how she might think, and maybe it was messed up, but all of this was kinda making Tamara feel better. "No, please. I'm not, like, gonna be weird. Just keep going. You need to talk about it." She parroted the words her school guidance counselor had always told her.

Bitty gave a tight smile and went on, "I don't mean to be a downer, but coming home to that small apartment, filled with almost nothing, and having nothing sentimental even to make it feel like home—well, it was miserable. And I didn't want to leave. When I did, I was gossiped about and treated with superficial smiles I could almost *feel* vanish from their faces the second I turned my back. I couldn't win. The only thing I could do was move away and start over. But I have no connection to anywhere. To any*one* anywhere. And to go out and date now is . . . Ugh."

Colleen was watching her intently as she spoke, doing the

Colleen thing: taking it all in, deciding how she felt, setting those feelings aside, and seeing how the sad person felt. Then reevaluating her own feelings on it.

"But you know what?" Bitty spoke to the two of them, but glanced at Tamara in the eyes before going on. "I was the most hopeless I have ever been in my life. I felt just about as awful as I believe a person can feel in my situation. And whatever stuff happened in between, I'm here now, on the other side of it. Glad I'm not with him. Glad I'm not dead. Glad I can move on."

Tamara nodded. The silence now between them, and the cacophony outside, made her want to be honest. To say what had happened. She said it fast, the way her confessions always came out. Like ripping off a Band-Aid.

"When I left home, I agreed to give my stupid, cheating boyfriend a blow job. And he recorded it. And I didn't know at first. And now it's all over the Internet."

That was another slap in the face for them. Colleen looked immediately sick, while Bitty looked like she was trying not to look intrigued *as well as* concerned.

Tam nodded. "It's eating away at me, and I feel like I needed to say it out loud. I *know* how bad it is. I *know* I was an idiot. I *know* there's—"

Tamara had been talking into her hands, but was cut off by Colleen's arms around her. At first she didn't know what to do, but then as Colleen squeezed her, she felt an emotional catch in her throat. Was Tamara really going to cry again? What a lot of *that* she'd been doing for the last couple of weeks.

It was weird, but she had been happier in the last few weeks than in the past few years. And some of the worst stuff that could have happened had all happened *in* that two weeks. Especially the night in St. Augustine.

She always pictured Rock Bottom as a well. A cold, dark, slimy, wet well. So if she had been rappelling down into this well for however long now, being pushed down by Vince and anyone else—mostly herself—then on this trip, she had definitely landed on the bottom. But now, and maybe it was kind of lame or whatever, but it felt like she was reaching around on that grimy wet ground and had found a key. A key that might unlock some happiness for her. All she had to do was climb back out of that well, and not slip on the way up.

CHAPTER TWENTY-FIVE

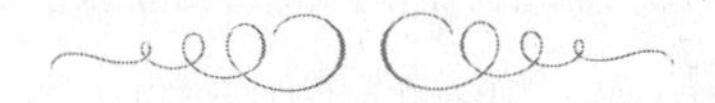

Colleen

"GAAAWD," COLLEEN WHISPERED TO BITTY SOTTO VOCE WHEN THEY stepped outside and left Tamara asleep in the trailer. "Can you believe what that poor kid has been through?" She was distinctly tipsy. Distinctly.

Bitty, however, was pretty sober. And she agreed. "It's awful."

"We need to save her."

"How?"

"You." Colleen jabbed a finger toward Bitty. "You should adopt her."

Bitty gave a laugh. "I—I don't think she's up for adoption."

"Just think how much fun you guys could have! Doing girl stuff together, shopping, mani-pedis, face masks, eating junk food while you watch *The Sound of Music* for the zillionth time—"

"Colleen."

"Mmm?"

"It sounds like you're thinking how much fun *you* could have with her."

She was. She was she was she was. But would she and Tam always have some small vestige of resentment between them for Colleen's telling on her? It had been on her own mind a lot, but she hadn't wanted to bring it up. Then again, Tam's revealing her story had been a big leap of faith. "I— Do you really think I could?"

"Are you kidding? Aunts and uncles take over for their lame siblings like that all the time. It's whatever's in the best interest of the child, right? Do you think Kevin's brother would object?"

"I don't know," she said honestly. Colleen had no doubt Chris would be overjoyed to be able to unload this burden onto someone else. But she was not so sure his pride would let him admit his failure in that way. So he might hold on to her, damaging her more and more each day, all in the name of saving face.

What would it really be like, having Tamara at the house full-time? It wasn't like this was the first time she'd met her or anything, but it was significant that this was the first time she'd *liked* her.

Then again, this was the first time she'd gotten to know Tamara at all. How could she have formed a real decision before this?

Now that she knew Tamara, and they'd talked as much as they had, and she'd really gotten to know her better, she was already thinking about weekend visits, maybe a trip to New York. And, yeah, maybe if Tam hadn't seen *The Sound of Music,* they could have a movie and popcorn night.

Maybe everything in her life—every coincidence, every uncertainty, all the stuff with Kevin and her meeting with Julia—maybe all of it had been some grand design, proving that she and Kevin were a good and strong alliance and they had the love and strength together to help raise this troubled kid alongside their own. Maybe—though this might be a stretch—maybe that was why they'd never been able to have another child, the daughter Colleen had longed for so much, maybe that was because that girl was already out there, waiting for them to find her.

Her conviction was strong, but she wasn't sure her argument would be right now. "How do I sound?" she asked Bitty. "Do you think I could have a conversation with Kevin that wouldn't be totally invalidated by all that—" She gestured toward the trailer. "—whatever it was that I had?"

Bitty considered, then, after a moment, said, "I think you have something important to say, and you have a lot of conviction right now. And, yes, you're tipsy. But you don't sound hammered or anything. So, yeah, give him a call. See what he says."

"I'm going to."

Bitty nodded. "I'll go back in the trailer."

"Bitty."

She stopped and turned back. "Yeah?"

"Is there more of that stuff in there?"

Bitty took a look. "Several cans."

"Good." Colleen heaved a sigh of relief. "I'm gonna need it."

Two minutes later, she was pitching the idea to Kevin. No intro to the idea, no laying of groundwork; she felt strongly about this, and all she needed to do was communicate that to him.

"Hon," he said, "a week and a half ago, when you were leaving, you were absolutely dreading having to take her with you."

"I know. But I didn't really know her then. Obviously. She was a reputation more than a person. Now that I've gotten to know her,

Kevin, she's so vulnerable. She has so many needs. I've got to tell you I'm scared of what will happen if she stays with Chris."

There was a long exhalation on the other line. "It's true, I never would have pegged Chris as Father of the Year."

"Think about Jay," she said. "Think about how many times we've had to walk on eggshells to preserve his self-esteem and confidence. No one has *ever* done that for this girl. But it's not too late." She thought of the story of the video and what Tamara potentially had to go back to if she couldn't come and live with Colleen. It was horrible to imagine that all her progress—and her opening up and talking about her feelings—might be for nothing if she had to go back to that sand trap.

"Sixteen isn't quite so old as you might think," Kevin pointed out, and she knew he was scratching his head the way he did when he was seriously considering the pros and cons of an idea. "There's a lot ahead on that road. If we did this, we couldn't just give up if the going got tough."

"Going has gotten tough before, and I haven't given up," she said. "Don't forget Jay's shoplifting phase."

"A gag golf tee from Sports Authority. I hardly think that constitutes a 'shoplifting phase.' "

"So you condone it."

"No!"

"Not even a little?"

"Of course not."

"You're not okay with golf tee theft but uncool with, for example, smoking weed."

Kevin sighed. "I wouldn't put it in those words, no."

"There you go." She shrugged, even though he couldn't see her.

"One may be aruguably more damaging than the other, but right is right and wrong is wrong, and we encourage right and don't put up with wrong. Right?"

"You lost me a little."

"We wouldn't condone either activity."

"Correct."

"We'd have ramifications for both."

"Yes."

"So . . . there. I'm not saying it will be easy or anything. But I'm saying I just really don't see how we can do anything *but* take her in. She's in trouble. We can save her."

"Will she be a bad influence on Jay?"

Colleen had thought about that. It was her primary concern. The last thing she wanted was to upset her neat little applecart by exposing her child to any sort of danger. But she really and truly thought that Tamara was acting out of boredom and loneliness, not inherent delinquency. With a little—no, a lot—of love and care and attention, that behavior could surely be gotten under control.

And Colleen would make it absolutely clear to Tamara that one toe over *that* particular line would carry a *very* stiff penalty.

"I think she'll be a good influence on Jay," Colleen said. "And vice versa. Neither one of them ever had a sibling before. It might be kind of nice for them to see what that feels like, to have a peer in the house when the adults go batshit."

"I've never gone batshit."

She smiled to herself. "Do you remember why I had to take over the argument with the cable company?"

He hesitated. "They're idiots."

"So you're in?"

There was a long pause. This was a lot to ask him. Then again, Tamara was his blood. There should have been less for him to think about than for Colleen. "Are you sure about this?" he asked.

"I'm sure."

"This isn't just the wine talking?"

"What wine?"

He laughed, but kindly. "The wine you obviously had before you called me."

"Kevin, I swear, I didn't have one drop of wine. And yes, I'm really really sure about this. What do you think?"

That familiar exhale. He was in. "I'll talk to Chris."

"Just make sure that when you do, you're careful to make it clear we're not saying he's doing a shitty job."

"But he is."

"I *know,* but if he thinks we're trying to just take over because he's so bad at it, he'll keep her just to prove something. But he won't prove anything except that he's the world's worst dad."

She could picture Kevin nodding before he said, "Gotcha. And agreed."

"Okay, and Kevin?"

Pause. "Yes?"

"One more thing."

Even longer pause. "I'm afraid to ask."

"No, this is a *good* thing."

"Okay." He chuckled. "Hit me."

"I love you," she said, and felt tears forming in her eyes. "I really, really love you. I am so grateful to have you in my life, I can't even tell you."

"Aw, babe. I feel the same way about you. Double back."

She smiled and put her head down. "Really? You never wish you'd married . . . someone else?"

"Never," he said firmly. "Never ever."

"Thanks."

"You come on home, now, okay? I miss you. I want to show you just how glad I am to have married you."

THE NEXT MORNING was bright in that way that it seems to get only after a lot of rain. Everything was crisp and clear and brightly colored. Optimism surged in Colleen, even though she was feeling like the business side of the trip had been sort of a bust.

So when she saw a thrift store in a strip mall when they'd stopped at Piggly Wiggly for food and drinks, it didn't really inspire much hope, but she had taught herself a long time ago never to give up an opportunity like this, because there were weird stories of outrageous fortune all the time. Maybe there was a painting of kittens in here, or that "Hang In There" poster with a copy of the Declaration of Independence behind it. You never knew.

Of course, the minute she walked in, she felt like she knew. Nothing would be here. It smelled like every thrift shop everywhere, and the front displays—usually indicators of what they were most proud of—were of tired Madame Alexander dolls and American Girl–compatible accessories (versus American Girl–authentic accessories, which had taken on a lot of value in the past few years).

The elderly female clerk, with tall white hair and shabby chic clothes, could have been at the counter of any thrift store anywhere in America. Colleen felt like she'd seen her a million times. The woman didn't even raise her eyes when Colleen walked in, and barely registered her vague, "Just looking."

She poked around a little bit, passing the old paperbacks and a section of saggy furniture and frayed wicker rocking chairs. But one section, right in the midst of it all, had a load of smaller junk. An old gas can for five dollars that she knew was worth forty-five but not worth stinking up the trailer, and an ornate old screen door that would make a really cool mirror. The price on it was eleven dollars. Sold. She'd mirror it for about seventy bucks and sell it for maybe two hundred. If she could part with it, that was. It was really gorgeous.

She went and lifted the door and started to take it to the register—imagining Tamara and Bitty's faces when she came out with a door—when the bottom snagged on a lace tablecloth and pulled everything from the table onto the floor.

"Sorry!" she called to the clerk. "I'm picking it up." She started to pick up the things—brass candlestick holders, broken costume jewelry, a Fiesta ware bowl that, miraculously, hadn't broken—but when she got to a dirty ziplock bag of utensils, she paused. Every once in a while, a piece of real silver made it into a bag like this and would be well worth the four-dollar price tag.

She unzipped the bag and started looking through the pieces. Every one of them was the same pattern. Carved roses, front and back, intricate but filthy. She took one out. Tarnish. So they were silver-plated or—please, God—silver. She turned one over, looking, hoping, for a hallmark, and there it was.

She took out her phone and Googled a couple variations of

description until she found it: *Baltimore Rose by Schofield. Sterling. 1905.* An entire set, or close to it.

She'd hit pay dirt.

All but forgetting the door—she'd wanted to take her find and get away with it as soon as possible—she went to the clerk and tried to remain calm and casual despite a thumping heart, while it took seemingly forever to ring up the purchase and take out a calculator to figure out the twenty-four-cent sales tax. Colleen would have told her, but she probably wouldn't have believed it, and it would only have delayed the transaction further.

Finally the receipt was handed over, and Colleen burst out into the Carolina sunshine and took a deep breath. Weepy webs of kudzu hung from the trees behind the mall, swaying in the wind. She felt like they were congratulating her.

She had just paid for her trip tenfold.

CHAPTER TWENTY-SIX

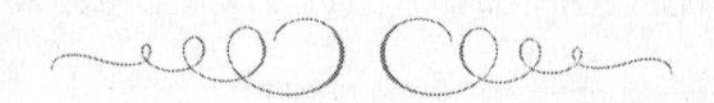

Bitty

Dear Stranger,

Last night was rough. Especially for Colleen and Tamara. We got stuck in the rain and had to hang out in the trailer with nothing but candlelight and several bottles of spiked whipped cream. I'm still not quite sure how they worked, though it was good stuff. Whipped cream fills me up so fast (in high school, I'd actually had an idea to start a Reddi-wip diet because it was filling and satisfying), I barely had any, while those two just went to town with it. Now, I don't know how a bottle of that stuff compares to, say, a bottle of wine or a decent amount of vodka, but by the looks of it, it was pretty strong.

And by the looks of them this morning, it has a lingering effect. I just hope they're okay back there with the car moving, because the last thing Colleen needs is vomit all over her new stuff.

Anyway, I ended up at the wheel, since Colleen is anxious to just end this trip now, and the more miles she can sleep through, the better. At least that was the original plan.

But here's the thing. I got to thinking about my conversations with Colleen regarding my marriage and my regrettably stupid handling of the Blake situation. God, what a child I was! So out of control, spoiled, selfish. And it went on, boy, my self-pity over his leaving clung to me like a spiderweb walked into in the dark. I couldn't even find all the strands of disenchantment.

Naturally, I thought of him over the years. Many, many times. You can't have a platonic marriage like mine without harking back to the big love of your life, who wanted you fiercely at all times. I'd felt thoroughly loved by Blake . . . until he left. Stupid how I made that about me, when he had so much serious stuff to worry about. Colleen was right about that—she'd tried to point it out, but I wouldn't hear it. Then and now. Poor me. That was all I could think.

Honestly, I probably deserved all the angst I suffered as a result.

So these were the thoughts that were chasing themselves around in my brain as I drove and that highway hypnosis took over, lines flipping under the car, boom boom boom boom, until sometime after the Florida/Georgia line, and almost in Savannah, I saw the exit that I remembered (how?) from the one and only time I'd gone to Blake's parents' house with him.

As I recalled, it wasn't that far off the highway, and it was only a few turns, but it would still be insanely selfish to take the exit while those two slept in the back, expecting to wake up well closer to home.

But what the hell? It was a beautiful day, the sun was shining but not burning, the top was down, the air was clean, and this was the chance in a lifetime—and, let's face it, I had absolutely no other plans. I still wasn't sure where I was even getting off this ride. Certainly not where I'd begun, in Henley, but maybe in Lumbarton, where I could rent a car and—what, slink back to the place that had already deemed me persona non grata?

No, I didn't want to go back to Winnington until I had a divorce settlement and a moving company, which meant this world was my oyster. I needed to keep my eyes open as I drove—figuratively, in addition to literally—because anyplace along the way could have been my new home. Savannah? Charleston?

Lunville. That was where he lived. The sign said 35 MILES. I pulled over gently, so as not to rock the trailer too much, and pulled up Google on my phone. Punched his name in, and there it was, on Maple Street, which I'd remembered, since it's hard to forget when someone *actually* lives on Maple Street.

This was a hell of a chance to take. A really stupid chance. He was undoubtedly married and maybe even unrecognizable. Maybe *I* was unrecognizable. Maybe it would be just a huge awkward exchange, but I was okay with that. I know that's hard to believe—I wouldn't believe it myself, as I've never exactly been *Zen* about embarrassing situations (see cat rescue, previously)—but this was one of those chances that not only felt worth taking, it felt *necessary*. So, with no questions about the integrity of my mission, I drove on, following the turn-by-turn instructions until I pulled up in front of a vaguely familiar Victorian house, dark blue, with a cheerful porch and a big black shiny Ford 150 out front.

No, not the same one he had in college. But completely consistent with Blake. I knew it was his.

My heart was pounding, and to be honest, part of me wanted to turn back and run. This could really be a fool's errand. I knew that. But the curiosity was deep. If nothing else, it would make a good story for Colleen when she woke up—and for a diary.

I parked and scrambled in the glove box for a piece of paper. On the back of a duplicate check, I wrote, "This is Blake's house, I'll be out soon," and taped it to the steering wheel with a Band-Aid from the first-aid kit that *of course* Colleen had.

And I went to the door.

I had to knock twice and was about to give up and leave—part of me wanted that, I think—when it opened, and there he was.

There is no *I would have known him anywhere* because he looked exactly the same. There was no way *not* to know him. I wasn't, however, sure the same could be said of me, and I was overwhelmed by a sense of insecurity and worry—what would I say? "I don't know if you remember me, but . . ."—until his surprise wore off enough for him to speak.

"I'll be damned."

"It's possible," I said.

"What the hell are you doing here?"

"Great question."

He glanced behind me, at the car and the trailer, and frowned. "That's . . . yours?"

"Um, no, it's—it's a friend's. I was driving and I saw the exit for your town and, well, I'd been thinking about you and just thought I'd stop by and see how you are. You know, how your life's gone, what you're up to, if you have . . . kids . . . or—"

"I'm fine, I'm a mechanic, I don't have kids or—" He smiled. "And I never would have seen this coming in a million years." He took a step back. "You, uh, you want to come in?"

"Sure." I glanced back at the car. They'd be fine. It's not like someone was going to come steal them. "For a minute, I guess."

He ushered me in and offered me water because he had to go to the store but hadn't so it was all he had. I took it. Water was about all I could deal with at that moment. Also that was a point for him, I was glad he wasn't drinking beer at the very stroke of 5 P.M. like so many overgrown, underdeveloped frat boys I'd known. Or like Lew, who drank Macallan 25 neat throughout the day like he'd been prescribed it.

We sat down on the couch and talked, small talk, for I don't know how long. It seemed like forever, given how little we were actually saying. It might as well have been the Sunday morning news, a lot of filler material and human interest stories, but not a lot of meat.

At one point, I thought I heard the distinctively thin slam of the trailer door, but no one came up to the house, thank God. I wouldn't have imagined Colleen would do that, but she might have been irked enough with the detour to do just about anything.

So it turned out, he'd never been married, though he'd been engaged for two years. To a woman who was nothing like me, so scratch that old wives' tale—he either didn't have a type or he never wanted to be with someone like me again. He'd dated like anyone else, had a few jobs before opening up his own repair and body shop, which did really well, thanks to some NASCAR connections he'd developed. His brother had married Blake's high school girlfriend—another imagined scenario to scratch—and now they lived just down the road, but Blake had taken his parents' house because he wanted to restore it to its original glory and he had the time and skill to do so.

No, he'd never gone back and finished college. He could have, he acknowledged. Still could. But what was the point now? He was doing great. He didn't need it.

His regrets about college had nothing to do with his education.

"I'm sorry," I told him when he said his mother had passed away just three months after his return. "Not just for your loss, because that's obvious, but I'm sorry I made the journey harder for you by . . . by punishing you for doing the only right thing."

The small talk came to a screeching halt as we started talking like real people again.

"I'm sorry it hurt you so much."

I held up a hand. I couldn't bear for him to apologize to me for *anything*, given what he'd gone through. "Please. Seriously."

He splayed his arms, universal signal for *Okay, whatever you say*, and a tense moment passed.

"Well, I'd better go," I said, standing up. "This was a crazy impluse, but I really just had to see how you were doing. I was really in the neighborhood, and strangely knew where you lived but not your phone number. I—I've thought about you so much."

"Me too." He touched my nose and looked down at me.

And suddenly all the awkwardness dissolved. That small gesture, and I melted. It was I who made the first move, without even thinking—and with years of inexperience and uncertainty under my belt since I'd last been intimate with any man—I snaked my hand up behind his neck and pulled him toward me, into a kiss.

Luckily he seemed to want the same—and I'm telling you, there were fireworks. It was bliss. It was like all the wrongs over the years bled away and left one tender new right, and this was it.

I sank against him, allowing him in, his mouth, his tongue, his breath, his soul. He reached down and pulled my shirt up and nudged his hand under the elastic of my undies and down. I already knew I was ready for him, but he smiled against my mouth when he felt it, and I felt a surge of even more desire for him.

"Let's go in the bedroom," he said, so quietly I almost couldn't hear him.

I swallowed. "Okay." But I didn't want to move. I didn't want his hands off me for even a second. I didn't want his mouth more than an inch away. I needed him inside me, not following me for an impossibly long ten or fifteen seconds into the bedroom and onto the bed.

He must have known, because he slipped his fingers into me, worked me for a moment, then eased me down to the floor. There wasn't time to go anywhere else. There wasn't a minute to be wasted. Even if we had all day, or all week, or all year, there wasn't a moment to be wasted. So much time had already been lost.

He needed to be inside me or we'd both explode.

I kicked my pants off and parted my legs under his hand, then gasped as he pressed his fingers in. He worked me for another moment while I tore at his belt and unzipped his pants and wrestled them off him. He sat up and pulled his shirt off, and I did the same with mine.

"You look so incredible," he said, and his gaze raked over me like something physical.

"I—" I didn't have an answer. Didn't need one, though, because again his mouth was on mine and I was slipping away. I felt him unhook my bra, and it fell away like a falling leaf.

He kissed his way down my neck and stopped at my breasts, alternately flicking his tongue across them and sucking so intensely that a coil of nerve shivered straight through my core. He glanced at me, then trailed his tongue across my stomach and abdomen and, not gently, moved his mouth onto me. He was good at this. He'd always been really good at this. His mouth was warm, his breath hot against me, but of course, that was only part of the art. The rest he did like it was instinct, always knowing where to touch me, when to back off and when to go stronger.

My nails scratched at the floor, nothing to hold on to or brace myself with as he moved his tongue expertly in just the right spot, driving me to the point of insanity, then instinctively moving his tongue down to enter me in tantalizing promise of what was to come.

I had missed this.

There was no other him. There would never be another him. No one would ever be able to play me in quite the way he could. Three months I could have waited, back then, and this would have been mine all this time, but, no, my selfishness and impatience had deprived us both of this for too long.

I would do my best to start to make it up to him now.

He moved back up my body and put an arm protectively across me, kissing the spot right under my ear.

I reached for him and took him in hand, feeling myself grow wetter at the feel of his hardness in my grasp. I had never wanted a man, anything about a man, the way I wanted him. I wanted to do everything with him, anything with him, I wanted to be the one to do everything he wanted. I think at the bottom of it all, my trust in him was so complete that I felt safer with him than I felt alone. He allowed me to think about things I never dared think about alone.

My mind was racing with all these thoughts. Thoughts I hadn't allowed into my mind in years.

"Come here," I managed to say, and he paused, then moved over so I could take him in my mouth. Another thing I'd never wanted from another man. But this one, I wanted everything. I wanted to taste everything. Everything about him made me want more. It had always been that way. It wasn't intellectual, I hadn't made a decision to want him or imagined him to be a superhero of some sort. I knew exactly who he was—that had been part of the problem, hadn't it?—but when we got close to each other, there was no controlling the physical attraction.

Tonight I knew I could not get enough.

He knelt beside me while I turned on my side and sucked him, bracing my hand on his leg, which was ripped with hard muscle. But his touch on my side was soft. He pressed hard into my mouth. I ran my tongue across him, hoping to make what was already hard into something he couldn't bear. I reached out and we twined fingers for a moment.

Camaraderie, it felt like.

In this together.

His breath grew labored and he drew back out of my mouth and moved over on top of me.

I was ready.

He braced his arms on either side of my face, looking down into my eyes. I got butterflies at that. In the thick of all this, that moment of softness made me feel like my crush had just looked at me from across the gym. I reached up and cupped my hands on his cheeks, his beard rough against my palms but that space on his cheekbones and toward his temples soft where my thumb grazed it. He was beautiful, no doubt about it. He'd never known it—maybe that was one of the things that was hot about him—but he was physically beautiful. In a way so classic that on anyone else, it might have been boring—the description was straight out of a romance novel: square jaw, cleft chin, dark eyes and hair, high cheekbones. If you left it at that, you'd have a soap star.

But add the details unique to him—the curved line of his lips that didn't tell you if he was pleased or pissed, the way his eyes got hooded and slight when he was tired, the nose that was broken but not obviously, and the perfect angle of his cheek down to his jaw, and that one slightly crooked tooth—and it added up to something that could never be duplicated.

Had the right person spotted him years ago, he'd probably be a movie star today. No, he would never have wanted anything like that. More than that, he'd just be "the one that got away" for some big-shot agent in addition to being that for me.

But at this moment, with his mouth moving on mine and his

hands running hot trails across my skin, he was nothing but mine.

He took my hand and guided me down to his hardness. Everything inside me screamed to life.

I caught my breath, just as I had every time.

He pressed his hand against my cheek and moved closer against me, catching my eye for just a moment and holding it while he pressed into me, suddenly and brutally, like a searing hot blade.

We both exhaled with relief. That was it, my favorite moment. The moment that drew me back to him again and again. Him filling me to the top, me sheathing him protectively. That moment of becoming almost one thing. This was perfect harmony.

He drew out, all the way, and I heard myself gasp at his absence.

"Come on," I whispered.

He got tantalizingly close but stopped short, and I shimmied down to him, wanting that feeling, needing that feeling of him pushing into me.

"Do it," I said.

He resisted—probably for only a few seconds, but it felt like forever—then stabbed into me with the searing force. And I wanted that, I wanted him to split me open. In this momentary time warp, I would have died, I would have happily bled to death on his altar if I could go under the force of his desire.

He pushed back in, keeping his eyes fixed on mine, and moved slowly inside me, gradually going faster and harder until eventually he was doing me as if I were the only one strong enough to take what he needed to give.

At that point, he took complete command. He was the man,

he was the aggressor; I was the woman, I received and accommodated. I was flexible to his convenience, no matter how he moved me, as soon as his cock slid into me, I was powerless to resist anything.

I couldn't say how much time passed. All I knew was that this was a moment I would replay again and again, and I wanted to live in it for as long as I could. He never faltered. Everything he did, everything he thought of, was always exactly right, sending agonizing twists of pleasure through every part of me. Pleasure rebounding and ricocheting like echoes inside me. I could have done it forever. I could have happily just lay beneath him and let him have me forever. I wouldn't have slept through it, but I wouldn't have missed sleep either. This was much, much better than sleep.

Much more restorative than sleep.

"Put your hands up," he said into my ear, moving my arms up and away from my body against the floor, holding me down by the wrists.

He kissed me hard, tangling his fingers in my hair and holding tight, then suspended himself over me and slid in and out while I skidded my fingers across the landscape of his hard triceps and back.

"Put your legs together."

I did.

He moved in me, and I felt him ripple against every nerve I had down there. I could barely breathe.

Don't stop. Don't ever stop.

And on it went. I moved at his whim. He flipped me over, drew me under, moved my legs like I was Circus Barbie. I did whatever he wanted, glad to give up the control I had to have in the rest of my life in order to defer to his strength for at least a couple of hours of relief.

Forget later. How could I worry about that when now felt so good?

I would, of course. Later I'd second-guess this. I'd be ashamed of my weakness in giving in to him so easily again. But I'd also suspect, I'd always suspect, that he needed this even more than I did. That with all the tension that drew him tight in the rest of his life, he needed my love and comfort a lot more than he'd admit.

If I hadn't believed that, I probably could have walked away.

Instead, I was ransomed by it. Like when I was a kid and my cousin threatened to put a needle in his eye if I left the basement where we were segregated to go up to the adults at the party upstairs. I'd sat down there for hours, scared to move, for fear he'd hurt himself if I made a wrong move and then it would be my fault forever.

There was no threat from Blake, but the imperative felt the same—he needed me. He needed warmth and touch and nurturing. He always had. As wild as he'd always been, there was a little boy in there who needed love. Craved it.

I'd always had to work to read him. It required thought and interpretation, despite the fact that, to him, I was a book that didn't even need words for him to decipher. I was *Where's Waldo? Good Dog, Carl.* Everything I thought and felt might as well have been pantomimed by schlocky, horrible actors—*A-Team* rejects—in front of me. He was Dostoyevsky to me, and I was Dr. Seuss to him.

But I thought I was good for him once.

Was I right?

And, if so, was I still?

His rhythm increased, and I recognized the change in his breathing. He wasn't the only one who knew this dance. I knew every movement, at this point. He was nearing the end. The crescendo. I wrapped my legs around him and held on, his back so strong, he didn't even seem to notice, and drew my arms tighter around his torso. Safety. That was one thing I got out of this. I felt safe beneath him.

I almost never felt safe anymore.

He grew stronger, his breath coming in forced bursts until the culmination.

I'd always tried to time this moment right, like a game. I closed my eyes and felt myself ratchet higher and higher up that mountain of physical need. Don't stop, don't think, don't interrupt, just feel. The sensation increased with his hard thrusts. It felt like he was getting even bigger in me, touching every spot inside and out, until finally my body reached fever pitch and went flying over the cliff into an orgasm so shudderingly strong that I shook.

Almost immediately, his breath quickened and he spilled into me. And in that one moment of vulnerability, I felt like the strong one.

His hands found mine again, and he sank down on me. I felt his heart pounding against mine, our breath ragged but synchronized. Every bit of his warmth felt good along the length of me.

This, I thought, was what sex was supposed to be. This was what was wrong with everyone else, all the gentlemen who would be so careful and quick. That wasn't how I wanted it. Sometimes I wanted it dirty, and hot, and sweaty, and raw. I wanted to feel so much need that there was nothing I'd stop at, nothing that would feel too far. I needed to be with someone who tasted perfect to me and smelled perfect to me, and felt perfect to me. Nothing else would do.

They were simple ingredients, but hard to find. And here he was, his skin on mine, his breath in my hair, his sweat under my hands on his back, but I knew I had to go, and when I did, maybe I would wish I hadn't done any of this.

A taste of honey's worse than none at all.

Was that true? Had this whole thing with him been a reawakening, or just some cruel tease, showing me a standard I should have stood up for a long time ago but hadn't, so I was screwed?

Better luck next life.

Hope you learned a lesson from this.

When Blake and I went our separate ways, had he missed this as much as I had, or was this ordinary to him? Maybe it was even subpar, I didn't know. Maybe he had a lot more experience than I did. Almost certainly, he'd had a lot better experience than I did, given that Lew and I had virtually *no* interaction. In believing this to be awesome, maybe I was a fool, some rube who'd never had real food and proclaimed rhubarb "the sweetest treat you can eat."

And that's where the Dr. Phils and Oprahs came back into my head. You should have let go, they said. Take your clean break and keep it. You can't go backwards. No one can go backwards.

I didn't have an answer for them.

So I pushed the feelings down and ran my fingertips along

his ribs and down his back. For the moment, this was enough. Later it wouldn't be, of course, I'd second-guess everything I'd done and would almost certainly think about doing again, but for the moment, just this moment, this was enough.

AFTERWARDS—AND I don't know how long afterwards it was—I told him the truth about the trailer, that Colleen and her niece were out there, sleeping off a hangover.

He was, needless to say, surprised. But, in a way, didn't it just figure? The last time he'd seen me, she and I had been two peas in a pod—and now, here we were, still. But it was getting later in the evening, and it was just about time for us to stop anyway. Why not stop here?

Man, I hoped I could convince them of that.

I went to the trailer and found a very impatient Tamara and Colleen sitting there, playing cards.

"I have to pee so bad, it's not even funny," Tamara said without preamble.

Colleen was not so impatient. "What is going *on*?"

"We're at Blake's—"

"Got that."

"He's fantastic, as wonderful as ever, I don't think I ever fell out of love with him." I could have gone on and on, it felt so good to be saying all of this. "I think maybe he feels the same way about me."

"Does he have indoor plumbing?" Tamara asked. "Because otherwise, he's going to have one hell of an embarrassing scene in front of his house in about two minutes."

"Yes," I said quickly. "He has plumbing. Come on in, you guys. He says we can stay the night." I raised an eyebrow at Colleen. "It saves the hotel money."

She quirked her mouth and narrowed her eyes. "And answers some long-unasked questions?"

"More than you know."

"We're in."

CHAPTER TWENTY-SEVEN

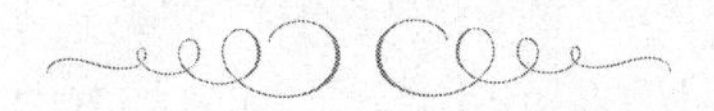

Tamara

ENDING UP AT BITTY'S OLD BOYFRIEND'S HOUSE. THAT WAS A TWIST Tamara hadn't expected. She wasn't part of the whole thing, and she was Undesirable No. I right now, so she did her best to sink into the hunter green walls and not be a bother. She slipped outside, catching a glimpse of side-eye from Colleen. This was farm country, though. They both knew Tamara couldn't go anywhere. And it's not like she would anyway. Hell no. Not after that night.

Things just weren't the same with Colleen ever since then. No, she wasn't being all pissy and brooding and angry like her dad would have been. She wasn't raising a hand in the air to slice the connection of their conversation. She wasn't even being bitchy or lecturing her. Yes, Colleen had lost it on her at first, but even Tamara understood that.

It was weird, actually. Tamara knew it was an old—now certainly unfunny, if it ever *was* funny—thing where someone with their face in a bucket on New Year's Day announces, "Ugh, I am never drinking again!"

But the morning after the night from hell, she wondered why she had ever thought that her current and regular life was worse than the potential feeling that her constant risks could land her with? Was a boring night worse than accidentally doing too many drugs and ending up God knows where with God knows who, covered in God doesn't even *want* to know *what*?

While Bitty, Colleen, and their friend chatted at the table, she walked outside. She had never gotten the farm or country thing. But this . . . was kind of awesome.

She looked up at the sky, where she could actually see stars. There were effing thousands of them. Even though Tamara knew that was obvious, it was more startling than she would have thought. Once for an Astronomy class, a bus had taken her and about twenty-three other less-than-interested students out to a big field an hour away, where there was less smog. But even that was nothing compared to this. It was like she had grown up with a Charlie Brown Christmas tree with one sad string of half-working lights, and this was the tree in Rockefeller Center. Except Charlie Brown's tree had its certain charm, and Catonsville with its gross streets and ugly private school–uniform navy sky had none. Of course, it was where she had lived forever.

Tamara had a strange urge to cry. She wasn't even sure if it was because she was happy or sad or guilty or angry or what. She thought of her mom, long gone. Then thought of her dad. He was cold and hard, but he was still her dad.

She bit her lip and stared at a spot in the field next to her before reaching in her pocket and pulling out her phone.

Tam clicked his number and let it dial.

Ring. Ring. Ring.

"Hello," came her father's voice on the other end. It was never a question when he answered. Never a warm greeting. Just what he knew he was to say when he picked up the phone. It was what you were obligated to say before it was someone else's turn to talk.

"Hey, Dad . . . um, so what's up?"

"If you're calling to say something in particular, just tell me. I don't want to chitchat until you break something to me. What is it?"

Again, not a question. A demand for a response, but not an invitation for one.

"No, Dad, nothing. I'm just calling because we haven't, like . . . talked at all this whole trip."

At first she felt offended and irritated that he was assuming she had something grave to call and announce. But then she realized that if she were being 100 percent honest, that probably *would* be why she was calling. But it wasn't, she figured, so screw him for assuming it.

"Oh," he said, still not sounding humble, sorry for asking, or like he even believed her. "How's the trip going, then?"

"It's good. . . . We've been stopping at some cool places. It's fun."

"Great, that's good. I'm glad Colleen's trip is a success."

Could he not just talk to her like family? Like they even really *knew* each other?

Which, she considered, maybe they really didn't.

"Look, Dad, I kind of did want to talk to you about something—but it's not bad!" she hastened to add the last part when he let out a humorless laugh and seemed to take a deep, exasperated breath.

"All right, then go for it."

She was losing her footing a little on what she had wanted to say.

"Well, it's just . . . I know how hard I have been for you. I am really sorry I have made you worry and I'm sorry that it's a constant, like, fight between us. Really. I'm going to be better when I get home." She nodded, even though he couldn't see her. "Really. I want to change. I want to be different. I don't want to be the jailbird mess-up girl anymore."

"You know, Tamara—" he started.

She mentally filled in his sentence. *You know, Tamara, that's all I've ever needed to hear from you.* Or maybe, *You know, Tamara, it's been a rough couple of years, but I love you. If you're going to change, let's do it together.* Or—

"—I've heard all of this horseshit before." He finished his sentence, cutting off her imaginary ones.

"No, listen—"

"No, you listen, Tamara Jane. This is enough. It's all well and good you want to change. Great for you. But I'm not going to believe anything until I see it. And even then, I'm still not going to have blind faith in you that you won't just keep this same cycle of making the same old mistakes over and over. It's just a matter of keeping you out of prison until you're eighteen, as far as I'm concerned. And then you're on your own, sweetheart."

She felt like she'd been slapped hard in the face. Not slapped by just anyone, but hit with the same beastly hand her father had. It was as strong as his words. In fact, she was sure his words were stronger. Because this sting went not from her cheek to her stomach. It went from her ears to her heart, to her now-spinning head, and to her jelly knees.

The "sweetheart" at the end had been the real stinger.

"That's— Do you know how that makes me feel?"

"Do you know how you've made *me* feel?"

"I don't think you're capable of feeling anything!"

She was veering from the point now. The point was that she wanted to make a change, and wasn't that the first step? But instead, all he did was take this as an opportunity to yell at her some more.

"I didn't call you to get yelled at, Dad. I called you because I haven't talked to you in forever and because I *do* want to make a change. Jesus! What would you do if I hadn't called, or if I'm not around? Do you just yell at the cabinets and faucets? Is it just that you have to yell and scream and I'm there at the right time?"

No more humorless laugh from him now. Just stony silence.

"Whatever, Dad." She was shaking now. "I call you and try to tell you I want to make a change, and you can't give me two fucking seconds of support on it! I— What—erghh!"

She ended the call and hurled the phone onto the ground. This time she didn't care if it was broken or not. Didn't care at all what her father might say, do, or think of her.

Tamara collapsed onto the ground into crossed legs, pretzel legs, as they had called it in elementary school. That long-since-passed era, when she had been a little brunette thing with pretty eyelashes and wide, unjaded eyes. Tamara of thirteen years ago, sitting pretzel-legged on a rugged, flat classroom carpet, was unrecognizable to Tamara now. The Tamara who sat with crossed legs in the dirt, five seconds out of a screaming match with her distant father, her mother gone, star of a porn video on the Internet, who couldn't even hang on to a boyfriend she had always *considered* lucky to have her. But really, who was lucky? He had a family with parents who talked to him and bought him presents, and a group of friends. Even if she didn't like his group of friends, *he* did, and that's more than she had for herself.

She had known for so long that she was smarter than the people she surrounded herself with. Smarter than her choices. And she had figured that by being smart enough to *know* all that, that meant she was doing okay. She was being young. Playing the part of messed-up teenager. Getting the experiences out of the way before she went off to college where she—what?

Another imaginary scenario popped into her head. Of her, maybe in a sorority. Her hair lightened up to its enhanced natural color. Her makeup neat and minimal. Her skin clear. A little insignia on her face as she cheered for a football team with her girlfriends. She imagined herself in those soft flannel pajamas and a college T-shirt, a crooked ponytail and light bags under her eyes as she stayed up late into the night, studying for a final.

That's what she envisioned for herself. And she pictured herself being good enough for a cute guy with a good head on his shoulders. But Conor, who had given her a shot in the beginning despite his probable better judgment, was too smart for a girl like her. What guy was going to continue talking to a girl when he saw a video of her blowing some other guy? On the Internet? On some amateur porn Web site?

No one who didn't have the understanding and patience of Gandhi.

So no. She wasn't as bad as she had been acting. She wasn't. And now she was. Now she really was the girl who constantly reeked of weed, who had a handful of bad trips under her belt, and who craved a cigarette when times got hard, instead of just wanting to treat herself to a piece of chocolate cake because she deserved it. She was everything she thought she was masquerading as just to get by.

She didn't deserve the cute older guy with good taste in music. She didn't deserve a tenth "second chance" from her father. She wasn't giving him the win, but she was giving him enough. Giving him understanding. Which was more than he would ever be able to give to her.

And Colleen . . . Colleen, who had probably dreaded taking her on her trip as much as, or more than, she had dreaded going. She had gone and screwed her. What must she have been thinking that whole night and morning? Tamara shuddered and sobbed a little harder. The kind of crying that leaked from everywhere and you just couldn't give a damn.

"I'm sorry. . . . I'm so sorry. *Shit. I'm sorry* . . . ," she muttered into her own lap, her voice echoing in the cave created by her folded arms and legs.

She wasn't sure who she was apologizing to most—her dad, her mother . . .

Her mother. The woman who had been her everything when she was a kid. Tamara could still so distinctly recall her reaching a hand out at the store or pulling her in tight to sleep at night when "Daddy" had been away. She remembered sitting at the counter, waiting for macaroni and cheese to get made, and the patience in her mother's posture as Tamara had sung and talked until she exhausted herself.

Then the decline in her mom. Tamara had been too young to know much or understand a lot about what exactly had put her on the path that led to her death. When she pieced together the memories, she decided that a growing distance and stomach-numbing cold from Tamara's father had led to her accidental increase in prescription intake. Which led to a higher tolerance. A high dosage.

Higher increase in side effects. Forgotten pills, then double-taken pills, then the ultimate side effect—which was not her death, but the zombie she became first.

She moved slowly; she didn't talk or think right. Sometimes her personality was there to lead you into a false sense of security, but then she was gone again in the blink of an eye, and you weren't even sure when it had happened. Like talking to a crazy person that you don't know is crazy—first you think *you're* crazy. Then you realize you're not. And you kind of wish you were. Because at least *that* you could control.

Some of her apologies were for her mother. For letting her sad and unintentional self-destruction be an explanation for everything Tamara herself was doing to self-destruct. She had been fighting fire with fire for years now. And that didn't work. It just didn't.

But mostly, as Tamara sobbed harder and harder into herself, her chest aching with breaths she couldn't take all the way in, she was apologizing to the bright-eyed little girl on the classroom floor. The one who had no idea that her light would be so dimmed by older-Tamara. That little girl laughing hysterically at a rhyming book had no idea that those laughing, rosebud lips would one day be so tainted by the bad choices that older-Tamara was too stupid not to make.

The damsel in distress she had thought she was didn't deserve to be rescued. She was just a stupid girl with too much black liner on who had tied herself to the tracks and screamed dares at the train to hit her.

No. She was not going to be rescued. And she was not going to sit out here until Colleen came to find her, or until a bear—or, she didn't know, a wolf?—came to put her out of her misery.

She got up, dirt sticking to her hands and tear-drenched knees, and walked inside. She could be embarrassed to walk in like that. But she needed someone. And if she could possibly have someone for a minute . . . she needed it.

Tamara walked into the kitchen. It was just Bitty sitting at the table. She hadn't really allowed for that possibility. In her head, it had just been Colleen alone or Colleen still with the others.

"Tamara?" Bitty leaned forward.

"Hi . . ."

"What's—? Are you okay? Obviously not, what's going on?"

She didn't want to be rude and ask where Colleen was, but her quick, "Um—" and look around must have told Bitty enough.

"Colleen is in the back barn with Blake. Apparently, he has a lot of interesting pieces he's been saving but hasn't known what to do with. Do you want me to get her?"

Tamara sniffed and shook her head, taking a seat at the table.

"I'm sorry for crying."

"Don't be absurd," said Bitty. "If you don't want to talk about it, you don't have to. But if you want to . . . I'm here."

Tam considered her cuticles for a minute, her head aching. "I have made the worst possible choices. Over and over. And it's like I expect the world to feel bad for me or something. Like I think I'm owed more than I'm earning, and I"—another sob enveloped her—"I don't."

She let her head fall into the crook of her elbow, as if she were playing Heads Up, Seven Up.

"I thought I deserved saving or something, but it's not like anyone can tell I do if I don't act like I'm worth it. Or, I don't know, I'm not making sense," she went on. "It's just that my life continues to suck, no matter how much I blame other people, and nothing changes because, *duh*."

Tamara looked up. Bitty's eyebrows were furrowed—or they seemed like they would be if they could be—and she no longer looked concerned or confused. She looked something else entirely.

"Realizing that," she said slowly, considering her carefully, "is far more important than anything that led up to it."

Tamara sniffed again, her breath finally calming. The two stared at each other for a moment, Tamara not sure what it was she was seeing in Bitty, exactly, but knowing that she understood. She knew that Bitty, whoever this odd, bug-catching, scrawny—less so now—woman was, she was someone who confirmed for Tamara that feeling this rock-bottom awful sure did suck. But that maybe it didn't always have to.

A moment later, there was laughter, and the sound of a screen door swinging open with a squeak.

"Right? I drive all this way with all these stops and get a third of what— Tam? What happened?"

Like her father's questions, it was not a curious invitation for a reply; it was a demand for a response. But it was a different thing coming from Colleen.

"Nothing, it's fine—"

"Tam, come on. Blake, if it's really fine we stay here, then I think I'll take her up." Colleen had a firm but warm hand on Tamara's shoulder. "Thanks again for everything. We'll see you two in the morning."

With that, Tamara was guided upstairs, away from the grown-ups, and taken to bed.

CHAPTER TWENTY-EIGHT

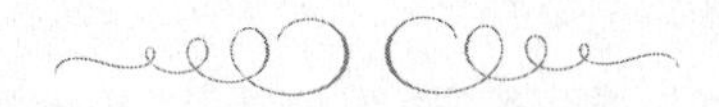

Tamara

IN THE MORNING, BITTY HAD THAT SEX-GLOW THING GOING ON. There was no other explanation for it. Her cheeks were pink, her eyes were bright, she looked like she'd just won the Miss America contest or something.

And, noticably, she wasn't dressed. She wasn't *un*dressed, but she was wearing a big T-shirt, obviously Blake's, and some of those yoga pants they'd had to stop at Target for. No shoes.

"Um . . . Bitty?" Colleen raised an eyebrow. "We're leaving now."

Bitty's cheeks flushed even pinker, if possible. "I'm"—she glanced at Blake—"I think I'm going to stay here a little longer."

"Mmmn." Colleen nodded. Total understanding. Even Tamara got it. Bitty had no place to go, her husband was a piece of shit, and she was like a dandelion wisp on the wind. "I guess Blake can get you to a car rental place when you're ready to go."

"Of course," he said with a sly smile, and he and Colleen locked eyes, the knowing exchange of old friends.

It was kind of hard to imagine a guy that hot was so into Bitty, but whatever. Lucky her. At least she had a life she could be happy in finally.

"Well, then." Colleen went over to him and gave him a hug. "It was really good to see you, Blake. I hope I'll see you again soon."

"Anytime, you name it." He kissed her cheek. "Say hey to your old man."

"Boy, he's not even going to *believe* this story. I think I'll save it for when we're in person so I can see his reaction."

Blake laughed. "I can imagine it."

Colleen nodded. "Me too." She turned her gaze to Bitty. "How about you walk us out?"

"Obviously. My stuff's still in the car." She laughed.

They walked out into the bright sun. The sky was blue and the clouds were so low and puffy, they looked like dog toys in the air.

"I'm not even going to ask if you're sure of what you're doing," Colleen said, "because this is long overdue. But I do need to make sure this isn't going to hurt your case against Lew at all."

"Nah. I'll give him what he feels like is a deal. I think he's going to be more afraid of what I can do to him. He's worked a long time to hide his truth. It's a shame, and I don't honestly think I'd reveal it, because I don't think being gay is what he has to be ashamed of—I think being an asshole is."

Colleen and Tamara both laughed at the unexpected bluntness from Bitty.

Bitty hugged Colleen hard and said, "I still can't believe we ran into each other like this. If I didn't believe in fate before, I do now. I am just so happy we've reconnected."

"Don't lose touch this time." Colleen wiped a tear from her eye. "You know I'm going to be wondering how on earth this story ends."

"Me too," Tam added.

Bitty let go of Colleen and went to her. "I want *you* to stay in touch too, got it? Do you have my number?"

Tam raised her phone. "Right here."

"Well, text me, at least. Even though I'm blind as a bat and can barely punch out words on the screen, I will answer."

Tam laughed. "That should be fun to see."

Bitty took her by the shoulders. "Listen to me. We're saying good-bye now, and later on you'll say good-bye to Colleen and go back to your dad, but we will *always* be here for you, got it? You are not alone. Don't make the same mistakes I did. Don't keep everything bottled up inside. Open up. It's like"—she looked around, then gestured at the car—"it's like driving with the top down. Technically, you're more vulnerable, and everyone can see what would otherwise be hidden inside, but it's the only way to really see, feel, and smell everything around you. It's the only way to fully enjoy the sun and the wind and *life.* It's so much better than keeping it all closed up!"

Tamara was surprised by this unexpected bit of wisdom from Bitty, but her advice made sense.

They got into the car and Colleen asked Tam to program the way back to 95 into her phone and navigate. With one last wave, they said good-bye to their third musketeer and headed north.

Tamara was dreading it.

THE RIDE BACK felt like it was flying by. She thought time was supposed to fly when you were having fun, not when you're miserable and dreading going home.

The very thought of her stark bedroom, complete with grayish white walls and a crappy, springy bed, made her heart sink. Seriously, the bed was so bad that when you sat down on it, it sounded like it had a waterproof plastic thing on it. If ever she had anyone over, she would have felt the need to explain that, no, she wasn't a bed wetter—this was just the cot she'd ended up with.

She leaned her head on the seat belt. Her brain was filled with so many fears and unspent complaints that she didn't know what to do. She couldn't even think anymore.

"You all right, Tam?"

Colleen's voice took her by surprise for some reason. Maybe because what she needed more than anything was to be asked what was wrong, and here she was being asked. No one ever asked her what was wrong. Ever.

"Yeah," she found herself saying anyway. No. She should talk to someone. Just this once. They were only six hours from home. From reality. From the gray room and gray life. "No. I'm not really all right."

"What's going on?" Colleen lowered the music. It was Tamara's phone playing the Neighbourhood, which Colleen said she liked. Maybe she was just saying that to make Tamara feel good. Or maybe she really did like them. Either way, it was cool. There was swearing in the songs too, and she didn't even get all weird or stiff when it happened.

"I don't really know exactly what's wrong. Well"—she gave a dry laugh—"I do, everything is wrong."

"No, not everything. You've got all the time in the world to figure it out."

"Yeah, but when I left, I had a boyfriend and a routine, and everything was like, *fine,* you know? It wasn't great, but still. Now I've been cheated on, my boyfriend—my *ex-boyfriend*—leaked a video that will never go away, I feel like, and . . . just everything. My house sucks. My dad sucks. My school sucks. It's like I want to start over, but I can't even. My reputation is already fuc—already shot—and the kids at my school are all, like, total bums. No one there is really trying. It's too late to start playing a sport, as if I'd even be good at one. Like, I know everything is different now, but it's gonna be the same too."

Colleen listened and then looked thoughtful. "Why is everything different now?"

"Be*cause* Vince is a scumbag—"

"Vince was always a scumbag."

"Okay, truth, but I didn't know it."

"Did you really not? When he took that video, had you trusted him completely, and he broke that trust?"

"No. I was always afraid he would do something like this. Or. Exactly this."

"Did you trust him with other girls?"

Tamara thought of her immediate instincts on the redhead. "No."

"Okay, so as far as Vince is concerned, it's not like your life has been turned upside down. You just finally got to see the whole picture. Like that game where you see only one-eighth of a photo, and you try to guess what it is. Now you see." She paused. "Turned out the picture was of a dick."

Tamara actually gasped. "Oh my god!"

"Sorry, that wasn't appropriate." But Colleen looked pleased with herself.

"Seriously, don't apologize—that was hilarious. And true—"

"Okay, so what else is so different from when you left?"

"I guess . . . I don't have any desire to smoke or do anything like that. That night was so bad—sorry again—that I can't even imagine wanting to feel anything close to that ever again."

"So that's good."

"I know. And I don't feel like going to parties. I don't like anyone I know." That might not be entirely true. "Well, I did like one guy kind of."

"Oh yeah? Who?"

"This guy Conor. I've known of him for a while, but I never met him until right before I left. He's actually the one who told me about the video. Someone had sent it to him. He doesn't seem to want to talk to me now. And I get why."

Colleen shrugged. "The thing is, Tamara, this is what a parent can't do for you. We can't punish you for something like this video." She heard herself say "we" like she was the parent, but she didn't correct herself. It felt right. "It *is* the punishment. You know it wasn't something you should have let happen. Now you have learned the real-world result of your actions. I'm sorry, really, *so* sorry that you have to live knowing it's out there. Why didn't you stop Vince?"

"I don't know."

"Sure you do."

"No, really I don't."

"You were afraid of something, or you wouldn't have let him do it. It obviously wasn't because you trusted him or because you didn't care."

"No." When Colleen didn't go on, it became clear she wasn't going to speak again until Tamara did. "Okay, I guess I kind of live in a weird fear of upsetting people. I would always rather pay the price and be uncomfortable rather than make someone *else* uncomfortable."

"And? Are you glad now that you're paying the price instead of temporarily pissing off this creep *Vince*?"

"No, of course not." She thought. "No. Definitely not."

Colleen nodded. "I'm sorry, honey, but that's a life lesson learned. All you can do is look at this like that. Yes, it sucks. It's embarrassing. And, yeah, it's gross. But now rise above it. Look back on that as a person you once were. All of it, Tam. When you get home, you don't have to feel like the same girl trying to fit into old shoes that don't fit anymore. You can look back on that with a wiser eye and a roll of the eyes now. That lesson is learned."

Tamara pictured it: Her, at her best. Pretty, clean, her natural best, alert and never altered. Confident and smart. No longer looked at like a hood rat. Like some kind of an Audrey Hepburn or something.

"That would be cool," she said.

"It *will* be. Seriously. We have all made mistakes."

"This is all pretty grimy, though."

"Yep, not going to deny that, chickadee. But it's over. It happened already. You know that's not going to change."

"Right. But still, so now I go home, and the only way to avoid all of it is to pull away from it all. To not talk to anyone I used to talk to. Which I can do—I'm not saying I'll miss it or be tempted back into anything. I'm just saying it's gonna suck. I'll only be able to spend time at home, especially since my dad freaks if I do anything. I can't even get permission to go to Starbucks and read a book or something at this point, because for one thing, he doesn't trust me. For another thing, that's how it all started. He didn't let me do *anything* at all, so eventually I didn't just do what I was allowed to because that was *nothing*. So I lied and did everything."

Colleen took in a deep breath. "Right."

"So I'll just hang out in my ugly stupid room. He doesn't even pay for Internet, Colleen. I can't even watch shows or anything. I'll become so hopelessly bored. That was always the problem. I might not have liked what I was doing, but at least it was *something*. And weed or getting wasted made time pass more quickly."

"I can't really tell you how to avoid that. That is something of a crap situation."

"Yyyyup." Tamara looked back out the window, her momentary hopefulness squashed back down a little.

"I'm sure you'll figure something out," said Colleen.

"Me too."

It was sometime later that they stopped at another rest stop. Colleen always had to pee, but on her way out, she stopped and took out her phone. In the distance, Tam could hear her saying her name, and mentioning taking her home. She was probably telling her husband how desperate she was to get rid of the loser, take her home, drop her off, and never have to deal with her again.

He probably owed her big-time for this.

Tamara turned on her phone, hesitated, then went to the amateur porn site. After a moment, she clicked over to "her video." Ugh.

She didn't want to watch it. She scrolled down quickly so she wasn't looking at her messed-up face and started looking at the comments. Facing the music, kind of. To see just how bad it was going to be to return to all those same people.

The first few comments she'd seen before. Congratulations to Vince from his lame buddies, virtually high-fiving him.

But then she saw: *Wow, you're a creep!*

And: *Good luck ever getting another girlfriend, slime ball.*

Why R U showing the world you have a tiny dick?

Tamara read on, surprised and increasingly bolstered at how thoroughly the video had backfired on Vince. It was awesome. It didn't lessen the humiliation for her, of course, but it made her feel better that he was being totally slammed for it publicly.

As he should be.

Maybe he'd see the comments and be humiliated enough to take the video down. Was that too much to hope for?

Okay, say he didn't. She still needed to own what she'd done. She needed to get past it, or make people *think* she had; she had to *own* it.

She went to her messaging icon and pulled up Conor. *Why not?* She asked herself. *What's the worst he can do? Ignore me?* That was about it. If he ignored her, she'd never know for sure what that meant, but it wasn't the worst thing that could happen.

Hey, she wrote. *Trip's almost over. What's going on back home?* She paused, then took a chance: *Did the academy call about my award?* She took a deep breath and watched the phone for a moment. Nothing. No ellipsis, no answer.

There could be a million reasons for that. It wasn't worth sweating it now. She put the phone aside and waited for Colleen.

When Colleen got back in the car, she had a strange expression on her face.

"What's wrong?" Tam asked, instantly thinking of weird scenarios in which her text was such a colossal mistake that her dad had received a cease-and-desist letter in the past five minutes and told Colleen.

"Nothing." Colleen turned down the corners of her mouth and shook her head, then started the car, put it in gear, and started rounding the back of the building. She drove onto the exit and pulled smoothly onto the highway before taking a breath, starting to say something, then stopping.

Tamara's nerves thrummed. Was she in trouble? Had Colleen told her dad what had happened, and was she heading home to a firing squad or maybe a dungeon?

"Tam," she said at last.

"What?" Tam answered too fast.

"I have a proposal for you, but I want you to think about it carefully before answering, okay?"

What could this mean? Nerves fluttered in Tam's stomach. "Go on."

"Your uncle Kevin and I were wondering if, by any chance, you might be interested in coming and staying with us for a while."

"Staying with you."

"Mm-hm." Colleen nodded.

She didn't understand. "What, you mean, like, tonight?"

Colleen glanced at her and smiled. "No, I mean maybe finish high school with us."

Silence.

Was this *true*?

"Are you serious?" Tam asked.

"Very."

"Did my dad say this was okay?" She believed he'd want to scrape her off, but this would be such an admission of defeat, she couldn't imagine he'd give permission for it. Her heart was racing with possibility. She didn't want to sound too eager.

"He did," Colleen said. "And not because he doesn't want you—so don't even go there. He has a lot of travel for work coming up in the next year, and he needs to be sure you're safe and sound."

He didn't want her. She knew that. She couldn't even take it personally, because he had not wanted her before he ever knew her. "What about Jay? Wouldn't he be pissed if someone else moved in?"

Colleen smiled. "Trust me, he needs a sister to torture him. I'd *pay* you to whip him into shape."

Tamara kneaded her hands in her lap. "Do I have to think about this?"

Colleen's face fell. "I guess not."

"Because the answer is yes. Absolutely. Yes, yes, yes. I don't have to think for one second about this."

Oh great, more tears were gracing her Maybelline mascara'd eyelashes.

Colleen smiled, then smiled broader. "You're sure?"

"Are *you*?"

"Never more sure of anything. We'll have a blast."

Tam tried to catch her breath. "I can't even believe this—"

"Okay, so now that we've got that piece of business out of the way, here are the rules: No smoking, no drugs, no drinking, no whipped cream alcohol exceptions, no Vince. No one even *like* Vince. Can you live with that?"

Tam nodded. "I think I can. Except, maybe a little whipped cream on Christmas?"

"We'll see."

"Deal."

Tamara's phone dinged. A message from Conor.

Haha, nope, no calls. New pizza place came in, though, and it's pretty decent. Hit me up when you're back and it's on me. Want to talk about the last ep of Breaking Bad. It was amazing!!

And just like that, it was over. At least as far as Conor was concerned. And she wasn't used goods, dirty, tainted, anything; she was still Tam, and he wanted to take her out for pizza.

"Whatcha smiling about there?" Colleen asked.

"Everything," Tam said. "Absolutely everything."

Colleen pressed the accelerator and Tam tipped her head back, turning toward the sun. Bitty had been absolutely right: There was nothing better than opening up and driving with the top down.

EPILOGUE

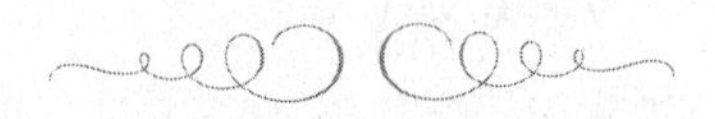

ONCE UPON A TIME, THERE WERE THREE HAPPY GIRLS, NONE OF whom were born into easy, uncomplicated lives. They had each been through their own hell, and come out on the other side. Each one could look back on some moments in the past and shudder or cringe, hoping those memories never saw the light of day again, and each one could look back at other past moments with a smile and a coo of nostalgic wistfulness. Each one had a life that didn't follow the yellow brick road they always hoped it would. But the road they ended up on had put them in a far better place.

First, there was Bitty. Since the road trip that had changed the direction of her life, she had changed. When she looked in the mirror now, she didn't see an extra ounce of fat on her hip bones or a wrinkle by her eyes that she really ought to take care of. Not because the ounces or wrinkles weren't there, but because she saw herself. She just saw Bitty now. Ounces and wrinkles be damned.

On this particular Saturday, Bitty was tossing on her favorite baggy red sweater, paired with a pair of simple black leggings, and black boots. Her hair was a little longer and less tamed than she used to wear it. She wondered now why she'd gone so long the other way—it looked way better this way.

"Come on, babe, we're gonna miss breakfast if you don't hurry your cute ass up!" Blake shouted up the stairs.

She laughed. A real laugh, not a polite one because someone had made a joke. He couldn't hear her either way. "I'm coming!"

"You wearin' those leggings I like?"

Screw makeup, she'd rather head down the stairs than even fuss with eye shadow. She left their room and stopped at the top of the stairs.

"Are these the leggings you like?"

He tilted his head and looked thoughtful. "I'm not sure if they are. Could you turn around for me?"

She gave an indulgent roll of the eyes and turned.

"Yup, those are the ones."

Bitty laughed again and went down the stairs. He gave her a wink as she walked past him and then a smack on the ass. "Let's get moving."

Out she trotted to his truck, and into the passenger seat. He climbed in himself, and they set off for breakfast. After, they were stopping at the hardware store. He had some tools to get of some kind, and Bitty had talked him into letting her paint the bathroom, and she was dying to look at the color swatches.

An Eagles song played on the radio, Blake was singing along—badly—and they set off, the truck jostled by the uneven road. And Bitty had never been happier.

A FEW STATES north, Colleen was in the kitchen. A timer was going off, the sink was running, and everything was ready at once—which is not exactly the dream come true, because that means everything needs action all at once.

"Tam, shut off the timer, will you?"

"Uhhh—" She rushed over, her mismatched fuzzy socks almost making her slide into the wall. She looked at the microwave, and pressed a button. The fan came on, adding to the cacophony. She pressed more buttons until she got it.

"Okay, now can you go outside and grab the tray that's been cooling out there?"

"Got it." She went off to complete the task, clearly glad that this one made perfect sense.

She heard the front door open, and Kevin came into the kitchen. Zuzu was all claws-on-hardwood as she scrambled to him. "Hey, there, Zuzu, let's get you outside." He did so.

A moment later, Jay came in the back door, laughing at Tam, who was saying, "Don't make fun of me!"

"I'm not! Okay, no, I totally am."

Kevin shut the door on the dog and turned off the sink. "It smells incredible in here."

"Right?" agreed Tam. "It smells like a restaurant or something."

"All I can smell is me, and I smell like cats from the Shapiros' house," said Jay.

"Gross! Go take a shower, nasty!" Tam said after getting a whiff. "And hurry, cuz, I am not waiting for you to eat."

She looked very seriously at him. Colleen smiled. Their interaction had surprised her. She had taken on a "responsible for Jay's well-being, even if it means tough love" sort of attitude, and he had adopted one that said "I don't have to listen to you, but it seems like it's good for you when I do, so I will" attitude. It worked out.

"I'll go change really quick and come back down." Kevin went off, and Colleen was left alone in the kitchen. Okay, finally everything was handled, everything was done.

They sat at the table together, as they did sometimes nowadays. Tam had a boy she liked, Jay had met a teacher who seemed really on his side, and Jay didn't want to mess that up. Kevin was doing great at work. Colleen's business was doing great with all her "domestic imports" as she was calling them.

After dinner, once Jay had retreated to his room and Tam had gone upstairs to get ready for the movie she was going to with her friends and—ooh, the boy!—Colleen and Kevin were left alone. She stood at the sink doing dishes.

"That dinner was incredible, Col, as always."

"Thank you, and I *know,* that seasoning I got in Georgia was really the—" She stopped as he kissed her on the neck from behind.

"Colleen, I have something I want to tell you."

There was a small drop in her stomach as she turned. She didn't even have to keep wondering or work up any fear, however. He was smiling at her when she looked at him. His hands were planted on the counter behind her. "What is it, Kevin?"

"I know you said you're almost out of stuff to sell. And I know how well you did with all of that. And . . . I was a little jealous last time that I didn't get to go along."

Colleen laughed. "Oh, I'm so sure."

"Hey. I had a great time. But you weren't trapped with a bunch of dudes and one cackling cougar-wannabe that whole time."

A small win for Colleen. "True."

"So." He pulled out an envelope from his back pocket. "I was thinking maybe now that we've got the built-in babysitter"—he indicated upstairs, where Tam was—"maybe you'd be interested in taking a little you-and-me trip."

"Really?"

He opened the envelope and handed it to her. "Really."

She pulled out two plane tickets. "Two one-way tickets to Portland?"

He nodded. "I thought maybe we could start at the top and drive down the other coast. You can get some different stuff over there, and we can see some new sights together, and then get a flight back or drive back, whatever we feel like. Neither of us have ever been there. I thought it would be pretty cool. I remember in college you used to talk about some program in California you had considered."

"Yeah—wait, the program . . . That was before I even knew you."

"Yeah, before we *dated*. But I remember you talking about it with other people, and I was there. Being a creep and eavesdropping on the hot girl with big dreams."

He gave her that grin that had always gotten a smile out of her.

She wrapped her arms around him. "This is so exciting. I love you so much."

"I love you too."

Yes, dinner had been a catastrophe as always. It was a madhouse between the teenagers, the dog, the beeping oven, and everything else. But she was happy. Truly, truly happy. This was exactly the kind of life she could never have planned for herself.

UPSTAIRS, TAM'S PHONE lit up with a text from her friend Kelly.

Hey b-face, I'm here!

K, be right out!

Don't spend too long getting ready just because kylllle is commmmingggg

Shhhh!

Tam laughed and put on her jacket before going down the stairs, where Kevin and Colleen were hugging.

"I'm not looking at you guys, but I'm leaving, K—love you, bye!"

She heard them laugh as she got to the front door. Colleen yelled after her, "Text me when you get there, and don't be out past midnight or I'll murder you!"

"I knowwww!"

She shut the door, to which she had a hot pink key to now, and got in the car. On the way to the movies, Kelly and Tam blasted the new Justin Timberlake album and sang their hearts out. There was a whole bunch of them meeting up for the movie, but she was mostly excited to see Kyle. Who, when she walked up, handed her a movie ticket with a shy smile and said, "I grabbed you one, so I'm glad you came." He laughed. "It didn't occur to me till after I bought it that you might not."

She bit her lip, biting back the huge grin she wanted to wear. "I thought about bailing." She gave him a look to let him know she was kidding, and they all went in to the movie.

Finally she was able to play it cool. Be the girl someone wanted. Be the girl she had always wanted to be, and envied. The one with dark, damaged hair and a drinking problem seemed like a stranger now. But the girl walking into the movies with a group of friends who would have been disappointed if she hadn't come was a happy girl. One who had herself together. One who had climbed out of that well, key in hand, and set out to find the lock.